mystery

THE DAUGHTERS OF CAIN

AND

THE JEWEL THAT WAS OURS

Colin Dexter graduated from Cambridge University in 1953 and has lived in Oxford since 1966.

His first novel, *Last Bus to Woodstock*, was published in 1975. There are now twelve novels in the Inspector Morse series, most recently *The Daughters of Cain* and *Death is Now My Neighbour*.

The Way Through the Woods and *The Wench is Dead* were awarded Gold Daggers by the Crime Writers' Association for best crime novel of the year, and Colin Dexter has also been awarded Silver Daggers for *Service of all the Dead* and *The Dead of Jericho*. *Death is Now My Neighbour* went straight to the top of the best-seller lists on first publication in 1996.

In 1997 Colin Dexter was awarded the CWA Cartier Diamond Dagger for outstanding services to crime literature.

The Inspector Morse novels have been adapted for the small screen, with huge success, in Carlton/Central Television's series starring John Thaw and Kevin Whately.

THE INSPECTOR MORSE NOVELS

Last Bus to Woodstock
Last Seen Wearing
The Silent World of Nicholas Quinn
Service of All the Dead
The Dead of Jericho
The Riddle of the Third Mile
The Secret of Annexe 3
The Wench is Dead
The Way Through the Woods
The Daughters of Cain
Death is Now My Neighbour
The Remorseful Day

Also available in Pan Books

Morse's Greatest Mystery and other stories
The First Inspector Morse Omnibus
The Second Inspector Morse Omnibus
The Third Inspector Morse Omnibus
The Fourth Inspector Morse Omnibus

COLIN DEXTER

THE DAUGHTERS OF CAIN

AND

THE JEWEL THAT WAS OURS

PAN BOOKS

The Daughters of Cain first published 1994 by Macmillan.
First published in paperback 1995 by Pan Books.
The Jewel That Was Ours first published 1991 by Macmillan.
First published in paperback 1992 by Pan Books.

This omnibus edition published 2003 by Pan Books
an imprint of Pan Macmillan Ltd
Pan Macmillan, 20 New Wharf Road, London N1 9RR
Basingstoke and Oxford
Associated companies throughout the world
www.panmacmillan.com

ISBN 0 330 43675 9

1 3 5 7 9 8 6 4 2

A CIP catalogue record for this book is available from
the British Library.

Printed and bound in Great Britain by
Mackays of Chatham PLC, Chatham, Kent

THE DAUGHTERS OF CAIN

For the staff of the Pitt Rivers Museum,
Oxford, with my gratitude to them for
their patient help.

Acknowledgements

The author and publishers wish to thank the following who have kindly given permission for use of copyright materials:

Extract from *A Cornishman at Oxford* © A. L. Rowse;

Extract from *The Lesson* by Roger McGough, reprinted by permission of Peters Fraser & Dunlop Group Ltd;

Extracts by Cyril Connolly reproduced by kind permission of the Estate of Cyril Connolly c/o Rogers, Coleridge & White Ltd, 20 Powis Mews, London W11 1JN, © 1944 Cyril Connolly;

Extract from *The Observer* © by Oliver Sacks, 9 January 1994;

Faber & Faber Ltd for the extract from *New Year Letter* by W. H. Auden;

Extract from *Oxford* by Jan Morris, published by permission of Oxford University Press;

Extract from *Back to Methuselah* granted by The Society of Authors on behalf of the Bernard Shaw Estate;

Extract from *The Pitt Rivers Museum, A Souvenir Guide to the Collections* © Pitt Rivers Museum 1993;

Extract from *The Pitt Rivers Museum* taken from *The Memory of War and Children in Exile: Poems 1968–1983*, James Fenton, published by Penguin © 1982;

Kate Champkin for the extracts from *The Sleeping Life of Aspern Williams* by Peter Champkin;

N. F. Simpson for the extract from *One-Way Pendulum*;

Extract from *Berlioz, Romantic and Classic* by Ernest Newman published by Dover Publications;

Extract from *The Times* by Matthew Parris, published 7 March 1994;

Extract from *Marriage and Morals* by Bertrand Russell, published by permission of Routledge (Unwin Hyman);

Extracts from *The New Shorter Oxford English Dictionary*, published by permission of Oxford University Press;

Faber & Faber Ltd for the extract from 'La Figlia Che Piange' in *Collected Poems 1909–1962* by T. S. Eliot.

Oxford is the Latin quarter of Cowley
(Anon)

PROLEGOMENA

Wednesday, 25 May 1994

(i)

Natales grate numeras?
(Do you count your birthdays with gratitude?)
(HORACE, *Epistles II*)

ON MONDAYS to Fridays it was fifty-fifty whether the postman called before Julia Stevens left for school.

So, at 8.15 a.m. on 25 May she lingered awhile at the dark blue front door of her two-bedroomed terraced house in East Oxford. No sign of her postman yet; but he'd be bringing something a bit later.

Occasionally she wondered whether she still felt just a little love for the ex-husband she'd sued for divorce eight years previously for reasons of manifold infidelity. Especially had she so wondered when, exactly a year ago now, he'd sent her that card – a large, tasteless, red-rosed affair – which in a sad sort of way had pleased her more than she'd wanted to admit. Particularly those few words he'd written inside: 'Don't forget we had some good times too!'

If anyone, perhaps, shouldn't she tell *him?*

Then there was Brenda: dear, precious, indispensable Brenda. So there would certainly be *one* envelope lying on the 'Welcome' doormat when she returned from school that afternoon.

Aged forty-six (today) the Titian-haired Julia Stevens would have been happier with life (though only a little) had she been able to tell herself that after nearly twenty-three years she was still enjoying her chosen profession. But she wasn't; and she knew that she would soon have packed it all in anyway, even if . . .

Even if . . .

But she put that thought to the back of her mind.

It wasn't so much the *pupils* – her thirteen- to eighteen-year-olds – though some of them would surely have ruffled the calm of a Mother Teresa. No. It wasn't that. It was the way the *system* was going: curriculum development, aims and objectives (whatever the difference between those was supposed to be!), assessment criteria, pastoral care, parent consultation, profiling, testing . . . God! When was there any time for *teaching* these days?

She'd made her own views clear, quite bravely so, at one of the staff meetings earlier that year. But the Head had paid little attention. Why should he? After all, he'd been appointed precisely *because* of his cocky conversance with curriculum development, aims and objectives and the rest . . . A young, shining ideas-man, who during his brief spell of teaching (as rumour had it) would have experienced considerable difficulty in maintaining discipline even amongst the glorious company of the angels.

There was a sad little smile on Julia's pale face as she fished her Freedom Ticket from her handbag and stepped on to the red Oxford City double-decker.

Still, there was one good thing. No one at school knew of her birthday. Certainly, she trusted, none of the pupils did, although she sensed a slight reddening under her high cheekbones as just for a few seconds she contemplated her embarrassment if one of her classes broke out into 'Happy Birthday, Mrs Stevens!' She no longer had much confidence in the powers of the Almighty; but she almost felt herself praying.

But if she were going to target any prayer, she could surely so easily find a better aim (or was it an 'objective'?) than averting a cacophonic chorus from 5C, for example. And in any case, 5C weren't all that bad, really; and she, Julia Stevens, *mirabile dictu,* was one of the few members of staff who could handle that motley and unruly crowd. No. If she were going to pray for anything, it would be for something that was of far greater importance.

Of far greater importance for herself . . .

As things turned out, her anxieties proved wholly groundless. She received no birthday greetings from a single soul, either in the staff-room or in any of the six classes she taught that day.

Yet there was, in 5C, just the one pupil who knew Mrs Stevens' birthday. Knew it well, for it was the same as his own: the twenty-fifth of May. Was it that strange coincidence that had caused them all the trouble?

Trouble? Oh, yes!

In the previous *Sunday Mirror*'s horoscope column, Kevin Costyn had scanned his personal 'Key to Destiny' with considerable interest:

> **GEMINI**
>
> Now that the lone planet voyages across your
> next romance chart, you swop false hope for
> thrilling fact. Maximum mental energy helps
> you through to a hard-to-reach person who
> is always close to your heart. Play it cool.

'Maximum mental energy' had never been Kevin's strong point. But if such mighty exertion were required to win his way through to such a person, well, for once he'd put his mind to things. At the very least, it would be an improvement on the 'brute-force-and-ignorance' approach he'd employed on that earlier occasion – when he'd tried to make amorous advances to one of his school-mistresses.

When he'd tried to rape Mrs Julia Stevens.

(ii)

> Chaos ruled OK in the classroom
> as bravely the teacher walked in
> the havocwreakers ignored him
> his voice was lost in the din
> (ROGER MCGOUGH, *The Lesson*)

AT THE AGE of seventeen (today) Kevin Costyn was the dominant personality amongst the twenty-four pupils, of both sexes, comprising Form 5C at the

Proctor Memorial School in East Oxford. He was fourteen months or so above the average age of his class because he was significantly below the average Intelligence Quotient for his year, as measured by orthodox psychometric criteria.

In earlier years, Kevin's end-of-term reports had semi-optimistically suggested a possible capacity for improvement, should he ever begin to activate his dormant brain. But any realistic hopes of academic achievement had been abandoned many terms ago.

In spite of – or was it because of? – such intellectual shortcomings, Kevin was an individual of considerable menace and power; and if any pupil was likely to drive his teacher to retirement, to resignation, even to suicide, that pupil was Kevin Costyn. Both inside and outside school, this young man could be described only as crude and vicious; and during the current summer term his sole interest in class activities had focused upon his candidature for the British National Party in the school's annual mock-elections.

Teachers were fearful of his presence in the classroom, and blessed their good fortune whenever he was (allegedly) ill or playing hookey or appearing before the courts or cautioned (again!) by the police or being interviewed by probation officers, social workers, or psychiatrists. Only rarely was his conduct less than positively disruptive; and that when some overnight dissipation had sapped his wonted enthusiasm for selective subversion.

Always he sat in the front row, immediately to the right of the central gangway. This for three reasons. First, because he was thus enabled to turn round and thereby the more easily to orchestrate whatever disruption he had in mind. Second, because (without ever admitting it) he was slightly deaf; and although he had little wish to listen to his teachers' lessons, his talent for verbal repartee was always going to be diminished by any slight mis-hearing. Third, because Eloise Dring, the sexiest girl in the Fifth Year, was so very short-sighted that she was compelled (refusing spectacles) to take a ring-side view of each day's proceedings. And Kevin wanted to sit next to Eloise Dring.

So there he sat, his long legs sticking way out beneath his undersized desk; his feet shod in a scuffed, cracked, decrepit pair of winkle-pickers, two pairs of which had been bequeathed by some erstwhile lover to his mother – the latter a blowsy, frowsy single parent who had casually conceived her only son (as far as she could recall the occasion) in a lay-by just off the Cowley Ring Road, and who now lived in one of a string of council properties known to the largely unsympathetic locals as Prostitutes Row.

Kevin was a lankily built, gangly-boned youth, with long, dark, unwashed hair, and a less than virile sprouting on upper lip and chin, dressed that day in a gaudily floral T-shirt and tattered jeans. His sullen, dolichocephalic face could have been designed by some dyspeptic El Greco, and on his left forearm – covered this slightly chilly day by the sleeve of an off-white sweatshirt – was a tattoo. This tattoo was known to everyone of any status in the school, including the Head; and indeed the latter, in a rare moment of comparative courage, had called Costyn into his study the previous term and demanded to know exactly what the epidermal epigram might signify. And Kevin had been happy to tell him: to tell him how the fairly unequivocal slogan ('Fuck 'em All') would normally be interpreted by anyone; even by someone with the benefit of a university education.

Anyway, that was how Kevin reported the interview.

Whatever the truth of the matter though, his reputation was now approaching its apogee. And with two sentences in a young offenders' unit behind him, how could it have been otherwise? At the same time, his influence, both within the circle of his immediate contemporaries and within the wider confines of the whole school, was significantly increased by two further factors. First, he even managed in some curious manner to exude a crude yet apparently irresistible sexuality, which drew many a girl into his magnetic field. Second, he was – had been since the age of twelve – a devotee of the Martial Arts; and under the tutelage of a diminutive Chinaman who (rumour had it) had once single-handedly left a gang of street-muggers lying pleading for mercy on the pavement, Kevin could appear, often *did* appear, an intimidating figure.

'KC.' That was what was written in red capital letters in the girls' loo: Kevin Costyn; Karate Champion; King of the Condoms; or whatever.

Tradition at the Proctor Memorial School was for pupils to rise to their feet whenever any teacher entered the classroom. And this tradition perpetuated itself still, albeit in a dishonoured, desultory sort of way. Yet when Mrs Stevens walked into 5C, for the first period on the afternoon of her birthday, the whole class, following a cue from Kevin Costyn, rose to its feet in synchronized smartness, the hum of conversation cut immediately . . . as if some maestro had tapped his baton on the podium.

And there was a great calm.

(iii)

As I heard the tread of pupils coming up my
ancient creaking stairs, I felt like a tired tart
awaiting her clients
    (A. L. ROWSE, *On Life as an Oxford Don*)

'IT'S ONLY ME,' he'd spoken into the rusted, serrated Entryphone beside the front door.

He'd heard a brief, distant whirring; then a click; then her voice: 'It's open.'

He walked up the three flights of shabbily carpeted stairs, his mind wholly on the young woman who lived on the top floor. The bone structure of her face looked gaunt below the pallid cheeks; her eyes (for all McClure knew) might once have sparkled like those of glaucopis Athene, but now were dull – a sludgy shade of green, like the waters of the Oxford canal; her nose – tip-tilted in slightly concave fashion, like the contour of a nursery ski-slope – was disfigured (as he saw things) by two cheap-looking silver rings, one drilled through either nostril; her lips, marginally on the thin side of the Aristotelian mean, were ever thickly daubed with a shade of bright orange – a shade that would have been permanently banned from her mouth by any mildly competent beautician, a shade which clashed horribly with the amateurishly applied deep-scarlet dye that streaked her longish, dark-brown hair.

But why such details of her face? Her hair? The mind of this young woman's second client that day, Wednesday, May 25, was firmly fixed on other things as a little breathlessly he ascended the last few narrow, squeaking stairs that led to the top of the Victorian property.

The young woman turned back the grubby top-sheet on the narrow bed, kicked a pair of knickers out of sight behind the shabby settee, poured out two glasses of red wine (£2.99 from Oddbins), and was sitting on the bed, swallowing the last mouthful of a Mars bar, when the first knock sounded softly on the door.

She was wearing a creased lime-green blouse, buttoned up completely down the front, black nylon stockings – whose tops came only to mid-thigh, held by a white suspender-belt – and red high-heeled shoes. Nothing more. That's how he wanted her; that's how she was. Beggars were proverbially precluded from overmuch choice and (perforce) 'beggar' she had become, with a triple burden of liabilities: negative equity on her 'studio flat', bought five years earlier at the height of the property boom; redundancy (*in*voluntary) from the sales office of a local engineering firm; and a steadily increasing consumption of alcohol. So she had soon taken on a ... well, a new 'job' really.

To say that in the course of her new employment she was experiencing any degree of what her previous employer called 'job satisfaction' would be an exaggeration. On the other hand, it was certainly the easiest work she'd ever undertaken, as well as being by far the best paid – and (as she knew) she was quite good at it. As soon as she'd settled her bigger debts, though, she'd pack it all in. She was quite definite about that. The sooner the quicker.

The only thing that sometimes worried her was the possibility of her mother finding out that she was earning her living as a cheap tart. Well, no, that wasn't true. An expensive tart, as her current client would soon be discovering yet again. Yes, fairly expensive; but that didn't stop her feeling very cheap.

At the second knock, she rose from the bed, straightened her left stocking, and was now opening the door. Within only a couple of minutes opening her legs, too, as she lay back on the constricted width of the bed, her mascara'ed eyes focusing on a discoloured patch of damp almost immediately above her head.

Almost immediately above *his* head, too.

It was all pretty simple, really. The trouble was it had never been satisfying, for she had rarely felt more than a minimal physical attraction towards any of her clients. In a curious way she wished she *could* so feel. But no. Not so far. There was occasionally a sort of wayward fondness, yes. And in fact she was fonder of this particular fellow than any of the others. Indeed, she had once surprised herself by wondering if when he died – well, he *was* nearly sixty-seven – she might manage to squeeze out a dutiful tear.

It had not occurred to her at the time that there are other ways of departing this earthly life; had not occurred to her, for example, that her present client,

Dr Felix McClure, former Ancient History don of Wolsey College, Oxford, might fairly soon be murdered.

(iv)

A highly geological home-made cake
(CHARLES DICKENS, *Martin Chuzzlewit*)

ONLY ONE communication, it appeared, was awaiting Julia Stevens that same day when she returned home just after 5 p.m.: a brown envelope (containing a gas bill) propped up against the table-lamp just inside her small entrance-hall.

The *white* envelope, unsealed, lay on the table in the living-room; and beside it was a glacé-iced cake, the legend 'Happy Birthday, Mrs Stevens' piped in purple on a white background, with an iced floral arrangement in violet and green, the leaves intricately, painstakingly crafted, and clearly the work of an expert in the skill.

Although Brenda Brooks had been Julia's cleaning-lady for almost four years now, she had never addressed her employer as anything but 'Mrs Stevens'; addressed her so again now, just as on the cake, in the letter folded inside the (NSPCC) birthday card.

Dear Mrs S,
Just a short note to wish you a very happy
birthday & I hope you will enjoy your surprise.

Don't look at it too closely as I had a little
'accident' & the icing isn't perfect. When I'd
made the flowers & when they were drying a
basin fell out of the cupboard & smashed the lot.
After saying something like 'oh bother' I had to
start again. Never mind I got there in the end.

Regarding my 'accident' I will tell you what
really happened. My husband decided to pick a
fight a few weeks ago & my doctor thinks he
could have broken a bone in my hand & so I
can't squeeze the bag very well. I was due to start
another icing course next week but he has saved
me £38.00!

Have a lovely day & I will see you in the
morning – can't wait.

Love & best wishes,
Brenda (Brooks)

After re-reading the letter, Julia looked down lovingly at the cake again, and suddenly felt very moved – and very angry. Brenda (she knew) had hugely enjoyed the cake-decorating classes at the Tech. and had become proudly proficient in the icer's art. All right, the injury was hardly of cosmic proportions, Julia realized that; yet in its own little-world way the whole thing was so terribly sad. And as she looked at the cake again, Julia could now see what Brenda had meant. On closer inspection, the 'Mrs' was really a bit of a mess; and the loops in each of the 'y's in 'Happy Birthday' were rather uncertain – decidedly wobbly, in fact – as if formulated with tremulous fingers. 'Lacks her usual Daedalian deftness' was Julia the Pedagogue's cool appraisal; yet something warmer, something deeper inside herself, prompted her to immediate action. She fetched her broadest, sharpest kitchen knife and carefully cut a substantial segment of the cake, in such a way as to include most of the mis-handled 'Mrs'; and ate it all, straightaway.

The sponge-cake was in four layers, striated with cream, strawberry jam, and lemon-butter icing. Absolutely delicious; and she found herself wishing she could share it with someone.

Ten minutes later, the phone rang.

'I didn't say nuffin' in class, Miss, but I want to say 'appy birfday.'

'Where are you phoning from, Kevin?'

'Jus' down the road – near the bus-shelter.'

'Would you like to come along and have a piece of birthday cake with me? I mean, it's *your* birthday too, isn't it?'

'Jus' try stoppin' me, Miss!'

The phone went dead. And thoughtfully, a slight smile around her full lips, Julia retraced her steps to the living-room, where she cut two more segments of cake, the second of which sliced through the middle of the more obviously malformed 'y'; cut them with the same knife – the broadest, sharpest knife she had in all her kitchen armoury.

(v)

> After working for two weeks on a hard crossword
> puzzle, Lumberjack Hafey, a teacher in Mandan,
> became a raving maniac when unable to fill in
> the last word. When found, he was in the alcove
> of the old homestead sitting on the floor, pulling
> his hair and shrieking unintelligible things
>
> (*Illinois Chronicle*, 3 October 1993)

MUCH EARLIER that same day, Detective Sergeant Lewis had found his chief sitting well forward in the black-leather chair, shaking his head sadly over *The Times* crossword puzzle.

'Not finished it yet, sir?'

Morse looked up briefly with ill-disguised disdain. 'There is, as doubtless you observe, Lewis, one clue and one clue only remaining to be entered in the grid. The rest I finished in six minutes flat; and, if you must know, without your untimely interruption—'

'Sorry!'

Morse shook his head slowly. 'No. I've been sitting here looking at the bloody thing for ten minutes.'

'Can I help?'

'Extremely improbable!'

'Don't you want to try me?'

Reluctantly Morse handed over the crossword, and Lewis contemplated the troublesome clue: 'Kick in the pants?' (3–5). Three of the eight letters were entered: – I – – L– S –.

A short while later Lewis handed the crossword back

across the desk. He'd tried so hard, so very hard, to make some intelligent suggestion; to score some Brownie points. But nothing had come to mind.

'If it's OK with you, sir, I'd like to spend some time down at St Aldate's this morning – see if we can find some link between all these burglaries in North Oxford.'

'Why not? And good luck. Don't give 'em *my* address though, will you?'

After Lewis had gone, Morse stared down at the cross-word again. Seldom was it that he failed to finish things off, and that within a pretty smartish time, too. All he needed was a large Scotch ... and the answer (he knew) would hit him straight between the eyes. But it was only 8.35 a.m. and—

It hit him.

Scotch!

As he swiftly filled in the five remaining blank squares, he was smiling beatifically, wishing only that Lewis had been there to appreciate the *coup de grâce*.

But Lewis wasn't.

And it was only many months later that Lewis was to learn – and then purely by accident – the answer to that clue in *The Times* crossword for 25 May 1994, a day (as would appear in retrospect) on which so many things of fateful consequence were destined to occur.

PART ONE

CHAPTER ONE

Pension: generally understood to mean monies grudgingly bestowed on aging hirelings after a lifetime of occasional devotion to duty
  (*Small's Enlarged English Dictionary*, 12th Edition)

JUST AFTER noon on Wednesday, 31 August 1994, Chief Inspector Morse was seated at his desk in the Thames Valley Police HQ building at Kidlington, Oxon – when the phone rang.

'Morse? You're there, are you? I thought you'd probably be in the pub by now.'

Morse forbore the sarcasm, and assured Chief Superintendent Strange – he had recognized the voice – that indeed he was there.

'Two things, Morse – but I'll come along to your office.'

'You wouldn't prefer me—?'

'I need the exercise, so the wife says.'

Not only the wife, mumbled Morse, as he cradled the phone, beginning now to clear the cluttered papers from the immediate desk-space in front of him.

Strange lumbered in five minutes later and sat down heavily on the chair opposite the desk.

'You may have to get that name-plate changed.'

Strange and Morse had never really been friends, but never really been enemies either; and some good-natured bantering had been the order of the day following the recommendation of the Sheehy Report six months earlier that the rank of Chief Inspector should be abolished. *Mutual* bantering, since Chief Superintendents too were also likely to descend a rung on the ladder.

It was a disgruntled Strange who now sat wheezing methodically and shaking his head slowly. 'It's like losing your stripes in the Army, isn't it? It's . . . it's . . .'

'Belittling,' suggested Morse.

Strange looked up keenly. '"Demeaning" – that's what I was going to say. Much better word, eh? So don't start trying to teach *me* the bloody English language.'

Fair point, thought Morse, as he reminded himself (as he'd often done before) that he and his fellow police-officers should never underestimate the formidable Chief Superintendent Strange.

'How can I help, sir? Two things, you said.'

'Ah! Well, yes. That's *one*, isn't it? What we've just been talking about. You see, I'm jacking the job in next year, as you've probably heard?'

Morse nodded cautiously.

'Well, that's it. It's the, er, pension I'm thinking about.'

'It won't affect the pension.'

'You think not?'

'Sure it won't. It's just a question of getting all the paperwork right. That's why they're sending all these forms around—'

'How do you know?' Strange's eyes shot up again, sharply focused, and it was Morse's turn to hesitate.

'I – I'm thinking of, er, jacking in the job myself, sir.'

'Don't be so bloody stupid, man! This place can't afford to lose me *and* you.'

'I shall only be going on for a couple of years, whatever happens.'

'And . . . and you've had the forms, you say?'

Morse nodded.

'And . . . and you've actually filled 'em *in*?' Strange's voice sounded incredulous.

'Not yet, no. Forms always give me a terrible headache. I've got a phobia about form-filling.'

No words from Morse could have been more pleasing, and Strange's moon-face positively beamed. 'You know, that's exactly what I said to the wife – about headaches and all that.'

'Why doesn't *she* help you?'

'Says it gives her a headache, too.'

The two men chuckled amiably.

'You'd like me to help?' asked Morse tentatively.

'Would you? Be a huge relief all round, I can tell you. We could go for a pint together next week, couldn't we? And if I go and buy a bottle of aspirin—'

'Make it *two* pints.'

'I'll make it two bottles, then.'

'You're on, sir.'

'Good. That's settled then.'

Strange was silent awhile, as if considering some matter of great moment. Then he spoke.

'Now, let's come to the second thing I want to talk about – far more important.'

Morse raised his eyebrows. 'Far more important than *pensions*?'

'Well, a bit more important perhaps.'

COLIN DEXTER

'Murder?'

'Murder.'

'Not *another* one?'

'Same one. The one near you. The McClure murder.'

'Phillotson's on it.'

'Phillotson's *off* it.'

'But—'

'His wife's ill. Very ill. I want you to take over.'

'But—'

'You see, you haven't got a wife who's very ill, have you? You haven't got a wife at all.'

'No,' replied Morse quietly. No good arguing with that.

'Happy to take over?'

'Is Lewis—?'

'I've just had a quick word with him in the canteen. Once he's finished his egg and chips . . .'

'Oh!'

'*And*' – Strange lifted his large frame laboriously from the chair – 'I've got this gut-feeling that Phillotson wouldn't have got very far with it anyway.'

'*Gut*-feeling?'

'What's wrong with that?' snapped Strange. 'Don't *you* ever get a gut-feeling?'

'Occasionally . . .'

'After too much booze!'

'Or mixing things, sir. You know what I mean: few pints of beer and a bottle of wine.'

'Yes . . .' Strange nodded. 'We'll probably both have a gut-feeling soon, eh? After a few pints of beer and a bottle of aspirin.'

6

He opened the door and looked at the name-plate again. 'Perhaps we shan't need to change them after all, Morse.'

CHAPTER TWO

Like the sweet apple which reddens upon the
   topmost bough,
A-top on the topmost twig – which the pluckers
   forgot somehow –
Forgot it not, nay, but got it not, for none could
   get it till now
      (D. G. ROSSETTI, *Translations from Sappho*)

IT WAS to be only the second time that Morse had ever taken over a murder enquiry after the preliminary – invariably dramatic – trappings were done with: the discovery of the deed, the importunate attention of the media, the immediate scene-of-crime investigation, and the final removal of the body.

Lewis, perceptively, had commented that it was all a bit like getting into a football match twenty-five minutes late, and asking a fellow spectator what the score was. But Morse had been unimpressed by the simile, since his life would not have been significantly impoverished had the game of football never been invented.

Indeed, there was a sense in which Morse was happier to have avoided any *in situ* inspection of the corpse, since the liquid contents of his stomach almost inevitably curdled at the sight of violent death. And he knew that the death there *had* been violent – very violent indeed. Much blood had been spilt, albeit now caked and dirty-brown – blood that would still (he supposed) be much in evidence around the chalk-lined contours of the spot on the saturated beige carpet where a man had been found with an horrific knife-wound in his lower belly.

'What's wrong with Phillotson?' Lewis had asked as they'd driven down to North Oxford.

'Nothing wrong with him – except incompetence. It's his wife. She's had something go wrong with an operation, so they say. Some, you know, some internal trouble . . . woman's trouble.'

'The womb, you mean, sir?'

'I don't *know*, do I, Lewis? I didn't ask. I'm not even quite sure exactly where the womb is. And, come to think of it, I don't even *like* the word.'

'I only asked.'

'And I only answered! His wife'll be fine, you'll see. It's him. He's just chickening out.'

'And the Super . . . didn't think he could cope with the case?'

'Well, he couldn't, could he? He's not exactly perched on the topmost twig of the Thames Valley intelligentsia, now is he?'

Lewis had glanced across at the man seated beside him in the passenger seat, noting the supercilious, almost arrogant, cast of the harsh blue eyes, and the complacent-looking smile about the lips. It was the sort of conceit which Lewis found the least endearing quality of his chief: worse even than his meanness with money and his almost total lack of gratitude. And suddenly he felt a shudder of distaste.

Yet only briefly. For Morse's face had become serious again as he'd pointed to the right; pointed to Daventry

Avenue; and amplified his answer as the car braked to a halt outside a block of flats:

'You see, we take a bit of beating, don't we, Lewis? Don't you reckon? Me and you? Morse and Lewis? Not *too* many twigs up there above us, are there?'

But as Morse unfastened his safety-belt, there now appeared a hint of diffidence upon his face.

'*Nous vieillissons, n'est-ce pas?*'

'Pardon, sir?'

'We're all getting older – that's what I said. And that's the only thing that's worrying me about this case, old friend.'

But then the smile again.

And Lewis saw the smile, and smiled himself; for at that moment he felt quite preternaturally content with life.

The constable designated to oversee the murder-premises volunteered to lead the way upstairs; but Morse shook his head, his response needlessly brusque:

'Just give me the key, lad.'

Only two short flights, of eight steps each, led up to the first floor; yet Morse was a little out of breath as Lewis opened the main door of the maisonette.

'Yes' – Morse's mind was still on Phillotson – 'I reckon he'd've been about as competent in this case as a dyslexic proofreader.'

'I like that, sir. That's good. Original, is it?'

Morse grunted. In fact it had been Strange's own appraisal of Phillotson's potential; but, as ever, Morse was perfectly happy to take full credit for the *bons mots* of others. Anyway, Strange himself had probably read it somewhere, hadn't he? Shrewd enough, was Strange: but hardly perched up there on the roof of Canary Wharf.

Smoothly the door swung open ... The door swung open on another case.

And as Lewis stepped through the small entrance-hall, and thence into the murder room, he found himself wondering how things would turn out here.

Certainly it hadn't sounded all that extraordinary a case when, two hours earlier, Detective Chief Inspector Phillotson had given them an hour-long briefing on the murder of Dr Felix McClure, former Student – late Student – of Wolsey College, Oxford ...

Bizarre and bewildering – that's what so many cases in the past had proved to be; and despite Phillotson's briefing the present case would probably be no different.

In this respect, at least, Lewis was correct in his thinking. What he could not have known – what, in fact, he never really came to know – was what unprecedented anguish the present case would cause to Morse's soul.

CHAPTER THREE

Myself when young did eagerly frequent
   Doctor and Saint, and heard great Argument
   About it and about: but evermore
Came out by the same Door as in I went
   (EDWARD FITZGERALD, *The Rubaiyat of Omar*
                          Khayyam)

DAVENTRY COURT (Phillotson had begun), comprising eight 'luxurious apartments' built in Daventry Avenue in 1989, had been difficult to sell. House prices had tumbled during the ever-deepening recession of the early nineties, and McClure had bought in the spring of 1993 when he'd convinced himself (rightly) that even in the continuing buyers' market Flat 6 was a bit of a snip at £99,500.

McClure himself was almost sixty-seven years old at the time of his murder, knifed (as Morse would be able to see for himself) in quite horrendous fashion. The knife, according to pathological findings, was unusually broad-bladed, and at least five inches in length. Of such a weapon, however, no trace whatsoever had been found. Blood, though? Oh, yes. Blood almost everywhere. Blood on almost everything. Blood on the murderer too? Surely so.

Blood certainly on his shoes (trainers?), with footprints – especially of the right foot – clearly traceable from the murder scene to the staircase, to the main entrance; but thence virtually lost, soon completely lost, on the gravelled forecourt outside. Successive scufflings by other residents had obviously obliterated all further traces of blood. Or had the murderer left by a car parked close to the main door? Or left on a bicycle chained to the nearest drainpipe? (Or taken his shoes off, Lewis thought.) But intensive search of the forecourt area had revealed nothing. No clues from the sides of the block either. No clues from the rear. No clues at all outside. (Or perhaps just the one clue, Morse had thought: the clue that there *were* no clues at all?)

Inside? Well, again, Morse would be able to see for himself. Evidence of extraneous fingerprints? Virtually none. Hopeless. And certainly no indication that the assailant – murderer – had entered the premises through any first-floor window.

'Very rare means of ingress, Morse, as you know. Pretty certainly came in the same way as he went out.'

'Reminds me a bit of Omar Khayyam,' Morse had muttered.

But Phillotson had merely looked puzzled, his own words clearly not reminding himself of anyone. Or anything.

No. Entry from the main door, surely, via the Entryphone system, with McClure himself admitting whomsoever (not Phillotson's word) – be it man or woman. Someone known to McClure then? Most likely.

Time? Well, certainly after 8.30 a.m. on the Sunday he was murdered, since McClure had purchased two newspapers at about 8 a.m. that morning from the newsagent's in Summertown, where he was at least a well-known face if not a well-known name; and where he (like Morse, as it happened) usually catered for both the coarse and the cultured sides of his nature with the *News of the World* and *The Sunday Times*. No doubts here. No hypothesis required. Each of the two news-sheets was found, unbloodied, on the work-top in the 'all-mod-con kitchen'.

After 8.30 a.m. then. But before when? Preliminary findings – well, *not* so preliminary – from the pathologist firmly suggested that McClure had been dead for about twenty hours or so before being found, at 7.45 a.m. the following morning, by his cleaning-lady.

Hypothesis here, then, for the time of the murder? Between 10 a.m., say, and noon the previous day. Roughly. But then everything was 'roughly' with these wretched pathologists, wasn't it? (And Morse had smiled sadly, and thought of Max; and nodded slowly, for Phillotson was preaching to the converted.)

One other circumstance most probably corroborating a pre-noon time for the murder was the readily observable, and duly observed, fact that there was no apparent sign, such as the preparation of meat and vegetables, for any potential Sunday lunch in Flat 6. Not that that was conclusive in itself, since it had already become clear, from sensibly orientated enquiries, that it had not been unusual for McClure to walk down the Banbury Road and order a Sunday lunch – 8oz Steak, French Fries, Salad – only £3.99 – at the King's Arms, washed down with a couple of pints of Best Bitter; no sweet; no coffee. But there had been no sign of steak or chips or lettuce or anything much else when the pathologist had split open the white-skinned belly of Dr

Felix McClure. No sign of any lunchtime sustenance at all.

The body had been found in a hunched-up, foetal posture, with both hands clutching the lower abdomen and the eyes screwed tightly closed as if McClure had died in the throes of some excruciating pain. He was dressed in a short-sleeved shirt, vertically striped in maroon and blue, a black Jaeger cardigan, and a pair of dark-grey flannels – the lower part of the shirt and the upper regions of the trousers stiff and steeped in the blood that had oozed so abundantly.

McClure had been one of those 'perpetual students in life' (Phillotson's words). After winning a Major Scholarship to Oxford in 1946, he had gained a First in Mods, a First in Greats – thereafter spending forty-plus years of his life as Ancient History Tutor in Wolsey College. In 1956 he had married one of his own pupils, an undergraduette from Somerville – the latter, after attaining exactly similar distinction, duly appointed to a Junior Fellowship in Merton, and in 1966 (life jumping forward in decades) running off with one of her own pupils, a bearded undergraduate from Trinity. No children, though; no legal problems. Just a whole lot of heartache, perhaps.

Few major publications to his name – mostly a series of articles written over the years for various classical journals. But at least he had lived long enough to see the publication of his *magnum opus*: *The Great Plague at Athens: Its Effect on the Course and Conduct of the Peloponnesian War*. A long title. A long work.

Witnesses?

Of the eight 'luxurious apartments' only four had

been sold, with two of the others being let, and the other two still empty, the 'For Sale' notices standing outside the respective properties – one of them the apartment immediately below McClure's, Number 5; the other Number 2. Questioning of the tenants had produced no information of any value: the newly-weds in Number 1 had spent most of the Sunday morning a-bed – sans breakfast, sans newspapers, sans everything except themselves; the blue-rinsed old lady in Number 3, extremely deaf, had insisted on making a very full statement to the effect that she had heard nothing on that fateful morn; the couple in Number 4 had been out all morning on a Charity 'Save the Whales' Walk in Wytham Woods; the temporary tenants of Number 7 were away in Tunisia; and the affectionate couple who had bought Number 8 had been uninterruptedly employed in redecorating their bathroom, with the radio on most of the morning as they caught up with *The Archers* omnibus. (For the first time in several minutes, Morse's interest had been activated.)

'Not *all* that much to go on,' Phillotson had admitted; yet all the same, not without some degree of pride, laying a hand on two green box-files filled with reports and statements and notes and documents and a plan showing the full specification of McClure's apartment, with arcs and rulings and arrows and dotted lines and measurements. Morse himself had never been able to follow such house-plans; and now glanced only cursorily through the stapled sheets supplied by Adkinsons, Surveyors, Valuers, and Estate Agents – as Phillotson came to the end of his briefing.

16

'By the way,' asked Morse, rising to his feet, 'how's the wife? I meant to ask earlier . . .'

'Very poorly, I'm afraid,' said Phillotson, miserably.

'Cheerful sod, isn't he, Lewis?'

The two men had been back in Morse's office then, Lewis seeking to find a place on the desk for the bulging box-files.

'Well, he must be pretty worried about his wife if—'

'Pah! He just didn't know where to go next – that was his trouble.'

'And we *do*?'

'Well, for a start, I wouldn't mind knowing which of those newspapers McClure read first.'

'If either.'

Morse nodded. 'And I wouldn't mind finding out if he made any phone-calls that morning.'

'Can't we get British Telecom to itemize things?'

'Can we?' asked Morse vaguely.

'You'll want to see the body?'

'Why on earth should I want to do that?'

'I just thought—'

'I wouldn't mind seeing that shirt, though. Maroon and blue vertical stripes, didn't Phillotson say?' Morse passed the index finger of his left hand round the inside of his slightly tight, slightly frayed shirt-collar. 'I'm thinking of, er, expanding my wardrobe a bit.'

But the intended humour was lost on Lewis, to whom it seemed exceeding strange that Morse should at the same time apparently show more interest in the dead man's shirt than in his colleague's wife. 'Apparently' though ... that was always the thing about Morse: no one could ever really plot a graph of the thoughts that ran through that extraordinary mind.

'Did we learn anything – from Phillotson, sir?'

'You may have done: I didn't. I knew just as much about things when I went into his office as when I came out.'

'Reminds you a bit of Omar Khayyam, doesn't it?' suggested Lewis, innocently.

CHAPTER FOUR

Krook chalked the letter upon the wall – in a very curious manner, beginning with the end of the letter, and shaping it backward. It was a capital letter, not a printed one.

'Can you read it?' he asked me with a keen glance

(CHARLES DICKENS, *Bleak House*)

THE sitting-cum-dining-room – the murder room – 12′ × 17′2″ as stated in Adkinsons' (doubtless accurate) specifications, was very much the kind of room one might expect as the main living-area of a retired Oxford don: an oak table with four chairs around it; a brown leather settee; a matching armchair; TV; CD and cassette player; books almost everywhere on floor-to-ceiling shelves; busts of Homer, Thucydides, Milton, and Beethoven; not enough space really for the many pictures – including the head, in the Pittura Pompeiana series, of Theseus, Slayer of the Minotaur. Those were the main things. Morse recognized three of the busts readily and easily, though he had to guess at the bronze head of Thucydides. As for Lewis, he recognized all four immediately, since his eyesight was now keener than Morse's, and the name of each of those immortals was inscribed in tiny capitals upon its plinth.

For a while Morse stood by the armchair, looking all round him, saying nothing. Through the open door of the kitchen – 6′10″ × 9′6″ – he could see the Oxford Almanack hanging from the wall facing him, and finally went through to admire 'St Hilda's College' from a watercolour by Sir Hugh Casson, RA. Pity, perhaps, it was the previous year's, for Morse now read its date, 'MDCCCCLXXXXIII'; and for a few moments he found himself considering whether any other year in the twentieth century – in *any* century – could command any lengthier designation. Fourteen characters required for '1993'.

Still, the Romans never knew much about numbers.

'Do you know how many walking-sticks plus umbrellas we've got in the hall-stand here?' shouted Lewis from the tiny entrance area.

'Fourteen!' shouted Morse in return.

'How the – how on earth—?'

'For me, Lewis, coincidence in life is wholly unexceptional; the readily predictable norm in life. You know that by now, surely?'

Lewis said nothing. He knew well where his duties lay in circumstances such as these: to do the donkey-work; to look through everything, without much purpose, and often without much hope. But Morse was a stickler for sifting the evidence; always had been. The only trouble was that he never wanted to waste his own time in helping to sift it, for such work was excessively tedious; and frequently fruitless, to boot.

So Lewis did it all. And as Morse sat back in the settee and looked through McClure's *magnum opus,* Lewis started to go through all the drawers and all the letters and all the piles of papers and the detritus of the litter-bins – just as earlier Phillotson and his team had done. Lewis didn't mind, though. Occasionally in the past he'd found some item unusual enough (well, unusual enough to Morse) that had set the great mind scurrying off into some subtly sign-posted avenue, or cul-de-sac; that had set the keenest-nosed hound in the pack on to some previously unsuspected scent.

Two things only of interest here, Lewis finally informed Morse. And Phillotson himself had pointed out the potential importance of the first of these, anyway: a black plastic W. H. Smith Telephone Index, with eighteen alphabetical divisions, the collocation of the less common letters, such as 'WX' and 'YZ', counting as one. The brief introductory instructions (under 'A') suggested that the user might find it valuable to record therein, for speed of reference, the telephone numbers of such indispensable personages as Decorator, Dentist, Doctor, Electrician, Plumber, Police . . .

Lewis opened the index at random: at the letter 'M'. Six names on the card there. Three of the telephone numbers were prefixed with the Inner London code, '071'; the other three were Oxford numbers, five digits each, all beginning with '5'.

Lewis sighed audibly. Eighteen times six? That was a hundred and eight . . . Still it might be worthwhile ringing round (had Phillotson thought the same?) provided there were no more than half a dozen or so per page. He pressed the index to a couple of other letters. 'P': eight names and numbers. 'C': just four. What about the twinned letters? He pressed 'KL': seven, with six of them 'L'; and just the one 'K' – and that (interestingly enough?) entered as the single capital letter 'K'. Who was K when he was at home?

Or she?

'What does "K" stand for, sir?'

Morse, a crossword fanatic from his early teens, knew some of the answers immediately: ' "King"; "Kelvin" – unit of temperature, Lewis; er, "thousand"; "kilometre", of course; "Köchel", the man who catalogued Mozart, as you know; er . . .'

'Not much help.'

'Initial of someone's name?'

'Why just the initial?'

'Girl's name? Perhaps he's trying to disguise his simmering passion for a married woman – what about that? Or perhaps all the girls at the local knocking-shop are known by a letter of the alphabet?'

'Didn't know you had one up here, sir.'

'Lewis, we have everything in North Oxford. It's just a question of knowing where it is, that's the secret.'

Lewis mused aloud. 'Karen . . . or Kirsty . . .'

'Kylie?'

'You've heard of *her*, sir?'

'Only just.'

'Kathy . . .'

'Well, there's one pretty simple way of finding out, isn't there? Can't you just ring the number? Isn't that what you're supposed to be doing? That sort of thing?'

Lewis picked up the phone and dialled the five-digit number – and was answered immediately.

'Yeah? Wha' d'ya wan'?' a woman's voice bawled at him.

'Hullo. Er – have I got the right number for "K"?'

'Yeah. You 'ave. Bu' she's no' 'ere, is she?'

'No, obviously not. I'll try again later.'

'You a dur'y ol' man, or sump'n?'

Lewis quickly replaced the receiver, the colour rising in his pale cheeks.

Morse, who had heard the brief exchange clearly, grinned at his discomfited sergeant. 'You can't win 'em all.'

'Waste of time, if that's anything to go by.'

'You think so?'

'Don't *you?*'

'Lewis! You were only on the phone for about ten seconds but you learned she was a "she", probably a she with the name of "Kay".'

'I didn't!'

'A she of easy virtue who old Felix here spent a few happy hours with. Or, as you'd prefer it, with whom old Felix regularly spent a few felicitous hours.'

'You can't just say that—'

'Furthermore she's a local lass, judging by her curly Oxfordshire accent and her typical habit of omitting all her "t"s.'

'But I didn't even *get* the woman!'

Morse was silent for a few seconds; then he looked up, his face more serious. 'Are you sure, Lewis? Are you quite sure you haven't just been speaking to the cryptic "K" herself?'

Lewis shook his head, grinned ruefully, and said nothing. He knew – knew again now – why he'd never rise to any great heights in life himself. Morse had got it wrong, of course. Morse nearly always got things hopelessly, ridiculously wrong at the start of every case. But he always seemed to have thoughts that no one else was capable of thinking. Like now.

'Anyway, what's this other thing you've found?'

But before Lewis could answer, there was a quiet tap on the door and PC Roberts stuck a reverential, unhelmeted head into the room.

'There's a Mrs Wynne-Wilson here, sir, from one of the other flats. Says she wants a word, like.'

Morse looked up from his Thucydides. 'Haven't we already got a statement from her, Lewis?'

But it was Roberts who answered. 'She says she made a statement, sir, but when she heard someone else was in charge – well, she said Inspector Phillotson didn't really want to know, like.'

'Really?'

'And she's, well, she's a bit deaf, like.'

'Like what?' asked Morse.

'Pardon?'

'Forget it.'

'Shall I show her in, sir?'

'What? In here? You know what happened here, don't you? She'd probably faint, man.'

'Doubt it, sir. She says she was sort of in charge of nurses at some London hospital.'

'Ah, a matron,' said Morse.

'They don't call them "matrons" any longer,' interposed Lewis.

'Thank you very much, Lewis! Send her in.'

CHAPTER FIVE

O quid solutis est beatius curis,
Cum mens onus reponit, ac peregrino
Labore fessi venimus larem ad nostrum,
Desideratoque acquiescimus lecto?

(What bliss! First spot the house – and then
Flop down – on one's old bed again)

(CATULLUS, *31*)

JULIA STEVENS had returned home that same afternoon.

The flight had been on time (early, in fact); Customs had been swift and uncomplicated; the Gatwick–Heathrow–Oxford coach had been standing there, just waiting for her, it seemed, welcoming her back to England. From the bus station at Gloucester Green she had taken a taxi (no queue) out to East Oxford, the driver duly helping her with two heavyweight cases right up to the front door of her house – a house which, as the taxi turned into the street, she'd immediately observed to be still standing there, unburned, unvandalized; and, as she could see as she stood inside her own living-room – at long last! – blessedly unburgled.

How glad she was to be back. Almost always, on the first two nights of any holiday away from home, she experienced a weepy nostalgia. But usually this proved to be only a re-adjustment. Usually, too, at least for the

COLIN DEXTER

last two days of her statutory annual fortnight abroad, she felt a similar wrench on leaving her summer surroundings; on bidding farewell to her newly made holiday friends. One or two friends in particular.

One or two men, as often as not.

But such had not been the case this time on her package tour round the Swiss and Italian lakes. She couldn't explain why: the coach-driver had been very competent; the guide good; the scenery spectacular; the fellow-tourists pleasantly friendly. But she'd not enjoyed it at all. My god! What was happening to her?

(But she knew exactly what was happening to her.)

Not that she'd said anything, of course. And Brenda Brooks had received a cheerful postcard from a multi-starred hotel on Lake Lucerne:

> Wed.
> Having a splendid time here with a nice lot of people. My room looks right across the lake. Tomorrow we go over to Triebschen (hope I've spelt that right) where Richard Wagner spent some of his life. There was a firework display last night – tho' nobody told us why. Off to Lugano Friday.
> Love Julia
> PS Give St Giles a big hug for me.

As Julia walked through her front door that afternoon, her house smelt clean and fragrant; smelt of pine and polish and Windolene. Bless her – bless Brenda Brooks!

Then, on the kitchen table, there was a note – the sort of note that she, Julia, had ever come to expect:

> Dear Mrs S,
> I got your card thankyou & I'm glad you had a good time. St Giles has been fine, there are two more tins of Whiskas in the fridge. See you Monday. There's something I want to tell you about & perhaps you can help – I hope so. Welcome home!!
> Brenda (Brooks)

Julia smiled to herself. Brenda invariably appended her (bracketed) surname as though the household boasted a whole bevy of charladies. And always that deferential 'Mrs S'. Brenda had worked for her for four years now, and at fifty-two was nearly seven years her senior. Again Julia smiled to herself. Then, as she re-read the penultimate sentence, for a moment she found herself frowning slightly.

It was a pleasant sunny day, with September heralding a golden finale to what had been a hot and humid summer. Indeed, the temperature was well above the average for an autumn day. Yet Julia felt herself shivering slightly as she unlocked and unbolted the rear door. And if a few moments earlier she may have looked a little sad, a little strained – behold now a metamorphosis! A ginger cat parted the ground-cover greenery at the bottom of the small garden and peered up at his mistress; and suddenly Julia Stevens looked very happy once again.

And very beautiful.

CHAPTER SIX

Envy and idleness married together beget curiosity
(THOMAS FULLER, *Gnomologia*)

MORSE DECIDED to interview Laura Wynne-Wilson, should that good lady allow it, in her own ground-floor apartment. And the good lady did so allow.

She was, she admitted, very doubtful about whether that previous policeman had attended to her evidence with sufficient seriousness. Indeed, she had formed the distinct impression that he had listened, albeit politely, in a wholly perfunctory way to what she had to say. Which was? Which was to do with Dr McClure – a nice gentleman; and a *very* good neighbour, who had acted as Secretary of the Residents' Action Committee and written such a *splendid* letter to that cowboy outfit supposedly responsible for the upkeep of the exterior of the properties.

She spoke primly and quietly, a thin smile upon thin lips.

'And what exactly have you got to tell us?' bawled Morse.

'Please don't *shout* at me, Inspector! Deaf people do *not* require excessive volume – they require only clarity of speech and appropriate lip-movement.'

Lewis smiled sweetly to himself as the small, white-haired octogenarian continued:

'What I have to tell you is this. Dr McClure had a fairly regular visitor here. A . . . a lady-friend.'

'Not all that unusual, is it?' suggested Morse, with what he hoped was adequate clarity and appropriate lip-movement.

'Oh, no. After all, it might well have been some female relative.'

Morse nodded. Already he knew that McClure had no living relatives apart from a niece in New Zealand; but still he nodded.

'And then again, Inspector, it might *not*. You see, he had no living relatives in the United Kingdom.'

'Oh.' Morse decided that, unlike Phillotson, he at least would treat the old girl with a modicum of respect.

'No. It was his "fancy woman", as we used to call it. By the way, I quite like that term myself, don't you?'

'Plenty of worse words, madam,' interposed Lewis, though apparently with less than adequate clarity.

'Pardon?' Laura W-W turned herself in the approximate direction of the man taking notes, as if he were merely some supernumerary presence.

And now it was Morse's turn to smile sweetly to himself.

'As I was saying, this . . . this woman came to see him several times – certainly three or four times during the last month.'

'What time of day was that?'

'Always at about half-past seven.'

'And you, er, you actually saw her?'

'"Actually" is a ridiculous word, isn't it? It's a weasel word, Inspector. It means nothing whatsoever. It's a space-filler. Whether I *actually* saw her, I don't know. What I *do* know is that I *saw* her. All right?'

Touché.

Morse's eyes wandered over to the wooden-frame casement, where the thin white lace curtains were pulled back in tight arcs at each side, with potted geraniums at either end of the window ledge, and three tasteful pieces of dark-blue and white porcelain positioned between them. But nothing there to clutter the clear view, from where Morse was sitting, over the whole front area of the apartments, especially of the two square, yellow-brick pillars which stood at either side of the entrance drive; and through which, per-force, everyone coming into Daventry Court must surely pass. Everyone except a burglar, perhaps. Or a murderer ... And this nosey old woman would delight in observing the visitors who called upon her fellow residents, Morse felt confident of that.

'This could be very helpful to our enquiries, you realize that, don't you? If you saw her clearly ... ?'

'My eyesight is not what it was, Inspector. But I had a good view of her, yes.' She glanced keenly at Morse. 'You see, I'm a nosey old woman with very little else to do – that's what you're thinking, anyway.'

'Well, I – we all like to know what's going on. It's only human nature.'

'Oh, no. I know several people who aren't in the *slightest* bit interested in "what's going on", as you put it. But I'm glad *you're* nosey, like me. That's good.'

Lewis was enjoying the interview immensely.

'Can you tell us something about this woman? Anything?'

COLIN DEXTER

'Let's say I found her interesting.'

'Why was that?'

'Well, for a start, I envied her. She was less than half his age, you see – good deal less, I shouldn't doubt.'

'And he,' mused Morse, 'was sixty-six . . .'

'Sixty-seven, Inspector, if he'd lived to the end of the month.'

'How—?'

'I looked him up in *Distinguished People of Today*. He's a Libra.'

Like me, thought Morse. And I wonder how old you are, you old biddy.

'And I'm eighty-three in December,' she continued, 'just in case you're wondering.'

'I was, yes,' said Morse, smiling at her, and himself now beginning to enjoy the interview.

'The other thing that struck me was that she wasn't at *all* nice-looking. Quite the opposite, in fact. Very shabbily dressed – darkish sort of clothes. Sloppy loose blouse, mini-skirt right up to . . .'

'The top of her tibia,' supplied Morse, enunciating the 't' of the last word with exaggerated exactitude.

'Absolutely! And she had a big old shoulder-bag, too.'

I wonder what was in that, thought Morse.

'Anything else you can remember?'

'Long – longish – dark hair. Earrings – great brassy-looking things about the size of hula-hoops. And she had a ring in her nose. I could see that. For all I know, she could have had *two* rings in her nose.'

God helps us all, thought Morse.

32

'But I'm not sure about that. As I say, my eyesight isn't what it used to be.'

I wonder what it used to be like, thought Lewis.

'Did she come by car?' asked Morse.

'No. If she did, she left it somewhere else.'

'Did she come in from . . . ?' Morse gestured vaguely to his left, towards the Banbury Road.

'Yes. She came from the Banbury Road – not the Woodstock Road.'

'Would you recognize her again?'

For the first time the old lady hesitated, rubbing the thin ringless fingers of her left hand with her right.

'Oh dear. Do you think she may have *murdered* him? I only—'

'No, no. I'm sure she didn't.' Morse spoke with the bogus confidence of a man who was beginning to wonder if she had.

'I only wanted to help. And I'm not at *all* sure if I would recognize her. Perhaps if she dolled herself up in some decent outfit and . . .'

Took that bull-ring out of her nose, thought Morse.

'. . . and took that ring out of her nose.'

Phew!

But some of the bounce had gone out of the old girl, Morse could see that. It was time to wind things up.

'Do you think they went to bed when she came?'

'I expect so, don't you?'

'Things must have changed a good deal since your day, Miss Wynne-Wilson.'

'Don't be silly, Inspector! I could teach some of these young flibbertigibbets a few things about going to bed

33

with men. After all, I spent most of my life looking after men in bed, now didn't I? And, by the way, it's *Mrs* Wynne-Wilson. I don't wear a wedding ring any longer . . .'

Phew!

Morse got to his feet. He had only one more question: 'Were you looking out of the window on Sunday morning – you know, about the time perhaps when Dr McClure was murdered?'

'No. On Sunday mornings I always hear the omnibus edition of *The Archers* on the wireless, that's from ten to eleven. Lovely. I have a really good long soak – and hear everything again.'

Dangerous thing that – having a radio in the bathroom, thought Lewis.

'It's dangerous they tell me – having a wireless propped up on the bath-rail. But I do so enjoy doing silly things, now that I'm so old.'

Phew!

It had not been much of a contest, Lewis appreciated that; but from his scorecard he had little hesitation in declaring Mrs W-W the winner, way ahead of Morse on points.

Quite mistakenly, of course.

CHAPTER SEVEN

For 'tis in vain to think or guess
At women by appearances
(SAMUEL BUTLER, *Hudibras*)

'WHAT DID you make of that, then?' asked Lewis,
when the two detectives had returned to McClure's
apartment.

Morse appeared disappointed. 'I'd begun to think
he was a civilized sort of fellow – you know . . .' Morse
gestured vaguely around the bookshelves.

'But he wasn't?'

'We-ell.'

'You mean . . . this woman he was seeing?'

Morse's features reflected disapproval. 'Rings in her
nose, Lewis? Pretty tasteless, isn't it? Like drinking lager
with roast beef.'

'For all you know she may be a lovely girl, sir. You
shouldn't really judge people just by appearances.'

'Oh?' Morse's eyes shot up swiftly. 'And why the hell
not?'

'Well . . .' But Lewis wasn't sure why. He did have a
point, though; he knew he did. Morse was always
making snap judgements. All right, one or two would
occasionally turn out to be accurate; but most of them
were woefully wide of the mark – as, to be fair, Morse
himself readily acknowledged.

Lewis thought of events earlier in the day; thought

35

of Phillotson's withdrawal from the present case; thought of Morse's almost contemptuous dismissal of the man's excuses. Almost automatically, it seemed, Morse had assumed him to be parading a few phoney pretexts about his wife's hospitalization in order to avoid the humiliation of failure in a murder case. Agreed, Phillotson wasn't exactly Sherlock Holmes, Lewis knew that. Yet Morse could be needlessly cruel about some of his colleagues. And why did he have to be so *sharp*? As he had been just now?

Still, Lewis knew exactly what to do about his own temporary irritation. Count to ten! – that's what Morse had once told him – before getting on to any high horse; and then, if necessary, count to twenty. Not that there was much sign that Morse ever heeded his own advice. *He* usually only counted to two or three. If that.

Deciding, therefore, the time to be as yet inopportune for any consideration of the old lady's testimony, Lewis reverted to his earlier task. There was still a great deal of material to look through, and he was glad to get down to something whose purpose he could readily grasp. The papers there, all the papers in the drawers and those stacked along the shelves, had already been examined – clearly that was the case. Not radically disturbed, though; not taken away to be documented in some dubious filing-system until sooner or later, as with almost everything in life, being duly labelled 'OBE'.

Overtaken By Events.

Glancing across at Morse, Lewis saw the chief abstracting another book from a set of volumes beautifully bound in golden leather; a slim volume this time;

a volume of verse by the look of it. And even as he watched, he saw Morse turning the book through ninety degrees and apparently reading some marginalia beside one of the poems there. For the present, however, the Do Not Disturb sign was prominently displayed, and with his usual competence Lewis resumed his own considerable task.

Thus it was that for the next half-hour or so the two men sat reading their different texts; preparing (as it were) for their different examinations; each conscious of the other's presence; yet each, for the moment, and for different reasons, unwilling to speak his own immediate thoughts.

Especially Morse.

Yet it was the latter who finally broke the silence.

'What did you make of her, then? Our Mrs Wynne-Wilson?'

'"*Mrs*", sir?' asked Lewis slowly.

Morse threw an interested, inquisitive look at his sergeant. 'Go on!'

'Well, I'd noticed from the start she wasn't wearing a wedding ring. As you did, of course.'

'Of course.'

'But I couldn't see any, you know, any mark of any ring like you'd normally have, wouldn't you? A sort of, you know, pale ring of skin, sort of thing, where the ring had been – before she took it off.'

'Not a particularly fluent sentence that, Lewis, if I may say so.'

'But you noticed that too?'

'Me? Your eyesight's far better than mine.'

'Makes you wonder, though.'

'You reckon she was making it up – about her marriage?'

'Wouldn't surprise me, sir.'

'And apart from that?'

'She seemed a pretty good witness. Her mind's pretty sharp. She got you weighed up all right.'

'Ye-es ... So you don't think she was making anything else up?'

'No. Do you?'

'Lew-is! When will you learn. She's a phoney. She's a phoney from A to Z.'

Lewis's look now was one of semi-exasperation. 'There you go again! I think you're far too quick—'

'Let me tell you something. She just about takes the biscuit, that woman – give or take one or two congenitally compulsive liars we've had in the past.'

Lewis shook his head sadly as Morse continued:

'Wedding ring? You're right. Odds strongly against her having worn one recently. Not necessarily the same as *not* being married though, is it? Suggestive, though, yes. Suggestive that she might be telling a few other fibs as well.'

'Such as?'

'Well, it was obvious she wasn't deaf at all. She heard everything I said. Easy. *Kein Problem.*'

'She didn't hear *me*.'

'She didn't want to hear you, Lewis.'

'If you say so, sir.'

'What about her eyesight? Kept telling us, didn't she, that she couldn't see half as well as she used to? But that didn't stop her giving us a detailed description of the woman who came to visit McClure. She knew she'd got a ring in one of her nostrils – at twenty-odd yards, Lewis! And the only reason she couldn't tell us if she'd got *two* rings in her nose was because she saw her in profile – like she sees everyone in profile coming in through that entrance.'

'Why don't you think she was making all *that* up too, sir – that description she gave?'

'Good point.' Morse looked down at the carpet briefly. 'But I don't think so; that bit rang true to me. In fact, I reckon it was the only thing of any value she did come up with.'

'What about—?'

'Lewis! She's a phoney. She's not even been a *nurse* – let alone a matron or whatever you call 'em.'

'How can you say that?'

'You heard her – we both heard her. Mini-skirt up to mid-tibia – remember me saying that? Mid-*tibia*? Your tibia's *below* your knee, Lewis. You know that. But *she* doesn't.'

'Unless she's deaf, and misheard—'

'She's not deaf, I told you that. She just doesn't know her tibia from her fibula, that's all. Never been near a nursing manual in her life.'

'And you deliberately tricked her about that?'

'*And*, Lewis – most important of all – she claims she's an *Archers* addict, but she doesn't even know when the omnibus edition comes on on a Sunday morning. Huh!'

'I wouldn't know—'

'She's a Walter Mitty sort of woman. She lives in a world of fantasy. She tells herself things so many times – tells other people things so many times – that she thinks they're true. And for her they *are* true.'

'But not for us.'

'Not for us, no.'

'Not even the time she was in the bath?'

'If she was in the bath.'

'Oh.'

'Anyway, I don't somehow think it's going to be of much importance to us, what time the murderer made his entrance . . .'

Morse was whining on a little wearily now; and like Miss (or Mrs) W-W he seemed to be running out of steam.

Both men became silent again.

And soon Lewis was feeling pleased with himself, for he was beginning to realize that the 'second thing' he'd found for Morse was looking far more promising.

And Morse himself, with melancholy mien, sat ever motionless, his eyes staring intently at the page before him: that selfsame page in the book of Latin poetry.

CHAPTER EIGHT

Caeli, Lesbia nostra, Lesbia illa,
Illa Lesbia, quam Catullus unam
Plus quam se atque suos amavit omnes,
Nunc in quadriviis et angiportis
Glubit magnanimi Remi nepotes
(CATULLUS, *Poems LVIII*)

WHEN HE was a boy – well, when he was fifteen – Morse had fallen deeply in love with a girl, a year his junior, who like him had won a scholarship to one of the two local grammar schools: one for boys, one for girls. The long relationship between the pair of them had been so formative, so crucial, so wonderful overall, that when, three years later, he had been called up for National Service in the Army, he had written (for the first twelve weeks) a daily letter to his girl; only to learn on his first weekend furlough, to learn quite accidentally, that one of his friends (friends!) had been openly boasting about the sensually responsive lips of his beloved.

Morse told himself that he had finally grown up that weekend: and that was good. But he'd realized too, at the same time, that his capacity for jealousy was pretty nearly boundless.

It was only many years later that he'd seen those deeply wise words, embroidered in multi-coloured silks, in a B&B establishment in Maidstone:

41

– If you love her, set her free
– If she loves you, she will gladly return to you
– If she doesn't she never really loved you anyway

Such thoughts monopolized Morse's mind now as he looked again at Poem LVIII – a poem which his Classics master at school had exhorted the class to ignore, as being totally devoid of artistic merit. Such condemnation was almost invariably in direct proportion to the sexual content of the poem in question; and immediately after the lesson was over, Morse and his classmates had sought to find the meaning of that extraordinary word which Catullus had stuck at the beginning of the last line.

Glubit.

In the smaller Latin dictionary, *glubo, -ere* was given only as 'libidinously to excite emotions'. But in the larger dictionary there was a more cryptic, potentially more interesting definition . . . And here, in the margin of the book he was holding, McClure had translated the same poem.

To totters and toffs – in a levelish ratio –
My darling K offers her five-quid fellatio.
Near Carfax, perhaps, or at Cowley-Road Palais,
Or just by the Turf, up any old alley:
Preferring (just slightly) some kerb-crawling gent
High in the ranks of Her Majesty's Government.

Morse gave a mental tick to 'Carfax' for *quadriviis*; but thought 'Palais' a bit adolescent perhaps. Had his own translation been as good? Better? He couldn't remember. He doubted it. And it didn't matter anyway.

Or did it?

In the actual text of the poem, McClure had underlined in red Biro the words *Lesbia nostra, Lesbia illa, Illa Lesbia*: my Lesbia, that Lesbia of mine, that selfsame Lesbia.

Jealousy.

That most corrosive of all the emotions, gnawing away at the heart with a greater pain than failure or hatred – or even despair. But it seemed that McClure, like Catullus, had known his full share of it, with an ever-flirting, ever-hurting woman with whom he'd fallen in love; a woman who appeared willing to prostitute, at the appropriate price, whatever she possessed.

And suddenly, unexpectedly, Morse found himself thinking he'd rather like to meet the mysterious 'K'. Then, just as suddenly, he knew he wouldn't; unless, of course, that ambivalent lady held the key to the murder of Felix McClure – a circumstance which (at the time) he suspected was extremely improbable.

CHAPTER NINE

And like a skylit water stood
The bluebells in the azured wood
(A. E. HOUSMAN, *A Shropshire Lad, XLI*)

MORSE SNAPPED Catullus to.

'You didn't hear what I just said, did you, sir?'

'Pardon? Sorry. Just pondering – just pondering.'

'Is it leading us anywhere, this, er, pondering?'

'We're learning quite a bit about this girl of his, aren't we? Building up quite an interesting—'

'The answer's "no" then, is it?'

Morse smiled weakly. 'Probably.'

'Not like you, that, sir – giving up so quickly.'

'No. You're right. We shall have to check up on her.'

'Find out where she lives.'

'What? Not much of a problem there,' said Morse.

'Really?'

'She came on foot, we know that. From the Banbury Road side.'

'I thought you said Mrs Thingummy was making everything up?'

But Morse ignored the interjection. 'Where do *you* think she lives?'

'Just round the corner, perhaps?'

'Doubt it. Doubt he'd meet any local girl locally, if you see what I mean.'

'Well, if she did have a car, she couldn't park it in the Banbury Road, that's for certain.'

'So she hasn't got a car?'

'Well, if she has, she doesn't use it.'

'She probably came by bus then.'

'If you say so, sir.'

'Number twenty-something: down the Cowley Road, through the High to Carfax, along Cornmarket and St Giles', then up the Banbury Road.'

'Has she got a season-ticket, sir?'

'Such flippancy ill becomes you, Lewis.'

'I'm not being flippant. I'm just confused. You'll be telling me next what colour her eyes are.'

'Give me a chance.'

'Which street she lives in . . .'

'Oh, I think I know that.'

Lewis grinned and shook his head. 'Come on, sir, tell me!'

'Pater Street, Lewis – that's where she lives. Named after Walter Pater, you know, the fellow who described the Mona Lisa as a woman who'd learned the secrets of the grave.'

'Pater Street? That's out in Cowley, isn't it?'

Morse nodded. 'McClure mentions Cowley in something he wrote here.' Morse tapped Catullus. 'And then there's this.'

He handed across the postcard he'd found marking the relevant page of notes at the back of the volume – notes including a chicken-hearted comment on *Glubit*: '*sensus obscenus*'.

Lewis took the card; and after glancing at the

coloured photograph, 'Bluebells in Wytham Woods', turned to the back where, to the left of McClure's address, he read the brief message, written boldly in black Biro:

> **P St out this Sat –**
> **either DC or wherever**   **K**

The unsmudged postmark gave the date as 10 August 1994.

'Ye-es. I see what you mean, sir. They'd arranged to meet at her place, perhaps, P-something Street, on the Saturday; then on the Wednesday something cropped up . . .'

'She may have had the decorators in.'

'. . . so it had to be "DC", Daventry Court, or "wherever".'

'Probably some hotel room.'

'Cost him, though. Double room'd be – what? – £70, £80, £90?'

'Or a B&B.'

'Even so. Still about £40, £50.'

'Then he's got to pay her for her services, don't forget that.'

'How much do you think, sir?'

'How the hell should *I* know?'

'Maybe she was worth every penny of it,' Lewis suggested quietly.

'Do you know, I very much doubt that,' asserted Morse with surprising vehemence, now walking over to the phone, consulting the black index, and dialling a number.

'Could be *Princess* Street, sir? That's just off the Cowley Road.'

Morse put his palm over the receiver and shook his head. 'No, Lewis. It's *Pater* Street. Hullo?'

'Yeah? Wha' d'ya wan'?'

'Have I got the right number for "K", please?'

'You 'ave. Bu' she ain't 'ere, is she?'

'That's what I hoped you'd be able to tell me.'

'You another dur'y ol' man or somethin'?'

'If I am, I'm a dirty old police inspector,' replied Morse, in what he trusted was a cultured, authoritative tone.

'Oh, sorry.'

'You say she's not there?'

'She's bin away for a week in Spain. Sent me a topless photo of 'erself from Torremolinos, didn't she? Only this mornin'.'

'A week, you say?'

'Yeah. Went las' Sa'dy – back this Sa'dy.'

'Does she have a . . . a client in North Oxford?'

'An' if she does?'

'You know his name?'

'Nah.'

'What about *her* name?'

'She in some sort of trouble?' Suddenly the voice sounded anxious, softer now – with a final 't' voiced upon that 'sort'.

'I could get all this information from Kidlington Police HQ – you know that, surely? I just thought it would save a bit of time and trouble if you answered me over the phone. Then when we've finished I can thank you for your kind co-operation with the police in their enquiries.'

Hesitation now at the other end of the line.

Then an answer: 'Kay Blaxendale. That's "Kay", K-A-Y. She jus' signs herself "K" – the letter "K".'

'Is that her real name? It sounds a bit posh?'

'It's her professional name. Her real name's Ellie Smith.'

'What about your name?'

'Do you have to know?'

'Yes.'

'Friday Banks – that's me.'

'Have *you* got another name?'

'No.'

'You've got another accent though, haven't you?'

'Pardon?'

'When you want to, you can speak very nicely. You've got a pleasant voice. I just wonder why you try to sound so cheap and common, that's all.'

'Heh! Come off it. I may be common, mista, but I ain't cheap – I can tell yer tha'.'

'All right.'

'Tha' all?'

'Er, do you like bluebells, Miss Banks?'

'Bluebells, you say? Bloody *blue*bells?' She snorted her derision. 'She does, though – Kay does. But me, I'm a red-rose girl, Inspector – if you're thinkin' of sendin' me a bunch of flowers.'

'You never know,' said Morse, as he winked across at Lewis.

'Tha' all?' she repeated.

'Just your address, please.'

'Do you have to know?' (An aspirated 'have'.)

'Yes.'

'It's 35 Princess Street.'

And now it was Lewis's turn, as he winked across at Morse.

CHAPTER TEN

A long time passed – minutes or years – while the
two of us sat there in silence. Then I said something, asked something, but he didn't respond. I
looked up and I saw the moisture running down
his face

(EDUARDO GALEANO, *The Book of Embraces*)

MORSE'S FACE, after he had cradled the phone,
betrayed a suggestion of satisfaction; but after a short
while a stronger suggestion of *dis*satisfaction.

'Ever heard of a girl called Friday, Lewis?'

'I've heard of that story – *The Man Who Was
Thursday.*'

'It's a diminutive of Frideswide.'

'Right. Yes. We learnt about her at school – St
Frideswide. Patron saint of Oxford. She cured somebody who was blind, I think.'

'Somebody, Lewis, she'd already herself struck blind
in the first place.'

'Not a very nice girl, then.'

'Just like our girl.'

'Anyway, you can cross her off the list of suspects.'

'How do you make that out, Lewis?'

'Unless you still think that girl on the phone's a
phoney too.'

'No. I don't think that. Not now.'

'Well, she said McClure's girlfriend was in Spain when he was murdered, didn't she?'

'It's impolite to eavesdrop on telephone conversations.'

Lewis nodded. 'Interesting, too. I felt sure you were going to ask her to send you the photo – you know, the topless photo from Torremolinos.'

'Do you know,' said Morse quietly, 'I think, looking back on it, I should have done exactly that. I must be getting senile.'

'You can still cross her off your list,' maintained an unsympathetic Lewis.

'Perhaps she was never on it in the first place. You see, I don't think it was a woman who murdered McClure.'

'We shall still have to see her, though.'

'Oh yes. But the big thing we've got to do is learn more about McClure. The more we learn about the murdered man, the more we learn about the murderer.'

Music to Lewis's ears. 'But no firm ideas yet, sir?'

'What?' Morse walked over to the front window, but his eyes seemed not so much to be looking out as looking in. 'I once went to hear a panel of writers, Lewis, and I remember they had to answer an interesting question about titles – you know, how important a title is for a book.'

'*The Wind in the Willows* – that's my favourite.'

'Anyway, the other panellists said it was the most difficult thing of the lot, finding a good title. Then this last woman, she said it was no problem for her at all. Said she'd got half a dozen absolutely dazzling titles – but

51

she just hadn't got any books to go with them. And it's the same with me, Lewis, that's all. I've got plenty of ideas already, but nothing to pin 'em to.'

'Not yet.'

'Not yet,' echoed Morse.

'Do you think Phillotson had any ideas – ideas he didn't tell us about?'

'For Christ's sake, forget Phillotson! He wouldn't know what to do if some fellow walked into his nearest nick with a knife dripping with blood and said he'd just murdered his missus.'

At least that's something you're never likely to do, thought Lewis. But the thought was not translated into words.

'Now,' continued Morse, 'just tell me about this second great discovery of yours.'

'Just give me ten more minutes – nearly ready.'

Morse ambled somewhat aimlessly around the rooms so splendidly cited by Messrs Adkinson: Sitting/Dining-Room; Fully Fitted Modern Kitchen; Cloaks/Shower Room; Guest Bedroom; Master Bedroom Suite; Luxury Bathroom. But nothing, it appeared, was able to hold his attention for long; and soon he returned to the murder room.

For Lewis, this brief period of time was profitable. His little dossier – well, three items held together by a paper-clip – was now, he thought, complete. Interesting. He was pleased with himself; trusted that Morse would be pleased with him, too.

Not that Morse had looked particularly pleased with anything these last few minutes; and Lewis watched him taking a few more books from the shelves, seemingly in

THE DAUGHTERS OF CAIN

random manner, opening each briefly at the title page, then shaking it quite vigorously from the spine as if expecting something to fall out. And even as Lewis watched, something did fall out from one of them – nothing less than the whole of its pages. But Lewis's cautious amusement was immediately stifled by a vicious scowl from Morse; and nothing was said.

In fact, over only one of the title pages had Morse lingered for more than a few moments:

THE GREAT PLAGUE AT ATHENS

*Its Effect on the Course and Conduct
of the Peloponnesian War*

BY

FELIX FULLERTON MCCLURE M.A., D.PHIL.
Student of Wolsey College, Oxford

Correction.
Late Student of Wolsey College, Oxford . . .

At 5.45 p.m. PC Roberts knocked, and entered in response to Morse's gruff behest.

'Super just rung through, sir—'

'"Rang" through,' muttered Morse.

'—and wanted me to tell you straightaway. It's Mrs Phillotson, sir. She died earlier this afternoon. Seems she had another emergency op . . . and well, she didn't pull through. He didn't tell me any more. He just wanted you to know, he said.'

Roberts left, and Lewis looked on as Morse slowly sat down in the brown leather armchair, staring, it seemed, at the design on the carpet – the eyes, usually so fierce and piercing, now dull and defeated; a look of such self-loathing on his face as Lewis had never seen before.

It was five minutes later that Lewis made an offer which (as he knew) could hardly be refused.

'Fancy a beer, sir? The King's Arms down the road's open – Open All Day, it says outside.'

But Morse shook his head, and sat there in continued silence.

So for a while Lewis pretended to complete an already completed task. Perhaps he should have felt puzzled? But no. He wasn't puzzled at all.

Tomorrow was Thursday . . .

And the next day was Friday . . .

Strange how they'd both cropped up already that day: the Man Who Was Thursday and the Girl Who Was Friday. Yet at this stage of the case, as they sat together in Daventry Court, neither Morse nor Lewis had the vaguest notion of how crucial one of the two was soon to become.

CHAPTER ELEVEN

You; my Lady, certainly don't dye your hair to
deceive the others, nor even yourself; but only to
cheat your own image a little before the looking-
glass

(LUIGI PIRANDELLO, *Henry IV*)

WHEN FOR a second time she had put down the phone,
Eleanor Smith stared at her own carpet, in this case
a threadbare, tastelessly floral affair that stopped, at
each wall, about eighteen inches short of the chipped
skirting-boards.

The calls hadn't been unexpected. No. Ever since
she'd read of McClure's murder in the *Oxford Mail*
she'd half expected, half feared that the police would
be in touch. Twice, at least twice, she remembered
sending him a postcard; and once a letter – a rambling,
adolescent letter written just after they'd first met when
she'd felt particularly lonely on a dark and cloudy day.
And knowing Felix, even a bit, she thought he'd
probably have kept anything she might have sent him.

Their first meeting for a drink together had been in
the Chapters Bar of The Randolph. Good, that had
been. No pretences then, on either side. But he'd
gently refused to consider her a 'courtesan' if only for
the reason (as he'd smilingly informed her) that ana-
grammatically, and appropriately, the word gave rise to
'a sore——'.

Yes, quite good really, that first evening – that first night, in fact – together. Above all perhaps, from her point of view, it had marked a nascent interest in crossword puzzles, which Felix had later encouraged and patiently fostered . . .

They'd found her telephone number in his flat – of course they had. Not that it was any great secret. Not exactly an ex-directory, exclusive series of digits. A number, rather, that in the early days had been slipped into half the BT phone-boxes in East Oxford, on a card with an amateurishly drawn outline of a curvaceous brunette with bouncy boobs. Her! But it was there; there in that telephone-thing of his on the desk. She knew that, for she'd seen it there. Odd, really. She'd have expected someone with such a fine brain as Felix to have committed her five-figure number to a permanent place in his memory. Seemingly not, though.

Poor old Felix.

She'd never loved anyone in life really – except her mum. But amongst her clients, that rather endearing, kindly, caring sort of idiot, Felix, had perhaps come nearer than anyone.

He'd never mentioned any enemies. But he must have had at least one – that much was certain. Not that she could help. She knew nothing. If she *had* known something, she'd have volunteered the information before now.

Or would she?

The very last thing she wanted was to get involved with the police. With *her* job? Come off it! And in any case there was no point in it. The last time she'd been round to Felix's apartment had been three weeks ago, when he'd cooked steak for the two of them, with a bottle of vintage claret to wash it down; *and* two bottles of expensive champagne, one before . . . things; and one after.

Poor old Felix.

A very nice person in the very nasty world in which she'd lived these last few years.

Easy enough fooling the fuzz! Just said she wasn't there, hadn't she? Just said she was in Spain. Just said there'd been this photo of a bare-breasted tourist in Torremolinos. Been a bit of a problem if that second copper'd asked for the photo, though. But he'd sounded all right – they'd both sounded all right. Just not very bright, that's all. Would they check up on her? But what if they did? They'd soon understand why she'd told a few fibs. It was a joke. Bit of fun. No one wanted to get involved in a murder enquiry.

And whatever happened she *couldn't* be a suspect. Felix had been murdered on Sunday 28th August, hadn't he? And on that same Sunday she'd left Oxford at 6.30 a.m. (yes!) on a coach-trip to Bournemouth. Hadn't got back, either, until 9.45 p.m. So there! And thirty-four witnesses could testify to that. Thirty-five, if you included the driver.

Nothing to worry about, then – nothing at all.

And yet she couldn't *help* worrying: worrying about who, in his senses, would want to murder such an inoffensive fellow as Felix.

Or in *her* senses . . .

Was there some history, some incident, some background in Felix's life about which she knew nothing? Sure to be, really. Not that he'd ever hinted—

Then it struck her.

There *was* that one thing. Just over a year ago, late May (or was it early June?) when that undergraduate living on Felix's staircase had jumped out of his third-floor window – and broken his neck.

'That undergraduate'? Who was she fooling?

Poor Matthew!

Not that she'd had anything to do with that, either. Well, she'd fervently prayed that she hadn't. After all, she'd only met him once, when Felix had become so furiously jealous.

Jealousy!

At *his* age – forty-one years older than she was. A grandfather, almost. A father, certainly. Yet one of the very few clients who meant anything to her in that continuum of carnality which passed for some sort of purpose in her present life.

Yes, a father-figure.

A foster-father, perhaps.

Not a bloody *step*-father, though! Christ, no.

She looked at herself in the mirror of the old-fashioned dressing-table. The pallor of her skin looked ghastly; and her dark hair, streaked with a reddish-orange henna dye, looked lustreless – and cheap. But she felt cheap all over. And as she rested her oval face on her palms, the index finger of each hand stroking the silver rings at either side of her nostrils, her sludgy-green eyes stared back at her with an expression of dullness and dishonesty.

Dishonesty?

Yes. The truth was that she probably hadn't given a sod for McClure, not really. Come to think of it, he'd been getting something of a nuisance: wanting to monopolize her; pressurizing her; phoning at inconvenient moments – once at a *very* inconvenient moment. He'd become far too obsessive, far too possessive. And what was worse, he'd lost much of his former gaiety and humour in the process. Some men were like that.

Well, hard luck!

Yes, if she were honest with herself, she was glad it was all over. And as she continued to stare at herself, she was suddenly aware that the streaks of crimson in her hair were only perhaps a physical manifestation of the incipient streaks of cruelty in her heart.

CHAPTER TWELVE

To run away from trouble is a form of cowardice
and, while it is true that the suicide braves death,
he does it not for some noble object but to escape
some ill

(ARISTOTLE, *Nicomachean Ethics*)

MORSE HAD finished the previous evening with four
pints of Best Bitter (under an ever-tightening waist-
belt) at the King's Arms in Banbury Road; and had
followed this with half a bottle of his dearly beloved
Glenfiddich (in his pyjamas) at his bachelor flat in the
same North Oxford.

Unsurprisingly, therefore, he had not exactly felt as
fit as a Stradivarius when Lewis had called the following
morning; and it was Lewis who now drove out to
Leicester.

It was Lewis who *had* to drive out to Leicester.

As the Jaguar reached the outskirts of that city,
Morse was looking again through the items (four of
them now, not three) which Lewis had seen fit to
salvage from McClure's apartment, and which – glory
be! – Morse had instantly agreed could well be of
importance to the case. Certainly they threw light upon
that murky drink-drugs-sex scene which had established
itself in some few parts of Oxford University. First was a
cutting from the *Oxford Mail* dated Tuesday, 8 June
1993 (fourteen months earlier):

DRUG LINK WITH
DREAM SON'S SUICIDE

At an inquest held yesterday, the Coroner, Mr Arnold Hoskins, recorded a verdict of suicide on the death of Mr Matthew Rodway, a third-year undergraduate reading English at Oxford.

Rodway's body had been discovered by one of the college scouts in the early hours of Friday, 21 May, at the foot of his third-floor window in the Drinkwater Quad of Wolsey College.

There was some discrepancy in the statements read out at the inquest, with suggestions made that Mr Rodway may perhaps have fallen accidentally after a fairly heavy drinking-party in his rooms on Staircase G.

There was also clear evidence, however, that Mr Rodway had been deeply depressed during the previous weeks, apparently about his prospects in his forthcoming Finals examination.

What was not disputed was that Rodway had taken refuge amongst one or two groups where drugs were regularly taken in various forms.

Dr Felix McClure, one of Rodway's former tutors, was questioned about an obviously genuine but unfinished letter found in Rodway's rooms, containing the sentence 'I've had enough of all this'.

Whilst he stoutly maintained that the words themselves were ambivalent in their implication, Dr McClure agreed with the Coroner that the most likely explanation of events was that Rodway had been driven to take his own life.

Pathological evidence substantiated the fact that Rodway had taken drugs, on a regular basis, yet there appeared no evidence to suggest that he was a suicidal type with some obsessive death-wish.

In his summing up, the Coroner stressed the evil nature of trafficking in drugs, and pointed to the ready availability of such drugs as a major contributory factor in Rodway's death.

Taken in the first place to alleviate anxiety, they had in all probability merely served to aggravate it, with the tragic consequences of which the court had heard.

Matthew's mother is reluctant to accept the Coroner's verdict. Speaking from her home in Leicester, Mrs Mary Rodway wished only to recall a bright, caring son who had every prospect of success before him.

'He was so talented in many ways. He was very good at hockey and tennis. He had a great love of music, and played the viola in the National Youth Orchestra.

'I know I'm making him sound like a dream son. Well, that's what he was.' (See Leader, p.8)

Morse turned to the second cutting, taken from the same issue:

A DEGREE TOO FAR

A recently commissioned study highlights the increasing percentage of Oxford graduates who fail to find suitable employment. Dr Clive Hornsby, Senior Reader in Social Sciences at Lonsdale College, has endorsed the implications of these findings, and suggests that many students, fully aware of employment prospects, strive for higher-class degrees than they are competent to achieve. Others, as yet mercifully few, adopt the alternative course of abandoning hope, of seeking consolation in drink and drugs, and sometimes of concluding that life is not worth the living of it. It may well be that Oxford University, through its various advisory agencies and helplines, is fully aware of these and related problems, although we are not wholly convinced of this. The latest suicide in an Oxford college (see p.1) prompts renewed concern about the pressures on our undergraduate community here, and the ways in which additional advice and help can be provided.

Morse now turned again to the third cutting, taken from the *Oxford Times* of Friday, 18 June 1993: a shorter article, flanked by a photograph of 'Dr F. F. Maclure', a clean-shaven, rather mournful-looking man, pictured in full academic dress.

PASTORAL CARE DEFENDED

Following the latest in a disturbing sequence of suicides, considerable criticism has been levelled against the University's counselling arrangements. But Dr Felix McLure, former Senior Lecturer in Ancient History at Wolsey College, has expressed his disappointment that so many have rushed into the arena with allegations of indifference and neglect. In fact, according to Dr MacClure, the University has been instrumental over the past year in promoting several initiatives, including the formation of Oxford University Counselling and Help (OUCH) of which he was a founder-member. 'More should be done,' he told our reporter. 'We all agree on that score. But there should also be some recognition of the University's present concern and commitment.'

'You'll soon know those things off by heart,' ventured a well-pleased Lewis as he stopped in a leafy lane on the eastern side of the London Road and briefly consulted his street-map, before setting off again.

'It's not that. It's just that I'm a slow reader.'

'What if you'd been a quick reader, sir? Where would you be now?'

'Probably been a proofreader in a newspaper office. They could certainly do with one,' mumbled Morse as he considered 'Maclure' and 'McLure' and 'MacClure' in the last cutting, with still no sign of the genuine article, 'former Senior Lecturer . . .'

Interesting, that extra little piece of the jigsaw – that 'former' . . .

Lewis braked gently outside Number 14 Evington Road South; then decided to continue into the drive, where the low-profile tyres of the Jaguar crunched into the deep gravel.

CHAPTER THIRTEEN

Whatever crazy sorrow saith,
No life that breathes with human breath
Has ever truly longed for death
(ALFRED, LORD TENNYSON, *The Two Voices*)

MRS MARY RODWAY, a smartly dressed, slim-figured, pleasantly featured woman in her late forties, seemed quite willing to talk about herself – at least for a start.

Four years previously (she told the detectives) her husband, a highly-salaried constructional engineer, had run off with his Personal Assistant. The only contact between herself and her former marriage-partner was now effected via the agency of solicitors and banks. She lived on her own happily enough, she supposed – if anyone could ever live happily again after the death of an only child, especially a child who had died in such dubious circumstances.

She had seen McClure's murder reported in *The Independent*; and Morse wasted no time in telling her of the specific reason for his visit: the cuttings discovered among the murdered man's papers which appeared firmly to underline his keen interest in her son, Matthew, and perhaps in the reasons for his suicide.

'He was quite wrong – the Coroner. You do realize that?' Mary Rodway lit another cigarette and inhaled deeply.

'You don't believe it was suicide?'

'I didn't say that. What I do say is that the Coroner was wrong in making such a big thing about those hard drugs. That's what they call them: "hard" as opposed to "soft". It's just the same with pornography, I believe, Inspector.'

Whilst Morse nodded his head innocently, Mrs Rodway shook her own in vague exasperation. 'Life's a far more *complicated* thing than that – Matthew's was – and that Coroner, he made it all sound so ... *un*complicated.'

'Don't be too, er, hard on him, Mrs Rodway. A Coroner's main job isn't dealing with right and wrong, and making moral judgements, and all that sort of thing. He's just there to put the bits and pieces into some sort of pattern, and then to stick some verdict, as best he can, in one of the few slots he's got available to him.'

If Mrs Rodway was at all impressed by this amalgam of metaphors, she gave no indication of it. Perhaps she hadn't even been listening, for she continued in her former vein: 'There were two things – two quite separate things – and they ought to have been *considered* separately. It's difficult to put it into words, Inspector, but you see there are causes of things, and symptoms of things. And in Matthew's case this drugs business was a symptom of something – it wasn't a cause. I *knew* Matthew – I knew him better than anyone.'

'So you think ... ?'

'I've stopped thinking. What on earth's the good of churning things over and over again in your mind for the umpteenth time?'

She stubbed out a half-smoked cigarette savagely, and immediately lit another.

'You don't mind me smoking?'

'No, no.'

'Can I offer you gentlemen one?' She held out a packet of King-Size Dunhill International, first to Lewis who shook his head with a smile; then to Morse who shook his head with stoical resolve, since only that same morning, when he'd woken up just before six with parched mouth and pounding head, he had decided to forgo – for evermore – the spurious gratification not only of alcohol but of nicotine also.

Perhaps his decision could wait until tomorrow for its full implementation, though; and he relented. 'Most kind, Mrs Rodway. Thank you . . . And it's very valuable, what you're saying. Please do go on.'

'There's nothing more to say.'

'But if you felt – feel – so strongly, why didn't you agree to give evidence at the Inquest?'

'How could I? I couldn't even bear to switch on the TV or the radio in case there might be something about it. *You* couldn't bear that, could you, Inspector? If it had been your child?'

'I – I take your point,' admitted Morse awkwardly.

'You know usually, when things like that happen, you get all the rumour and all the gossip as well. But we didn't have any of that – at the Inquest.'

Three times now Mary Rodway inhaled on her cigarette with such ferocity that she seemed to Lewis hell-bent on inflicting some irreparable damage to her respiratory tract.

But Morse's mind for a few seconds was far away, a glimmer of light at last appearing at the far end of a long, black tunnel.

'So ...' he picked his slow words carefully, 'you'd hoped that there might be some other evidence given at the Inquest, but you didn't want to provide any of it yourself?'

'Perhaps it wasn't all that important anyway.'

'Please tell me.'

'No.'

Morse looked around the large lounge. The day was warm already, yet he suspected (rightly) that the two long radiators were turned up to full capacity. Much space on the walls was devoted to pictures: prints of still-life paintings by Braque, Matisse, Picasso; photographs and watercolours of great buildings and palaces, including Versailles and Blenheim – and Wolsey College, Oxford. But virtually no people were photographed or represented there. It was as if those 'things' so frequently resorted to by Mrs Rodway in her conversation were now figuring more prominently than people.

'You knew Dr McClure, I think,' said Morse.

'I met him first when Matthew went up to Oxford. He was Matthew's tutor.'

'Didn't he have rooms on the same staircase as Matthew?' (Lewis had spent most of the previous evening doing his homework; *and* Morse's homework.)

'The first year, and the third year, yes. He was out of college his second year.'

'Where was that, do you remember?'

Did Lewis observe a flicker of unease in Mary Rodway's eyes? Did Morse?

'I'm not sure.'

'Oh, it doesn't matter. Sergeant Lewis here can check up on that easily enough.'

But she had her answer now. 'It was in East Oxford somewhere. Cowley Road, was it?'

Morse continued his questioning, poker-faced, as if he had failed to hear the tintinnabulation of a bell: 'What did you think of Dr McClure?'

'Very nice man. Kindly – genuine sort of person. And, as you say, he took a real interest in Matthew.'

Morse produced a letter, and passed it across to Mrs Rodway: a single handwritten sheet, on the pre-printed stationery of 14 Evington Road South, Leicester, dated 2 June, the day after the Coroner's verdict on Matthew Rodway's death.

Dear Felix

I was glad to talk to you on the phone however briefly. I was so choked I could hardly speak to you. Please do as we agreed. If you find anything else among M's things which would be upsetting please get rid of them. This includes any of my letters he may have kept. He had two family photos in his room, one a framed one of the two of us. I'd like both of them back. But all clothes and personal effects and papers – get rid of them all for me.

I must thank you for all you tried to do for Matthew. He often spoke of your kindness, as you know. I'm so sorry, I can't go on with this letter any more.

Sincerely yours
Mary

Morse now accepted a second cigarette; and as Mrs Rodway read through the letter Lewis turned his head away from the exhalation of smoke. He was not over-much concerned about the health risks supposedly linked with passive smoking, but it must have some effect; had already *had* its effect on the room here, where a thin patina of nicotine could be seen on the emulsioned walls. In fact the whole room could surely do with a good wash-down and redecoration? The corners of the high ceiling were deeply stained, and just above one of the radiators an oblong of pristinely bright magnolia served to emphasize a slight neglect of household renovation.

'Did you write that?' asked Morse.

'Yes.'

'Is there anything you want to tell us about it?'

'Pretty clear, isn't it?'

'Did Dr McClure find anything in Matthew's rooms?'

'I don't know.'

'Would he have told you if, let's say, he'd found some drugs?'

'I doubt it.'

'Did he think Matthew was taking drugs?'

It was hard for her to say it. But she said it: 'Yes.'

'Did you ever find out where he got his drugs from?'

'No.'

'Did he ever say anything about his friends being on drugs?'

'No.'

'Do you think they may have been?'

'I only met one or two of them – on the same staircase.'

'Do you think drugs were available inside the college?'

'I don't know.'

'Would Dr McClure have known, if they were?'

'I suppose he would, yes.'

'Was Matthew fairly easily influenced by his friends, would you say?'

'No, I wouldn't.'

The answers elicited from Mrs Rodway hardly appeared to Lewis exciting; or even informative, for that matter. But Morse appeared content to keep his interlocution at low key.

'Do you blame anyone? About the drugs?'

'I'm in no position to blame anyone.'

'Do you blame yourself?'

'Don't we all blame ourselves?'

'What about Dr McClure – where did he put the blame?'

'He did say once . . . I remember . . .' But the voice trailed off as she lit another cigarette. 'It was very odd really. He was talking about all the pressures on young people these days – you know, about youth culture and all that sort of thing, about whether standards were declining in . . . well, in everything, I suppose.'

'What exactly did he say?' prompted Morse gently.

But Mary Rodway was not listening. 'You know, if only Matthew hadn't . . . killed himself that night, whatever the reason was – reason or reasons – he'd probably have been perfectly happy with life a few days later, a week later . . . That's what I can't . . . I can't get over.'

Tears were dropping now.

And Lewis looked away.

But not Morse.

'What exactly did he say?' he repeated.

Mrs Rodway wiped her tears and blew her nose noisily. 'He said it was always difficult to apportion blame in life. But he said . . . he said if he had to blame anybody it would be the students.'

'Is that all?'

'Yes.'

'Why was that an "odd" thing to say, though?'

'Because, you see, he was always on the students' side. Always. So it was a bit like hearing a trade-union boss suddenly siding with the Conservative Party.'

'Thank you. You've been very kind, Mrs Rodway.'

Clearly (as Lewis could see) it was time to depart; and he closed his notebook with what might have passed for a slight flourish – had anyone been interested enough to observe the gesture.

But equally clearly (as Lewis could also see) Morse was momentarily transfixed, the blue eyes gleaming with that strangely distanced, almost ethereal gaze, which Lewis had observed so often before – a gaze which usually betokened a breakthrough in a major case.

As now?

The three of them rose to their feet.

'Did you get to university yourself?' asked Morse.

'No. I left school at sixteen – went to a posh secretarial college – did well – got a good job – met a nice boss – became his PA – and he married me . . . As I told you, Inspector, he's got a weakness for his PAs.'

Morse nodded. 'Just one last question. *When* did your husband leave you?'

'I told you, don't you remember? Four years ago.' Suddenly her voice sounded sharp.

'When *exactly*, Mrs Rodway?' Suddenly Morse's voice, too, sounded sharp.

'November the fifth – Bonfire Night. Not likely to forget the date, am I?'

'Not *quite* four years ago then?'

Mrs Rodway made no further reply.

CHAPTER FOURTEEN

Everyone can master a grief but he that has it
(SHAKESPEARE, *Much Ado About Nothing*)

'BIG THING you've got to remember is that it's a great healer – time. Just give it a while, you'll see.'

It was just before lunchtime that same day, in his office at Kidlington Police HQ, that Chief Superintendent Strange thus sought to convey his commiserations to Detective Chief Inspector Phillotson – going on to suggest that an extended period of furlough might well be a good thing after ... well, after things were over. And if anyone could help in any way, Phillotson only had to mention it.

'Trouble with things like this,' continued Strange, as he rose from behind his desk and walked round to place a kindly hand on his colleague's shoulder, 'is that nothing really helps much at all, does it?'

'I don't know about that, sir. People are being very kind.'

'I know, yes. I know.' And Strange resumed his seat, contemplating his own kindliness with some gratification.

'You know, sir, I've heard from people I never expected to show much sympathy.'

'You have?'

'People like Morse, for instance.'

'Morse? When did you see Morse? He told me he was off to Leicester this morning.'

'No. He put a note through the letter-box, that's all. Must have been latish last night – it wasn't there when I put the milk-tokens out . . .'

'I'd say he probably wrote it in a pub, knowing Morse.'

'Does it matter where he wrote it, sir?'

'Course not. But I can't imagine *him* being much comfort to anybody. He's a pagan, you know that. Got no time for the Church and . . . Hope and Faith and all that stuff. Doesn't even believe in God, let alone in any sort of life after death.'

'Bit like some of our Bishops,' said Phillotson sadly.

'Like some Theology dons in Oxford, too.'

'I was still glad to get his letter.'

'What did he say?'

'Said what you just said really, sir; said he'd got no faith in the Almighty; said I just ought to forget all this mumbo-jumbo about meeting . . . meeting up again in some future life; told me just to accept the truth of it all – that she's gone for good and I'll never see her again; told me I'd probably never get over it, and not to take any notice of people who gave you all this stuff about time healing—' Phillotson suddenly checked himself, realizing what he'd just said.

'Doesn't sound much help to me.'

'Do you know, though, in an odd sort of way it was. It was sort of *honest*. He just said that he was sad, when he heard, and he was thinking of me . . . At the end, he said it was always a jolly sight easier in life to face up to the truths than the half-truths. I'm not quite sure what he meant ... but, well, somehow it helps, when I remember what he said.'

Phillotson could trust himself to say no more, and he rose to leave.

At the door he turned back. 'Did you say Morse went to Leicester this morning?'

'That's where he said he was going.'

'Funny! Odds are I'd have been in Leicester myself. I bet he's gone to see the parents of that lad who killed himself in Wolsey a year or so ago.'

'What's that got to do with things?'

'There were a few newspaper articles, that's all, about the lad, among McClure's papers. *And* a letter from the mother. She started it off "Dear Felix" – as if they'd known each other pretty well, if you see what I mean.'

Strange grunted.

'Do you think I should mention it to Morse, sir?'

'No. For Christ's sake don't do that. He's got far too many ideas already, you can be sure of that.'

CHAPTER FIFTEEN

Say, for what were hop-yards meant
Or why was Burton built on Trent?
Oh many a peer of England brews
Livelier liquor than the Muse,
And malt does more than Milton can
To justify God's ways to man
(A. E. HOUSMAN, *A Shropshire Lad, LXII*)

THE TURF TAVERN, nestling beneath the old walls of New College, Oxford, may be approached from Holywell Street, immediately opposite Holywell Music Room, via a narrow, irregularly cobbled lane of mediaeval aspect.

A notice above the entrance advises all patrons (although Morse is not a particularly tall man) to mind their heads (DUCK OR GROUSE) and inside the rough-stoned, black-beamed rooms the true connoisseur of beers can seat himself at one of the small wooden tables and enjoy a finely cask-conditioned pint; and it is in order to drink and to talk and to think that patrons frequent this elusively situated tavern in a blessedly music – Muzak – free environment.

The landlord of this splendid hostelry, a stoutly compact, middle-aged ex-Royal Navy man, with a grizzled beard and a gold ring in his left ear, was anticipatorily pulling a pint of real ale on seeing Morse enter, followed by the dutiful Lewis, at 1.50 p.m.

The latter, in fact, was feeling quite pleased with himself. Only sixty-five minutes from Leicester. A bit over the speed-limit all the way along (agreed); but fast-driving was one of his very few vices, and the jazzy-looking maroon Jaguar had been in a wonderfully slick and silky mood as it sped down the M40 on the last stretch of the journey from Banbury to Oxford.

Morse had resisted several pubs which, *en route*, had paraded their credentials – at Lutterworth, Rugby, Banbury. But, as Lewis knew, the time of drinking, and of thinking, was surely soon at hand.

In North Oxford, Morse had asked to be dropped off briefly at his flat: 'I ought to call in at the bank, Lewis.' And this news had further cheered Lewis, since (on half the salary) it was invariably *he* who bought about three-quarters of the drinks consumed between the pair of them. Only temporarily cheered, however, since he had wholly misunderstood the mission: five minutes later it was he himself who was pushing a variety of old soldiers through their appropriate holes (White, Green, Brown) in the Summertown Bottle Bank.

Thence, straight down the Banbury Road to the Martyrs' Memorial, where turning left (as instructed) he had driven to the far end of Broad Street. Here, as ever, there appeared no immediate prospect of leaving a car legitimately, and Morse had insisted that he parked the Jaguar on the cobblestone area outside the Old Clarendon building, just opposite Blackwell's.

'Don't worry, Lewis. All the traffic wardens know my car. They'll think I'm on duty.'

'Which you are, sir.'

'Which I am.'

'How are we, Chief Inspector?'

'Less of the "Chief". Sheehy's going to demote me. I'll soon be just an insignificant Inspector.'

'The usual?'

Morse nodded.

'And you, Sergeant?'

'An orange juice,' said Morse.

'Where've you parked?' asked Biff. It was a question which had become of paramount importance in Central Oxford over the past decade. 'I only ask because they're having a blitz this week, so Pam says.'

'Ah! How *is* that beautiful lady of yours?'

'I'll tell her you're here. She should be down soon anyway.'   Morse stood at the bar searching through his pockets in unconvincing manner. 'And a packet of – do you still sell cigarettes?'

Biff pointed to the machine. 'You'll need the right change.'

'Ah! Have you got any change on you by any chance, Lewis . . . ?'

When, at a table in the inner bar, Morse was finally settled behind his pint, his second pint, he took from his inside jacket-pocket the used envelope on which Lewis had seen him scribbling certain headings on their return to Oxford.

'Did you know that Wolsey College is frequently referred to, especially by those who are in it, as "The House"?'

'Can't say I did, no.'

'Do you know why?'

'Let me concentrate on the orange juice, sir.'

'It's because of its Latin name, *Aedes Archiepiscopi*, the House of the Bishop.'

'Well, that explains it, doesn't it?'

'Another peculiarity is that in all the other colleges they call the dons and the readers and the tutors and so on – they call them "Fellows". You with me? But at Wolsey they call them "Students".'

'What do they call the students then?'

'Doesn't *matter* what they call 'em, does it? Look! Let's just consider where we are. We've discovered a couple of possible links in this case so far: McClure's fancy woman; and the Rodway woman, the mother of one of his former pupils. Now neither of 'em comes within a million miles of being a murderer, I know that; but they're both adding to what we know of McClure himself, agreed? He's a respected scholar; a conscientious don—'

'"Student", sir.'

'A conscientious Student; a man who's got every sympathy with his stu—'

Lewis looked across.

' – with the young people he comes into contact with; a founder member of a society to help dedicated druggies; a man who met Matthew's mum, and probably slipped in between the sheets with her—'

Lewis shook his head vigorously. 'You *can't* just say that sort of thing.'

'And why not? How the hell do you think we're going to get to the bottom of this case unless we make the odd hypothesis here and there? You don't know?

Well, let me tell you. We think of anything that's unlikely. That's how. Any bloody idiot can tell you what's *likely*.'

'If you say so, sir.'

'I *do* say so,' snapped Morse. 'Except that what I say is *not* particularly unlikely, is it? They obviously got on pretty well, didn't they? Take that salutation and vale-diction, for instance.'

Lewis lifted his eyebrows.

'All Christian-name, palsy-walsy stuff, wasn't it? Then there's this business of her husband leaving her – you'll recall I pressed her on that point? And for a very good reason. It was November, a month or so after her precious Matthew had first gone up to Oxford. And it occurred to me, Lewis – and I'm surprised it didn't occur to you – that things may well have been the other way round, eh? She may have left *him*, and it was only then that he started playing around with his new PA.'

'We could always look at a copy of the divorce proceedings.'

'What makes you think they're divorced?'

Lewis surrendered, sipped his orange juice, and was silent.

'But it doesn't matter, does it? It's got bugger-all to do with McClure's murder. You can make a heap of all the money you've got and wager it on *that*. No risk there!'

Lewis fingered the only money he had left in his pockets – three pound coins – and decided that he was hardly going to become a rich man, however long the odds that Morse was offering. But it was time to mention something. Had Morse, he wondered, seen that oblong patch of pristine magnolia . . . ?

'There was,' Lewis began slowly, 'a light-coloured patch on the wall in Mrs Rodway's lounge, sir—'

'Ah! Glad you noticed that. Fiver to a cracked piss-pot that was a picture of *him*, Lewis – of McClure! That's why she took it down. She didn't want us to see it, but something like that's always going to leave its mark, agreed?'

'Unless she put something else up there to cover it.'

Morse scorned the objection. 'She wouldn't have taken a photo of her *son* down, would she? Where's the point of that? Very unlikely.'

'You just said that's exactly what we're looking for, sir – something "unlikely".'

Morse was spared any possible answer to this astute question by the arrival of the landlady, a slimly attractive brunette, with small, neat features, and an extra sparkle in her eyes as she greeted Morse with a kiss on his cheek.

'Not seen you for a little while, Inspector.'

'How's things, beautiful?'

'Another beer?'

'Well, if you insist.'

'I'm not really insisting—'

'Pint of the best bitter for me.'

'You, Sergeant?'

'He's driving,' said Morse.

Biff, the landlord, came over to join them, and the four sat together for the next ten minutes. Morse, after explaining that the word 'Turf' had appeared in the margin of one of McClure's books, asked whether they, either landlord or landlady, would have known the murdered man if they had seen him in the pub ('No');

whether they'd ever seen the young man from Wolsey who'd committed suicide ('Don't think so'); whether they'd ever seen a young woman with rings in her nose and red streaks in her hair ('Hundreds of 'em').

Yet the landlady had one piece of information.

'There's one of the chaps comes in here sometimes who was a scout on that staircase ... when, you know ... I heard him talking to somebody about it.'

'That's right.' The landlord was remembering too. 'Said he used to go to the Bulldog – or was it the Old Tom, Pam?'

'Can't remember.'

'He was a scout, you say?' asked Morse.

'Yeah. Only started coming in here after he moved – moved to the Pitt Rivers, I think it was. Well, only just up the road, isn't it?'

'He still comes?'

Biff considered. 'Haven't seen him for a little while now you come to mention it. Have you, love?'

Pam shook her pretty head.

'Know his name?' asked Lewis.

'Brooks – Ted Brooks.'

'Just let me get this clear,' said Lewis, as he and Morse left the Turf Tavern, this time via St Helen's Passage, just off New College Lane. 'You're saying that Mrs Rodway misunderstood what McClure said to her – about the "students"?'

'You've got it. What he meant was that he blamed the dons, the set-up there, the authorities. He wasn't saying they were a load of crooks – just that they should

84

have known what was going on there, and should have done something about it.'

'*If* anything was going on, sir.'

'Which'll be one of our next jobs, Lewis – to find out exactly that.'

It was Lewis who spotted it first: the traffic-warden's notice stuck beneath the near-side windscreen-wiper of the unmarked Jaguar.

By three o'clock that afternoon, Mary Rodway had assembled the new passe-partout for the picture-frame. Like most things in the room (she agreed) it had been getting very dingy. But it looked splendid now, as she carefully replaced the re-mounted photograph, standing back repeatedly and adjusting it, to the millimetre – that photograph of herself and her son which Felix had sent to her as she'd requested.

Nothing further of any great moment occurred that day, except for one thing – something which for Lewis was the most extraordinary, the most 'unlikely' event of the past six months.

'Come in a minute and let me pay you for those cigarettes,' Morse had said, as the Jaguar came to a stop outside the bachelor flat in North Oxford.

CHAPTER SIXTEEN

And sidelong glanced, as to explore,
In meditated flight, the door
(SIR WALTER SCOTT, *Rokeby*)

WHAT MORSE had vaguely referred to as the 'authorities' at Wolsey were immediately co-operative; and at 10 a.m. the following day he and Lewis were soon learning many things about the place: specifically, in due course, about Staircase G in Drinkwater Quad, on which Dr McClure had spent nine years of his university life, from 1984 until his retirement from academe at the end of the Trinity Term, 1993.

From his rooms overlooking the expansive quad ('Largest in Oxford, gentlemen – 264 by 261 feet') the Deputy Bursar had explained, rather too slowly and too pedantically for Morse's taste, the way things, er, worked in the, er, House, it clearly seeming to this former Air-Vice Marshal ('Often mis-spelt, you know – and more often mis-hyphenated') that these non-University people needed some elementary explanations.

Scouts?

Interested in *scouts*, were they?

Well, each scout ('Interesting word – origin obscure') looked after one staircase, and one staircase only – with that area guarded as jealously as any blackbird's territory in a garden, and considered almost as a sort of mediaeval fiefdom ('If you know what I mean?'). Several of the scouts had been with them, what, twenty, thirty years? Forty-nine years, one of them! What exactly did they do? Well, it would be sensible to go and hear things from the horse's mouth, as it were. What?

Escorted therefore through Great Quad, and away to the left of it into what seemed to Morse the unhappily named 'Drinkwater Quad', the policemen thanked their cicerone, the Air-hyphen-Vice Marshal ('One "l"') and made their way to Staircase G.

Where a surprise was in store for them.

Not really a scout at all – more a girl-guide.

Susan Ewers, too, was friendly and helpful – a married woman (no children yet) who was very happy to have the opportunity of supplementing the family income; very happy, too, with the work itself. The majority of scouts were women now, she explained: only three or four men still doing the job at Wolsey. In fact, she'd taken over from a man – a man who'd left to work at the Pitt Rivers Museum.

'Mr Brooks, was that?' asked Morse.

'Yes. Do you know him?'

'Heard of him, er . . . please go on.'

Her duties? Well, everything really. The immediate area outside; the entrance; the porchway; the stairs; the eight sets of rooms, all of them occupied during term-time, of course; and some of them during the vacs, like now, by delegates and visitors to various do's and conferences. Her first job each morning was to empty all the rubbish-baskets into black bags; then to clean the three WCs, one on each floor (no *en suite* facilities as yet); same with the wash-basins. Then, only twice a week, though, to Hoover all the floors, and generally to dust around, polish any brasswork, that sort of thing; and in general to see that the living quarters of her charges were kept as neat and tidy as could be expected with young men and young women who would (she felt) probably prefer to live in – well, to live in a bit of a mess, really. No bed-making, though. Thank goodness!

Willingly she showed the detectives the rooms at G4, on the second floor of her staircase, where until fourteen months previously the name 'Dr F. F. McClure' had been printed in black Gothic capitals beside the Oxford-blue double doors.

But if Morse had expected to find anything of significance in these rooms, he was disappointed. All fixtures befitting the status of a respected scholar had been replaced by the furniture of standard undergraduate accommodation: a three-seater settee; two armchairs; two desks; two bookcases . . . It reminded Morse of his own unhappy, unsuccessful days at Oxford; but made no other impact.

It might have been helpful to move quietly around the lounge and the spacious bedroom there, and seek to detect any vibrations, any reverberations, left behind by a cultured and (it seemed) a fairly kindly soul.

But clearly Morse could see little point in such divination.

'Is G8 free?' he asked.

'There *is* a gentleman there. But he's not in at the minute. If you want just a quick look inside?'

'It's where Matthew Rodway, the man who . . .'

'I know,' said Susan Ewers quietly.

But G8 proved to be equally disappointing: a three-seater settee, two (faded fabric) armchairs . . . cloned and cleaned of every reminder of the young man who had thrown himself down on to the paved area below the window there – the window at which Morse and Lewis now stood for a little while. Silently.

'You didn't know Mr Rodway, either?' asked Morse.

'No. As I say, I didn't come till September last year.'

'Do people on the staircase still take drugs?'

Mrs Ewers was taken aback by the abruptness of Morse's question.

'Well, they still have parties, like, you know. Drink and . . . and so on.'

'But you've never seen any evidence of drugs – any packets of drugs? Crack? Speed? Ecstasy? Anything? Anything at all?'

Had she?

'No,' she said. Almost truthfully.

'You've never smelt anything suspicious?'

'I wouldn't know what they smell like, drugs,' she said. Truthfully.

As they walked down the stairs, Lewis pointed to a door marked with a little floral plaque: 'Susan's Pantry'.

'That where you keep all your things, madam?'

She nodded. 'Every scout has a pantry.'

'Can we take a look inside?'

She unlocked the door and led the way into a fairly

small, high-ceilinged room, cluttered – yet so neatly cluttered – with buckets, mops, bin-liners, black plastic bags, transparent polythene bags, light bulbs, toilet rolls, towels, sheets, two Hoovers. And inside the white-painted cupboards rows of cleaners and detergents: Jif, Flash, Ajax, Windolene ... And everything so clean – so meticulously, antiseptically clean.

Morse had little doubt that Susan Ewers was the sort of housewife to polish her bath-taps daily; the sort to feel aggrieved at finding a stray trace of toothpaste in the wash-basin. If cleanliness were next to saint-liness, then this lady was probably on the verge of beatification.

So what?

Apart from mentally extending his lively sympathies to *Mr* Ewers, Morse was aware that his thought-processes were hardly operating *vivamente* that morning; and he stood in the slightly claustrophobic pantry, feeling somewhat feckless.

It was Lewis who, as so frequently, was the catalyst.

'What's your husband do, Mrs Ewers?'

'He's – well, at the minute he's unemployed, actually. He did work at the old RAC offices in Summertown, but they made him redundant.'

'When was that?'

'Last year.'

'When exactly?' (If Morse could ask such questions, why not Lewis?)

'Last, er, August.'

'Good thing you getting the job then. Help tide things over a bit, like.'

Lewis smiled sympathetically.

And Morse smiled gratefully.

Bless you, Lewis – bless you!

Gestalt – that's what the Germans call it. That flash of unified perception, that synoptic totality which is more than the sum of the parts into which it may be logically analysable; parts, in this case, like drugs and scouts and a suicide and a murder and a staircase and changing jobs and not having a job and retirement and money and times and dates ... Yes, especially times and dates ...

Most probably, in the circumstances, Matthew Rodway's rooms would not have been re-occupied for the few remaining weeks at the end of Trinity Term the previous year; and if (as now) only *some* of the rooms were in use during the Long Vac, it might well be that Mrs Ewers had been the very first person to look closely around the suicide's chambers. But no; that was wrong. McClure had already gone through things, hadn't he? Mrs Rodway had asked him to. But would he have been half as thorough as this newly appointed woman?

He'd questioned her on the point already, he knew that. But he hadn't asked the right questions, perhaps? Not quite.

'Just going back a minute, Mrs Ewers ... When you got Mr Rodway's old rooms ready for the beginning of the Michaelmas term, had anyone else been in there – during the summer?'

'I don't think so, no.'

'But you still didn't find anything?'

'No, like I just said—'

'Oh, I believe you. If there'd been anything to find, you'd have found it.'

She looked relieved.

'In his rooms, that is,' added Morse slowly.

'Pardon?'

'All I'm saying is that you've got a very tidy mind, haven't you? Let's put it this way. I bet I know the first thing you did when you took over here. I bet you gave this room the best spring-clean – best autumn-clean – it's ever had – last September – when *you* moved in – and the previous scout moved out.'

Susan Ewers looked puzzled. 'Well, I scrubbed and cleaned the place from top to bottom, yes – filthy, it was. Two whole days it took me. But I never found anything – any drugs – honest to God, I didn't!'

Morse, who had been seated on the only chair the room could offer, got to his feet, moved over to the door, and put his penultimate question:

'Do you have a mortgage?'

'Yes.'

'Big one?'

She nodded miserably.

As they stood there, the three of them, outside Susan's Pantry, Morse's eyes glanced back at the door, now closed again, fitting flush enough with the jambs on either side, but with a two-centimetre gap of parallel regularity showing between the bottom of the turquoise-blue door and the linoed floor of the landing.

Morse asked his last question simply and quietly: 'When did the envelopes first start coming, Susan?'

And Susan's eyes jumped up to his, suddenly flashing the unmistakable sign of fear.

CHAPTER SEVENTEEN

Examination: trial; test of knowledge and, as also may be hoped, capacity; close inspection (especially med.)
(*Small's Enlarged English Dictionary*, 1812 Edition)

ON FRIDAY, 2 September, two days after Julia Stevens' return to Oxford, there were already three items of importance on her day's agenda.

First, school.

Not as yet the dreaded restart (three whole days away, praise be!) but a visit to the Secretary's Office to look through the GCSE and A-level results, both lists having been published during her fortnight's absence abroad. Like every self-respecting teacher, she wanted to discover the relative success of the pupils she herself had taught.

In former days it had often been difficult enough for some pupils to *sit* examinations, let alone pass them. And even in the comparatively recent years of Julia's girlhood several of her own classmates had been deemed not to possess the requisite acumen even to attempt the 11 Plus. It was a question of the sheep and the goats – just like the division between those who were lost and those who were saved in the New Testament – a work with which the young Julia had become increasingly familiar, through the crusading fervour of a local curate with whom (aged ten and a half) she had fallen passionately in love.

How things had changed.

Now, in 1994, it was an occasion for considerable surprise if anyone somehow managed to *fail* an examination. Indeed, to be recorded in the Unclassified ranks of the GCSE was, in Julia's view, a feat of quite astonishing incompetence, which carried with it a sort of bravura badge of monumental under-achievement. And as far as Christian doctrine was concerned, it was becoming far easier to cope with sin, now that Hell was (semi-officially) abolished.

She looked through 5C's English results. Very much as she'd expected. Then looked a little more closely at the results of the only pupil in the class whose name had begun with 'C'. Costyn, K: Religious Education, 'Unclassified'; English, 'D'; Maths, 'Unclassified'; Geography, 'Unclassified'; Metalwork, 'Unclassified'. Well, at least he'd got something – after twelve years of schooling ... thirty-six terms. But it was difficult to imagine him getting much further than the Job Centre. Nowhere else for him to go, was there – except to jail, perhaps?

How she wished that 'D' had been a 'C', though.

At 10.30 a.m. she hurried fairly quickly away from the school premises and made her way on foot to the Churchill Hospital where her appointment at the clinic was for 11 a.m.; and where a few minutes ahead of schedule she was seated in the upstairs waiting-room, no longer thinking of Kevin Costyn and his former classmates – but of herself.

'How are you feeling?' asked Basil Shepstone, a large, balding, slightly stooping South African.

'You want me to undress?'

'I'd love you to undrress,' he said with that characteristic rolling of the 'r'. 'No need today, though. Next time, I'll insist.'

His friendly brown eyes were suddenly sad, and he reached across to place his right hand on her shoulder.

'You want the good news first? Or the bad news?' he asked quietly.

'The good news.'

'Well, your condition's fairly stable. And that's good – that's very good news.'

Julia found herself swallowing hard. 'And the bad news?'

'Well, it's not exactly bad news. Shall I read it?'

Julia could see the Oxfordshire Health Authority heading on the letter, but no more. She closed her eyes.

'It says . . . blah, blah, blah . . . "In the event of any deterioration, however, we regret to have to inform Mrs Stevens that her condition is inoperable."'

'They can't operate if it gets worse, they mean?'

Shepstone put down the letter. 'I prrefer your English to theirs.'

She sighed deeply; then opened her eyes and looked at him, knowing that she loved him for everything he'd tried to do for her. He had always been so gentle, so kindly, so professional; and now, watching him, she could understand why his eyes remained downcast as his Biro hatched the 'O' of 'Oxfordshire'.

'How long?' she asked simply.

He shook his head. 'Anyone who prredicts something like that – he's a fool.'

'A year?'

'Could be.'

'Six months?'

He looked defeated as he shrugged his broad shoulders.

'Less?'

'As I say—'

'Would you give up work if you were me?'

'Fairly soon, I think, yes.'

'Would you tell anyone?'

He hesitated. 'Only if it were someone you loved.'

She smiled, and got to her feet. 'There are not many people I love. You, of course – and my cleaning-lady – with whom incidentally' – she consulted her wristwatch – 'in exactly one hour's time, I have a slap-up lunch engagement at the Old Parsonage.'

'You're not inviting me?'

She shook her head. 'We've got some very private things to discuss, I'm afraid.'

After Mrs Stevens had left, the consultant took a handkerchief from his pocket and quickly wiped his eyes. What the dickens was he supposed to say? Because it never really did much good to lie. Or so he believed.

He blamed himself, for example, for lying so blatantly to the woman who'd died only two days previously – lying to Mrs Phillotson.

Not much difference in the case-histories.

No hope in either.

CHAPTER EIGHTEEN

Dead flies cause the ointment of the apothecary to send forth a stinking savour: so doth a little folly him that is in reputation for wisdom and honour

(*Ecclesiastes*, ch. 10, v. 1)

MORSE NOW realized that he would have few, if any, further cases of murder to solve during his career with Thames Valley CID. All right, orchestral conductors and High Court judges could pursue their professions into their twilight years, regardless – indeed sometimes completely oblivious – of their inevitably deteriorating talents. But more often than not policemen finished long before any incipient senility; and Morse himself was now within a couple of years of normal retirement.

For many persons it was difficult to tell where the dividing line came between latish middle-age and advisable pensionability. Perhaps it had something to do with the point at which nostalgia took over from hope; or perhaps with a sad realization that it was no longer possible to fall in love again; or, certainly in Morse's case, the time when, as now, he had to sit down on the side of the bed in order to pull his trousers on.

Such and similar thoughts were circulating in Morse's mind as on Saturday, 3 September, the morn-

ing after his visit with Lewis to Wolsey (and the statement made, immediately thereafter, by Mrs Ewers), he
sat in the Summertown Health Centre.

A mild cold had, as usual with Morse, developed into
a fit of intermittently barking bronchitis; but he comforted himself with the thought that very shortly, after
a sermon on the stupidity of cigarette-smoking, he
would emerge from the Centre with a slip of paper
happily prescribing a dose of powerful antibiotics.

Clutching his prescription, Morse was about to leave
when he remembered *The Times*, left in his erstwhile
seat in the waiting-room. Returning, he found that his
earlier companions – the anorexic girl and the spotty-
faced, overweight youth – had now been joined by a
slatternly looking, slackly dressed young woman, with
rings in her nostrils; a woman to whom Morse took an
immediate and intense dislike.

Predictably so.

From the chair next to the newcomer he picked up
his newspaper, without a word; though not without a
hurried glance into the woman's dull-green eyes, the
colour of the Oxford Canal along by Wolvercote. And
if Morse had waited there only a few seconds longer,
he would have heard someone call her name: 'Eleanor
Smith?'

But Morse had gone.

She'd already got the address of an abortion clinic;
but one of her friends, an authority in the field,
had informed her that it was now closed. So! So she'd
have to find some other place. And the quack ought to

be able to point her somewhere not too far away, surely? That's exactly the sort of thing quacks were there for.

In a marked police car, standing on a Strictly Doctors Only lot in the Centre's very restricted parking-area, Lewis sat thinking and waiting; waiting in fact, quite patiently, since the case appeared to be developing in a reasonably satisfactory way.

When, the previous afternoon, Susan Ewers had made (and signed) her statement, many things already adumbrated by Morse had dawned at last on Lewis's understanding.

Suspicion, prima facie, could and should now be levelled against Mr Edward Brooks, the man who had been Mrs Ewers' immediate predecessor as scout on Staircase G in Drinkwater Quad. Why? Morse's unusually simple and unspectacular hypothesis had been stated as follows:

It should be assumed, in all probability, that Brooks had played a key role, albeit an intermediary one, in supplying a substantial quantity of drugs to the young people living on his staircase – including Matthew Rodway; that Rodway's suicide had necessarily resulted in some thorough investigation by the college authorities into the goings-on on the staircase; that McClure, already living on the same staircase anyway, had become deeply involved – indeed had probably been the prime mover in seeing that Brooks was 'removed' from his post (coincidentally at the same time as McClure's retirement); that, as Mrs Ewers had now testified, the former scout had continued his trafficking in drugs, and that this information had somehow reached McClure's ears; that McClure had threatened Brooks with exposure, disgrace, criminal prosecution, and almost certain imprisonment; that finally, at a showdown in Daventry Court, Brooks had murdered McClure.

Such a hypothesis had the merit of fitting all the known facts; and if it could be corroborated by the new facts which would doubtless emerge from the meeting arranged for that afternoon at the Pitt Rivers Museum ...

Yes.

But there was the 'one potential fly in the ointment', as Lewis had expressed himself half an hour earlier.

And Morse had winced at the phrase. 'The cliché's bad enough in itself, Lewis – but what's a "potential fly" look like when it's on the window-pane?'

'Dunno, sir. But if Brooks *was* ambulanced off that Sunday with a heart attack—'

'Wouldn't *you* be likely to have a heart attack if you'd just killed somebody?'

'We can check up straightaway at the hospital.'

'All in good time,' Morse had said. 'You'll have *me* in hospital if you don't get me down to the Health Centre ...'

Still thinking and still waiting, Lewis looked again at the brief supplementary report from the police pathologist, which had been left on Morse's desk that morning.

Attn. Det. C.I. Morse.

No more re time of McClure's death – but
confirmation re probable 'within which':
8 a.m.–12 a.m. 28 Aug. Little more on knife/
knife-thrust: blade unusually (?) broad, 4–5 cms
and about 14–15 cms in length/penetration.
Straight through everything with massive internal
and external bleeding (as reported). Blade not
really sharp, judging by ugly lacerations round
immediate entry-area. Forceful thrust. Man
rather than woman? Perhaps woman with good
wrist/arm (or angry heart?). Certainly one or two
of our weaker (!) sex I met a year ago on a
martial arts course.

Full details available if required.
All very technical – but possibly helpful?

Laura Hobson

'At least she understands the full-stop,' Morse had
said.

Never having really mastered the full-stop himself,
Lewis had refrained from any comment.

Yet they both realized the importance of finding the
knife. Few murder prosecutions were likely to get off
on the right foot without the finding of a weapon. But
they hadn't found a weapon. A fairly perfunctory search
had earlier been made by Phillotson and his team; and
Lewis himself had instigated a very detailed search of
the area surrounding Daventry Court and the gardens
of the adjacent properties. But still without success.

Anyway, Morse was never the man to hunt through
a haystack for a needle. Much rather he'd always seek

to intensify (as he saw it) the magnetic field of his mind and trust that the missing needle would suddenly appear under his nose. Not much intensification as yet, though; the only thing under Morse's nose lately – and that under a towel – had been a bowl of steaming Friar's Balsam.

But here came Morse at last (10.40 a.m.), cum prescription. And Lewis could predict the imminent conversation:

'Chemist just around the corner, Lewis. If you'd just nip along and ... I'd be grateful. Only problem' – searching pockets – 'I seem ...'

Lewis was half right anyway.

'There's a chemist's just round the corner. If you'd be so good? I don't know how much these wretched Tories charge these days but' – searching pockets – 'here's a tenner.'

Lewis left him there on the reserved parking lot, just starting *The Times* crossword; and walked happily up to Boots in Lower Summertown.

What was happening to Morse?

The third item appearing on Julia Stevens' agenda the previous day had been postponed. On her arrival at the Old Parsonage Hotel, a telephone message was handed to her: Mrs Brooks would not be able to make the lunch; she was sorry; she would ring later if she could, and explain; please not to ring her.

Understandably, perhaps, Julia had not felt unduly

disappointed, for her mind was full of other thoughts, especially of herself. And she enjoyed the solitude of her glass of Bruno Paillard Brut Premier Cru (daring!) seated on a high stool at the Parsonage Bar, before walking down to the taxi-rank by the Martyrs' Memorial and thence being driven home in style and in a taxi gaudily advertising the Old Orleans Restaurant and Cocktail Bar.

It was not until later that evening that her brain began to weave its curious fancies about what exactly could have caused the problem . . .

Brenda Brooks rang (in a hurry, she'd said) just before the *Nine O'Clock News* on BBC1. Could they make it the next day, Saturday? A bit earlier? Twelve – twelve noon, say?

After she had put down the phone, Julia sat silently for a while, staring at nothing. A little bit odd, that – Brenda ringing (almost certainly) from a telephone-box when she had a phone of her own in the house. It would be something – everything – to do with that utterly despicable husband of hers. For from the very earliest days of their marriage, Ted Brooks had been a repulsive fly in the nuptial ointment; an ointment which had, over the thirteen increasingly unhappy and some-times desperate years (as Julia had learned), regularly sent forth its stinking savour.

CHAPTER NINETEEN

The true index of a man's character is the health
of his wife

(CYRIL CONNOLLY)

AS BRENDA BROOKS waited at the bus-stop that Saturday morning, then again as she made her bus journey down to Carfax, a series of videos, as it were, flashed in a nightmare of repeats across her mind; and her mood was an amalgam of anticipation and anxiety.

It had been three days earlier, Wednesday, 31 August, that she'd been seen at the Orthopaedic Clinic . . .

'At least it's not made your fracture.'

'Pardon, doctor?' So nervous had she been that so many of his words made little or no sense to her.

'I said, it's not a major fracture, Mrs Brooks. But it *is* a fracture.'

'Oh deary me.'

But she'd finally realized it was something more than a sprain – that's why she'd eventually gone to her GP, who in turn had referred her to a specialist. And now she was hearing all about it: about the meta-something between the wrist and the fingers. She'd try to look it up in that big dark-blue *Gray's Anatomy* she'd often dusted on one of Mrs Stevens' bookshelves. Not too difficult to remember: she'd just have to think of 'met a couple' – that's what it sounded like.

'And you'll be very sensible, if you can, to stop using your right hand completely. No housework. Rest! That's what it needs. The big thing for the time being is to give it a bit of support. So before you leave, the nurse here'll let you have one of those "Tubigrips" – fits over your hand like a glove. And, as I say, we'll get you in just as soon as, er . . . are you a member of BUPA, by the way?'

'Pardon?'

'Doesn't matter. We'll get you in just as soon as we can. Only twenty-four hours, with a bit of luck. Just a little op to set the bone and plaster you up for a week or two.'

'It's not quite so easy as that, Doctor. My husband's been in hospital for a few days. He's had a bit of a heart attack, and he's only just home this morning, so . . .'

'We can put you in touch with a home-help.'

'I can do a *little* bit of housework, can't I?'

'Not if you're sensible. Can't you get a cleaning-lady in for a couple of days a week?'

'I *am* a cleaning-lady,' she replied, at last feeling that she'd rediscovered her bearings; re-established her identity in life.

She'd hurried home that morning, inserting and turning the Yale key with her left hand, since it was becoming too painful to perform such an operation with her right.

'I'm back, Ted!'

Walking straight through into the living-room, she

found her husband, fully dressed, lounging in front of the TV, his fingers on the black control-panel.

'Christ! Where the 'ell a' you bin, woman?'

Brenda bit her lip. 'There was an emergency – just before my turn. It held everything up.'

'I thought *you* were the bloody emergency from all the fuss you've bin making.'

'Baked beans all right for lunch?'

'*Baked beans?*'

'I've got something nice in for tea.'

A few minutes later she took a tin of baked beans from a pantry shelf; and holding it in her right hand beneath a tin-opener fixed beside the kitchen door, she slowly turned the handle with her left. Slowly – yes, very slowly, like the worm that was finally turning . . .

And why?

If ever Brenda Brooks could begin to contemplate the murder of her husband, she would surely acknowledge as her primary, her abiding motive, the ways in which mentally and verbally he had so cruelly abused her for so long.

But no!

Belittlement had been her regular lot in life; and on that score he was, in reality, robbing her at most of a dignity that she had never known.

Would the underlying motive then be found in the knowledge of her husband's sexual abuse of an adolescent and increasingly attractive step-daughter?

Perhaps.

But it was all so much simpler than that. One thing there had been in her life – just the one thing – in which she could rejoice, in which until so very recently she *had* rejoiced: the skills she had acquired with her hands. And Edward Brooks had robbed her of them; had robbed her even of the little that she had, which was her all.

And for that she could never forgive him.

Brenda decided she needn't replay *all* that last bit to Mrs Stevens; but she did need to explain what had gone wrong the day before. Not that there was much to say, really. What was it *he*'d said when she'd told him she'd been invited out to lunch with Mrs S?

'Well if you think you're going to leave me this lunchtime, you bloody ain't, see? Not while I'm feeling groggy like this.'

Why had she ever married the man?

She'd known it was a mistake even before that ghastly wedding – as she'd prayed for God to boom down some unanswerable objection from the hammer-beam roof when the vicar had invited any just cause or impediment. But the Voice had been silent; and the invited guests were seated quietly on each side of the nave; and the son of Brenda's only sister (a sub-postmistress in Inverness), a spotty but mellifluous young soprano, was all rehearsed to render the 'Pie Jesu' from the Fauré *Requiem*.

Often in life it was difficult enough to gird up one's loins and go through with one's commitments. On this occasion, though, it had been far more difficult *not* to do so . . .

*

But at least Ted Brooks had relented somewhat, that previous evening – *and she knew why.* He'd decided he was feeling a whole lot better. He thought he might venture out – *would* venture out – into the big wide world again: the big wide world in this case being the East Oxford Conservative Club, well within gentle walking distance, where (he said) he'd be glad to meet the lads again, have a pint – even try a frame of snooker, perhaps. *And* he'd have a bite to eat in the club there; so she needn't bother 'erself about any more bloody baked beans.

Brenda had almost been smiling to herself that evening, when on the pretext of getting another pint of milk from the corner-shop she'd given Mrs S a quick ring from the nearby BT kiosk, just before nine o'clock.

But what . . . what about those other two things?

She was a good ten minutes early; and in leisurely, but tremulous, fashion, she crossed the Broad and walked up St Giles'; past Balliol College; past St John's College; past the Lamb and Flag; and then, waiting for the traffic lights just before Keble Road, she'd quickly checked (yet again) that the letter was there in her handbag.

For a few moments this letter almost assumed as much importance as that second thing – the event which had caught her up in such distress, such fear, since the previous Sunday, when her husband had returned home, the stains on the lower front of his shirt and the top of his grey flannel trousers *almost* adequately concealed by a beige summer cardigan (new from M&S); but only by the *back* of this cardigan, since the front of it was saturated with much blood. And it was only later that she'd noticed the soles of his trainers . . .

Opposite her, the Green Man flashed, and the bleeper bleeped; and Mrs Brenda Brooks walked quickly over to the Old Parsonage Hotel, at Number 1, Banbury Road.

CHAPTER TWENTY

When you live next to the cemetery, you cannot
weep for everyone

(Russian proverb)

THE OLD PARSONAGE HOTEL, dating back to 1660,
and situated between Keble College to the east and
Somerville College to the west, stands just north of the
point where the broad plane-tree'd avenue of St Giles'
forks into the Woodstock Road to the left and the
Banbury Road to the right. Completely refurbished a
few years since, and now incorporating such splendid
twentieth-century features as *en suite*, centrally-heated
bedrooms, the stone-built hotel has sought to preserve
the intimacy and charm of former times.

With success, in Julia Stevens' judgement.

In the judgement, too, of Brenda Brooks, as she
seated herself in a wall-settee, in front of a small, highly
polished mahogany table in the Parsonage Bar, lushly
carpeted in avocado green with a tiny pink-and-peach
motif.

'Lordy me!' Brenda managed to say in her soft
Oxfordshire burr, gently shaking her tightly curled grey
hair.

Whether, etymologically speaking, such an expression of obvious approval was a conflation of 'Lord'
and 'Lumme', Julia could not know. But she was
gratified with the reaction, and watched as Brenda's

eyes surveyed the walls around her, the lower half painted in gentle gardenia; the upper half in pale magnolia, almost totally covered with paintings, prints, cartoons.

'Lordy me!' repeated Brenda in a hushed voice, her vocabulary clearly inadequate to elaborate upon her earlier expression of delight.

'What would you like to drink?'

'Oh, coffee, please – that'll be fine.'

'No it won't. I insist on something stronger than coffee. Please!'

Minutes later, as they sipped their gins and slimline tonics, they read through the menu: Julia with the conviction that this was an imaginative selection of goodies; Brenda with more than a little puzzlement, since many of the imported words therein – Bagel, Couscous, Hummus, Linguini, Mozzarella – had never figured in her own cuisine. Indeed, the sight of such exotic fare might well, a decade or so back, have prompted within her a stab of some sympathy with a husband constantly complaining about baked beans, about sardines, about spaghetti . . .

In the past, yes.

But no longer.

'What's it to be, then?'

Brenda shook her head. 'I'm sorry, but I just can't eat anything. I'm all – I'm all full up, Mrs Stevens, if you know what I mean.'

Julia was too sensible to argue; and in any case she understood only too well, for she'd experienced exactly the same the day before when she'd sat on a bar-stool there, alone, feeling ... well, feeling 'all full up', as Brenda had so economically phrased it.

Half an hour later, as she was finishing her Poached Salmon with Lemon Butter, Salad, and New Potatoes, Julia Stevens had been put in the (latest) picture about Ted Brooks. She'd known all about the verbal abuse which had led to a broken heart; and now she learned of the physical abuse which had led to a broken hand.

'I'm so wicked – did you know that? You know why? I wished' (she whispered closely in Julia's ear) 'I wished him dead! Can you believe that?'

Most people in your position would have *murdered* him, you dear old thing, said Julia, but only to herself. And suddenly the realization that such a viciously cruel man should have ruined the life of such a sweet and lovable woman made her so very angry. Yet, at the same time, so very much in control.

Was it perhaps that the simultaneous keeping of her *own* secret with the hearing of *another's* was an unsuspected source of strength? But Julia had no opportunity of pursuing this interesting line of thought, for Brenda now opened her handbag and passed over the letter she'd received the previous Tuesday – not through the post, but pushed by hand through her letter-box.

'Just read it, please! No need to say anything.'

As Julia put on her school-ma'amish spectacles, she was aware that the woman seated beside her was now in tears.

*

The silent weeping had subsided into intermittent snuffling as Julia finished reading the agonized and agonizing pages.

'My God,' she whispered.

'But that's not all. There's something else – something even worse. I shall just have to tell somebody, Mrs Stevens – if you can bear it.'

CHAPTER TWENTY-ONE

Hate is the consequence of fear; we fear something before we hate it. A child who fears becomes
an adult who hates
        (CYRIL CONNOLLY, *The Unquiet Grave*)

Dear mum – dearest mum!
Its been a long time hasn't it and I didn't really
want to write but I can't talk about it, I just can't.
I was never much good with words but I'm going
to try. Its about why I left home and how I
couldn't really ever tell you about it. I'm writing
now because my friend at the hospital told me
about <u>him</u> and she said he's a lot better and
going home soon – and all I want you to do is let
him get very much worse again and don't look
after him – just let him die that's what I want
because he bloody deserves it! You thought I left
because I hated school and dreamt of boys and
sex and got mixed up with drugs and all the
punk scene and all that, and you were right in a
way because I did. But you got upset about the
wrong things, that's what I'm saying. Why did I
leave <u>you</u> mum – tell me that. You can't think it
was much fun for me with sod all to pay for
anything and nowhere to bloody go, I'd just got
one thing going for me and that was what you
and dear old dad gave me, a good pair of thighs

and a good pair of tits all the randy buggers wanted to get their hands on and believe me they paid good money for it. All I'm saying mum is I never really had to slum it after those first few weeks in London anyway. I never had the guts to tell you why but I've got to tell you now so here goes. Don't get too upset about it all, well not about me anyway, just about that horny bastard you married thirteen years ago.

I was thirteen when it started and we had the flu together him and me and so you remember we were both in bed when you went off cleaning one Thursday morning, you see I even remember the day of the week, and he came into my bedroom about eleven and brought me a cup of bovril and he said how nice looking I was getting and what a nice little figure I was getting and all that bullshit and how proud he was to have a daughter like me, well a step-daughter. Then he put his arm round me and started rubbing my neck and back a bit through my pajamas and told me to relax because that would do me good and soon I was lying down again with my back to him, and then I'm not sure how it happened but he was lying down and I could feel his hand inside my pajama top and he was feeling me, and I didn't know what to do because for a start I just thought he was being affectionate and I didn't want to upset him because we'd both be embarassed if I tried to push him away. Please mum try to understand! Perhaps its difficult to know where the line comes between affection

and sex but I knew because I felt something hard
against me and I knew what it was. I just felt
scared then like that first day in school when I
was in a room I shouldn't have been in and when
I just got kept in for what wasn't my fault at all,
but I thought it was my fault. Oh mum I'm not
explaining things very well. And then he grabbed
my hand and pulled it back behind him and
pushed it inside his pajamas and told me to rub
him, and I just didn't know what I was doing. It
was the first time I'd ever felt a man like that and
he was sort of silky and warm and I felt afraid
and fascinated at the same time. All I know is I'd
done what he wanted before I had the chance of
thinking about what I was doing and suddenly
there was all that sticky stuff all over my pajama
bottoms, and you won't remember but when you
came home I told you I'd put them in the
washing machine because I'd been sweating.
Afterwards he kept on saying that it was me
who'd agreed to do it, me who'd started it all not
him. Mum! He was a wicked liar, but even if it
was just one per cent me you've got to forgive
me. He made the most of everything, my God he
did. He said if I told you about what he'd done
he'd tell you about what I done, and I got scared
stiff you'd find out, and it was like blackmail all
the time those next three awful years when he
made me do everything he wanted. You could
never believe how I loathed him, even the sight
of him, I hated him more than I've ever hated
anybody since. Well that's it mum, I wonder what

your thinking. He's a shit and I never never
never want to see him again unless its to stick a
bloody great big knife in his great fat gut and
watch him squirm and hear him squeal like the
great fat pig he is. And if you want any help with
sticking the fucking pig you just let me know
because I'll only be too glad to help. There's only
one other thing to tell you and perhaps its why
I've written to you now. I've always kept in touch
with Auntie Beryl, its been a secret but she's
always let me know how you are and she wrote a
fortnight ago and told me how he's been treating
you mum – you must have let her know. Your
mad to stick it, your a matyr that's what you are.
I've just read through all this and I know one
thing I said you can do but you can't – not yet –
and that's get in touch with me, but its better
that way though don't be surprised if you see me.
Not just yet though, its been such a long long
time and I can't quite face it, not yet. I love you
mum, I shall always love you better than anybody.
One last thing and its odd really but I read in the
Oxford—

Julia turned over the page but that was the finish:
the last part of the letter was missing.

CHAPTER TWENTY-TWO

We all wish to be of importance in one way or another

(RALPH WALDO EMERSON, *Journals*)

LEWIS, on his way for an appointment with the House Matron of Wolsey, had dropped Morse in the Broad, where the Chief Inspector had swilled down a double dosage of penicillin pills with a pint of Hook Norton in the White Horse, before making his way to the Pitt Rivers Museum of Ethnology and Pre-History – for his own appointment.

Sooner or later, inevitably, a golden afternoon will captivate the visitor to Oxford; and as he walked leisurely up Parks Road, past the front of Wadham on his right, past the blue wrought-iron gates at the back of Trinity on his left, Morse felt deeply grateful that he had been privileged to spend so much of his lifetime there.

And one of those captivated visitors might have noticed a smile of quiet satisfaction around Morse's lips that early afternoon as he turned right, just opposite Keble, into the grounds of the Oxford University Museum – that monument to the nineteenth-century Gothic Revival, and the home of the Dodo and the Dinosaur. Some clouds there were in the pale blue sky that September day: some white, some grey; but not many.

No, not many, Morse.

Oddly, he'd enjoyed the short walk, although he believed that the delights of walking were often ludicrously exaggerated. *Solvitur ambulando*, though, as the Romans used to say; and even if the 'ambulando' was meant to be a figurative rather than a physical bit of 'walking' – well, so much the better. Not that there was anything intrinsically wrong with the occasional bit of physical walking; after all, Housman had composed some of his loveliest lyrics while walking around the Backs at Cambridge, after a couple of lunchtime beers.

Solvitur ambulando, yes.

Walk along then, Morse, since perhaps you are now walking towards the solution.

On the stone steps leading up to the entrance porch, he read the notice:

> ## THIS MUSEUM IS OPEN
> ## TO THE PUBLIC
> 12 a.m.–4.30 p.m. Mon–Sat.

It was already past noon, and on the grass a large party of visiting schoolchildren were unharnessing ruck-sacks and extracting packed lunches as Morse walked hurriedly by. It wasn't that he positively disliked schoolchildren; just that he didn't want to meet any of them.

Inside the glass-roofed, galleried building, Morse continued on his course, quickly past a huge reconstruction of a dinosaur ('Bipedal, but capable of quadripedal locomotion'); quickly past some assembled skeletons of African and Asian elephants. Nor was he long (if at all) detained by the tall show-cases displaying their specimens of the birds and insects of Australasia. Finally, after making his way between a statue of the Prince Consort and a well-stuffed ostrich, Morse emerged from the University Museum into the Pitt Rivers Museum; where he turned right, and knocked on the door of the Administrator.

Capital 'A'.

'Coffee?' she invited.

'No thanks. I've just had some.'

'Some beer, you mean.'

'Is it that obvious?'

'Yes.'

She was a tall, slim woman in her mid-forties, with prematurely white hair, and an attractively diffident smile about her lips.

'Some women,' began Morse, 'have an extraordinarily well-developed sense of smell—' But then he stopped. For a second or two he'd anticipated a little mild flirtation with Jane Cotterell. Clearly it was not to be, though, for he felt her clear, intelligent eyes upon him, and the tone of her voice was unambiguously no-nonsense:

'How can I help you?'

For the next ten minutes she answered his questions.

Brooks had joined the eight-strong team of attendants at the Pitt Rivers Museum – quite separate from the University Museum – almost exactly a year ago. He worked a fairly regular thirty-five-hour week, 8.30 a.m. to 4.30 p.m., with an hour off for lunch. The attendants had the job of cleaning and maintaining the premises; of keeping a watchful eye on all visitors, in particular on the many school-parties regularly arriving by coach from near and far; sometimes of performing specific tasks, like manning the museum shop; of being helpful and courteous to the public at all times – 'more friendly than fierce'; and above all, of course, of safeguarding the unrivalled collection of anthropological and ethnographic items housed in the museum . . .

'A unique museum, Inspector.'

'Do you ever get anybody trying to steal things?'

'*Very* rarely. Last summer we had someone trying to get into the case with the shrunken heads in it, but—'

'Hope you caught him.'

'*Her*, actually.'

'I'd rather rob a bank, myself.'

'I'd rather not rob at all.'

Morse was losing out, he realized that; and reverted to his questioning about Brooks.

The man was, in the Administrator's view, competent in his job, not frightened of work, punctual, reasonably pleasant with the public; private sort of person, though, something of a loner. There were certainly some of his colleagues with slightly more endearing qualities.

'If you'd known what you know now, would you have appointed him?'

'No.'

'Mind if I smoke?' asked Morse.

'I'd rather you didn't.'

'Did *he* smoke?'

'Not in the museum. No one smokes in the museum.'

'In the Common Room, or whatever you have?'

'I don't know.'

'You don't associate him with drugs at all?'

She glanced at him keenly before replying. 'There are no drugs here – not on my staff.'

'You'd know – if there were?'

'As you say, some women have a particularly well-developed sense of smell, Inspector.'

Morse let it go. 'Have you still got his references?'

The Administrator unlocked a filing-cabinet beside her and produced a green folder marked 'BROOKS, E'; and Morse looked through the half-dozen sheets it contained: Brooks's CV; a carbon of the letter appointing him wef 1 September 1993; a photocopied page giving details of Salary, National Insurance, Job Specification, Shift-Patterns; two open, blandly worded testimonials; and one hand-written reference, equally bland.

Morse read this last item a second time, slowly.

To the Administrator, Pitt Rivers Museum

Dear Madam,

I understand that Mr Edward Brooks has applied to you for the post (as advertised in the University Gazette, June '93) of Assistant Attendant at the Museum.

Brooks has worked as a scout at Wolsey College for almost ten years and I recommend to you his experience and diligence.

Yours sincerely,
Felix McClure (Dr)

Well, well.

'Did you know Dr McClure?' asked Morse.

'No. And I shan't have a chance of knowing him now, shall I?'

'You heard . . . ?'

'I read it in the *Oxford Mail*. I know all about Mr Brooks's illness too: his wife rang through early on Monday morning. But from what they say he's on the mend.'

Morse changed tack once more. 'I know a lot of the exhibits here are invaluable; but . . . but are there things here that are just plain *valuable*, if you know what I mean? Commercially valuable, saleable . . . ?'

'My goodness, yes. I wouldn't mind getting my fingers on some of the precious stones and rings here. Or do I mean *in* some of them?'

But Morse appeared to miss the Administrator's gentle humour.

'Does Mr Brooks have access to, well, to almost everything here really?'

'Yes, he does. Each of the attendants has a key to the wall-safe where we keep the keys to all the cabinets and drawers and so on.'

'So, if he took a fancy to one of your shrunken heads?'

'No problem. He wouldn't have to use a crow-bar.'

'I see.'

Jane Cotterell smiled, and thereby melted a little more of Morse's heart.

'Do I gather you want me to show you a bit about the security system here?'

'Not really,' protested Morse.

She rose to her feet. 'I'd better show you then.'

Twenty minutes later they returned to her office.

'Thank you,' said Morse. 'Thank you for your patience and your time. You're a very important person, I can see that.'

'Really? How—?'

'Well, you've got a capital "A" for a start; then you've got a wall-to-wall carpet; and for all I know you've not only got a parking space, you've probably got one with your name on it.'

'No name on it, I'm afraid.'

'Still . . .'

'What about you?'

'I've got my name on the door, at least for the present. But I've only got a little carpet, with a great big threadbare patch where my megapodic sergeant stands.'

'Is there such a word – "megapodic"?'

'I'll look it up when I get home. I've just treated myself to the *Shorter Oxford*.'

'Where is your home?'

'Top of the Banbury Road . . . Anywhere near you?'

'No. That's quite a way from where I live.' For a few seconds her eyes looked down at the carpet – that old carpet of hers, whose virtues had so suddenly, so unexpectedly expanded.

Only semi-reluctantly, a few minutes earlier, had Brenda Brooks been persuaded to hand over the last sheet of her daughter's letter. Its content, as Julia saw things, was very much as before. But, yes, it *was* a bit self-incriminating; especially that rather fine passage just before the end:

> He's undermined everything for me mum,
> including sex! But the very worst thing he ever
> did was to make me feel it could all have been
> my fault. Mum! Mum! He's bloody fucked up my
> life, and if he ever turns up murdered
> somewhere you'll know it was *me*, alright?

Strangely, however, Julia had experienced little sense of shock. A hardening of heart, rather; and a growing conviction that if Brooks *were* to turn up murdered somewhere his step-daughter would not be figuring alone on any list of possible suspects.

CHAPTER TWENTY-THREE

One night I contrived to stay in the Natural
History Museum, hiding myself at closing time in
the Fossil Invertebrate Gallery, and spending an
enchanted night alone in the museum, wandering
from gallery to gallery with a flashlight

(OLIVER SACKS, *The Observer*, 9 January 1994)

MORSE SPENT a while wandering vaguely around the
galleries. On the ground floor he gave as much of his
attention as he could muster to the tall, glass show-cases
illustrating the evolution of fire-arms, Japanese Noh
masks, the history of Looms and Weaving, old musical
instruments, shields, pots, models of boats, bull-roarers,
North American dress, and a myriad precious and semi-
precious stones . . .

Then, feeling like a man who in some great picture
gallery has had his fill of fourteenth-century crucifix-
ions, he walked up a flight of stone steps to see what
the Upper Gallery had to offer; and duly experienced
a similar sense of satiety as he ambled aimlessly along a
series of black-wood, glass-topped display-cases, sev-
erally containing scores of axes, adzes, tongs, scissors,
keys, coins, animal-traps, specialized tools . . . Burmese,
Siamese, Japanese, Indonesian . . .

In one display-case he counted sixty-four Early Medical Instruments, each item labelled in a neat manuscript, in black ink on a white card, with documentation

of provenance and purpose (where known). Among these many items, all laid out flat on biscuit-coloured backing-material (clearly recently renovated), his attention was drawn to a pair of primitive tooth-extractors from Tonga; and not for the first time he thanked the gods that he had been born after the general availability of anaesthetics.

But he had seen quite enough, he thought, wholly unaware, at this point, that he had made one extraordinarily interesting observation. So he decided it was time to leave. Very soon Lewis would be at the front waiting for him. Lewis would be on time. Lewis was always on time.

For the moment, however, he was conscious that there was no one else around in the Upper Gallery. And suddenly the place had grown a little forbidding, a little uncanny; and he felt a quick shiver down his spine as he made his way back into the main University Museum.

But even here it was quieter now, more sombre, beneath the glass-roofed atrium, as if perhaps a cloud had passed across the sun outside. And Morse found himself wondering what it would be like to be in this place, be locked in this place, when everyone else had gone; when the schoolchildren were back on their coaches; when the rest of the public, when the attendants, when the Administrator had all left ... Then perhaps, in the silent, eerie atmosphere, might not the spirits of the Dodo and the Dinosaur, never suspecting their curious extinction, be calling for their mates again on some primeval shore?

*

Jane Cotterell sat at her desk for several minutes after the door had closed behind Morse. She shouldn't really have said that about the beer. Silly of her! Why, she could just do with a drink herself, and it would have been nice if he'd asked her out for a lunchtime gin. She felt herself wishing that he'd forgotten something: a folding umbrella or a notebook or something. But as she'd observed, the Inspector had taken no notes at all; and outside, the sun now seemed to be shining gloriously once more.

CHAPTER TWENTY-FOUR

Cruelty is, perhaps, the worst kind of sin. Intellectual cruelty is certainly the worst kind of cruelty
(G. K. CHESTERTON, *All Things Considered*)

AFTER READING the (now complete) letter, Julia Stevens re-arranged the pages and read them again; whilst beside her, in a semi-distraught state, sat the original addressee; for whom, strangely enough, one of the most disturbing aspects of the letter was the revelation that her sister Beryl had told her niece the events of that terrible night. Had she (Brenda) made too much of everything when Ted had handled her so roughly? Had it been as much an accident as an incident? But no. No, it hadn't. And whether her account of it had been exaggerated or whether it had been understated – either to her sister over the phone or to her employer in person – certain it was that the recollection of that night in May would remain ever vivid in Brenda's memory . . .

'You're ever so late, Ted. What time is it?'

'Twelve, is it?'

'It's far later than that.'

'If you know what the bloody time is, why the 'ell do you ask me in the first place?'

'It's just that I can't get off to sleep when I know you're still out. I feel worried—'

'Christ! You want to worry when I start gettin' in 'alf-past bloody three, woman.'

'Come to bed now, anyway.'

'I bloody shan't – no!'

'Well, go and sleep in the spare room, then – I've got to get some sleep.'

'All the bloody same to me, innit – if I go in there, or if I stay in 'ere. Might just as well a' bin in different rooms all the bloody time, you know that. Frigid as a fuckin' ice-box! That's what you are. Always 'ave bin.'

'That's just not fair – that's not fair, what you just said!'

'If the bloody cap fits—'

'It can't go on like this, Ted – it just *can't*. I can't stick it any more.'

'Well, bloody *don't* then! Sling your 'ook and go, if you can't stick it! But just stop moanin' at me, d'you hear? Stop fuckin' *moanin'*! All right?'

She was folding her candlewick dressing-gown round her small figure and edging past him at the foot of the double bed, when he stopped her, grabbing hold of her fiercely by the shoulders and glaring furiously into her face before pushing her back.

'You stay where you are!'

Twice previously he had physically maltreated her in a similar way, but on neither occasion had she suffered physical hurt. That night, though, she had stumbled – *had* to stumble – against the iron fireplace in the bedroom; and as she'd put out her right hand to cushion the fall, something had happened; something had snapped. Not that it had been too painful. Not then.

As a young girl Brenda had been alongside when her mother had slipped in the snow one February morning and landed on her wrist; broken her wrist. And passers-by had been so concerned, so helpful, that as she'd sat in the Casualty Department at the old Radcliffe Infirmary, she'd told her daughter that it had almost been worthwhile, the accident – to discover such unsuspected kindness.

But that night Ted had just told her to get up; told her not to be such a bloody ninny. And she'd started to weep then – to weep not so much from pain or shock but from the humiliation of being treated in such a way by the man she had married . . .

Julia handed back the letter.

'I think she hates him even more than you do.'

Brenda nodded miserably. 'I must have loved him once, though, mustn't I? I suppose he was – well, after Sid died – he was just *there* really. I suppose I needed something – somebody – and Ted was there, and he made a bit of a fuss of me – and I was lonely. After that . . . but it doesn't matter any more.'

For a while there was a silence between the two women.

'Mrs Stevens?'

'Yes?'

'What about this other thing? What am I going to do about it? Please help me! Please!'

It was with anger that Julia had listened to Brenda's earlier confidences; with anger, too, that she had read the letter. The man was an animal – she might have known it; had known it. But the possibility that he was a *murderer*? Could Brenda have got it all wrong? Ridiculously wrong?

Julia had never really got to know Ted Brooks. In the early days of Brenda working for her, she'd met him a few times – three or four, no more. And once, only once, had she gone round to the Brooks's house, when Brenda had been stricken with some stomach bug; and when, as she had left, Ted Brooks's hand had moved, non-accidentally, against her breasts as he was supposedly helping her on with her mackintosh.

Take your horny hands off me, you lecherous sod, she'd thought then; and she had never seen him since that day. Never would, if she could help it. Yet he was not an ill-looking fellow, she conceded that.

The contents of the letter, therefore, had come as something less of a shock than may have been expected, since she had long known that Brenda had fairly regularly been on the receiving end of her husband's tongue and temper, and had suspected other things, perhaps . . .

But Brooks a *murderer*?

She looked across with a sort of loving distress at the busy, faithful little lady who had been such a godsend to her; a little lady dressed now in a navy-blue, two-piece suit; an oldish suit certainly, yet beautifully clean, with the pleats in the skirt most meticulously pressed for this special occasion. She felt an overwhelming surge of compassion for her, and she was going to do everything she could to help. Of course she was.

What about 'this other thing', though? My god, what could she do about that?

'Brenda? Brenda? You know what you said about . . . about the blood? Are you sure? Are you *sure*?'

'Mrs Stevens?' Brenda whispered. 'I wasn't going to tell you – I wasn't even going to tell *you*. But yes, I *am* sure. And shall I tell you why I'm sure?'

It was twenty-past two when Julia's taxi dropped Brenda – not immediately outside her house, but very close, just beside the Pakistani grocer's shop on the corner.

'Don't forget, Brenda! Make sure you run out of milk again tonight. Just before nine. And don't say or do anything before then. Agreed? Bye.'

On her way home, Julia spotted the *Oxford Mail* placard outside a newsagent's in the Cowley Road:

POLICE
HUNT
MURDER
WEAPON

and she asked the taxi-driver to stop.

Just before 3 p.m., Ted Brooks was lining up the shot, his eyes coolly assessing the angle between the white cue-ball and the last colour. Smoothly his cue drove through the line of his aim, and the black swiftly disappeared into the bottom right-hand pocket.

His opponent, an older man, slapped a pound coin down on the side of the table.

'Not done your snooker much harm, Ted.'

'No. Back at work in a fortnight, so the doc says. With a bit o' luck.'

CHAPTER TWENTY-FIVE

The older I grow, the more I distrust the familiar
doctrine that age brings wisdom

(H. L. MENCKEN)

AS MORSE had expected, Lewis was already sitting
waiting for him outside the museum.

'How did things go, sir?'

'All right.'

'Learn anything new?'

'Wouldn't go quite so far as that. What about you?'

'Interesting. That woman, well – she's a sort of major-
domo – Amazonian type, sir. I wouldn't like her as
Chief Constable.'

'Give it five years, Lewis.'

'Anyway, it's about Matthew Rodway. In the autumn
term—'

'We call it the Michaelmas Term here, Lewis.'

'In the Michaelmas Term, in his third year, when he
was back in college again—'

'In the House.'

'In the House again, he was sharing rooms with
another fellow—'

'Another undergraduate.'

'Another undergraduate called Ashley Davies. But
not for long, it seems. Davies got himself temporarily
booted out of college—'

'Rusticated.'

'Rusticated that term. Some sort of personal trouble, she said, but didn't want to go into it. Said we should see Davies for ourselves, really.'

'Like me, then, you didn't learn very much.'

'Ah! Just a minute, sir,' smiled Lewis. 'Mr Ashley Davies, our undergraduate, in the Michaelmas Term 1993, was rusticated from the House on the say-so of one Dr Felix McClure, former Student – capital "S", sir – of Wolsey College.'

'The plot thickens.'

'Bad blood, perhaps, sir? Ruined his chances, certainly – Davies was expected to get a First, she'd heard. And he didn't return this year, either. Murky circumstances . . . Drugs, do you think?'

'Or booze.'

'Or love.'

'Well?'

'I've got his address. Living with his parents in Bedford.'

'Did any good thing ever come out of Bedford?'

'John Bunyan, sir?'

'You go and see him, then. I can't do everything myself.'

'What's wrong?' asked Lewis quietly.

'I dunno. My chest's sore. My legs ache. My head's throbbing. I feel sick. I feel sweaty. It's the wrong question, isn't it? You mean, what's *right*?'

'Have you had your pills?'

'Course I have. Somebody's got to keep fit.'

'When were you last fit, sir?'

Morse pulled the safety-belt across him and fumbled for a few seconds to fix the tongue into the buckle.

'I don't ever remember feeling really fit.'

'I'm sure you'll blast my head off, sir, but—'

'I ought not to drink so much.'

'I wouldn't be surprised if you'd just washed your pills down with a pint.'

'Would you be surprised if you were quite wrong about that?'

'Washed 'em down with *two* pints, you mean?'

Morse smiled and wiped his forehead with a once-white handkerchief.

'You know the difference between us, sir – between you and me?'

'Tell me.'

'I got married, and so I've got a missus who's always tried to look after me.'

'You're lucky, though. Most people your age are divorced by now.'

'You never – never met a woman – you know, the right woman?'

Morse's eyes seemed focused far away. 'Nearly. Nearly, once.'

'Plenty of time.'

'Nonsense! You don't start things at my age. You pack 'em up. Like the job, Lewis.' Morse hesitated. 'Look, I've not told anybody yet – well, only Strange. I'm packing in the job next autumn.'

Lewis smiled sadly. 'Next Michaelmas, isn't it?'

'I could stay on another couple of years after that but . . .'

'Won't you miss things?'

'Course I bloody won't. I've been very lucky – at least in that respect. But I don't want to push the luck too far. I mean, we might get put on to a case we can't crack.'

'Not this one, I hope?'

'Oh no, Lewis, not this one.'

'What's the programme—?'

But Morse interrupted him: 'You just asked me if I'll miss things and I shan't, no. Only one thing, I suppose. I shall miss you, old friend, that's all.'

He had spoken simply, almost awkwardly, and for a little while Lewis hardly trusted himself to look up. Somewhere behind his eyes he felt a slight prickling; and somewhere – in his heart, perhaps – he felt a sadness he could barely comprehend.

'Not getting very far sitting here, Lewis, are we? What's the programme?'

'That's what I just asked you.'

'Well, there's this fellow from Bedford, you say?'

'Former undergraduate, sir.'

'Yes, well – is he at home?'

'Dunno. I can soon find out.'

'Do that, then. See him.'

'When—?'

'What's wrong with now? The way you drive you'll be back by teatime.'

'Don't *you* want to see him?'

Morse hesitated. 'No. There's something much more important for me to do this afternoon.'

'Go to bed, you mean?'

Slowly, resignedly, Morse nodded. 'And try to fix something up with Brooks. Time we paid him a little visit, isn't it?'

'Monday?'

'What's wrong with tomorrow? That'll be exactly a week after he murdered McClure, won't it?'

CHAPTER TWENTY-SIX

Three may keep a secret if two of them are dead
(BENJAMIN FRANKLIN)

BRENDA BROOKS was in a state of considerable agitation when she went through into the kitchen to put the kettle on. But at least she was relieved to be home before *him*; to have time for a cup of tea; to try to stop shaking. The anguish, the sheer misery of it all, were as strong as ever; with only her growing fear a new element in the tragedy . . .

After the first inevitable bewilderment – after the uncomprehending questions and the incomprehensible answers – her immediate reaction had been to wash the bloodstained clothing – shirt, trousers, cardigan; but instead, she had followed the fierce instructions given from the invalid's bed that the clothes be carted off to the rubbish dump, and that the affair never be referred to again.

Yet there the event stood – whatever had happened, whatever it all meant – forming that terrible and terrifying secret between them, between husband and wife. No longer a proper secret, though, for she had shared that secret . . . those secrets; or would it not be more honest to say that she had betrayed them? Particularly, therefore, did her fear centre on his return now: the fear that when he came in he would only have to

140

look at her – *to know*. And as she squeezed the tea-bag with the tongs, she could do nothing to stop the constant trembling in her hands.

Automatically almost, between sips of tea, she wiped the tongs clean of any tannin stain and replaced them in the drawer to the right of the sink, in the compartment next to the set of beautifully crafted knives which her sister Beryl had given her for her first wedding – knives of many shapes and sizes, some small and slim, some with much longer and broader blades, which lay there before her in shining and sharpened array.

The phone rang at 2.45 p.m.: the Pitt Rivers Museum.

The phone rang again just before 3 p.m.: Mrs Stevens.

'Is he home yet?'

'No.'

'Good. Now listen!'

The front door slammed at 3.20 p.m., when, miraculously as it seemed to Brenda, the shaking in her hands had ceased.

Almost invariably, whenever he came in, she would use those same three words: 'That you, Ted?' That afternoon, however, there was a change, subconscious perhaps, yet still significant.

'That you?' she asked in a firm voice. Just the two words now – as if the query had become depersonalized,

as if she could be asking the information of anyone; dehumanized, as if she could be speaking to a
dog.

As yet, still holding out on the battle-field, was a
small fortress. It was likely to collapse very soon, of
course; but there was the possibility that it might hold
out for some little time, since it had been recently
reinforced. And when the door had slammed shut she
had been suddenly conscious – yes! – of just a little
power.

'That you?' she repeated.

'Who do you think it is?'

'Cup o' tea?'

'You can get me a can o' beer.'

'The museum just rang. The lady wanted to know
how you were. Kind of her, wasn't it?'

'Kind? Was it fuck! Only wanted to know when I'd
be back, that's all. Must be short-staffed – that's the
only reason she rung.'

'You'd have thought people would be glad of a job
like that, with all this unemployment—'

'Would be, wouldn't they, if they paid you decent
bloody rates?'

'They pay you reasonably well, surely?'

He glared at her viciously. 'How do you know that?
You bin lookin' at my things when I was in 'ospital?
Christ, you better not 'a bin, woman!'

'I don't know what they pay you. You've never told
me.'

'Exackly! So you know fuck-all about it, right? Look
at *you*! You go out for that bloody teacher and what's
'er rates, eh? Bloody slave-labour, that's what you are.

Four quid an hour? Less? Christ, if you add up what *she* gets an hour – all those 'olidays and everything.'

Brenda made no answer, but the flag was still flying on the small fortress. And, oddly enough, he was right. Mrs Stevens *did* pay her less than £4 an hour: £10 for three hours – two mornings a week. But Brenda knew why that was, for unlike her husband her employer had told her exactly where she stood on the financial ladder: one rung from the bottom. In fact, Mrs Stevens had even been talking that lunchtime of having to get rid of her B-registration Volvo, which stood in one of the rundown garages at the end of her road, rented at £15 per calendar month.

As Brenda knew, the protection which that rusting, corrugated shack could afford to any vehicle was minimal; but it did mean that the car had a space – which was more than could be said for the length of road immediately outside Julia's own front door, where so often some other car or van was parked, with just as much right to do so as she had (so the Council had informed her). It wasn't that the sale of the old Volvo ('£340, madam – no, let's make it £350') would materially boost her current account at Lloyds; but it would mean a huge saving on all those other wretched expenses: insurance, road tax, servicing, repairs, MOT, garaging . . . what, about £800 a year?

'So why keep it?' that's what Julia had asked Brenda.

She would have been more honest if she had told Brenda why she was going to sell it. But that lunchtime, at least, the telling of secrets had been all one-way traffic.

*

143

After dropping off the drooping Morse, Lewis returned to Kidlington HQ, where before doing anything else he looked at the copy of the *Oxford Mail* that had been left on Morse's desk. He was glad they'd managed to get the item in – at the bottom of page 1:

MURDERED DON

The police are appealing for help in their enquiries into the brutal murder of Dr Felix McClure, discovered knifed to death in his apartment in Daventry Court, North Oxford, last Sunday.

Det. Sergeant Lewis, of Thames Valley C.I.D., informed our reporter that in spite of an extensive search the murder weapon has not been discovered.

Police are asking residents in Daventry Avenue to help by searching their own properties, since it is believed the murderer may have thrown the knife away as he left the scene.

The knife may be of the sort used in the kitchen for cutting meat, probably with a blade about 2″ broad and 5–6″ in length. If found it should be left untouched, and the police informed immediately.

CHAPTER TWENTY-SEVEN

Men will pay large sums to whores
For telling them they are not bores
(W. H. AUDEN, *New Year Letter*)

LATER THAT afternoon it was to be the B–B–B route: Bicester–Buckingham–Bedford. Fortunately for Lewis the detached Davies' residence was on the western outskirts of Bedford; and the door of 248 Northampton Road was answered immediately – by Ashley Davies himself.

After only a little skirmishing Davies had come up with his own version of the events which had preceded the showdown between himself and Matthew Rodway ... and Dr Felix McClure: an old carcass whose bones Lewis had been commissioned to pick over yet again.

Davies had known Matthew Rodway in their first year together. They'd met in the University Conservative Association (Lewis felt glad that Morse was abed); but apart from such political sympathy, the two young men had also found themselves fellow members of the East Oxford Martial Arts Club.

'Judo, karate – that sort of thing?' Lewis, himself a former boxer, was interested.

'Not so much the physical side of things – that was part of it, of course. But it's a sort of two-way process, physical and mental; mind and body. Both of us were more interested in the yoga side than anything. You know, "union" – that's what yoga means, isn't it?'

Lewis nodded sagely.

'Then you get into TM, of course.'

'TM, sir?'

'Transcendental Meditation. You know, towards spiritual well-being. You sit and repeat this word to yourself – this "mantra" – and you find yourself feeling good, content ... happy. Everything was OK, between Matthew and me, until this girl, this woman, joined. I just couldn't take my eyes off her. I just couldn't think of anything else.'

'The TM wasn't working properly?' suggested Lewis helpfully.

'Huh! It wasn't even as if she was attractive, really. Well, no. She *was* attractive, that's the whole point. Not beautiful or good-looking, or anything like that. But, well, she just had to look at you really, just look into your eyes, and your heart started melting away.'

'Sounds a bit of a dangerous woman.'

'You can say that again. I took her out twice – once to the Mitre, once to The Randolph – and she was quite open about things. Said she'd be willing to have sex and so on: fifty quid a time; hundred quid for a night together. No emotional involvement, though – she was very definite about that.'

'You agreed?'

'Well, I couldn't afford that sort of money. Hundred? Plus a B&B somewhere? But I did ask her about coming up to my room one evening – that was just after I'd started sharing with Matthew – when he had to go home for a family funeral. But it was a Tuesday, I remember, and she said she had to be very careful which day of the week it was. She could only do Saturday or perhaps Sunday because she knew somebody on the staircase and she wasn't prepared to take any risks.'

'What risks?'

'I don't know.'

'One of the other students – undergraduates there?'

For the first time the casually dressed, easy-mannered Davies hesitated. 'She didn't say.'

'Who else could it have been?'

Davies shrugged, but made no reply.

'There were two dons on the staircase, I understand – "Students" don't you call them?'

'Only a bloody pedant would call 'em Students these days.'

'I see. And, er, Dr McClure was one of those dons.'

'You've done your homework.'

'Go on please, sir.'

'Well, I had to go up for a Civil Service Selection thing on November the fifth, Bonfire Night, in Whitehall. Whole weekend of it – Friday, Saturday, Sunday. Anyway, I got so pissed off with all the palaver that I didn't stay for the Sunday session. I caught the ten-something from Paddington back to Oxford on Saturday night and when I got back to the staircase – well, there they were. We had two single beds in the one room, you see; and she was in his bed, and he was in mine. I don't quite know why, but it just made me see red and . . .'

'You'd tried to do the same yourself, though, so you said?'

'I know, yes.'

'You were just jealous, I suppose?'

'It was more than that. It's difficult to explain.'

'You mean, perhaps, if she'd been in *your* bed . . . ?'

'I don't know. You'd have to ask Freud. Anyway, I went berserk. I just went for him, that's all. He'd got nothing on – neither of 'em had – and soon we were wrestling and punching each other and knocking everything all over the bloody place, and there must have been one helluva racket because there was this great banging on the door and, well, we quietened down and I opened the door and there – there he was: that stuffed prick McClure. Well, that's about it, really. Matthew'd got a cut on his mouth and one of his eyes was badly bruised; I'd got a gash on my left arm but . . . no great damage, not considering. McClure wanted to know all about it, of course: who the girl was—'

'Who was she?'

'She called herself Ellie – Ellie Smith.'

'Then?'

'Well, they put me in one of the guest rooms in Great Quad, and Ellie went off – I think McClure put her in a taxi – and that was that. The Senior Tutor sent for me the next morning, and you know the rest.'

'Why didn't Mr Rodway get rusticated too?'

'Well, I'd started it. My fault, wasn't it?'

'Wasn't he disciplined at all?'

'Warned, yes. You get a warning in things like that. Then, if it happens again . . .'

Lewis thought he was beginning to get the picture. 'And perhaps you'd already had a warning yourself, sir?' he asked quietly.

Unblinking, the thickset Davies looked for several seconds into Lewis's eyes before nodding. 'I'd had a fight in a pub in my first year.'

'Much damage done then?'

'He broke his jaw.'

'Don't you mean *you* broke his jaw, sir?'

It was a pleasant little rejoinder, and perhaps Davies should have smiled. But Lewis saw no humour, only what he thought may have been a hint of cruelty, in the young man's eyes.

'You've got it, Sergeant.'

'Was that over a woman as well?'

'Yeah, 'fraid so. There was this other guy and he kept, you know, messing around a bit with this girl of mine.'

'Which pub was that?'

'The Grapes – in George Street. I think this guy thought it was called The Gropes.'

'And you hit him.'

'Yeah. I'd told him to fuck off.'

'And he hadn't.'

'Not straightaway, no.'

'But later he wished he had.'

'You could say that.'

'How did it get reported?'

'The landlord called the police. Bit unlucky, really. Wasn't all that much of a fight at all.'

Lewis consulted his notes. 'You wouldn't say you "went berserk" on that occasion?'

'No.'

'Why do you reckon you got so violent with Mr Rodway, then?'

Davies stared awhile at the carpet, then answered, though without looking up. 'It's simple, really. I was in love with her.'

'And so was Mr Rodway?'

Davies nodded. 'Yeah.'

'Have you seen her since?'

'A few times.'

'Recently?'

'No.'

'Can you tell me why you didn't go back to Oxford – to finish your degree? You were only rusticated for a term, weren't you?'

'Rest of the Michaelmas *and* all the Hilary. And by the time I was back, what with Finals and everything . . . I just couldn't face it.'

'How did your parents feel about that?'

'Disappointed, naturally.'

'Have you told them why I'm here today?'

'They're on a cruise in the Aegean.'

'I see.' Lewis stood up and closed his notebook and walked over to the window, enviously admiring the white Porsche that stood in the drive. 'They've left you the car, I see?'

'No, that's mine.'

Lewis turned. 'I thought you – well, you gave me the impression, sir, that fifty pounds might be a bit on the expensive side . . .'

'I came into some money. That's perhaps another reason I didn't go back to Oxford. Rich aunt, bless her! She left me . . . well, more than enough, let's say.'

Lewis asked a final question as the two men stood

in the front porch: 'Where were you last Sunday, sir?'

'Last *Sunday*?'

'Yes. The day Dr McClure was murdered.'

'Oh dear! You're not going to tell me . . . ? What possible reason could I have—'

'I suppose you could say it was because of Dr McClure that . . .'

'That they kicked me out? Yes.'

'You must have hated him for that.'

'No. You couldn't really hate him. He was just an officious bloody bore, that's all.'

'Did you know that he fell in love with Ellie Smith too?'

Davies sighed deeply. 'Yes.'

'Last Sunday, then?' repeated Lewis.

'I went bird-watching.'

'On your own?'

'Yes. I went out – must've been about nine, half-nine? Got back about three.'

'Whereabouts did you go?'

Davies mentioned a few names – woods or lakes, as Lewis assumed.

'Meet anyone you knew?'

'No.'

'Pub? Did you call at a pub? Hotel? Snackbar? Shop? Garage?'

'No, don't think so.'

'Must have been quite a lot of other bird-watchers around?'

'No. It's not the best time of year for bird-watching. Too many leaves still on the trees in late summer.

Unless you know a bit about flight, song, habitat – well, you're not going to spot much, are you? Do you know anything about bird-watching, Sergeant?'

'No.'

As Lewis left, he noticed the RSPB sticker on the rear window of a car he would have given quite a lot to drive. Perhaps not so much as fifty pounds, though.

Chapter Twenty-Eight

I do not love thee, Doctor Fell,
The reason why I cannot tell,
But this one thing I know full well:
I do not love thee, Doctor Fell
(THOMAS BROWN, *I Do Not Love Thee, Doctor Fell*)

STANDING QUITE still behind the curtained window of the first-floor front bedroom, she looked down across the drive at the departing policeman. She had a very good idea of what the interview had been about. Of course she had.

She was completely naked except for the dressing-gown (his) draped around a figure which was beginning to wobble dangerously between the voluptuous and the overblown – the beginnings of a pot-belly quite certainly calling for some fairly regular visits to the Temple Cowley pool in East Oxford, to plough through some thirty or forty lengths a time (for she was an excellent swimmer).

The smell of her was seductive though, she knew that. How else, with that posh eau-de-toilette just squirted everywhere about her person? 'Mimosa Pour Moi' – the last thing Felix had bought her.

Felix . . .

Always (above all perhaps?) he'd adored the sight and the smell of her when she'd just finished drying herself after one of her frequent baths. And how she treasured that letter – well, sort of letter – he'd written that morning in a posh London hotel as he'd sat waiting (and waiting and waiting) to go down to breakfast whilst she reclined luxuriously, reluctant to make any decisive move from the bath-tub.

How she loved a long, hot bath.

Yummy!

And how she loved what he'd written – one of the very few things she carried around in that scuffed shoulder-bag of hers:

I ask my darling if she is ready for breakfast; and
she stands in front of me; and with a
synchronized circular swish of her deodorant-
can, she sprays first her left armpit, then her
right.
   But she gives no answer.
I ask my darling if she has been thinking of me
during our night together; and she forms her lips
into a moue and rocks her right hand to and fro,
as if she was stretching it forward to steady a
rickety table on the stone-flagged floor at The
Trout.
   But she gives no answer.
I ask my darling why she can't occasionally be
more punctual for any rendezvous with me; and I
would be so glad if she could speak and dip into
a pool of unconvincing excuses.
   But she gives no answer.
I ask my darling what she loves most of all in her
life; and she smiles (at last, a smile!) and she
points behind her to the deep, scented water in

which she has just been soaking and poaching,
her full breasts seemingly floating on the surface.

It is, I must suppose, the nearest I shall ever
come to an answer.

She'd read it many, many times. Above all she
enjoyed reading about herself in the third person. It
was as if she were a key character in some *roman-à-clef*
(Felix had told her about that sort of book – told her
how to pronounce it): a character far more important
on the page than in reality. Oh, yes. Because in real life
she wasn't important at all; nor ever would be. After all,
she wouldn't exactly be riding up to the abortion clinic
that Wednesday in a Roller, now would she? God, no.
Just standing on that perishing Platform Number 2,
waiting for the early bloody train up to bloody
Birmingham.

Ashley Davies opened the bedroom door and walked
up behind her, unloosening the belt of her (his)
dressing-gown.

'God, am I ready—'

But she slipped away from him – and slipped out of
the dressing-gown, fixing first her black suspender-belt,
then her black bra; then pulling a thin dark blue dress
over her ridiculously colourful head before hooking a
pair of laddered black stockings up her legs.

Davies had watched her, silently. He felt almost as
sexually aroused by watching her dress as watching her
undress.

At last he spoke:

'What's the matter? What have I done wrong?'

She made no reply, but stood tip-tilting her chin towards the dressing-table mirror as she applied some transparent substance to her pouting lips.

'Ellie!'

'I'm off.'

'What d'you mean, you're off? I'm taking you out to lunch, remember?'

'I'm off.'

'You can't do this to me!'

'Just watch me!'

'Is it the police?'

'Could be.'

'But he's gone – it's over – it's all right.'

She picked up a small, overnight grip of faded pink canvas, inscribed with the names of pop groups and punk stars.

'I'm off.'

'When do I see you again?'

'You don't.'

'Ellie!'

'I don't want to see you any more.' (It seemed a long sentence.)

Davies sat down miserably on the side of the double bed in which he and Ellie had slept – half slept – the previous night.

'You don't love me at all, do you?'

'No.'

'Have you ever loved me?'

'No.'

'Did you love Matthew?'

'No.'

'Don't tell me you loved McClure? Don't tell me you loved *that* prick?'

'About the only thing about him I did love.'

'Christ! You shouldn't *say* things like that.'

'Why ask, then?'

'Have you ever loved anybody?'

'Me mum, yeah.'

'Nobody else?'

'Me dad – me real dad, I suppose. Can't remember.'

With a series of upward brushes she applied some black colouration to her eyelashes.

'Where d'you think you're going now?'

'Oxford.'

Davies sighed miserably, stood up, and reached inside his trouser-pocket for his car-keys.

'Come on, then.'

'I'm not going with *you.*'

'What's that supposed to mean?'

'I'll hitch a lift.'

'You can't do that.'

'Course I bloody can. That's all they're lookin' for, most of these lecherous sods. All I gotta do—'

'*Ellie!*'

'First car, like as not. You see.'

In fact, Ellie Smith's prediction was unduly optimistic, since the first car drove past her with little observable sign of interest, no detectable sign of deceleration.

The second car did exactly the same.

But not the third.

CHAPTER TWENTY-NINE

My predestinated lot in life, alas, has amounted to
this: a mens not particularly sana in a corpore not
particularly sano
(VISCOUNT MUMBLES, *Reflections on My Life*)

ON THE following day, Sunday 4 September, Ted
Brooks was sitting up in bed, two pillows behind his
back, reading the more salacious offerings in the *News
of the World*. It was exactly 11.30 a.m., he knew that,
since he had been looking at his wristwatch every
minute or so since 11.15.

Now, for some reason, he began to feel slightly less
agitated as the minute-hand moved slowly up in the
climb towards the twelve – the 'prick of noon', as
Shakespeare has it. His mind, similarly, was moving
slowly; perhaps it had never moved all that quickly
anyway.

Whatever happened, though, he was going to make
the most of his heart attack – his 'mild' heart attack, as
they'd assured him in the Coronary Care Unit. Well, he
hoped it was mild. He didn't want to die. Course he
bloody didn't. Paradoxically, however, he found himself wishing it wasn't *all that* mild. A heart attack
– whatever its measurement on the Richter Scale – was
still a heart attack; and the maximum sympathy and
attention should be extracted from such an affliction,
so Brenda'd better bloody understand *that*.

He shouted downstairs for a cup of Bovril. But before the beverage could arrive, he heard the double-burred ring of the telephone: an unusual occurrence in the Brooks's household at any time; and virtually unprecedented on a Sunday.

He got out of bed, and stood listening beside the bedroom door as Brenda answered the call in the narrow entrance-hall at the bottom of the stairs.

'Oh, I see . . .'

'I do understand, yes . . .'

'Look, let me try to put him on . . .'

She found him sitting on the side of the bed, pulling on his socks.

'Thames Valley Police, Ted. They want to come and talk to you.'

'Christ!' he hissed. 'Don't they know I've only just got out of 'ospital?'

Brenda's upper lip was trembling slightly, but her voice sounded strangely calm. 'Would you like to speak to him yourself? Or tell me what to say? I don't care – but don't let's keep him waiting.'

'What's 'is name, this feller?'

'Lewis. Detective Sergeant Lewis.'

Lewis put down the phone.

Like Brooks a few minutes earlier, he was sitting on the side of the bed – Morse's bed.

'That's fixed that up, then, sir. I still feel you'd be better off staying in bed, though.'

'Nonsense!'

Lewis looked with some concern across at his chief,

lying back against three pillows, in pyjamas striped in maroon, pale blue, and white, with an array of bottles and medicaments on the bedside table: aspirin, Alka Seltzer, indigestion tablets, penicillin, paracetamol – and a bottle of The Macallan, almost empty.

He looked blotchy.

He looked ghastly.

'No rush, is there, sir?' he asked in a kindly manner.

'Not much danger of me rushing today.' He put down the book he'd been reading, and Lewis saw its title: *The Anatomy of Melancholy*.

'Trying to cheer yourself up, sir?'

'Oddly enough, I am. Listen to this: "There is no greater cause of melancholy than idleness; no better cure than busyness" – that's what old Burton says. So tell me all about Bedford.'

So Lewis told him, trying so very hard to miss nothing out; and conscious, as always, that Morse would probably consider of vital importance those things he himself had assumed to be obviously trivial.

And vice versa, of course.

Morse listened, with only the occasional interruption.

'So you can see, sir, he's not got much of an alibi, has he?'

'Lew-is! We won't *want* another suspect. We know who killed McClure: the fellow we're off to see this afternoon. All we're looking for is a bit more background, a slightly different angle on things. We can't take Brooks in yet – well, we *can*; but he's not going to run away. We ought to wait for a bit more evidence to accumulate.'

'We certainly haven't got much, to be truthful, have we?'

'You've still got people looking for the knife?'

Lewis nodded. 'Eight men on that, sir. Doing the houses Phillotson's lads didn't – along most of the road, both sides.'

Morse grunted. 'I don't like this fellow Brooks.'

'You've not even *seen* him yet.'

'I just don't like this drugs business.'

'I doubt if Davies had any part in that. Didn't seem the type at all.'

'Just in on the sex.'

'He fell for that woman in a pretty big way, no doubt about that.'

'Mm. And you say there may have been somebody in the house while you were there?'

'As I say, I heard the loo flushing.'

'Well, a trained detective like you would, wouldn't he?'

'When the cat's away . . .'

'Looks like it.'

'I think he's the sort of fellow who just welcomes all the floozies with open arms—'

'And open flies.'

'You don't think . . .' The thought struck Lewis for the first time. 'You don't think . . . ?'

'The loo-flusher was one and the same as our stair-case Lulu? No. Not a chance. Forget it! The really interesting thing is what Davies told you about her – about Ellie Smith, or whatever her name is.'

Morse broke off, wearily, wiping the glistering perspiration from his forehead with a grubby white handkerchief taken from his pyjama top – top number three, in fact, for he had already sweated his way through two pairs of pyjamas since taking to his bed the previous afternoon.

'Did you take your dose this morning, sir?'

Morse nodded. 'Double dose, Lewis. That's always been the secret for me.'

'I meant the medicine, not the Malt.'

Morse grinned weakly, his forehead immediately prickling with moisture once more, like a windscreen in persistent drizzle.

He lit a cigarette; and coughed revoltingly, his chest feeling like a chunk of excoriated flesh. Then spoke:

'She said she couldn't see him on a weekday, right? Saturday OK, though, and perhaps Sunday. Why? Pretty clearly because she knew somebody there on the staircase; and you thought – be honest, now! – you thought it must be somebody who buggered off to his cottage in the Cotswolds somewhere every weekend, and left the coast clear. You thought it was one of the two Students, didn't you? You thought it was McClure.'

'To be honest with you, I didn't, no. I thought it was somebody who didn't work after Saturday lunchtime until starting up again on Monday morning. I thought it was the scout. I thought it was Brooks.'

'Oh!'

'Wasn't I supposed to think that?'

Morse wiped his brow yet again. 'I'm not really up to things at the minute, am I?'

'No, I don't think you are.'

'Oh!'

'I think Brooks wasn't just a pusher; I think he was a

pimp as well. And it was probably too risky for him to let any of his girls get into the college – into the *House*, sir. So, if this particular girl *was* going to get in, it was going to be at weekends, when he wasn't there, when she could make her own arrangements, take her own risks, and set her own fee – without cutting him in at all.'

Morse was coughing again. 'Why don't I put you in charge of this case, Lewis?'

'Because I couldn't handle it.'

'Don't you think you can handle Brooks?'

'No.'

'You think we ought to wait a couple of days, don't you – before we see him?'

'Yes.'

'And you think I'll agree to that?'

'No.'

Morse closed Burton's immortal work, and folded the duvet aside.

'Will you do me a quick favour, Lewis, while I get dressed?'

'Course.'

'Just nip out and get me the *News of the World*, will you?'

CHAPTER THIRTY

Randolph, you're not going to like this, but I was
in bed with your wife
   (*Murder Ink: Alibis we never want to hear again*)

AT 1.15 P.M., on the way to the Brooks's residence in
East Oxford, they had called briefly at Daventry
Avenue. Still no sign of any murder weapon.

'Give 'em a chance,' Lewis had said.

Morse had insisted on taking the Jaguar, with Lewis
driving: he thought the finale of *Die Walküre* might well
refresh his drooping spirits, and the tape (he said) was
already in position there. But strangely enough he
hadn't turned it on; even more strangely he appeared
ready to engage in conversation in a car.

Most unusual.

'You ought to invest in a bit of Wagner, Lewis. Do
you far more good than all that rubbish you play.'

'Not when you're there, I don't.'

'Thank God!'

'I don't get on to you, for what you like.'

'What do *you* like best?'

Lewis came up to the roundabout at the Plain, and
took the second exit, the one after St Clements, into
the Cowley Road.

'I'll tell you what I can't stand, sir – the bagpipes.'

Morse smiled. 'Somebody once said that was his

favourite music – the sound of bagpipes slowly fading away into the distance.'

It was a quarter-to two when Ted and Brenda Brooks, side by side on the living-room settee, sat facing the two detectives: Morse in the only armchair there, Lewis on an upright chair imported for the occasion from the kitchen.

Brooks himself, in his late forties, dressed in a white, short-sleeved shirt and well-pressed grey slacks, looked pale and strained. But soon he appeared to relax a little, and was confirming, with an occasional nod of his greying head, the background details which Morse now briefly rehearsed: his years as a scout at Wolsey, where he had got to know Matthew Rodway ('Yup'); and Dr McClure ('Yup'); his present employment at the Pitt Rivers Museum ('Yup').

The skirmishing had been very civilized, and Mrs Brooks asked them all if they'd like a cup of tea.

But Morse declined, speaking, as it appeared, for all three of them, and turning back to Brooks and to the trickier part of the examination paper.

'Do you want your wife to be here, sir, while I ask you – I'm sorry – some rather awkward questions?'

'She stays. You stay, don't you, Bren? Nothing she shouldn't know about, Inspector.'

Lewis watched the man carefully, but could see no greater signs of nervousness than was normal among witnesses being interviewed by the police. Wasn't *she*, Mrs Brooks, the more obviously nervous of the two?

'Mr Brooks,' Morse began. 'I know you've been in

hospital, but please bear with me. We have evidence that there was some trading in drugs on your old staircase over the last three or four years.'

'Nothin' to do wi' me if there was.'

'You knew nothing of it?'

'No.'

'It's difficult for us, you see, because we have a statement to the effect that you did know something about it.'

'Christ! I'd like to know who it was as told you that. Load o' bloody lies!'

'You'd have no objections to coming along to HQ and going through that statement with us?'

'I can't – not just now, I can't – but I will – I'll be 'appy to – when I'm better. You don't want to give me another bloody 'eart attack, do you?'

Brooks's manner of speaking, which had begun in a gentle Oxfordshire burr, had suddenly switched into the coarse articulation with which he was wont to address his wife.

'Would you have known, Mr Brooks, if there had been drugs?'

'No job o' mine to interfere. Everybody's got their own lives to live.'

'There were parties there, on the staircase?'

'You try an' stop 'em!'

'Did *you* try?'

'If you talk to people they'll all tell you I were a good scout. That's all that worried me.'

'I'm afraid we shan't be able to talk to Dr McClure, shall we?'

'There's others.'

'Did you like Dr McClure?'

'OK, yeah.'

'You both left at the same time, I believe.'

'So wha'?'

'I just wondered if you had a farewell drink together, that's all.'

'Don't know much about Town and Gown, do you?'

Morse turned to Lewis. 'Sergeant?'

'We've obviously got to interview anyone, sir, who had a link with Dr McClure. That's why we're here, as I told you on the phone. So I shall have to ask you where you were last Sunday – Sunday the twenty-eighth of August.'

'Huh! Last Sunday?' He turned to his wife. 'Hear that, Bren? Not bloody difficult, that one, is it? You tell 'em. You remember better 'an I do. Bloody 'ell! If you reckon I 'ad anything to do wi' *that* – last *Sunday*? Christ!'

Brenda Brooks folded her hands nervously in her lap, and for the first time Morse noticed that the right hand, beneath an elastic support, might be slightly deformed. Perhaps she held them to stop them shaking? But there was nothing she could do about her trembling upper-lip.

'Well ... Ted woke me about three o'clock that Sunday morning—'

'More like 'alf-two.'

'—with this awful pain in his chest, and I got up to find the indigestion tablets and I made a cup o' tea and you seemed better, didn't you, Ted? Well, a bit better anyway and I slept a bit and he did, just a bit, but it was a bad night.'

'Terrible!'

'I got up at six and made some more tea and asked Ted if he wanted any breakfast but he didn't and the pain was still there, and I said we ought to ring the doctor but Ted said not yet, well, you know, it was Sunday and he'd have to come out special, like. Anyway he got up about ten because I remember we sat in the kitchen listening to *The Archers* at quarter-past while I got the meat ready – lamb and mint sauce – but Ted couldn't face it. Then about half-past one, quarter-to two, it got so bad, well, it was no good hanging on any longer and I rang the ambulance and they came in about ... well, it was only about ten minutes – ever so quick. He was on a machine at half-past two – about then, weren't you, Ted?'

'Intensive Care,' said the ex-scout, not without a touch of pride. 'The pain 'ad got t'rific – I knew it were summat serious. Told you so at the time, didn't I, Bren?'

Brenda nodded dutifully.

It had immediately become clear to Morse that there was now a very considerable obstacle between him and any decision to arrest Edward Brooks on suspicion of murder; a considerable objection even to leaving his name on the list of suspects – which indeed would be a dramatic set-back for the whole case, since Brooks's name was the *only* one appearing on Morse's list.

He looked across now at the faithful little lady sitting there in her skirt and summer blouse next to her husband. If she persisted in her present lies (for Morse was convinced that such they were) it was going to be extremely difficult to discredit her testimony, appearing, as she did, to possess that formidable combination of nervousness and innocence. Any jury would strongly sympathize.

Morse changed tack completely.

'Do you know, I'm beginning to feel a bit thirsty, Mrs Brooks. Does that offer of a cuppa still stand?'

After Mrs Brooks had put the kettle on and taken the china cups from the dresser, she stood close to the kitchen door. Her hearing was still good. It was the white-haired one who was speaking . . .

'Have you got a car, sir?'

'Not 'ad one for ten year or more.'

'How do you get to work?'

'Still go on the bus, mostly.'

'You don't bike?'

'Why d'you ask that?'

'I saw your cycling helmet in the hall, that's all.'

'So?'

'Didn't mind me asking, did you?'

'Why the 'ell should I?'

'Well, Dr McClure was knifed to death, as you know, and there was an awful lot of blood all over the place – and all over the murderer, like as not. So if he'd driven off in a car, well . . . these clever lads in the labs, they can trace the tiniest speck of blood . . .'

'As I said, though, I 'aven't got a car.'

'I still think we'd quite like to have a look at your bike. What do you think, Sergeant Lewis?'

'Not a question of "liking", sir. I'm afraid we shall *have* to take it away.'

'Well, that's where you're wrong, 'cos I 'aven't got no bike no longer, 'ave I? Bloody stolen, wasn't it?

Sat'day lunchtime, that were – week yesterday. Just went to the Club for a pint and when I got out – there it was, gone! Lock 'n' all on the back wheel. Ten bloody quid, that fancy lock cost me.'

'Did you report the theft, sir?'

'Wha'? Report a stolen bike? In Oxford? You must be jokin'.'

Mrs Brooks came in with a tray.

'I must ask you to report the theft of your bike, sir,' said Lewis quietly. 'To St Aldate's.'

'Milk and sugar, Inspector?'

For the first time her eyes looked unflinchingly straight into his, and suddenly Morse knew that behind the nervousness, behind the fear, there lay a look of good companionship. He smiled at her; and she, fleetingly, smiled back at him.

And he felt touched.

And he felt poorly again.

And he felt convinced that he was sitting opposite the man who had murdered Felix McClure; felt it in his bones and in his brains; would have felt it in his soul, had he known what such a thing was and where it was located.

When ten minutes later Mrs Brooks was about to show them out, Morse asked about the two photographs hanging on the wall of the entrance-hall.

'Well, that one' – she pointed to a dark, broody-looking girl in her mid-teens or so – 'that's my daughter. That's Ellie. Her first name was Kay, really, but she likes to be called Ellie.'

Phew!

With an effort, Lewis managed not to exchange glances with Morse.

'That one' – she pointed to a photograph of herself arm-in-arm, in front of a coach, with a younger, taller, strikingly attractive woman – 'that's me and Mrs Stevens, when we went on a school-party to Stratford last year. Lovely, it was. And with a bit of luck I'll be going with her again this next week. She teaches at the Proctor Memorial School. I clean for her . . . Well, as I say . . . I clean for her.'

It seemed for a few seconds that she was going to add a gloss to that last repeated statement. But her husband had shouted from within, and Morse managed not to look down at that disfigured palm again as Brenda Brooks's hands indulged in a further spasm of floccillation.

CHAPTER THIRTY-ONE

There is nothing which has yet been contrived by
man by which so much happiness is produced as
by a good tavern

(SAMUEL JOHNSON, *Obiter Dictum*,
21 March 1776)

'WELL, *well*! What do you make of all that?'

The Jaguar was gently negotiating half a dozen
traffic-calming humps, before reaching the T-junction
at the Cowley Road.

'Not now, Lewis!'

'How're you feeling, sir?'

'Just change the first letter of my name from "M" to
"W".'

'You should be in bed.'

Morse looked at his wristwatch. 'Nearest pub, Lewis.
We need to think a little.'

Morse was comparatively unfamiliar with the part of
Oxford in which he now found himself. In his own
undergraduate days, it had seemed a long way out,
being dubbed a 'Bridge Too Far' – on the farther side,
the eastern side, the *wrong* side, of Magdalen Bridge –
beyond the pale, as it were. Yet even then, three
decades earlier, it had been (as it still was) a cosmopol-
itan, commercial area of fascinating contrasts: of the
drab and the delightful; of boarded-up premises and
thriving small businesses; of decay and regeneration –

a Private Sex Shop at the city-centre end, and a police station at the far Ring Road end, with almost everything between, including (and particularly) a string of highly starred Indian restaurants. Including too (as Morse now trusted) a local pub selling real ale.

Lewis himself knew the area well; and after turning right at the T-junction, he almost immediately turned left into Marsh Road, pulling up there beside the Marsh Harrier.

Ashley Davies, he thought, would almost certainly have approved.

The *Good Pubs of Oxford* guide always reserved its highest praise for those hostelries where conversation was not impeded (let alone wholly precluded) by stentorian juke-boxes. And certainly Morse was gratified to find no music here. Yet he appeared to Lewis clearly ill-at-ease as he started – well, almost finished really – his first swift pint of Fuller's 'London Pride'.

'What's worrying you, sir?'

'I dunno. I've just got a sort of premonition—'

'Didn't know you believed in them.'

'—about this copy-cat-crime business. You know, you get a crime reported in the press – somebody pinching a baby from outside a supermarket, say – and before you can say "Ann Robinson" somebody else's having a go at the same thing.'

Lewis followed the drift of Morse's thought. 'The article we placed in the *Oxford Mail*?'

'Perhaps.'

'You mean, we shouldn't perhaps . . . ?'

'Oh, no! It was our duty to print that. And for all we know it could still produce something. Though I doubt it.'

Morse drained his beer before continuing: 'You know, that knife's somewhere, isn't it? The knife that someone stuck into McClure. The knife that *Brooks* stuck into McClure. That's the infuriating thing for me. Knowing that the bloody thing's *somewhere*, even if it's at the bottom of the canal.'

'Or the Cherwell.'

'Or the Isis.'

'Or the gravel-pits . . .'

But the conversation was briefly interrupted whilst Lewis, on the landlord's announcement of Last Orders, was now despatched to the bar for the second round.

Perhaps it was Morse's bronchial affliction which was affecting his short-term memory, since he appeared to be suffering under the misapprehension that it was he who had purchased the first.

Whatever the case, however, Morse quite certainly looked happier as he picked up his second pint, and picked up the earlier conversation.

'Brooks wouldn't have been too near any water, would he?'

'Not that far off, surely. And he'd have to go over Magdalen Bridge on his way home, anyway.'

'On his blood-saddled bike . . .'

'All he'd need to do was drop his knife over the bridge there – probably be safe till Kingdom Come.'

Morse shook his head. 'He'd have been worried about being seen.'

Lewis shrugged. 'He could have waited till it was dark.'

'It was bloody *morning*, Lewis!'

'He could've ditched it earlier. In a garden or somewhere.'

'No! We'd have found it by now, surely.'

'We're still trying,' said Lewis, quietly.

'You know' – Morse sounded weary – 'it's not quite so easy as you think – getting rid of things. You get a guilt-complex about being seen. I remember a few weeks ago trying to get rid of an old soldier in a rubbish-bin in Banbury Road. And just after I'd dropped it in, somebody I knew drove past in a car, and waved . . .'

'He'd seen you?'

'What makes you think it was a "he"?'

'You felt a bit guilty?'

Morse nodded. 'So it's vitally important that we find the knife. I just can't see how we're going to make a case out against Brooks unless we can find the murder weapon.'

'Have you thought of the other possibility, sir?'

'What's that?' Morse looked up with the air of a Professor of Mathematics being challenged by an innumerate pupil.

'He took the knife home with him.'

'No chance. We're talking about instinctive behaviour here. You don't stab somebody – and then just go back home and wash your knife up in Co-op detergent with the rest of the cutlery – and put it back in the kitchen drawer.'

'There'd be a knife missing, though – from a set, perhaps.'

'So what? Knives get lost, broken . . .'

'So *Mrs* Brooks would probably know?'

'But she's not going to tell us, is she?'

Morse seemed to relax as he leaned back against the wall-seat, and looked around him.

'You sure it *was* Brooks?' asked Lewis quietly.

'Too many coincidences, Lewis. All right, they play a far bigger part in life than most of us are prepared to admit. But not in this case. Just think! Brooks left Wolsey, for good, on exactly the same day as the man who was murdered – McClure. Not only that, the pair of them had been on the same staircase together – exactly the same staircase – for several years. Then, a year later, Brooks has a heart attack on exactly the same day as McClure gets murdered. Just add all that up – go on, Lewis!'

'Like I say, though, you've always believed in coincidences.'

'Look! I could stomach two, perhaps – but not *three*.'

Lewis, who'd believed that Morse could easily stomach at least four, was not particularly impressed; and now, looking around him, he saw that he and Morse were the only clients left in the Marsh Harrier.

It was 3.10 p.m.

'We'd better be off, sir.'

'Nonsense! My turn, isn't it?'

'It's way past closing time.'

'Nonsense!'

But the landlord, after explaining that serving further drinks after 3 p.m. on Sundays was wholly against the law, was distinctly unimpressed by Morse's assertion that he, the latter, *was* the law. And a minute or so later it was a slightly embarrassed Lewis who was unlocking the passenger door of the Jaguar – before making his way back to North Oxford.

CHAPTER THIRTY-TWO

These are, as I began, cumbersome ways
to kill a man. Simpler, direct and much more neat
is to see he is living somewhere in the middle
of the twentieth century, and leave him there
(EDWIN BROCK, *Five Ways to Kill a Man*)

PERPETUALLY, on the drive back to North Oxford, Morse had been wiping the perspiration from his forehead; and Lewis was growing increasingly worried, especially when, once back home, Morse immediately poured himself a can of beer.

'Just to replace the moisture,' Morse had averred.

'You ought to get the doc in, you know that. And you ought not to be drinking any more, with all those pills.'

'Lewis!' Morse's voice was vicious. 'I appreciate your concern for my health. But never again – never! – lecture me about what I drink. Or if I drink. Or when I drink. *Is – that – clear?*'

In a flush of anger, Lewis rose to his feet. 'I'll be getting back—'

'Siddown!'

Morse took out a cigarette, and then looked up at the still-standing Lewis. 'You don't think I ought to smoke, either?'

'It's your life, sir. If you're determined to dig yourself an early grave . . .'

'I don't want to die, not just yet,' said Morse quietly.

And suddenly, as if by some strange alchemy, Lewis felt his anger evaporating; and, as bidden, he sat down.

Morse put the cigarette back in its packet. 'I'm sorry – sorry I got so cross. Forgive me. It's just that I've always valued my independence so much – too much, perhaps. I just don't like being told what to do, all right?'

'All right.'

'Well, talk to me. Tell me what you thought about Brooks.'

'No, sir. You're the thinker – that's why you get a bigger pay-packet than me. You tell *me*.'

'Well, I think exactly the same as I did before. After young Rodway's suicide, McClure found out about the availability of drugs on the staircase there – cannabis, amphetamines, cocaine, crack, ecstasy, LSD, heroin, whatever – and he also found out that it was Brooks who was supplying them, and making a pretty penny for himself in the process. Then, at some point, McClure told Brooks he'd got two options: either he packed up his job as a scout and left; or else he'd be reported to the University authorities – and probably the police – and faced with criminal proceedings. So Brooks had just about enough nous to read the writing on the wall: he resigned, and got another job, with a reluctant McClure providing a luke-warm testimonial to the Pitt Rivers Museum. But there were too many links with his former clients – and not just on the old staircase; and he kept up his lucrative little sideline *after* he'd left Wolsey – until McClure somehow got wind of the situation – and confronted him – and told him that this time it wasn't just an empty threat. I suspect Brooks must have had some sort of hold on McClure, I don't know. But Brooks said he was ready to step into line, and do whatever McClure wanted. *And he arranged a meeting with McClure* – at McClure's place in Daventry Court, a week ago today. That's the way I see it.'

'So you don't believe a word of his alibi?'

'No. And it isn't *his* alibi at all – it's hers. Mrs Brooks's alibi for him.'

'And you think he biked up to see McClure?'

'He biked, yes. Whether he'd already decided to murder McClure then, I don't know. But he took a murder weapon with him, a knife from his wife's kitchen drawer; and I've not the slightest doubt he took as many precautions as he could to keep himself from being recognized – probably wrapped a scarf round his face as if he'd got the toothache. And with his cycling helmet—'

'You're making it all up, sir.'

Morse wiped his brow once more. 'Of *course* I am! In a case like this you've got to put up some ... some scaffolding. You've got to sort of take a few leaps in the dark, Lewis. You've got to hypothesize ...'

'Hypothesize about the knife then, sir.'

'He threw it in the canal.'

'So we're not going to find it?'

'I'm sure we're not. We'd have found it by now.'

'Unless, as I say, he took it home with him – and washed it up and wiped it dry and then put it back in the kitchen drawer.'

'Ye-es.'

'Probably he *did* mean to throw it in the canal, or

somewhere. But something could have stopped him, couldn't it?'

'Such as?'

'Such as a heart attack,' suggested Lewis gently.

Morse nodded. 'If he suddenly realized he hadn't got any time to . . . if he suddenly felt a terrible pain . . .'

' "T'rific", that's what he said.'

'Mm.'

'What about the bike, though? He must have ridden it up to Daventry Court, mustn't he? So if he'd felt the pain starting, you'd have thought he'd get back home as fast as he could.'

Morse shook his head. 'It doesn't add up, does it? He must have ditched his bike somewhere on the way back.'

'Where, though?'

Morse pondered the problem awhile. Then, remembering Brooks's contempt for anyone taking the trouble to report a bicycle-theft in Oxford, he suddenly saw that it had ceased to be a problem at all.

'Do you know a poem called "Five Ways to Kill a Man"?'

'No.'

Wearily Morse rose to his feet, fetched an anthology of modern verse from his shelves, looked up Brock in the index, turned to the poem – and read the last stanza aloud.

But Lewis, though not unaccustomed to hearing Morse make some apposite quotation from the poets between draughts of real ale, could see no possible connexion in logic here.

'I'm not with you.'

181

Morse looked down at the stanza again; then slowly recited his own parody of the lines:

'There are several cumbersome ways
of losing a bike – like pushing it in the canal.
Neater and simpler, though, is to take it somewhere
like Cornmarket in Oxford – and just leave it there.'

'You ought to have been a poet, sir.'
'I am a poet, Lewis.'

Morse now coughed violently, expectorating into a tissue a disgusting gobbet of yellowish-green phlegm streaked with bright blood.

Lewis, although he saw it, said nothing.

And Morse continued:

'First thing is to get Brooks in, and go through Susan Ewers' statement with him. She's a good witness, that one – and he'll have to come up with something better than he gave us this afternoon.'

'When shall we bring him in, though? He's got a point, hasn't he? We don't want to give him another heart attack.'

'Don't we?'
'Day or two?'
'Day or three.'

Morse finished his beer. It had taken that swift drinker an inordinately long time to do so; and if Morse had experienced a premonition earlier, Lewis himself now sensed that his chief was seriously ill.

'What about the photograph, sir? Mrs Brooks's daughter?'

'Interesting question. I wonder. I wonder where that young lady fits into the picture.'

'Pretty well everywhere, wouldn't you say?'

'Ye-es. "Kay" – "K" – "Eleanor" – "Ellie" – we've got to assume she's the same girl, I suppose: Mrs B's daughter – Mr B's step-daughter – staircase-tart for Messrs Rodway and Davies – mistress for Dr McClure . . .'

'She must be quite a girl.'

'But what about that other photograph, Lewis? The school-mistress? D'you know, I've got a feeling she might be able to shed a little light—'

But Morse was coughing uncontrollably now, finally disappearing into the bathroom, whence was heard a series of revolting retches.

Lewis walked out into the entrance hall, where he flicked open Morse's black plastic telephone-index to the letter 'S'. He was lucky. Under 'Summertown Health Centre' he found an 'Appointments' number; and an 'Emergency' number.

He rang the latter.

That same afternoon, just after four o'clock, Dr Richard Rayson, Chaucerian scholar, and fellow of Trinity College, Oxford, strolled round his garden in Daventry Avenue. For almost three weeks he had been away with his family in the Dolomites. Gardening, in truth, had never been the greatest passion of his life; and as he stood surveying the state of his neglected front lawn, the epithet which sprang most readily to his literate mind was 'agrestal': somewhat overgrown; run to seed; wild, as the *Shorter Oxford* might define it.

Yet strangely, for such an unobservant man, he'd spotted the knife almost immediately – a couple of feet or so inside the property, between an untrimmed laurel bush and the vertical slats of a front fence sorely in need of some re-creosoting. There it was, lying next to a semi-squashed tin of Coca Cola.

Nina Rayson, a compensatingly practical sort of partner, had welcomed her husband's discovery, promptly washing it in Sainsbury's 'Economy' washing-up liquid, and forthwith adding it to her own canteen of cutlery. A good knife, it was: a fairly new, sturdy, unusually broad-bladed instrument, in no immediate need of any further sharpening.

That same evening, at nine-thirty, Brenda Brooks was aware that her jangled nerves could stand very little more that day. Paradoxically, though, she felt almost competent about coping with the loathsome man she'd just seen to bed, with a cup of tea, two digestive biscuits, and one sleeping tablet. At least she knew him: knew the *worst* about him – for there was nothing but the worst to know. It was now the *unknown* that was worrying her the more deeply: that strange technical jargon of the doctors and nurses at the hospital; the brusque yet not wholly unsympathetic questions of the two policemen who had earlier called there.

She found herself neurotically dreading any phone-call; any ringing of the door-bell. Anything.

What was that?

What was *that?*

Was she imagining things – imagining noises?

There it was again: a muffled, insistent, insidious, tapping . . .

Fearfully, she edged towards the front door.

And there, behind the frosted glass, she saw a vaguely human silhouette; and she turned the Yale lock, and opened the door, her heart fluttering nervously.

'You!' she whispered.

185

CHAPTER THIRTY-THREE

It is an inexorable sort of festivity – in September 1914 they tried to cancel it, but the Home Secretary himself admitted that he was powerless to do so

(JAN MORRIS, *Oxford*)

OXFORD'S St Giles' Fair is held annually on the first Monday and Tuesday after the first Sunday every September, with the whole area of St Giles' brought into use, from the Martyrs' Memorial up to (and beyond) St Giles' Church at the northern end, where the broad, tree-lined avenue bifurcates to form the Woodstock Road to the left and the Banbury Road to the right.

In mid-afternoon on Tuesday, 6 September (two days after Lewis had telephoned the Summertown Health Centre), Kevin Costyn was sauntering under the plane trees there, along the various rides and amusements and candy-floss stalls. Nothing could really kindle his imagination or interest, for the Naked Lady of earlier years, in her rat-infested cage, no longer figured in the fair's attractions. And as Kevin considered the jazzy, jolty, vertiginous cars and carriages, he felt no real wish to part with any of his limited money.

That day the children in the state schools in Oxfordshire had returned to their classrooms; and for the first time in twelve years Costyn himself was not one of them. No more school. But no job yet, either. He'd signed on at the Job Centre. Even taken away some literature on *Youth Employment Schemes and Opportunities.* Not that he was going to read that bumf. He wasn't interested in jobs. Just money. Well, not *just* money, no.

Smugly he grinned to himself as he stood outside the Bird and Baby and watched the gigantic, gyrating structure of the Big Wheel.

The previous month he'd been part of a three-man ram-raid at a Summertown supermarket, but it hadn't proved the windfall they'd expected. Shop windows – *replaced* shop windows – were being made of tougher glass; and several regular, and formerly profitable, targets were now protected by concrete frontal pillars. That wasn't the real trouble, though. It was getting rid of the stuff that was getting trickier all the time. Cigarettes had usually been the best bet: lightweight, handy to stack, easy to sell. But booze was becoming one helluva job to sell; and the cases of whisky, gin, and vodka they'd got away with then had changed hands for a miserly £850, though according to Costyn's (admittedly less than competent) calculation their street-value would have been four times that amount. It was the police – becoming far cannier at tracking down the wholesale-market contacts – they were the real trouble.

There must be easier ways of being able to afford the life of Riley, surely?

Yes, occasionally there were . . .

It had been Kevin Costyn himself who had answered the door the previous afternoon, to find Mrs Stevens standing there – a subtly scented Mrs Stevens, with a moist, red beauty at her lips.

Could she come in? She'd come in.

Would he listen to what she had to say? He'd listened.

Would he be willing to do as she asked? He'd be willing.

Would he be able to do what she wanted? He'd be able.

Payment? What about payment? Did he understand she had very little money? He'd understood.

How would he like her to pay him, then?

Well . . .

'What time's your mother back?' she'd asked.

No one over the past few years had deemed it necessary, or deemed it wise, to challenge Costyn's minority; nor did the young barmaid now, as she pulled him a pint of Burton Ale in the Bird and Baby ('Open All Day').

Ten minutes later he made his way to the Gents, where he spat a globule of phlegm on to the tiled floor, and where his left hand was directing his urination whilst his right hand was seeking, wholly ineffectually, to spell out FUCK in red Biro on the corrugated surface of the wall in front of him.

'Fuck' was a key word in Costyn's limited vocabulary. Had already been so for many years, ever since, night after night, his mum and dad (*perhaps*, his dad) had bawled their mutual 'fuck-off's at each other. Until the day when his dad had apparently interpreted the injunction rather too literally – and just, well, 'fucked off'. Indeed, so significant had the word become to the sole son of that hapless, unhappy union, that he regularly inserted it, in its present-participial form, into any lengthy-ish word which seemed to invite some internal profanation. Such a process is known, in the Homeric epics, as 'tmesis' – although, in truth, Costyn knew of 'Homer' only as a breed of pigeon; for his father had once kept such a pigeon, trained (once released) to find its way home from the most improbable distances. Which is more than its owner had done, once he had left his home, and his wife, and his son ... and his pigeon.

Before leaving the Gents, Costyn made a purchase. The condom machine looked, even to him, pretty theft-proof; and he decided for once to pay for his potential pleasures. For a few seconds he mentally debated the respective merits of 'lubrication', 'sensitivity', and 'silkiness'; finally plumping for the latter as he thought – yet again! – of the blouse that he'd slowly eased down over the suntanned shoulders of Mrs Julia Stevens.

At 4 p.m., standing waiting for a Cowley Road bus outside Marks and Spencer in Queen's Street, Costyn recognized an ex-pupil of the Proctor Memorial immediately in front of him; and he put a hand on her untanned shoulder.

'Bin 'avin' a ride, darlin'?'

She turned round. 'Wha' d'you want?'

'What about a little ride with *me*, darlin'? I got the necessaries.'

'Fuck off!'

Few girls ever spoke to him in such a fashion. But Costyn felt little resentment as he fingered the two packets of Silken Dalliance in his pocket . . .

Payment for his services?

'Half now; half later,' that's what Mrs Stevens had promised. And as he sat upstairs on the Cowley Road bus, Costyn savoured yet again that intoxicating cocktail of excitement and sensuality.

Half later . . . when the job was done; when the jobs (plural, perhaps), were done.

Was it terribly risky, what he'd so willingly agreed to do? Especially since she wasn't exactly sure of when she'd be calling on him. So what? Much riskier for her than for him. Not that she'd ever need to worry about *him*: he'd never breathe a word of it to any living soul.

Never.

And anyone who thought he would was suffering under a misapprefuckinhension.

CHAPTER THIRTY-FOUR

The gaudy, blabbing, and remorseful day
Is crept into the bosom of the sea
(SHAKESPEARE, *Henry IV, Part II*)

(i)

ON WEDNESDAY, 7 September 1994, at 11.20 a.m., Ms Ellie Smith sat in a taxi, every half-minute or so nervously consulting her wristwatch and cursing herself for not having taken up Ashley Davies's offer.

Rightly or wrongly, before walking out on him the previous weekend, she'd informed him of her situation: she was twelve weeks' pregnant; she was determined to have another abortion; she had an appointment at a South Birmingham clinic for preliminary consultation and advice. But when Davies had rung her the previous afternoon, she'd turned down his offer of a lift – once again. He'd been quite insistent really, saying that he'd got to be in Oxford later the next day, anyway; and it was so quick to Brum now – M40, M42 – and in *his* car, well, they'd do it in an hour almost; save her no end of time and trouble – and the rail fare into the bargain.

But she'd refused.

She was going by train, catching the 9.11 a.m. from Oxford, due to arrive at Birmingham New Street at 10.30 a.m., which would give her a whole hour to get to the clinic, only five miles distant from the railway station.

That was the plan.

But with the combination of a 'signalling failure' just before Leamington Spa and a security scare at Coventry, the train had finally rumbled into New Street forty-eight minutes late – and she'd had no option but to take a taxi. Not that she need have bothered too much, for it was 11.55 a.m. before she was called into the consulting-room.

Looking back on things, Ms Smith knew that she had been strangely impressed by the small, white-coated Pakistani doctor – a kindly, compassionate man, with Spaniel eyes – who had gently encouraged her at least to consider the alternative: that of keeping the child she had conceived.

She felt glad that she had tried to present herself in rather more conventional guise, putting on bra and pants (both!) beneath her only presentable summer dress – *and* removing the rings from her nostrils. Admittedly that left her hair, still streaked with crimson like the horizon in an angry sunset; but she felt (dare she admit it to herself?) somehow . . . expiated!

She couldn't really think why.

No, she *could* think why.

It was something to do with being with her mum once more . . .

The 15.09 train from New Street, timetabled to arrive in Oxford at 16.31 p.m., arrived virtually on time. And half an hour later Ellie Smith was back at her flat, reading the brief note contained in the white envelope ('By Hand') which she'd found propped up at the foot of her white-painted door on the third floor:

> Hope things went OK. Any chance of you
> thinking again? If there's even a remote chance
> of its being mine, I'll marry you and make an
> honest woman of you yet. Don't be cross with me
> for badgering you.
>
> Ashley, with lots and lots of kisses.

As she put her key into the lock, Ellie Smith wondered whether she'd sadly misjudged Mr Ashley Davies.

(ii)

'THANKS for coming,' said a sombre Phillotson.

In vain Lewis sought to find some suitable rejoinder.

'Morse on the mend?'

'Out tomorrow, so they say.'

'Will he be fit enough to carry on – with the case?'

'Dunno, sir. I suppose he'll please himself whatever happens.'

'I suppose he will, yes.'

Lewis moved away, and briefly surveyed the wreaths laid out there, including a splendid display of white lilies from the Thames Valley Police HQ.

Phillotson's wife had lived a gently unspectacular life, and died at the age of forty-six. Not much of an innings, really; and not too much of a memorial either, although her husband, her next of kin, and all of her friends, would hope that the little rose-bush (*Rosa rubrifolia*), already happily stuck into a wodge of blackly-rich compost in the Garden of Remembrance, would thrive and prosper – and, metempsychotically, as it were, take over.

If Chief Inspector Morse had been present at the short service, he would have been impatient with what he saw as the pretentious prayers; and yet, almost certainly, he would have welcomed the hymn that was played there – 'O Love that wilt not let me go' – and his quiet unmusical baritone would probably have mingled with the singing.

But Morse was not one of the thirty-seven mourners Lewis counted at the Oxford Crematorium that Wednesday lunchtime.

(iii)

'WHAT EXACTLY'S *wrong* with you, Morse?'

'I'm only here for observation.'

'Yes, I know that. But what exactly is it they're *observing*?'

Morse drew a deep breath. 'I'm suffering from bronchi-something beginning with "e"; my liver and kidneys are disintegrating; my blood pressure isn't quite off the top of the scale – not yet; I'm nursing another stomach ulcer; and as if that wasn't enough I'm on the verge of diabetes, because my pancreas, they tell me, isn't producing sufficient insulin to counteract my occasional intake of alcohol. Oh yes, and my cholesterol's dangerously high.'

'I see. Perhaps I should have asked what exactly's *right* with you, Morse.'

Strange shifted his great bulk awkwardly on the small wooden chair beside Morse's bed in Ward 7 of the John Radcliffe Two Hospital out at Headington, whither, in spite of his every protestation of being in excellent health, Morse had been conveyed by ambulance, half an hour after the doctor had been summoned the previous Sunday afternoon.

'I had an endoscopy yesterday,' continued Morse.

'Sounds painful. Where do they stick that?'

'In the *mouth*, sir.'

'Ah. No more dramatic finds?'

'No more corpses under the floorboards.'

'Well, the wife'll be very pleased if you can last out till – fairly soon, isn't it? – when you've got a speaking engagement, I understand.'

'I *have*?'

'You know – the WI group-meeting in Kidlington. Likely to be a good crowd there, she says. So try to make it, old man. She's, er ... you know, she's the President this year. Means a lot to her.'

'Tell her I'll be there, even if they have to wheel me in.'

'Good. Good. "The Grislier Aspects of Murder." Nice little title, that.'

With which Morse's mind reverted to the investigation. 'If you see Lewis, sir, tell him to call in tonight, will you? I'd like to know how things are going.'

'He was going to Mrs Phillotson's funeral this lunchtime.'

'What? Nobody told me about that.'

'No, well ... we didn't want to, er ... Not a nice subject, death, is it.'

The clock showed 2.45 p.m. when Strange made his way out of Ward 7; and for several minutes Morse lay back on his pillows and pondered. Perhaps a hospital was an appropriate place to meditate on death, for there was plenty of it going on all around. But most men or women preferred not to think or talk about it. Morse had known only one person who positively relished discussing the topic – Max the police pathologist, who in a macabre kind of way had almost made a friend of Death. But Death had made no reciprocal arrangement; and Max was police pathologist no longer.

(iv)

ALTHOUGH THE autumn term had only begun the day before, clearly one or two of the local schools had been planning, well in advance, to despatch their pupils on some of the dreaded GCSE 'projects' at the earliest possible opportunity. Certainly, until about 4.05 p.m., twenty or so schoolchildren had still been studying a range of anthropological exhibits in the Upper Gallery of the Pitt Rivers Museum.

Which was rather worrying.

But by 4.15 p.m., the galleries were virtually – by 4.20 p.m., totally – deserted. And from where he stood, beside the collection made in the South Pacific by Captain Cook on his second visit there in 1772, the young man observed most carefully whilst a suntanned, balding attendant walked briskly round the Upper Gallery, doubtless checking that no bags or satchels or writing-pads had inadvertently been left behind; and in so doing, as was immediately apparent, giving a quick, upward 'lift' to each of the glass covers of the locked cabinets there, like a potential car-thief swiftly moving along a line of vehicles in a Park and Ride and testing the doors.

Two minutes later, the young man was following in the attendant's same pre-closure tracks; but stopping now, at a particular spot, where he looked down at a collection of knives – knives of all shapes and sizes, knives from many parts of the world – displayed in Cabinet Number 52.

Quickly, his heart pounding, he took a chisel from his summer sweatshirt and inserted its recently sharpened edge between the metal rim of the display-case top and the darkly stained wooden slat below it, into which the cabinet's lock was set.

Easy!

No great splintering of wood or moaning of metal. Just a single, quick 'click'. Yet it had been a bad moment; and the young man checked anxiously to his left, then to his right, before lifting the glass lid and putting a hand inside.

It was 4.29 p.m. when he walked through the museum shop. He might have bought a postcard of the forty-foot-high Haida Totem Pole (British Columbia), but an assistant was already totting up the takings, and he wished to cause no trouble. As the prominent notice had advised him as he'd entered, the Pitt Rivers Museum of Ethnology and Pre-History closed at 4.30 p.m. each day.

(v)

AT THE Proctor Memorial School, the take-up for the *Twelfth Night* trip to the Shakespeare Theatre had been encouraging. Before the end of the summer term, Julia Stevens had made her usual block-booking of thirty-one seats; and with twenty-three pupils (mostly fifth- and sixth-formers), two other members of staff, plus two parents, only three tickets had been going begging. Only *two*, in fact – and those soon to be snapped up with alacrity at the box office – because Julia Stevens had invited Brenda Brooks (as she had done the previous year) to join the school-party.

At the Stratford Coach Park, the three teachers had distributed the brown-paper-wrapped rations: two rolls, one with mayonnaised-curried-chicken, the other with a soft-cheese filling; one packet of crisps; and one banana – with a plastic cup of orangeade.

On the way back, though not on the way out, Mrs Stevens and Mrs Brooks sat side by side in the front seats: the former semi-listening (with some gratification) to her pupils' pronouncements on the performances of Sirs Toby Belch and Andrew Aguecheek; the latter, until Woodstock, trying to read the latest instalment of a romantic serial in *Woman's Weekly*, before apparently falling into a deep slumber, and not awakening therefrom until, two minutes before midnight on

Wednesday, 7 September, the coach made its first stop at Carfax Tower, from where the streets of Oxford looked strangely beautiful; and slightly sinister.

PART TWO

CHAPTER THIRTY-FIVE

In me there dwells
No greatness, save it be some far-off touch
Of greatness to know well I am not great
(ALFRED, LORD TENNYSON, *Lancelot and Elaine*)

AFTER RINGING the emergency number the previous
Sunday, it had been a sad sight that confronted Lewis
in the bathroom: Morse standing creased over the
pedestal basin, his cheeks wholly drained of colour, his
vomit streaked with blood forming a chrysanthemum
pattern, scarlet on white, across the porcelain.

Dr Paul Roblin had been adamant.

Ambulance!

Lewis had woken up to the truth an hour or so later:
for a while at least, he was going to be left alone with a
murder investigation.

Such a prospect would normally have daunted him;
yet the present case was unusual in that it had already
established itself into a pattern. In the past, the more
spectacular cases on which he and Morse had worked
together had often involved some bizarre, occasionally
some almost incredible, twists of fate. But the murder
of Dr Felix McClure appeared – surely *was* – a comparatively straightforward affair. There could be little
doubt – none in Morse's mind – about the identity of
the murderer. It was just a question of timing now,
and patience: of the accumulation, the aggregation of

evidence, against a man who'd had the means, the motive, and the opportunity, to murder McClure. Only concerning the actual commission of the crime was there lack of positive evidence. Lack of any evidence. And what a feather in his cap it would be if he, Lewis, could come up with something on *that*, during Morse's reluctant, yet enforced, immobility.

For the present, then, it was he who was sole arbiter of the course of further enquiries; of the most productive deployment of police resources. He had not been born great, Lewis was aware of that; nor did the rank of Detective Sergeant mark him out as a man who had achieved any significant greatness. Yet for a few days now, some measure of vicarious greatness was being thrust upon him; and he would have been encouraged by the Latin proverb (had he known it) that 'Greatness is but many small littles', since it was upon a series of 'small littles' that he embarked over the following three days – Monday, Tuesday, Wednesday, 5, 6, 7 September.

Over these few days many statements were taken from people, both Town and Gown, some fairly closely, some only peripherally, connected with the murdered man and with his putative murderer. And it was Lewis himself who had visited the JR2 on Tuesday afternoon for it to be confirmed, quite unequivocally, that Mr Edward Brooks had been admitted, via Casualty, to the Coronary Care Unit at 2.32 p.m. on Sunday, 28 August; that Brooks had spent twenty-four hours in Intensive Care before being transferred to Level 7, whence he had been discharged three days later.

Whilst in the hospital, Lewis had called in to see Morse (his second visit), but had refused to be drawn into any discussion of new developments in the enquiry. This for two reasons: first, that there were no new developments; and, second, that Superintendent Strange had strongly urged against such a course of action – 'Start talking about it, and he'll start thinking about it. And once he starts thinking, he'll start thinking about drinking, whatever the state of his innards . . .' So Lewis stayed only a few minutes that afternoon, taking a 'Get Well' card from Mrs Lewis, and a small bunch of seedless white grapes from himself, the latter immediately confiscated by the hawk-eyed ward-sister.

From the JR2, Lewis had gone on to interview the Brooks's family GP, Dr Philip Gregson, at the Cowley Road Health Centre.

The brief medical report on Edward Brooks which Lewis read there was quite optimistic: 'Mild heart attack – condition now stable – surprisingly swift recovery. GP appt 1 wk; JR2 out/p appt 2 wk.'

About Brenda Brooks, however, Gregson was more circumspect. She had, yes, suffered a very nasty little injury to her right hand; and, yes, he had referred her to a specialist. But he couldn't comment in any way upon his colleague's findings. If further information were considered necessary . . .

In such fashion was it that Lewis's queries were concluded late that Tuesday afternoon – with the telephone number of an orthopaedic surgeon, and with the knowledge that he was getting nowhere fairly slowly.

Yet only twenty-four hours were to elapse before the first major breakthrough in the case was destined to occur.

CHAPTER THIRTY-SIX

Is this a dagger which I see before me,
The handle towards my hand?
(SHAKESPEARE, *Macbeth*)

IT TOOK a long time, an inordinately long time, for
the penny to drop.

Dr Richard Rayson had been wholly unaware of the
great excitement which had been witnessed by the
residents of Daventry Avenue over the previous week.
Yet his inability to establish any connection between
the discovery of a knife and the death of a neighbour is
readily explicable. In the first place, the physical police
presence around Daventry Court had been withdrawn
on the day prior to his return from abroad. Then, too,
Rayson had not as yet re-instated his standing-order
with the Summertown newsagent for the daily delivery
of the *Oxford Mail*; he had therefore missed the brief
item tucked away at the bottom of page 3 on Monday
(would probably have missed it anyway). And finally,
and most significantly, his communications with his
neighbours, on either side, had been almost completely
severed of late – this breakdown occasioned by a series
of increasingly bitter differences of view over the maintenance of boundary fences, the planting of inter-
property trees, an application for planning permission,
and (most recently) the dangerous precedent of a
teenage party.

Thus, after spending the whole of the Monday and Tuesday with his wife in regrooming their garden, it was only at lunchtime on Wednesday, 7 September, that Rayson was re-introduced into the mainstream of Oxford life and gossip – at a cocktail reception in Trinity College to meet a group of librarians from Oklahoma.

'Fine drop of claret, what, Richard?' one of his colleagues had affirmed.

'Beautifully balanced little wine, George.'

'By the way, you must have known old McClure, I suppose? Lives only a few doors from you, what? *Lived*, rather.'

Rayson had frowned. 'McClure?'

'You know, the poor sod who got himself knifed?'

McClure. Felix McClure. Knifed.

The knife.

Just after five o'clock that afternoon, Detective Sergeant Lewis stood looking down at the prime exhibit, laid out on the Formica-topped surface of the kitchen in Rayson's elegant detached house in Daventry Avenue – seven properties distant, on the Woodstock Road side, from the scene of McClure's murder. As Rayson had explained over the phone, the knife had been found just inside the front fence, had been picked up, washed, dried, put away, picked up again, used to cut a roll of boiled ham, re-washed, re-dried, put away again – and picked up yet again when Rayson had returned from Trinity in the late afternoon, and examined it with a sort of ghoulish fascination.

With no prospects, therefore, of the exhibit retaining any incriminating fingerprints or blood-stains, Lewis in turn now picked up the black-handled knife, its blade unusually broad at the base, but tapering to a sharp-looking point at the end. And concurrently several thoughts coursed through his mind – exciting thoughts. There was the description, for a start, of the murder weapon – so very similar to this knife – which had appeared in the *Oxford Mail*, the description which was perhaps worrying Morse somewhat when he'd mentioned his premonition about the possibility of a copy-cat killing. Then there was the firm likelihood that the second of Morse's necessary prerequisites had now been met – not only a body, but also a weapon; and this one surely seemed to fit the bill so very nicely. And then – by far the most exciting thought of all – the strong possibility that the knife had come from a set of such knives, *one of which Lewis had seen so very recently*: that slim, elegant, black-handled little knife with which Mrs Brenda Brooks had sliced the Madeira cake the previous Sunday afternoon.

CHAPTER THIRTY-SEVEN

I enjoy convalescence; it is the part that makes the illness worth while

(GEORGE BERNARD SHAW)

ON THURSDAY, 8 September, as on the previous day, so many things were happening in close sequence that it is difficult for the chronicler to decide upon the most comprehensible way in which to record events, events which were to some degree contemporaneous but which also overlapped and which in their full implications stretched both before and beyond their strict temporal occurrence.

Let the account begin at Morse's flat in North Oxford.

Morse was due to be discharged at ten o'clock that morning. Lewis had rung through to the ward-sister half an hour earlier to save Morse any wait for an ambulance and to chauffeur him home in style – only to discover that his chief had already discharged himself, getting a lift from one of the consultants there who was on his way out to Bicester.

Lewis rang the door-bell at 9.45 a.m., experiencing a customary qualm of semi-apprehension as he waited outside that lonely flat – until a fully dressed Morse, his cheeks rosy-red, suddenly appeared on the threshold, panting like a breathless bulldog.

'I'm just starting a new regimen, Lewis. No more nicotine, limited – very limited – alcohol, plenty of fresh fruit and salad, and regular exercise. What about that? I've' – he paused awhile to get his breath – 'I've just done a dozen press-ups. You'd never have thought that possible a week ago, now, would you?'

'You must be feeling quite, er, elated, sir.'

'"Knackered" is the word I think you're looking for, Lewis. But come in! Good to see you. Have a drink.'

Almost as if he were trespassing, Lewis entered the lounge and sat down.

'Nothing for me, thanks.'

'I'll just . . .' Morse quickly drained a tumbler of some pale amber liquid that stood on one of the shelves of the book-lined room beside the Deutsche Grammophon cassettes of *Tristan und Isolde*. 'A small, celebratory libation, that, Lewis – in gratitude to whatever gods there be that temporarily I have survived the perils and dangers of this mortal life.'

Lewis managed a grin, half sad, half happy – and immediately told Morse about the knife.

'I don't believe it! We'd had those gardens searched.'

'Only up to six either side, sir. If only we'd gone a couple further.'

'But why didn't this fellow Rayson find it earlier? Is he blind or something?'

'He was in Italy.'

'Oh.'

'You don't sound all that pleased about it.'

'What? Course I am. Well done!'

'I know you were a bit worried about that *Oxford Mail* article . . .'

'I was?'

'You know, the premonition you had—'

'Nonsense! I don't even know what a premonition is.'

'Well, if that description's anywhere near accurate, sir, I think we've got the knife that was used to kill McClure. And I think I know where it came from. And I think you do, too.'

The small round-faced clock on the mantelpiece showed two minutes after ten, and for a while Morse sat in silence. Then, of a sudden, he jumped to his feet and, against all the medical advice he'd so meekly accepted over the previous few days, insisted on being driven immediately to police HQ, stopping (as it happened) only briefly along the journey, in a slip-road on the left, just opposite the Sainsbury supermarket in Kidlington, to buy a packet of Dunhill King-Size cigarettes.

Brenda Brooks had spent the previous night not in her own house in Addison Road but in the spare bedroom, the only other bedroom, of Julia Stevens' house in Baldwin Road. After Mrs Stevens had left for school at 8.15 a.m., Brenda had eaten a bowl of Corn Flakes and a round of toast and marmalade. Her appointment at the hairdresser's was for 9.15 a.m.; and fairly soon after her breakfast she was closing the Oxford-blue front door behind her, testing (as always) that the lock was firmly engaged, and walking down towards the Cowley Road for her Special Offer Wash-and-Perm.

On her way home, well over an hour and a half later, she bought two salmon fillets, a pack of butter, and a carton of ecologically friendly washing-up liquid.

The sun was shining.

As she turned into Addison Road she immediately spotted the marked police car, parked on the double-yellow lines across the road from her house; spotted a second car, too, the elegant-looking lovingly polished maroon-coloured Jaguar she'd seen the previous Sunday afternoon.

Even as she put her key into the Yale lock, she felt the hand on her shoulder, heard the man's voice, and heard, too, the ringing of the telephone just inside the hall.

'Get a move on,' said Morse quickly. 'You may just catch it.'

But the ringing stopped just before she could reach the phone; and taking off her lightweight summer coat, and gently patting the back of her blue-rinsed curls, she turned to the two men who stood just outside, the two men she'd seen the previous Sunday afternoon.

'If it's Ted you want, you'll have to come back later, I'm afraid. He's up at the JR2 – he's got an Outpatient appointment.'

'When do you expect him back?' asked Lewis.

'I don't know really. He'll be back for lunch, I should think, unless he calls in at the Club for a game of snooker.'

'How did he get to the hospital?'

Mrs Brooks hesitated. 'I ... I don't know.' The

fingers of her left hand were plucking their way along the invisible rosary she held in her right. 'You'd better come in, hadn't you?'

Haltingly, nervously, as they sat again in the lounge, in the same sedentary formation as before, Mrs Brooks sought to explain the situation. She had been to Stratford the previous evening with a friend and hadn't returned until late – about midnight – as she'd known she would, anyway. And she'd stayed with this person, this friend, at her house – overnight. Ted knew all about the arrangement. He was due at Outpatients the next morning, and she hadn't wanted to disturb his night's sleep – *hadn't* disturbed his night's sleep. He was getting along quite nicely and the doctors said how important it was to rest – to have regular rest and sleep. He hadn't shown her the little blue appointments card from the Oxfordshire Health Authority, but she thought he was due at the hospital somewhere between nine and ten.

'You haven't been here, in this house, since – since when?' asked Morse, rather brusquely.

'Four o'clock, yesterday afternoon. Or just before. The coach left at five.'

'You don't seem to have been too worried about Mr Brooks coping . . . with meals, that sort of thing?'

'Don't you think so, Inspector?' Her eyes, rather sad and weary now, looked into Morse's; and it was Morse who was the first to look away.

Lewis sounded a kindlier note. 'You've just come back from the hairdresser's?'

She nodded the tightly permed hair. 'The Golden Scissors, in Cowley Road.'

213

'Er . . . what was the play, by the way?'

'*Twelfth Night.*'

'Did you enjoy it?'

She half-smiled. 'Well, I couldn't quite follow all the
– you know, what they were saying. But I loved it, yes,
and I'd love to see it again.'

'And you went with . . . with a friend, you say?'

'Yes, with a school-party.'

'And this friend . . . ?'

Lewis was noting her name and address when the
telephone rang once more; and this time Mrs Brooks
reached the hall swiftly. As she did so, Morse immediately pointed in the opposite direction, and Lewis,
equally swiftly, stepped quietly into the kitchen where
he opened a drawer by the side of the sink.

Morse meanwhile listened keenly to one side of a
telephone conversation.

'Yes?'

'Is he all right?'

'I don't understand.'

'What's happened, do you think?'

'No. I wasn't here, you see.'

'Of course I will.'

'Can you just give me the number again?'

'All right.'

Brenda Brooks put down the phone slowly, her face
anxious as she walked back into the lounge – only a few
seconds after Lewis, with a silent thumbs-up sign, had
re-appeared from the kitchen and quickly resumed his
seat.

'Anything important?' asked Morse.

214

'It was the hospital. Ted's not been there. Not yet. So the lady at Appointments says. He was due there at twenty-past nine, it seems.'

'What do you think's happened to him?' asked Morse quietly.

'That's what she asked me. I don't know.'

'I'm sure everything's fine,' continued Morse. 'He's probably just got the time wrong.'

'That's exactly what she said,' whispered Brenda Brooks.

'She'll ring you back – when he gets there.'

'That's . . . that's exactly . . .'

But the tears had started now.

She opened her handbag and took out a handkerchief, and said, 'Sorry'; said 'Sorry' five times. And then, 'Oh dear! Where's my purse? I must have . . .' She got up and went to the hall where she patted the pockets of her summer coat, and came back and looked rather fecklessly around. 'I must have . . .'

'You did some shopping, didn't you? You may have left it . . . ?' suggested Lewis.

A few minutes later, Mrs Brooks was seated in the back of the police car, impatient and worried; but so glad to be away from the two detectives – who now stood in her kitchen.

'What do you reckon, sir?'

'About Brooks? Buggered off, hasn't he – sensible chap! He must have guessed we were on his tail.'

'What about her? She seemed glad to get away.'

'She's worried about her purse – money, cards, keys . . .'

'More than that, I think.'

'Well, *you* made her feel a bit guilty, didn't you, checking up on her hairdresser – and Stratford.'

'What?'

'Quite right too, Lewis. She was telling us a load of lies, wasn't she? She knows exactly where he is! He may treat her like a skivvy, but she's still his missus.'

Lewis opened the drawer again, this time selecting four knives, of different sizes, but of the same basic pattern, of the same make – each with a black handle, one side of which, the side of the cutting-edge, was slightly sinuous, with an indented curve at the top to fit the joint of the index finger, and a similar curve at the lower end for the little finger.

Four knives.

Four from a set of five?

But if so, the fifth was missing ... yet not really all that far away, neatly docketed and safely stored as it was in an Exhibits Locker at Thames Valley Police HQ.

Oh, yes!

Lewis nodded to himself, and to Morse.

And Morse nodded to himself, and to Lewis.

It seemed to Morse no great surprise that Mr Edward Brooks, ex-scout of Wolsey, and current assistant-custodian of the Pitt Rivers Collection, had decided to make a bolt for it – once news of the discovery of that fatal fifth knife had leaked out.

Which it hadn't ...

Lewis had seen to that.

CHAPTER THIRTY-EIGHT

The museum has retained much of its Victorian
character. Painstakingly hand-written labels can
still be found attached to some of the artefacts in
the crammed black cases there
(The Pitt Rivers Museum, A Souvenir Guide)

THE DETAILS of what was to prove the key discovery
in the case – or, to be more accurate, the 'lack-of-key'
discovery in the case – were not communicated by the
City Police to Kidlington HQ until just after 1 p.m. that
same day, although the discovery had in fact been made
as early as 8.45 a.m.

Janis Lawrence, an unmarried young woman, lived
with her mother, an unmarried middle-aged woman,
on the Cutteslowe Estate in North Oxford. The household was completed by Janis's four-year-old son, Jason –
a name chosen not to commemorate the intrepid
leader of the Argonauts but the lead guitarist of a long-
forgotten pop group. Jason found it impossible to pass
by any stone or small brick without picking it up and
hurling it at anything which moved across his vision –
dogs, prams, pedestrians, motor-vehicles, and similar
obstructions. Thus it was that Janis Lawrence was ever
longing for the time when she could transfer complete
responsibility for the child to the hapless teachers of
the local Cutteslowe Primary School. And when she
had learned of a temporary (August to September)

217

cleaning job at the Pitt Rivers Museum, she had applied for it. And got it.

The Cutteslowe Estate in North Oxford, built in the 1930s, had achieved national notoriety because of the Cutteslowe Wall, a seven-foot high, spiked-topped, brick-built wall, which segregated the upper-middle-class residents of the Banbury Road from the working-class tenants of the Council Estate. But the wall had been demolished in 1959; and on the bright morning of Thursday, 8 September 1994, as on each weekday for the past month, Janis walked without hindrance up to the Banbury Road, where she caught a bus down to Keble Road, thence walking across to Parks Road, and into the museum itself, where from Mondays to Saturdays she began work at 8.30 a.m.

Her first job as always was to clear up any litter, such as the rings of zig-zag shavings often left behind by pupils who had sharpened their pencils the previous afternoon. And for a short while that morning, as she cleaned the floor and dusted the cabinets in the Upper Gallery, she paid little attention to the bright-yellow splinter of wood on the floor below one of the cabinets there – until she noticed that the glass-topped lid was not resting flush upon its base. Then, too, she became aware of the slight disarray of the cabinet's contents, since there appeared one unfilled space in the ranks of the exhibits there, with both the artefact to the left of this gap, and the artefact to the right of it, knocked somewhat askew on the light-beige hessian material which formed the backing for the display: 'Knives from Africa and South-East Asia'.

Janis reported her discovery immediately. And just after 9 a.m. Mr Herbert Godwin, attendant with responsibility for the Upper Gallery, was staring down at Cabinet 52.

'Oh dear!'

'Somebody's pinched somethin', Bert?'

'I reckon you could say that again.'

'What's gone?'

'Good question.'

'When could it have been, though?'

'Dunno. *After* I checked last night. Must have been. I allus check on these cabinets.'

'Well, it couldn't have been this morning. Nobody else's been here, 'cept me.'

'Have you got summat hidden in your knicker-pocket, Janis?'

'I've told you *before*, Bert. I only wear knickers on a Sunday.'

Gently Herbert Godwin patted the not-unattractive Janis on her ample bottom: 'We'd better go and inform our superiors, my love.'

Paradoxically Jane Cotterell, Administrator of the Museum, was attending a meeting that morning at the Ashmolean on 'Museum Security'. But straightway she was summoned to the telephone and was soon issuing her orders: the University Marshal was to be informed immediately, as were the police; the lower steps to the Upper Gallery were to be roped across, with the 'Temporarily Closed' sign positioned there; Dr Cooper, the Assistant Curator (Documentation) – and *only* Dr Cooper – should go along and, without touching

219

anything, seek to ascertain, from his inventory lists, which object(s) had been stolen. She herself would be back in the Pitt Rivers as soon as she could possibly manage it.

Which was three-quarters of an hour later, her return coinciding with the arrival of the police from St Aldate's; *and* with the production of a sheet of paper on which she found the following sketch:

'That's it!' exclaimed a jubilant-looking Dr Cooper, as if the museum had suddenly acquired a valuable new exhibit, instead of losing one. 'Forty-seven knives – forty-seven! – there were in that cabinet. And you know how many there are now, Jane?'

'Forty-*six*, perhaps?' suggested the Administrator innocently.

CHAPTER THIRTY-NINE

Yes
You have come upon the fabled lands where myths
Go when they die
       (JAMES FENTON, 'The Pitt Rivers Museum')

AT FIVE minutes to two, parked in front of the Radcliffe Science Library, Morse switched off *The Archers* (repeat).

'Well, we'd better go and have a look at things, I suppose.'

In retrospect, the linkage (if there were one) appeared so very obvious. Yet someone had to make it first, that someone being Jane Cotterell: the linkage between the earlier visit of the police; the museum's employment of Edward Brooks; the murder by knifing of Dr McClure; and now the theft of another knife, from one of the museum's cabinets.

Thus, it was Jane Cotterell herself who had argued that the City Police should link their enquiry into the theft with the Kidlington HQ enquiry into the murder of McClure; and Jane Cotterell herself who greeted Morse and Lewis, in the Pitt Rivers' Upper Gallery, at 2 p.m.

'It's what I was afraid of, though God knows why,' mumbled Morse to himself as he looked down at

Cabinet 52, now dusted liberally with fine aluminium fingerprint-powder.

Ten minutes later, whilst Lewis was taking statements from Janis Lawrence and Herbert Godwin, Morse was seated opposite the Administrator, quickly realizing that he was unlikely to learn (at least from her) more than two fairly simple facts: first, that almost certainly the cabinet had been forced between 4.15 and 4.30 p.m. the previous afternoon; second, since the contents of the cabinet had been fully documented only six months earlier – when exhibits had been re-arranged and cabinets re-lined – it could be stated quite authoritatively that one artefact, *and one only*, the Northern Rhodesian Knife, had been abstracted.

Yet Morse seemed uneasy.

'Could one of your own staff have pinched it?'

'Good Lord, no. Why should any of them want to do that? Most of them have access to the key-cupboard anyway.'

'I see.' Morse nodded vaguely; and stood up. 'By the way, what do you line your cabinets with? What material?'

'It's some sort of new-style hessian – supposed to keep its colour for yonks, so the advert said.'

Morse smiled, suddenly feeling close to her. 'Can I say something? I'd never have expected you to say "yonks".'

She smiled back at him, shyly. 'You wouldn't?'

It seemed a good moment for one of them to say something more, to elaborate on this intimate turn of the conversation. But neither did so. And Morse reverted to his earlier line of enquiry.

'You don't think anyone could have hidden himself, after closing time, and spent the night here in the museum?'

'Or herself? No. No, I don't. Unless they stood pretty motionless all through the night. You see, the place is positively bristling with burglar alarms. And anyway, it would be far too spooky, surely? I couldn't do it. Could *you*?'

'No. I've always been frightened of the dark myself,' admitted Morse. 'It's a bit eerie, this place, even in broad daylight.'

'Yes,' she said softly. 'When you come in here you enter a place where all the lovely myths go when they die.'

Suddenly Morse felt very moved.

After he had left her office, Jane felt guilty about not telling Morse that the 'myths' bit was far from original. And indeed she'd looked around to try to find him, to tell him so.

But he had left.

CHAPTER FORTY

Thursday is a bad day. Wednesday is quite a good day. Friday is an even better one. But Thursday, whatever the reason, is a day on which my spirit and my resolution, are at their lowest ebb. Yet even worse is any day of the week upon which, after a period of blessed idleness, I come face to face with the prospect of a premature return to my labours

(DIOGENES SMALL, *Autobiography*)

AN HOUR later, Morse was seated in the black leather chair in his office, still considering the sketch of the knife – when Lewis came back from the canteen carrying two polystyrene cups of steaming coffee.

'Northern Rhodesia, Lewis. Know where that is? Trouble is they keep changing all these place-names in Africa.'

'Zambia, sir. You know that.'

Morse looked up with genuine pain in his eyes. 'I never did any Geography at school.'

'You get a newspaper every day, though.'

'Yes, but I never look at the international news. Just the Crossword – and the Letters.'

'That's not true. I've often seen you reading the Obituaries.'

'Only to look at the years when they were born.'

Morse unwrapped the cellophane from his cigarettes, took one from the packet, and lit it, inhaling deeply.

'*You*'ll be in the obituary columns if you don't soon pack up smoking. Anyway, you said you *had* packed it up.'

'I have, Lewis. It's just that I need to make a sort of gesture – some sort of sacrifice. That's it! A sacrifice. All right? You see, I'm only going to smoke this one cigarette. Only one. And the rest of them?'

Morse appeared to have reached a fateful decision. He picked up the packet and flicked it, with surprising accuracy, into the metal waste-bin.

'Satisfied?'

Lewis reached for the phone and rang the JR2 Outpatients department: no news. Then he rang Brenda Brooks: no news.

Edward Brooks was still missing.

'You don't think somebody's murdered *him*, sir?'

But Morse, as he studied yet again the details of the stolen knife, appeared not to hear. 'Would you rather be a bishop – or a paramount chief?'

'I don't want to be either, really.'

'Mm. I wouldn't have minded if they'd made me a paramount chief.'

'I thought they had, sir.'

'Where would a paramount chief go from here, Lewis?'

'I just asked you, sir, whether—'

'I heard you. The answer's "no". Brooks is alive and well. No. He may not be well, of course – but he's alive. You can bet your Granny Bonds on that.'

'Where *do* we go from here, then?'

COLIN DEXTER

'Well, I'm going to spend the rest of the afternoon in bed. I want to feel fresh for this evening. I've got a date with a beautiful lady.'

'Who's she?'

'Mrs Stevens – Julia Stevens.'

'When did you fix that up?'

'While you were getting the coffee.'

'You want me to come along?'

'Lew-is! I just told you. It's a *date*.'

'Didn't you believe Mrs Brooks? About where she spent last night?'

'I believed *that* all right. It's just that I reckon she knows where her husband is, that's all. And it's on the cards that if she does know, she probably told her friend, Mrs Stevens.'

'What would you like me to do, sir?'

'I'd like you to go and see Mrs Brooks's daughter – Ellie Smith, or whatever she calls herself. She's a key character in this case, don't you reckon? McClure's mistress – and Brooks's step-daughter.'

'Shouldn't *you* be seeing her then?'

'All in good time. I'm only just out of hospital, remember?'

'You mean she's not so attractive as Mrs Stevens.'

'Purely incidental, that is.'

'Anything else?'

'Yes. You'd better get back to the museum for a while. I don't think we're going to get very far on the fingerprint front – but you never know.'

Lewis was frowning. 'I just don't see the link myself – between the McClure murder, and now this Pitt Rivers business.'

'*She* saw a link, though, didn't she? Jane Cotterell? Clever lass, that one.'

'But she said whoever else it was, it couldn't have been Brooks who took the knife.'

'Exactly.'

'So?'

'So what?'

'So where's the link?'

Morse's eyes remained unblinking for several seconds, staring at nothing it seemed, and yet perhaps staring at everything. 'I'm not at all sure now that there is a link,' he said quietly. 'To find some connection between one event and another ensuing event is often difficult; and especially difficult perhaps when they *appear* to have a connection . . .'

Morse was aware of feeling worried at the prospect – the actuality, really – of his return to work. For, in truth, he had little real idea of the correct answers to the questions Lewis had just asked. He needed some assistance from somewhere; and as he drove down to North Oxford he patted his jacket-pocket where he felt the reassurance of the square packet he had retrieved from the waste-bin immediately after Lewis had left for the Pitt Rivers Museum.

CHAPTER FORTY-ONE

His failing powers disconcerted him, for what he would do with women he was unsure to perform, and he could rarely accept the appearance of females who thought of topics other than *coitus*

(PETER CHAMPKIN, *The Sleeping Life of Aspern Williams*)

NOW JULIA STEVENS was very fair to behold, for there was a gentle beauty in the pallor of the skin beneath that Titian hair, and the softest invitation in the redness of her lips. And as he sat opposite her that evening, Morse was immediately made aware of an animal magnetism.

'Care for a drink, Inspector?'

'No – er, no thank you.'

'Does that mean "yes"?'

'Yes.'

'Scotch?'

'Why not?'

'Say when.'

'When.'

'Cheers!'

'Mind if I smoke?'

'Yes, I do.'

She left the room, and re-appeared with an ashtray. Perhaps they were beginning to understand each other.

'Mrs Brooks stayed the night here?' began Morse.

'Yes.'

'You see, her husband's gone missing – he failed to keep an appointment at the hospital this morning.'

'I know. Brenda rang me.'

'You'd both been to Stratford, I understand.'

'Yes.'

'Enjoy the play?'

'No.'

'Why?'

'My life will not be significantly impoverished if I never see another Shakespearian comedy.'

'Mrs Brooks enjoyed it though, I believe?'

Julia nodded, with a slow reminiscence. 'Bless her! Yes. She's not had much to smile about recently.'

'Have *you*?'

'Not much, really, no. Why do you ask that?'

But Morse made no direct answer. 'Isn't it just a bit odd, perhaps, that Mrs Brooks didn't call in to see if her husband was all right?'

'Odd? It's the most natural thing in the world.'

'Is it?'

'She hates him.'

'And why's that?'

'He treats her in such a cruel way – that's why.'

'How do you know that?'

'Brenda's told me.'

'You've no first-hand evidence?'

'I've always tried to avoid him.'

'Aren't you being a bit unfair, then?'

'I don't think so.'

'Have you any idea where he might be?'

'No. But I hope somebody's stuck a knife into him somewhere.'

As he looked across at the school-mistress, Morse found himself wondering whether her pale complexion was due not so much to that inherited colouration so common with the auburn type, as to some illness, possibly; for he had observed, in a face almost completely devoid of any other cosmetic device, some skin-tinted application to the darkened rings beneath her eyes.

'Did Mrs Brooks go out last night, after you'd got back?'

Julia smiled tolerantly. 'You mean, did she just nip out for a few minutes and bump him off?'

'*Could* she have gone out? That's all I'm asking.'

'Technically, I suppose – yes. She'd have a key to get back in here with. I just wonder what you think she did with the body, that's all.'

'She *didn't* go out – is that what you're telling me?'

'Look! The only thing I know for certain is that she was fast asleep when I took her a cup of tea just before seven this morning.'

'So she'd been with you the whole time since yesterday afternoon?'

'Since about a quarter-to four, yes. I would have picked her up in the car, but the wretched thing wanted to stay at home in the garage. Suffering from electrical trouble.'

Morse, who didn't know the difference between brake fluid and anti-freeze, nodded wisely. 'You should get a car like mine. I've got a *pre-*electrics model.'

Julia smiled politely. 'We took a bus up to school and, well, that's about it, really.'

'Did you actually go into the Brooks's house?'

'Well, I suppose I did, yes – only into the hallway, though.'

'Was Mr Brooks there?'

'Only just. He was getting ready to go out, but he was still there when we left.'

'Did you speak to him?'

'You mean ... ask him politely if he was feeling better? You must be joking.'

'Did his wife speak to him?'

'Yes. She said "goodbye".'

'She didn't say "cheerio" or "see you soon"?'

'No. She said "goodbye".'

'What about you? Did *you* go out last night?'

'Do you suspect me as well?'

'Suspect you of what, Mrs Stevens?'

Julia's clear, grey eyes sparkled almost gleefully. 'Well, if somebody's bumped off old Brooks—'

'You look as if you hope someone has.'

'Didn't I make that clear from the start, Inspector?'

'Have you actually *seen* Mrs Brooks since you left home this morning?'

'No. I've been in school all day. Bad day, Thursday! No free periods. Then we had a staff-meeting after school to try to decide whether we're all satisfying the criteria for the National Curriculum.'

'Oh.'

It was a dampener; and for a little while each was silent, with Morse looking around the neatly cluttered

room. He saw, on the settee beside Julia, a copy of
Ernest Dowson's *Poems*. He pointed to it:

'You enjoy Dowson?'

'You've *heard* of him?'

'They are not long, the weeping and the laughter,
    Love and desire and hate . . .'

'I'm impressed. Can you go on?'

'Oh, yes,' said Morse quietly.

For some reason, and for the first time that evening,
Julia Stevens betrayed some sign of discomfiture, and
Morse saw, or perhaps he saw, a film of tears across her
eyes.

'Anything else I can do for you, Inspector?'

Yes, you can take me to bed with you. I may feel no
love for you, perhaps, but I perceive the beauty and the
readiness of this moment, and soon there will be no
beauty and no readiness.

'No, I think that's all,' he said.

The phone rang as they walked into the narrow
hallway, and Julia quickly picked up the receiver.

'Hullo? Oh, hullo! Look, I'll ring you back in five
minutes, all right? Just give me the number, will
you?' She wrote down five digits on a small yellow
pad beside the phone, and said 'Bye' – as did a male
voice at the other end of the line (if Morse had heard
aright).

As they took leave of each other at the doorway, it
seemed for a moment that they might have embraced,
however perfunctorily.

But they did not do so.

It might have been possible, too, for Morse to have spotted the true importance of what Julia Stevens had told him.

But he did not do so.

CHAPTER FORTY-TWO

> You can lead a whore to culture
> but you can't make her think
> (Attributed to Dorothy Parker)

'HAVEN'T YOU got any *decent* music in this car?' she asked, as Lewis drove down the Iffley Road towards Magdalen Bridge.

'Don't you like it? That's your Mozart, that is. That's your slow movement of the Clarinet Concerto. I keep getting told I ought to educate my musical tastes a bit.'

'Bit miserable, innit?'

'Don't you go and say that to my boss.'

'Who's he when he's at home?'

'Chief Inspector Morse. Chap you're going to see. You're getting the VIP treatment this morning.'

'Don't you think I'm used to that, Sergeant?'

Lewis glanced across briefly at the young woman beside him in the front seat; but he made no reply.

'Don't believe me, do you?' she asked, a curious smile on her lips.

'Shall I . . . ?' Lewis's left hand hovered over the cassette 'on-off' switch.

'Nah! Leave it.'

She leaned back languorously; and even to the staid

234

Lewis, as he made his way up to Kidlington, she seemed to exude a powerful sexuality.

When he had rung her late the previous afternoon, Lewis had been unable to get an answer; also been unable to get an answer in the early evening, when he had called at the house in Princess Street, off the Iffley Road, where she had her bed-sitter-cum-bathroom, and where he had left a note for her to call him back as soon as possible. Which was not very soon at all, in fact, since it had been only at 9.45 that morning when she'd rung, expressing the preference to be interviewed at Kidlington, and when Morse (sounding, from his home, in adequate fettle) had stated his intention to be present at the interview.

After Lewis had parked outside the HQ building, his passenger eased herself out of the car; and then, standing on the tarmac in full view of a good many interested eyes, stretched out her arms horizontally, slowly pressing them back behind her as far as the trapezius muscles would allow, her breasts straining forward against her thin blouse. Lewis, too, observed the brazen gesture with a gentle smile – and wondered what Morse would make of Ms Eleanor Smith.

In fact the answer would appear to be not very much, for the interview was strangely low-key, with Morse himself clearly deciding to leave everything to Lewis. First, Ms Smith gave what (as both detectives knew) was a heavily censored account of her lifestyle, appearing in no way surprised that for a variety of reasons she should be worthy of police attention – even police suspicion, perhaps. She'd had nothing to do with the murder of poor Dr McClure, of course; and she was confident that she could produce, if it proved necessary, some corroborative witnesses to account for most of her activities on that Sunday, 28 August: thirty-five of them, in fact, including the coach-driver. Yes, she'd known Matthew Rodway – and liked him. Yes, she'd known, still knew, Ashley Davies – and liked him as well; in fact it was with Davies she had been out the previous evening when the police had tried to contact her.

'You must have been with him a long time?' suggested Lewis.

Ms Smith made no reply, merely fingering her right (re-ringed) nostril with her right forefinger.

She was dismissive with the series of questions Lewis proceeded to put about drugs, and her knowledge of drugs. Surely the police didn't need *her* to tell them about what was going on? The easy availability of drugs. Their widespread use? What century were the police living in, for God's sake? And Morse found himself quietly amused as Lewis, just a little disconcerted now, persisted with this line of enquiry like some sheltered middle-aged father learning all about sex-parties and the like from some cruelly knowing little daughter of ten.

Last Wednesday? Where had she been then? Well, if they must know, she'd been in Birmingham for most of that day, on … well, on a personal matter. She'd got back to Oxford, back to Oxford station, at about half-past four. The train – surprise, surprise! – had been on time. And then? (Lewis had persisted.) Then she'd invited one of her friends – one of her girlfriends – up to her flat – her bed-sit! – where they'd drunk a bottle of far-from-vintage champers; and this muted celebration (the occasion for which Eleanor failed to specify) was followed by a somewhat louder merry-making at the local pub; whence she had gone home, whence she'd been *escorted* home, at closing-time. And if they wanted to know whether she'd woken up with a bad head, the answer was 'yes' – a bloody *dreadful* head.

Why all this interest in Wednesday, though? Why Wednesday afternoon? Why Wednesday evening? That's what she wanted to know.

Morse and Lewis had exchanged glances then. If she were telling the truth, it was not this woman, not McClure's former mistress, not Brooks's step-daughter, who had stolen the knife from Cabinet 52 – or done anything with it afterwards. Not, at least, on the Wednesday evening, for Lewis had been making a careful note of times and places and names; and if Eleanor Smith had been fabricating so much detail, she was doing it at some considerable peril. And after another glance from Morse, and a nod, Lewis told her of the theft from the Pitt Rivers, which had now pretty certainly been pin-pointed to between 4.20 p.m. and 4.30 p.m. on Wednesday, the seventh; told her, too, of the disappearance of her step-father.

Ah, her step-father! Well, she could tell them something about him, all right. He was a pig. She'd buggered off from home because of him; and the miracle was that her mother hadn't buggered off from home because of him, too. She'd no idea (she claimed) that he was missing. But that wasn't going to cause her too much grief, was it? She just hoped that he'd remain missing, that's all; hoped they'd find him lying in a gutter somewhere with a knife – *that* knife – stuck firmly in his bloody guts.

The Chief Inspector had not spoken a single word to the woman he'd so recently heralded as his key-witness in the case; and the truth was that, like some maverick magnet, he had felt half repelled, half attracted by the strange creature seated there, with her off-hand (*deliberately* common, perhaps?) manner of speech; with her lack of any respect for the dignity of police procedure; with her contempt concerning the well-being of her step-father, Mr Edward Brooks.

A note had been brought into the room a few minutes earlier and handed to Morse. And now, with the interview apparently nearing its end, Morse jerked his head towards the door and led the way into the corridor. The press, he told Lewis, had got wind of the Pitt Rivers business, and questions were being asked about a possible linkage with the murder enquiry. Clearly some of the brighter news editors were putting two and two together and coming up with an aggregate considerably higher than the sum of the component parts. Lewis had better go and mollify the media, and not worry too much about concealing any confidential information – which shouldn't be terribly difficult since there *was* no confidential information. He himself, Morse, would see that Ms Smith was escorted safely home.

CHAPTER FORTY-THREE

The scenery in the play was beautiful, but the actors got in front of it
(ALEXANDER WOOLLCOTT)

SHE SPOKE as Morse came up to the first roundabout on his way towards Oxford:

'Have you got *any* decent music in this car?'

'Such as what?'

'Well, your nice sergeant played me some Mozart. Fellah playin' the clarinet.'

'Jack Brymer, was it?'

'Dunno. He was great, though. It'd pay him to join a jazz group.'

'You think so?'

'If he's lookin' to the future.'

'He's about eighty.'

'Really? Ah well, you're no chicken yourself, are you?'

Morse, unsmiling, kept his eyes on the road.

'Your sergeant said you was tryin' to educate his musical tastes.'

'Did he?'

'You don't think *I* need a bit of educatin'?'

'I doubt it. I'd guess you're a whole lot better educated than you pretend to be. For all I know, you're probably quite a sensitive and appreciative lass – underneath.'

'Yeah? Christ! What the 'ell's *that* s'posed to mean?'

Morse hesitated before answering her. 'I'll tell you what your trouble is, shall I? You're suffering from a form of inverted snobbery, that's all. Not unusual, you know, in girls – in young ladies of . . . in young ladies like you.'

'If that's supposed to be a bloody insult, mister, you couldn't a' done much bleedin' better, could you?'

'I'm only guessing – don't be cross. I don't know you at all, do I? We've never even spoken—'

'Except on the phone. Remember?'

Morse almost managed a weak smile as he waited at the busy Cutteslowe roundabout.

'I remember.'

'Great, that was. You know, pretendin' to be somebody else. I sometimes think I should a' been an actress.'

'I think you are an actress – that's exactly what I was saying.'

'Well, I'll tell you somethin'. Right at this minute there's one thing I'd swap even for an Oscar.'

'What's that?'

'Plate of steak and chips. I'm starvin'.'

'Do you know how much steak costs these days?'

'Yeah. £3.99 at the King's Arms just down the road here: salad and chips chucked in. I saw it on the way up.'

'It says "French Fries", though, on the sign outside. You see, that's exactly what I meant about—'

'Yeah, you told me. I'm sufferin' summat chronic from inverted snobbery.'

*

'Don't *you* ever eat?' demanded Ellie, wiping her mouth on the sleeve of her blouse, and draining her third glass of red wine.

'Not very often at meal-times, no.'

'A fellah needs his calories, though. Got to keep his strength up – if you know what I mean.'

'I usually take most of my calories in liquid form at lunchtimes.'

'Funny, isn't it? You bein' a copper and all that – and then drinkin' all the beer you do.'

'Don't worry. I'm the only person in Oxford who gets more sober the more he drinks.'

'How do you manage that?'

'Years of practice. I don't recommend it though.'

'Wouldn't help you much with a bleedin' breathalyser, would it?'

'No,' admitted Morse quietly.

'Do you know when you've had enough?'

'Not always.'

'You had enough now?'

'Nearly.'

'Can I buy *you* something?'

'You know, nineteen times out of twenty . . . But I've got to drive you home and then get back to give Sergeant Lewis his next music lesson.'

'What's all them weasel words s'posed to mean?'

'Pint of Best Bitter,' said Morse. 'If you insist.'

'Would you ever think of giving *me* a music lesson?' she asked, as after a wait at the lights in Longwall Street the Jaguar made its way over Magdalen Bridge.

'No.'

'Why not?'

'You want me to be honest?'

'Why not?'

'I just couldn't stick looking at those rings in your nose.'

She felt the insult like a slap across the face; and had the car still been queuing at the Longwall lights she would have jumped out of the Jaguar and left him. But they were travelling now quite quickly up the Iffley Road, and by the time they reached Princess Street she was feeling fractionally less furious.

'Look! Just tell your sergeant somethin' from me, will you?'

'*I'm* in charge of the case,' said Morse defensively, 'not Sergeant Lewis.'

'Well, you could a' fooled me. You never asked me nothin' – not at the station, did you? You hadn't said a single word till we got in the car.'

'Except on the phone. Remember?' said Morse quietly.

'Yeah, well, like I said, that was good fun . . .' But the wind had been taken from her sails, and she glanced across at Morse in a slightly new light. In the pub, as she'd noticed, he'd averted his gaze from her for much of the time. And now she knew why . . . He was a bit different – a lot different, really – from the rest of them; the rest of the men *his* age, anyway. Felix had once told her that she looked at people with eyes that were 'interested and interesting', and she would never forget that: it was the most wonderful compliment anyone had ever paid her. But this man, Morse, hadn't even looked at her eyes; just looked at his beer for most of the time.

What the hell, though.

Bloody police!

'Look, somethin' for you or your sergeant, OK? If he wants to check up about Wednesday, when I went to Brum, I went to an abortion clinic there. Sort o' consultation. But I decided I wasn't goin' to go through with it – not this time, OK? Then, about last night, I went out with Ashley – Ashley Davies – and he asked me to marry him. With or without me bloody nose-rings, mister, OK?'

With that she opened the near-side door and jumped out.

She slammed it so hard that for a moment Morse was worried that some damage might have been incurred by the Jaguar's (pre-electrics) locking mechanism.

'And you can stuff your fuckin' Mozart, OK?'

CHAPTER FORTY-FOUR

No small art is it to sleep: it is necessary to keep
awake all day for that purpose
(FRIEDRICH NIETZSCHE)

IT IS sometimes maintained, and with some cause, that
insomnia does not exist. The argument, put most
briefly, is that anyone unable to fall asleep has no real
need to fall asleep. But there were several key players in
the present drama who would have readily challenged
such an argument that night – the night of Friday, 9
September.

Morse himself, who only infrequently had the slightest
trouble in falling asleep, often had the contrary problem of 'falling awake' during the small hours, either to
visit the loo, or to drink some water – the latter liquid
figuring quite prominently with him during the night,
though virtually never during the day. Yet sleep was as
important to Morse as to any other soul; and specifically
on the subject of sleep, the Greek poets and the Greek
prose-writers had left behind several pieces of their
literary baggage in the lumber-room of Morse's mind.
And if, for him, the whole of the classical corpus had to
be jettisoned except for one single passage, he would
probably have opted for the scene depicting the death
of Sarpedon, from Book XVI of the *Iliad*, where those

swift companions, the twin brothers Sleep and Death, bear the dead hero to the broad and pleasant land of Lycia. And so very close behind Homer's words would have been those of Socrates, as he prepared to drink the hemlock, that if death were just one long and dreamless sleep then mortals could have nought to fear.

That night, though, Morse had a vivid dream – a dream that he was playing the saxophone in a jazz ensemble, yet (even in his dream) ever wondering whence he had acquired such dazzling virtuosity, and ever worried that his skill would at any second desert him in front of his adulatory audience – amongst whom he had spotted a girl with two rings in her nose; a girl who could never be Eleanor Smith, though, since the girl in the dream was disfigured and ugly; and Eleanor Smith could never be that . . .

Julia Stevens tossed back and forth in her bed that night, repeatedly turning over the upper of her two pillows as she sought to cool her hot and aching head. At half-past midnight, she got up and made herself another cup of Ovaltine, swallowing with it two further Nurofen. A great block of pain had settled this last week at the back of her head, and there was a ceaseless surge of something (blood?) that broke in rhythmic waves inside her ears.

During the daytime, she had so little fear of dying; but recently, in the hours of darkness, Fear had been stalking her bedroom, reporting to her its terrifying tales, and bullying her into confessing (Oh, God!) that, no, she didn't want to die. In her dream that night, when finally she drifted off into a fitful sleep, she beheld an image of the Pale Horse; and knew that the name of the one who rode thereon was Death . . .

Covering the space over and alongside the single bed pushed up against the inside wall of the small bedroom, were three large posters, featuring Jimi Hendrix, Jim Morrison, and Kurt Cobain – rock idols who during their comparatively short lives had regularly diced with drugs and death. At 1 a.m., still dressed, Kevin Costyn was sitting on the bed, his back against the creaking headboard, listening on his Walkman to some ear-blasting fury of punk music. In a perverse sort of way, he found it quite soothing. *Eroticon IV*, a crudely pornographic paperback, lay open on the bed beside him; but for the moment Kevin's mind was not beset with sexual fantasies.

Surprisingly, in a week of virtually unparalleled excitement, his thoughts were now centred more soberly on the nature of his surroundings: the litter-strewn front gardens along the road, with derelict, disembowelled cars propped up in drives; the shoddy, undusted, threadbare house in which he lived with his feckless mother; above all the sordid state of his own bedroom, and particularly of the dingy, soiled, creased sheets in which he'd slept for the past seven weeks or more. It was the contrast that had caught his imagination – the contrast between all this and the tidy if unpretentious terrace in which Mrs Julia Stevens lived; the polished, clean, sweet-smelling rooms in her house; above all, the snow-white, crisply laundered sheets on her inviting bed.

He thought he'd always known what makes the difference in life.

Money.

And as he took off his socks and trousers and got into bed, he found himself wondering how much money Mrs Stevens might have saved in life.

In the past few weeks Mrs Rodway was beginning to sleep more soundly. Sleeping pills, therapy, exercise, holidays, diet – none of them had been all that much help. But she had discovered something very simple which did help: she *counted*. One thousand and one; one thousand and two ... and after a little while she would stop her counting, and whisper some few words aloud to herself: 'And – there – was – a – great – calm' ... Then she would begin counting again, backwards this time: one thousand and five; one thousand and four ...

Sometimes, as she counted, she almost managed not to think of Matthew. On a few nights recently, she didn't have to count at all. But this particular night was not one of them ...

The previous evening, Ashley Davies had taken Ellie Smith to a motel near Buckingham where he, flushed with the success of his marriage proposal, and she, much flushed with much champagne, had slept between pale green sheets – an idyllic introit, one might have thought, to their newly plighted state.

And perhaps it was.

But as Davies lay awake, alone, this following night, he began to doubt that it was so.

His own sexual enjoyment had been intense, for *in medio coitu* she had surrendered her body to his with a wondrous abandon. Yet before and after their love-making – both! – he had sensed a disturbing degree of reserve in her, of holding back. Twice had she turned her mouth away from him when his lips had craved some full commitment, some deeper tenderness. And in retrospect he knew that there must be some tiny corner in her heart which she'd not unlocked as yet to any man.

In the early hours, she had turned fully away from him, seeming to grow colder and colder, as if sleep and the night were best; as if, too, somewhere within her was a secret passion committed already to someone else . . .

Restless, too, that night was the scout now given responsibility for Staircase G in the Drinkwater Quad at Wolsey. At 2 a.m. she went downstairs to the kitchen to make herself a cup of tea, looking in the mirror there at a neatly featured face, with its auburn hair cut in a fringe across the forehead: getting just a little long now, and almost covering a pair of worried eyes.

Susan had agreed to check and sign (at 10 o'clock

the following morning, Saturday) the statement earlier made to Sergeant Lewis. And the prospect worried her. It was like reporting some local vandals to the police, when there was always the fear that those same vandals would return to wreak even greater havoc, precisely for having been reported. In her own case, though – as Susan was too intelligent not to appreciate – the risk was considerably greater. This was not a case of vandalism; but of murder. As such, she'd had little option but to make a full (if guarded) statement; yet she feared she would now be open to some sort of retaliation – to threats of physical violence, perhaps, from a man who, by an almost unanimous verdict, was seen as a very nasty piece of work indeed.

Back in bed, Susan tried a cure she'd once been told: to close one's eyes gently (yes, *gently*) and then to look (yes, *look*) at a point about four or five inches in front of one's nose. Such a strategy, it was claimed, would ensure that the eyeballs remained fairly still, being focused as they were upon some specific point, however notional that point might be; and since it had been demonstrated that the rapid revolving of the eyeballs in their sockets was a major cause of sleeplessness, insomniacs most certainly should experiment along such lines.

That night, therefore, Mrs Susan Ewers had so experimented, though with only limited success. As it happened, however, her apprehension was wholly groundless, since Edward Brooks was never destined to become a threat to Susan or to any other living person. One of those twins from Morse's schooldays, the one whose name was Death, had already claimed him for his own; and together with his brother, Sleep, had borne him off, though not perhaps to the broad and pleasant land of Lycia, wherein Sarpedon lies.

CHAPTER FORTY-FIVE

Keep careful watch too on the moral faults of
your patients, which may cause them to tell
untruths about things prescribed – and things
proscribed

(*Corpus Hippocraticum*)

A WEEK in a murder enquiry, especially one in which
there is virtually no development, can be a wearisome
time. And so it was for Sergeant Lewis in the days
between Friday 9 and Friday 16 September.

The whereabouts and movements of key characters
in the Pitt Rivers enquiry, most particularly on the
evening and night of Wednesday the seventh, immediately after the knife had been stolen, had been checked
and in every case confirmed, with appropriate statements made and (with the more obvious mis-spellings
corrected) duly signed and filed. Nothing else, though.

Nothing else, either, on the murder scene. House-
to-house enquiries in Daventry Avenue had come to an
end; and come to nothing. Three former undergraduates from Staircase G on Drinkwater Quad had been
traced with no difficulty; but with no real consequence
either, since apart from confirming the general availability of drugs during their years in Oxford they had
each denied any specific knowledge of drug-trafficking
on their own staircase.

What worried Lewis slightly was that Morse appeared

just as interested in the disappearance of a knife as in the death of a don, as though the connection between the two events (Morse had yet again reversed his views) was both logically necessary and self-evidently true.

But *was* it?

And on the morning of Thursday, 15 September, he had voiced his growing doubt.

'Brooks, sir – Brooks is the only real connection, isn't he? Brooks who's top of your murder-suspects; and Brooks who's got a job at the Pitt Rivers.'

'Have you ever thought, Lewis, that it could have been Brooks who stole the knife?'

'You can't be serious?'

'No. Brooks didn't steal the knife. Sorry. Go on!'

'Well, you said so yourself early on: we often get people who do copy-cat things, don't we? And whoever stole the knife – well, it might not have anything to do with the murder at all. Somebody just read that bit in the *Oxford Mail* and . . .'

'Ye-es. To tell you the truth, I've been thinking the same.'

'It could just be a coincidence.'

'Yes, it could. Perhaps it was.'

'I mean, you've often said coincidences happen all the time; just that some of us don't spot 'em.'

'Yes, I've often thought that.'

'So there may be no causal connection after all—?'

'Stop sounding like a philosopher, Lewis, and go and get us some coffee.'

Morse, too, was finding this period of inactivity frustrating. *And* a time of considerable stress, since for three whole days now he had not smoked a single cigarette, and had arrived at that crucial point where his self-mastery had already been demonstrated, his victory over nicotine finally won. So? So it was no longer a question of relapsing, of re-indulging. If he wished to re-*start*, though ... for, in truth, the fourth day was proving even harder than the third.

The earlier wave of euphoria was ebbing still further on the fifth day, when it was his own turn to have a medical check-up, and when ten minutes before his appointment time he checked in at the Outpatients reception at the JR2 and sat down in the appropriate area to await his call, scheduled for 9.20 a.m. By some minor coincidence (yes!) this was the same time that Mr Edward Brooks had been expected for his own designated brand of Outpatient care – an appointment which had not been kept eight days earlier ... and which was unkept still.

After undergoing a fairly thorough examination; after skilfully parrying the questions put to him about avoirdupois and alcohol; after politely declining a suggested consultation with a dietitian; after going along the corridor to have three further blood-samples taken – Morse was out again; out into the morning sunshine, with a new date (six whole weeks away!) written into his little blue card, and with the look of a man who feels fresh confidence in life. What was it that the doc had said?

'You know, I'm not quite sure why, but you're over things pretty well. You don't deserve to be, Mr Morse; but, well, you seem surprisingly fit to me.'

Walking along to the southern car park and savouring still the happy tidings, Morse caught sight of a young woman standing at the bus-stop there. By some minor coincidence (yes!) they had earlier been present together in the same waiting-room at the Summertown Health Centre, where neither had known the other. And now, here they were together again, on the same morning, at the same time, at the same hospital, both of them (as it appeared) on their way back home.

'Good morning, Miss Smith!' said the cheerful Chief Inspector, taking care to articulate a clear 'Miss', and not (as he always saw it) the ugly, pretentious, fuzzy 'Ms'.

Little that morning could have dampened Morse's spirits, for the gods were surely smiling on him. Even had she ignored his greeting, he would have walked serenely past, with little sense of personal slight. Yet perhaps he would have felt a touch of disappointment too; for he had seen the sadness in her face, and knew that for a little while he wanted to be with her.

CHAPTER FORTY-SIX

I once knew a person who spoke in dialect
with an accent

(IRVIN COBB)

'THERE'S NO need really,' she said, manoeuvring herself into the passenger seat. 'I'm not short o' money, you know.'

'How long have you been waiting?'

'Long enough! Mind if I smoke?' she asked, as Morse turned left into Headley Way.

'Go ahead.'

'You want one?'

'Er, no thanks – not for me.'

'You *do* smoke, though. Else your wife does. Ashtray's full, innit? Think I'd make a good detective?'

'Which way's best?' asked Morse.

'Left at the White Horse.'

'Or *in* the White Horse, perhaps?'

'Er, no thanks – not for me,' she mimicked.

'Why's that?'

'They're not bloody open yet, that's why.' It was meant to be humorous, no doubt, but her voice was strained; and glancing sideways, Morse guessed that something was sorely wrong with her.

'Want to tell me about it?'

'Why the 'ell should I tell *you*?'

Morse breathed in deeply as she stubbed out her

cigarette with venom. 'I think you've been in hospital overnight. I could see a bit of a white nightie peeping out of the hold-all. The last time we met you told me you were expecting a baby, and the JR1 is where they look after babies, isn't it? They wouldn't normally take a mum who's had a miscarriage, though – that'd be the Churchill. But if you had a *threatened* miscarriage, with some internal bleeding, perhaps, then they might well get you into the JR1 for observation. That's the sort of thing a policeman gets to know, over the years. And please remember,' he added gently, 'I only asked if you wanted to tell me about it.'

Tears coursed down cheeks that were themselves wholly devoid of make-up; washing down with them, though, some of the heavy eye-shadow from around her dull-green eyes.

'I lost it,' she said, finally.

For a moment or two Morse considered placing his hand very gently, very lightly on hers, but he feared that his action would be misconstrued.

'I'm sorry,' he said simply, not speaking again until he reached Princess Street.

She got out of the car and picked up her hold-all from the back. 'Thank you.'

'I wasn't much help, I'm afraid. But if I *can* ever be of any help, you've only got to give me a ring.' He wrote down his ex-directory telephone number.

'Well, you could help now, actually. It's a lousy little place I live in – but I'd be quite glad if you'd come in and have a drink with me.'

'Not this morning.'

'Why the 'ell *not*, for Christ's sake? You just said to

give you a ring if I needed any help – and I bloody *do*, OK? *Now.*'

'All right. I'll come in and have one quick drink. On one condition, though.'

'What's that?'

'You don't slam the car-door. Agreed?'

'Doesn't seem *too* lousy a little place?' suggested Morse as, whisky in hand, he leaned back in the only armchair in the only room – the fairly large room, though – which was Eleanor Smith's bed-sitter-cum-bathroom.

'I can assure you it *is*. Crawling with all those microscopic creatures – you've seen photographs of them?'

Morse looked at her. Was he imagining things? Hadn't she just spoken to him with a degree of verbal and grammatical fluency that was puzzlingly at odds with her habitual mode of speech. 'Crawlin' wiv all them little bugs an' things' – wasn't *that* how she'd normally have expressed herself?

'I think I know why you're lookin' at me like that,' she said.

'Pardon?'

In answer, she placed an index finger on each nostril. On each ringless nostril.

And Morse nodded. 'Yes, I prefer you as you are now.'

'So you said.'

'You know that your step-father's still missing?'

'So what? You want me to break out into goose-pimples or something?'

'Why do you hate him so much?'

'Next question.'

'All right. You said you were going to get married. Does all this – the loss of your baby – does it make any difference?'

'Gettin' deep, ain't we? Cigarette?'

Ellie held out the packet; and stupidly, inevitably, Morse capitulated.

'You're still going ahead with getting married?'

'Why not? It's about time I settled down, don't you think?'

'I suppose so.'

'What else can I tell you?'

Well, if she was inviting questions (Morse decided) it was a good opportunity to probe a little more deeply into the heart of the mystery, since he was convinced that the key to the case – the key to *both* cases – lay somewhere in those late afternoon hours of Wednesday, 7 September, when someone had stolen the knife from the Pitt Rivers Museum.

'After your trip to Birmingham, you *could* have caught an earlier train back?'

She shrugged. 'Dunno. I didn't, though.'

'Do you remember exactly what time you asked your friend up here – when you got back that afternoon?'

'Exactly? Course, I can't. *She* might. Doubt it, though. We were both tight as ticks later that night.'

Was she lying? And if so, why?

'On that Wednesday—'

But she let him get no further. 'Christ! Give it a rest about Wednesday, will you? What's wrong with Tuesday? Or Monday? I 'aven't a bleedin' clue what I was doin' them days. So why *Wednesday*? Like I say, I know where I was all the bloody time that day.'

'It's just that there may be a connection between Dr McClure's murder and the theft of the knife.'

She seemed unimpressed, but mollified again. 'Drop more?'

'No, I must be off.'

'Please yourself.' She poured herself another Scotch, and lit another cigarette. 'Beginnin' to taste better. I hadn't smoked a fag for three days – three days! – before that one in your car. Tasted terrible, that first one.'

Morse rose to his feet and put his empty glass down on the cluttered mantelpiece, above which, on the white chimney-breast, four six-inch squares in different shades of yellow had been painted – with the name of each shade written in thick pencil inside each square: Wild Primrose, Sunbeam, Buttermilk, Daffodil White.

'Which d'you like best?' she asked. 'I'm considering some redecoration.'

There it was again, in that last sentence – the gear-shift from casual slang to elegance of speech. Interesting ...

'But won't you be leaving here – after you're married?'

'Christ! You can't leave it alone, can you? All these bloody questions!'

Morse turned towards her now, looking down at her as she sat on the side of the bed.

'Why did you invite me here? I only ask because you're making me feel I'm unwelcome – an intruder – a Nosey Parker. Do you realize that?'

She looked down into her glass. 'I felt lonely, that's all. I wanted a bit of company.'

'Haven't you told Mr Davies – about your miscarriage?'

'No.'

'Don't you think—'

'Augh, shut up! You wouldn't know what it feels like, would you? To be on your own in life . . .'

'I'm on my own all the time,' said Morse.

'That's what they all say, did you know that? All them middle-aged fellows like you.'

Morse nodded and half-smiled; and as he walked to the door he looked at the chimney-breast again.

'Yellow's a difficult colour to live with; but I'd go for the Daffodil White, if I were you.'

Leaving her still seated on the bed, he trod down the narrow, squeaking stairs to the Jaguar, where for a few minutes he sat motionless, with the old familiar sensation tingling across his shoulders.

Why hadn't he thought of it before?

CHAPTER FORTY-SEVEN

Given a number which is a square, when can we write it as the sum of two other squares?

(DIOPHANTUS, *Arithmetic*)

LEWIS WAS eager to pass on his news. Appeals on Radio Oxford and Fox FM, an article in the *Oxford Mail*, local enquiries into the purchase, description, and condition of Brooks's comparatively new bicycle, had proved, it appeared, successful. An anonymous phone-call (woman's voice) had hurriedly informed St Aldate's City Police that if they were interested there was a 'green bike' chained to the railings outside St Mary Mags in Cornmarket. No other details.

'Phone plonked down pronto,' the duty sergeant had said.

'Sure it wasn't a "Green dyke" chained to the railings?' Lewis had asked, in a rare excursion into humour.

Quite sure, since the City Police were now in possession of one bicycle, bright green – awaiting instructions.

The call had come through just after midday, and Lewis felt excitement, and gratification. Somebody – some mother or wife or girlfriend – had clearly decided to push the hot property back into public circulation. Once in a while procedure and patience paid dividends. Like now.

If it was Brooks's bike, of course.

Morse, however, on his rather late return from lunch, was to give Lewis no immediate opportunity of reporting his potentially glad tidings.

'Get on all right at the hospital, sir?'

'Fine. No problem.'

'I've got some news—'

'Just a minute. I saw Miss Smith this morning. She'd been in the JR1 overnight.'

'All right, is she?'

'Don't know about that. But she's a mixed-up young girl, is our Eleanor,' confided Morse.

'Not really a *girl*, sir.'

'Yes, she is. Half my age, Lewis. Makes me feel old.'

'Well, perhaps . . .'

'She gave me an idea, though. A beautiful idea.' Morse stripped the cellophane from a packet of cigarettes, took one out, and lit it from a box of matches, on which his eyes lingered as he inhaled deeply. 'You know the problem we're faced with in this case? We've got to square the first case – the murder of McClure.'

'No argument there.'

'Then we've got to square the second case – the theft of a Northern Rhodesian knife. And the connection between these two—'

'But you said perhaps there wasn't any connection.'

'Well, there is and now *I know what it is.*'

'I see,' said Lewis, unseeing.

'As I say, if we square the first case, and then we square the second case . . . all we've got to do is to work out the sum of the two squares.'

Lewis looked puzzled. 'I'm not quite following you, sir.'

'Have you heard of "Pythagorean Triplets"?'

'We did Pythagoras Theorem at school.'

'Exactly. The most famous of all the triplets, that is – "3, 4, 5": $3^2 + 4^2 = 5^2$. Agreed?'

'Agreed.'

'But there are more spectacular examples than that. The Egyptians, for example, knew all about "5961, 6480, 8161".'

'That's good news, sir. I didn't realize you were up in things like that.'

Morse looked down at the desk. 'I'm not. I was just reading from the back of this matchbox here.'

Lewis grinned as Morse continued.

'There was this fellow called Fermat, it seems – I called in at home and looked him up. He knew all about "things like that", as you put it: square-roots, and cube-roots, and all that sort of stuff.'

'Has he got much to do with *us*, though – this fellow?'

'Dunno, Lewis. But he was a marvellous man. In one of the books on arithmetic he was studying he wrote something like: "I've got a truly marvellous demonstration of this proposition which this margin is too narrow to contain." Isn't that a wonderful sentence?'

'If you say so, sir.'

'Well, I've worked out the square of three and the square of four and I've added them together and I've come up with – guess what, Lewis!'

'Twenty-five?'

'Much more! You see, this morning I suddenly realized where we've been going wrong in this case. We've been assuming what we were *meant* to assume ... No. Let me start again. As you know, I felt pretty certain almost from the beginning that McClure was murdered by Brooks. And I think now, though I can't be certain of course, that Brooks himself was murdered last week. And I know – listen, Lewis! – I now know what Brooks's murderer *wanted* us to think.'

Lewis looked at the Chief Inspector, and saw that not uncommon, strangely distanced, almost mystical look in the gentian-blue eyes.

'You see, Brooks's body is somewhere where we'll never find it – I feel oddly sure about that. Pushed in a furnace, perhaps, or buried under concrete, or left in a rubbish-dump—'

'Waste Reception Area, sir.'

'Wherever, yes. But consider the *consequences* of the body never being found. We all jump to the same conclusion – the conclusion our very intelligent Administrator at the Pitt Rivers jumped to: that there was a direct link between the murder of Brooks and the theft of the knife. Now, there was a grand deception here. The person who murdered Brooks wanted us to take one fact for granted, and almost – almost! – he succeeded.'

'Or she.'

'Oh, yes. Or she ... But as I say the key question is this: why was the knife stolen? So let me tell you. That theft was a great big bluff! For what purpose? To convince us that Brooks was murdered after 4.30 p.m. on that Wednesday the seventh. But he wasn't,' asserted

Morse slowly. '*He was murdered the day before* – he was murdered on Tuesday the sixth.'

'But he was seen alive on the Wednesday, sir. His wife saw him – Mrs Stevens saw him—'

'Liars!'

'Both of 'em?'

'Both of them.'

'You mean . . . you mean *they* murdered Brooks?'

'That's exactly what I do mean, yes. As I see things, it must have been Julia Stevens who supplied the brains, who somehow arranged the business with the knife. But what – *what*, Lewis – if Brooks was murdered by *another* knife – a household knife, let's say – a knife just like the one McClure was murdered with, the knife that was found in Daventry Avenue, the knife that was missing from the Brooks's kitchen.'

Lewis shook his head slowly. 'Why all this palaver, though?'

'Good question. So I'll give you a good answer. To give the murderer – murderers – watertight alibis for that *Wednesday*. I sensed something of the sort when I interviewed Julia Stevens; and I suddenly *knew* it this morning when I was interviewing our punk-wonder.'

'She's in it, too, you reckon?'

Morse nodded. 'All three of them have been telling us the same thing, really. In effect they've been saying: "Look! I don't mind being suspected of doing something on Tuesday – but *not on the Wednesday*." They're happy about not having an alibi for the day Brooks was murdered. It was for the day afterwards – the Wednesday – that for some reason they figured an alibi was vital. And – surprise, surprise! – they've each of 'em got a beautiful alibi for then. It's been very clever of them – this sort of casual indifference they've shown for the *actual* day of the murder, the Tuesday. You see, they all knew they'd be the likely suspects, and they've been very gently, very cleverly, pushing us all along in the direction they wanted.'

'All three of them, you think?'

'Yes. They'd *all* have gladly murdered Brooks, even if they hadn't known he was a murderer himself: the wife he'd treated so cruelly; the step-daughter he'd probably abused; and Julia Stevens, who could see how her little cleaner was being knocked about by the man she'd married. So they hatch a plot. They arrange for the knife to be stolen, having made sure that none of *them* could have stolen it—'

'Ellie Smith could have stolen it,' interposed Lewis quietly.

'Yes . . . perhaps she could, yes. But I don't think so. Didn't the attendant think it was more likely to have been a man? No. My guess is that they bribed someone to steal it – someone they could trust . . . someone *one* of them could trust.'

'Ashley Davies?'

'Why not? He's got his reward, hasn't he?'

'You think that's a reward, sir, marrying *her*?'

Morse was silent awhile. 'Do you know, Lewis, it might be. It might be . . .'

'What did they do with the knife?'

'That's the whole point. That's what I'm telling you. *They didn't use the stolen knife at all.* They just got rid of it.'

'But you can't just get rid of things like that.'

'Why not? Stick it in a black bag and leave it for the dustmen. You could leave a dismembered corpse in one of those and get away with it. *Kein Problem*. The only thing the dustmen won't take is garden-refuse – that's a well-known fact, isn't it?'

'You seem to be assuming an awful lot of brains somewhere.'

'Look, Lewis! There seems to be a myth going round these days that criminals are a load of morons and that CID personnel are all members of Mensa.'

'Perhaps I should apply then,' said Lewis slowly.

'Pardon?'

'Well, I've been very clever, sir, while you were away. I think I've found Brooks's bike.'

'You have? Why the hell didn't you tell me before?'

CHAPTER FORTY-EIGHT

It'll do him good to lie there unconscious for a
bit. Give his brain a rest

(N. F. SIMPSON, *One-Way Pendulum*)

AT THE Proctor Memorial School that Friday afternoon the talk was predominantly of a ram-raid made
on an off-licence in the Blackbird Leys Estate the
previous evening, when by some happy chance a routine police patrol-car had been cruising round the
neighbourhood just as three youths were looting the
smashed shop in Verbena Avenue; when, too, a little
later, the same police car had been only fifty or so yards
behind when the stolen getaway car had crashed at full
speed into a juggernaut lorry near the Horspath roundabout on the Eastern Ring Road . . .

When the chase was over one of the three was seated
dead in the driving seat, his chest crushed by the
collapsed steering-wheel; another, the one in the front
passenger seat, had his right foot mangled and trapped
beneath the engine-mounting; the third, the one seated
in the back, had severe lacerations and contusions
around the head and face and was still unconscious
after the firemen had finally cut free his colleagues in
crime from the concertina'ed Escort.

The considerable interest in this incident – accident
– is readily explicable, since two of the youths, the two
who survived the crash, had spent five years at the

Proctor Memorial School; had spent fifteen terms mocking the attempts of their teachers to instil a little knowledge and a few of the more civilized values into their lives. Had they received their education at one of the nation's more prestigious establishments – an Eton, say, or a Harrow, or a Winchester – the youths would probably have been designated 'Old Boys' instead of the 'former pupils' printed in the late afternoon edition of the *Oxford Mail.* And the former pupil who had been seated in the back of the car had left his Alma Mater only the previous term.

His name was Kevin Costyn.

Julia Stevens walked round to her former pupil's house during the lunch-break that Friday, wishing, if she could, to speak to Kevin's mother. But the door-bell, like most of the other fixtures there by the look of things, was out of order; and no one answered her repeated knockings. As she slowly turned and walked back through the neglected, litter-strewn front garden, a young woman, with two small children in a push-chair, stopped for a moment by the broken gate, and spoke to her.

'The people in there are usually out.'

That was all.

Perhaps, thought Julia Stevens, as she made her way thoughtfully back to school – perhaps that brief, some-what enigmatic utterance could explain more about her former pupil than she herself had ever learned.

*

In the Major Trauma Ward, on Level 5 of the JR2 in Headington, she explained to the ward-sister that she had rung an hour earlier, at 6 p.m., and been told that it would be all right for her to visit Mr Kevin Costyn.

'How is he?'

'Probably not quite so bad as he looks. He's had a CT test – Computerized Tomography – and there doesn't *seem* to be any damage but we're a little bit worried about his brain, yes. And he looks an awful mess, I'm afraid. Please prepare yourself, Mrs Stevens.'

He was awake, and recognized her immediately.

'I'm sorry,' he whispered, speaking through a dreadfully lop-sided mouth, like one who has just received half a dozen injections of local anaesthetic into one half of the jaw.

'Sh! I've just come to see how you're getting on, that's all.'

'I'm sorry.'

'Listen! I'm the teacher, remember? Just let *me* do the talking.'

'That were the worst thing I ever done in my life.'

'Don't talk about it now! *You* weren't driving.'

He turned his face towards her, revealing the left cheek, so terribly bloodied and stitched and torn.

'It's not that, Mrs Stevens. It's when I asked you for the money.' His eyes pleaded with her. 'I should never a' done that. You're the only person that was ever good to me, really – and then I go and . . .'

His words were faltering further, and there was a film of tears across his eyes.

'Don't worry about that, Kevin!'

'Will you promise me something? *Please?*'

'If I can, of course I will.'

'*You* won't worry if I don't worry.'

'I promise.'

'There's no need, you see. I won't ever tell anybody what I done for you – honest to God, I won't.'

A few minutes later, Julia was aware of movement behind her, and she turned to see the nurse standing there with a uniformed policeman, the latter clutching his flat hat rather awkwardly to his rib-cage.

It was time to go; and laying her hand for a few seconds on Kevin's right arm, an arm swathed in bandages and ribbed with tubes, she took her leave.

As she waited for the lift down to the ground floor, she smiled sadly to herself as she recalled the nurse's words: 'But we're a little bit worried about his brain' . . . just like almost all the staff at the Proctor Memorial School had been, for five years . . . for fifteen terms.

And then, as she tried to remember exactly where she'd parked the Volvo, she found herself, for some reason, thinking of Chief Inspector Morse.

CHAPTER FORTY-NINE

I sometimes wonder which would be nicer – an opera without an interval, or an interval without an opera

(ERNEST NEWMAN, *Berlioz, Romantic and Classic*)

OF THE four separate operas which comprise *Der Ring des Nibelungen* (an achievement which in his view ranked as one of the seven great wonders of the modern world), *Siegfried* had always been Morse's least favourite. And on the evening of Saturday, 17 September, he decided he would seek again to discover whether the fault lay with himself or with Wagner. But the evening was destined not to pass without its interruptions.

At 7.35 p.m. Lewis had rung through with the dramatic news that the handle-bars and the saddle on the bicycle recovered from the railings outside the parish church of St Mary Magdalene still bore traces of blood, and that preliminary tests pointed strongly to its being McClure's blood. Such findings, if confirmed, would provide the police with their first physical link between Felix McClure and Edward Brooks, since the latter's wife, Brenda, had now identified the bike as her husband's; as had one of the assistants at Halford Cycles on the Cowley Road, where Brooks had purchased the bike four months previously. A warrant, therefore, should be made out asap for the arrest of Mr Edward Brooks – with Morse's say-so.

And Morse now said so.

The fact that the person against whom the warrant would be issued was nowhere to be found had clearly taken some of the cream from Lewis's éclair. But Morse seemed oddly content: he maintained that Lewis was doing a wonderful job, but forbad him to disturb him again that evening, barring some quite prodigious event – such as the birth of another Richard Wagner.

So Morse sat back again, poured himself another Scotch, lit another cigarette, and turned *Siegfried* back on.

Paradise enow.

Very few people knew Morse's personal (ex-directory) telephone number, and in fact he had changed it yet again a few months earlier. When, therefore, forty minutes further into *Siegfried*, the telephone rang once more, Morse knew that it must be Lewis again; and thumping down his libretto with an ill grace, he answered tetchily.

'What do you want this time?'

'Hullo? Chief Inspector Morse?' It was a woman's voice, and Morse knew whose. Why had he been such a numbskull as to give his private number to the pink-haired punk-wonder?

'Yes?'

'Hi! You told me if ever I wanted any help, all I'd got to do was pick up the phone, remember?'

'How can I help?' asked Morse wearily, a hint of exasperation in his voice.

'You don't sound overjoyed to hear from me.'

'Just a bit tired, that's all.'

'Too tired for me to treat you to a pint?'

Morse wasn't quite sure at that moment whether his spirits were rising or falling. 'Sometime next week, perhaps?' he suggested.

'No. I want to see you tonight. Now. Right *now.*'

'I'm sorry, I can't see you tonight—'

'Why not?'

'Well, to tell you the truth, I'm in the bath.'

'Wiggle the water a bit so I can hear.'

'I can't do that – I'd get the phone wet.'

'So you didn't really mean what you said at all.'

'Yes, I did. I'll be only too glad to help. What's the trouble?'

'It's no good – not over the phone.'

'Why on earth not?'

'You'll see.'

'I don't follow you.'

'I'm just going out to catch a bus to the City Centre. With a bit of luck I'll be there in twenty minutes – outside Marks and Sparks – that's where it stops, and then I'm going to walk up St Giles', and I'm goin' in the Old Parsonage for a drink. I'll stay there half an hour. And if you've not turned up by then, I'll just take a taxi up to your place – OK with you?'

'No, it's not. You don't know where I live anyway—'

'Nice fellah, Sergeant Lewis. I could fall for 'im.'

'He's never told you my address!'

'Why don't you ring and ask 'im?'

Morse looked at his wristwatch: almost half-past eight.

'Give me half an hour.'

'Won't you need a bit longer?'

'Why's that?'

'Well, you've got to get yourself dried and then get dressed and then make sure you can find your wallet and then catch a bus—'

'Make it three-quarters of an hour, then,' said Morse, wondering, in fact, where his wallet was, for he seldom used it when Lewis was around.

Lewis himself rang again that evening, about ten minutes after Morse had left. The path lab had confirmed that the blood found on the recovered bicycle was McClure's; and on his way home (a little disappointed) he pushed a note to that effect through the front door of Morse's bachelor flat – together with the newspaper cutting from the previous week's *Oxford Times* received from one of his St Aldate's colleagues:

THIEVES PUT SPOKE IN THINGS

An optimistic scheme to provide free bicycles was scrapped yesterday by the Billingdon Rural District Council.

The cycles, painted green, and repaired by young offenders on community service, were put into specially constructed stands outside the church for villagers to use and then return.

However within thirty-six hours of the scheme being launched, all twelve cycles, purchased at a cost of £1100, had disappeared.

The chair of the Council, Mrs Jean Ashton, strongly defended the initiative. 'The bikes are still somewhere on the road,' she maintained.

DC Watson of the Thames Valley Police agreed: 'Most of them probably in Oxford or Banbury, resprayed a bright red.'

Ashley Davies also had repeatedly rung an Oxford number that Saturday evening, but with similar lack of success; and he (like Sergeant Lewis) felt some disappointment. Ellie had told him that she would be out all day, but suggested that he gave her a ring in the evening. His news could wait – well, it wasn't really 'news', at all. He just wanted her to know how efficient he'd been.

He'd visited the plush, recently opened Register Office in New Road, where he'd been treated with courtesy and competence. In the circumstances 'Notice by Certificate' (he'd been informed) would be the best procedure – with Saturday, 15 October a possible, probable, marriage date, giving ample time for the requisite notices to be posted both at Bedford and at Oxford. He'd agreed to ring the Registrar the following Monday with final confirmation.

A few 'family' to witness the ceremony would have been nice. But, as Ashley was sadly aware, his own mother and father had long since distanced themselves from 'that tart'; and although Ellie's mum could definitely be counted upon, no invitation would ever be sent to her step-father – and that not just because he had left no forwarding address, but because Ellie would never allow even the mention of his name.

Only one wedding guest so far then. But it would be easy to find a few others; and anyway the legal requirement (Ellie, oddly enough, had known all about this) was only for two.

Ashley rang her number again at 10 p.m. Still no answer. And for more than a few minutes he felt a surge of jealousy as he wondered where she was, and with whom she was spending the evening.

CHAPTER FIFTY

There is not so variable a thing in nature as a
lady's head-dress: within my own memory I have
known it rise and fall above thirty degrees
(JOSEPH ADDISON, *The Spectator*)

SHE WAS nowhere to be seen in the area known as the
Parsonage Bar, which (as we know) served as a combined bar and restaurant. There were, however, two
temporarily unescorted young women there, one
blonde, the other brunette. The former, immaculately
coiffured, and dressed in a white suit, would attract
interest wherever she went; the latter, her hair cut
stylishly short, and dressed in a fold-over Oxford-blue
creation, would perhaps attract her own fair share of
attention too, but her face was turned away from Morse,
and it was difficult for him to be certain.

With no real ale on offer, he ordered a glass of
claret, and stood at the bar for a couple of minutes
watching the main door; then sat on one of the green
bar-stools for a further few minutes, still watching the
main door.

But Miss Smith made no entrance.

'Are you on your own?'

The exaggeratedly seductive voice had come from
directly behind him, and Morse swivelled to find one of
the two women, the brunette, climbing somewhat in-
elegantly on to the adjoining stool.

'For the moment I am, yes. Er, can I buy – ?'

He had been looking at her hair, a rich dark brown, with bottled-auburn highlights. But it was not her hair that had caused the mid-sentence hiatus, for now he was looking into her eyes – eyes that were sludgy-green, like the waters of the Oxford Canal.

'Ye gods!' he exclaimed.

'Didn't recognize me, did you? I've been sittin' waitin'. Good job I've got a bit of initiative.'

'What will you have to drink?'

'Champagne. I fancy some champagne.'

'Oh.' Morse looked down at the selection of 'Wines available by the Glass'.

'Can't we stretch to a bottle?' she asked.

Morse turned over the price-list and surveyed 'A Selection of Vintage Champagnes', noting with at least partial relief that most of them were available in half-bottles. He pointed to the cheapest (cheapest!) of these, a Brut Premier Cru: £18.80.

'That should be all right, perhaps?'

She smiled at him slyly. 'You look a little shell-shocked, Inspector.'

In fact Morse was beginning to feel annoyed at the way she was mocking him, manipulating him. He'd show her!

'Bottle of Number 19, waiter.'

Her eyebrows lifted and the green eyes glowed as if the sun were shining on the waters. She had crossed her legs as she sat on the bar-stool, and Morse now contemplated a long expanse of thigh.

'"Barely Black" they're called – the stockings. Sort of sexy name, isn't it?'

Morse drained his wine, only newly aware of why Eleanor Smith could so easily have captivated (*inter alios*) Dr Felix McClure.

They sat opposite each other at one of the small circular-topped tables.

'Cheers, Inspector.'

'Cheers.'

He noticed how she held the champagne glass by the stem, and mentally awarded her plus-one for so doing; at the same time cancelling it with minus-one for the fingernails chewed down to the quicks.

'It's OK – I'm workin' on it.'

'Pardon?'

'Me fingernails – you were lookin' at 'em, weren't you? Felix used to tell me off about 'em.' She speared first a green, then a black olive.

'You can't blame me for not recognizing you. You look completely different – your hair . . .'

'Yeah. Got one o' me friends to cut it and then I washed it out – four times! – then I put some other stuff on, as near me own colour as I could get. Like it?'

She pushed her hair back from her temples and Morse noticed the amethyst earrings in the small, neat ears.

'Is your birthday in February?'

'I say! What a clever old stick you are.'

'Why this . . . this change of heart, though?'

She shook her head. 'Just change of appearance. You can't change your heart. Didn't you know that?'

'You know what I mean,' said Morse defensively.

'Well, like I told you, I'm gettin' spliced – got to be a respectable girl now – all that sort o' thing.'

Morse watched her as she spoke and recalled from the first time he'd seen her the glossy-lipsticked mouth in the powder-pale face. But everything had changed now. The rings had gone too, at least temporarily, from her nose; and from fingers, too, for previously she had worn a whole panoply of silverish rings. Now she wore just one, a slender, elegant-looking thing, with a single diamond, on the third finger of her left hand.

'How can I help you?' asked Morse.

'Well, I thought you might like to *see* me for starters – that wouldn't 'ave bin no good over the blower, would it?'

'Why do you have to keep talking in that sort of way? You've got a pleasant voice and you can speak very nicely. But sometimes you deliberately seem to try to sound like a . . .'

'A trollop?'

'Yes.'

Neither of them spoke for a while. Then it was Ellie:

'I wanted to ask you two things really.'

'I'm all ears.'

'Actually you've got quite nice ears, for a man. Has anyone ever told you that?'

'Not recently, no.'

'Look. You think my step-father's dead, don't you?'

'I'm not sure what I think.'

'If he is dead, though, *when* do you think . . . ?'

'As I say – I just don't know.'

'Can't you guess?'

'Not to you, Miss Smith, no.'

'Can't you call me "Ellie"?'

'All right.'

281

'What do I call you?'

'They just call me Morse.'

'Yes – but your Christian name?'

'Begins with "E", like yours.'

'No more information?'

'No more information.'

'OK. Let me tell you what's worrying me. You think Mum's had something to do with all this, don't you?'

'As I say—'

'I agree with you. She may well have had, for all I know – and good luck to her if she did. But *if* she did, it must have been before that Wednesday. You know why? Because – she doesn't know this – but I've been keeping an eye on her since then, and there's no way – *no way* – she could have done it after . . .'

'After what?' asked Morse quietly.

'Look, I've read about the Pitt Rivers business – everybody has. It's just that . . . I just wonder if something has occurred to you, Inspector.'

'Occasionally things occur to me,' said Morse.

'Have you got any cigarettes, by the way?'

'No, I've given up.'

'Well, as I was saying, what if the knife was stolen on the Wednesday afternoon to give everybody the impression that the murder – if there *is* a murder – was committed *after* that Wednesday afternoon? Do you see what I mean? OK, the knife was *stolen* then – but what if it wasn't *used*? What if the murder was committed with a *different* knife?'

'Go on.'

'That's it really. Isn't that enough?'

'You realize what you're saying, don't you? If your step-father *has* been murdered; if he was murdered *before* the theft of the knife, then your mother is under far more suspicion, not less. As you say, quite rightly, she's got a continuous alibi from the time she left for Stratford with Mrs Stevens on that Wednesday, but she hasn't got much of one for the day before. In fact she probably hasn't got one at all.'

Ellie looked down at the avocado-coloured carpet, and sipped the last of her champagne.

'Would you like me to go and get a packet of cigarettes, Inspector?'

Morse drained his own glass.

'Yes.'

Whilst she was gone (for he made no effort to carry out the errand himself) Morse sat back and wondered exactly what it was that Ellie Smith was trying to tell him ... or what it was that she was trying *not* to tell him. The point she had just made was exactly the one which he himself (rather proudly) had made to Sergeant Lewis, except that she had made it rather better.

'Now, second thing,' she said as each of them sat drinking again and (now) smoking. 'I want to ask you a favour. I said, didn't I, that me and Ashley—'

'Ashley and I.'

'Ashley and I are getting married, at the Registry Office—'

'Register Office,' corrected the pedantic Inspector.

'—and we wondered – *I* wondered – if you'd be willing to come along and be a witness.'

'Why me?'

'Because . . . well, no reason really, perhaps, except I'd like you to be there, with me mum. It'd make me . . . I'd be pleased, that's all.'

'When is it – the wedding?'

'"Wedding"? Sounds a bit posh, doesn't it? We're just getting married: no bridesmaids, no bouquets – and not too much bloody confetti, I hope.'

An avuncular Morse nodded, like an understanding senior citizen.

'Not like all the razzmatazz you probably had at your wedding,' she said.

Morse looked down at the carpet, as she had done earlier; then looked up again. For a second or two it was as though an electric current had shot across his forehead, and for some strange reason he found himself wanting to reach out across the table and just for a moment touch the hand of the young woman seated opposite.

'How are you getting home, Ellie?'

In the taxi ('Iffley Road – then the top of the Banbury Road,' Morse had instructed), Ellie had interlaced her fingers into his; and Morse felt moved and confused and more than a little loving.

'Did you see that watercolour?' she asked. 'The one just by our table? *Our* table?'

'No.'

'It was lovely – with fields and sheep and clouds. And the clouds . . .'

'What about them?' asked Morse quietly.

'Well, they were white at the top and then a sort of

middling, muddy grey, and then a darker grey at the bottom. Clouds are like that, aren't they?'

'Are they?' Morse, the non-Nephologist, had never consciously contemplated a cloud in his life, and he felt unable to comment further.

'It's just that – well, all I'm tryin' to say is that I enjoyed bein' with you, that's all. For a little while I felt I was on the top o' one o' them clouds, OK?'

After the taxi had dropped her off, and was making its way from East Oxford to North Oxford, Morse realized that he too had almost been on top of one of 'them clouds' that evening.

Back in his flat, he looked with some care at the only watercolour he had. The clouds there had been painted exactly as Ellie Smith had said. And he nodded to himself, just a little sadly.

CHAPTER FIFTY-ONE

Needles and pins, needles and pins,
When a man marries his trouble begins
(Old nursery rhyme)

IN THE waiting area of the Churchill Hospital, immediately Mrs Stevens had been called in to see her specialist, at 10.35 a.m. on Tuesday, 20 September, Brenda Brooks picked up a surprisingly recent issue of *Good Housekeeping*, and flicked through its glossy pages. But she found it difficult to concentrate on any particular article.

Brenda was a person who took much pleasure in the simple things of life. Others, she knew, had their yearnings for power or wealth or knowledge, but two of her own greatest delights were cleanliness and tidiness. What a joy she felt each week, for example, when she watched the dustmen casually hurl her black bags into the back of the yellow rubbish-cart – then seeing them no more. It seemed like Pilgrim finally ridding himself of his burden of sin.

For her own part, she had seldom made any mess at all in her life. But there was always an accumulation of things to be thrown away: bits of cabbage-leaves, and empty tins, and cigarette stubs from her husband's ashtrays ... Yes. It was always good to see the black bags, well, *disappear* really. You could put almost anything in them: bloodstained items like shirts, shoes, trousers – anything.

There were the green bags, too – the bags labelled 'Garden Waste', issued by Oxford City Council, at 50p apiece. Householders were permitted to put out two such bags every week; but the Brooks's garden was small, and Brenda seldom made use of more than one a fortnight.

Then there were those strong, transparent bags which Ted had brought home a couple of years ago, a heavy stack of them piled in the garden shed, just to the left of the lawn-mower. Precisely what purpose her husband had envisaged for such receptacles had been unclear, but they had occasionally proved useful for twigs and small branches, because the material from which they were manufactured was stout, heavy-duty stuff, not easily torn.

But the real joy of Brenda's life had ever centred on the manual skills – knitting, needlework, embroidery – for her hands had always worked confidently and easily with needles and crochet-hooks and bodkins and such things. Of late, too, she had begun to extend the area of her manual competence by joining a cake-icing class, although (as we have seen) it had been only with considerable and increasing pain that she had been able to continue the course, before finally being compelled to pack it up altogether.

She was still able, however, to indulge in some of her former skills; had, in fact, so very recently indulged in them when, wearing a leather glove instead of the uncomfortable Tubigrip, she had stitched the 'body-bag' (a word she had heard on the radio) in which her late and unlamented husband was destined to be wrapped. Never could she have imagined, of course, that the disposal of a body would cause a problem in her gently undemanding life. But it had, and she had seen to it. Not that the task had been a labour of love. Far from it. It had been a labour of hate.

She had watched, a few months earlier, some men who had come along and cut down a branch overarching the road there, about twelve feet long and about nine inches across. (Wasn't a human head about nine inches across?) The men had got rid of that pretty easily: just put it in that quite extraordinary machine they had – from which, after a scream of whirring, the thick wood had come out the other end . . . sawdust.

Then there was the furnace up at the Proctor Memorial School – that would have left even less physical trace perhaps. But (as Mrs Stevens had said) there was a pretty big problem of 'logistics' associated with such waste-disposal. And so, although Brenda had not quite understood the objection, this method had been discounted.

The Redbridge Waste Reception Area had seemed to her a rather safer bet. It was close enough, and there was no one there to ask questions about what you'd brought in your bags – not like the time she and Ted had come through Customs and the man with the gold on his hat had discovered all those cigarettes . . . No, they didn't ask you anything at the rubbish dump. You just backed the car up to the skip, opened the boot, and threw the bags down on to the great heap already there, soon to be carted away, and dumped, and bulldozed into a pit, and buried there.

But none of these methods had found favour.

Dis aliter visum.

The stiffish transparent bags measured 28½ inches by 36 inches, and Brenda had taken three. After slitting open the bottoms of two of them, she had stitched the three together cunningly, with a bodkin and some green garden string. She had then repeated the process, and prepared a second envelope. Then a third.

It was later to be recorded that at the time of his murder Mr Edward Brooks was 5 feet 8 inches in height, and 10½ stones in weight. And although the insertion of the body into the first, the second, and the third of the winding-sheets had been a traumatic event, it had not involved too troublesome an effort physically. Not for her, anyway.

Edward Brooks had been almost ready for disposal.

Almost.

By some happy chance, the roll of old brown carpet which had stood for over two years just to the right of the lawn-mower, measured 6 feet by 6 feet.

Ideal.

With some difficulty the body had been manipulated into its container, and four lengths of stout cord were knotted – very neatly! – around the bundle. The outer tegument made the whole thing a bit heavier, of course – but neater, too. And neatness, as we have seen, was an important factor in life (and now in death) for Brenda Brooks. The parcel, now complete, was ready for carriage.

It might be expected perhaps – expected certainly? – that such an experience would permanently have traumatized the soul of such a delicate woman as Mrs Brenda Brooks. But, strangely enough, such was not the case; and as she thought back on these things, and flicked through another few pages of *Good Housekeeping*, and waited for Mrs Stevens to re-emerge, she found herself half-smiling – if not with cruelty at least with a grim satisfaction . . .

There was an empty Walkers crisp-packet on the floor, just two seats away; and unostentatiously Brenda rose and picked it up, and placed it in the nearest wastepaper basket.

Mrs Stevens did not come out of the consulting-room until 11.20 a.m. that morning; and when she finally did, Brenda saw that her dearest friend in life had been weeping . . .

It had been that last little bit really.

'You've got some friends coming over from California, you say?'

'Yes. Just after Christmas. I've not seen them for almost ten years. I went to school with her – with the wife.'

'Can I suggest something? Please?' He spoke quietly.

'Of course.' Julia had looked up into the brown eyes of Basil Shepstone, and seen a deep and helpless sadness there. And she'd known what he was going to say.

'If it's possible . . . if it's at all possible, can you get your friends to come over, shall we say, a month earlier? A month or two earlier?'

CHAPTER FIFTY-TWO

I said this was fine utterance and sounded well
though it could have been polished and made to
mean less

(PETER CHAMPKIN, *The Sleeping Life of Aspern
Williams*)

THE CASE was not progressing speedily.

That, in his own words, is what Lewis felt embol-
dened to assert the following morning – the morning
of Wednesday, 21 September – as he sat in Morse's
office at HQ.

'Things are going a bit slow, sir.'

'That,' said Morse, 'is a figure of speech the literati
call "hyperbole", a rhetorical term for "exaggeration".
What I think you're trying to tell me is that we're
grinding to a dead halt. Right?'

Lewis nodded.

And Morse nodded.

They were both right . . .

Considerable activity had centred on the Brooks's
household following the finding of the bicycle, with
Brenda Brooks herself gladly co-operating. Yet there
seemed little about which she was able to co-operate,
apart from the retraction of her earlier statement that
her husband had been at home throughout the morn-

ing of Sunday, 28 August. In a nervous, gentle recantation, she was now willing (she'd said) to tell the police the whole truth. He had gone out on his bike, earlyish that morning; he had returned in a taxi, latish that morning – with a good deal of blood on his clothing. Her first thought, naturally enough, was that he'd been involved in a road accident. Somehow she'd got him into his pyjamas, into bed – and then, fairly soon afterwards, she'd called the ambulance, for she had suddenly realized that he was very ill. The bloodstained clothing she had put into a black bag and taken to the Redbridge Waste Reception Area the following morning, walking across the Iffley Road, then via Donnington Bridge Road to the Abingdon Road.

Not a very heavy load, she said.

Not so heavy as Pilgrim's, she thought.

That was almost all, though. The police could look round the house – of course, they could. There was nothing to hide, and they could take away whatever they liked. She fully understood: murder, after all, was a serious business. But no letters, no receipts, no addresses, had been found; few photographs, few mementos, few books; no drugs – certainly no drugs; nothing much at all apart from the pedestrian possessions of an undistinguished, unattractive man, whose only memorable achievement in life had been the murder of an Oxford don.

There had been just that one discovery, though, which had raised a few eyebrows, including (and particularly) the eyebrows of Brenda Brooks. Although only £217 was in Brooks's current account at Lloyds

Bank (Carfax branch), a building society book, found in a box beside Brooks's bed, showed a very healthy balance stashed away in the Halifax – a balance of £19,500. The box had been locked, but Brenda Brooks had not demurred when Lewis had asked her permission to force the lid – a task which he had accomplished with far more permanent damage than had been effected by the (still unidentified) thief at the Pitt Rivers Museum . . .

'You think he's dead?' asked Lewis.

'Every day that goes by makes it more likely.'

'We need a body, though.'

'We do. At least – with McClure – we had a body.'

'And a weapon.'

'And a weapon.'

'But with Brooks we've still not got a body.'

'And still not got a weapon,' added Morse rather miserably.

Ten minutes later, without knocking, Strange lumbered into the office. He had been on a week's furlough to the west coast of Scotland and had returned three days earlier. But this was his first day back at HQ, having attended a two-day Superintendents' Conference at Eastbourne.

He looked less than happy with life.

'How're things going, Morse?'

'Progressing, sir,' said Morse uneasily.

Strange looked at him sourly. 'You mean they're *not* progressing, is that it?'

'We're hoping for some developments—'

'Augh, don't give me that bullshit! Just tell me where we are – and don't take all bloody day over it.'

So Morse told him.

He knew (he said) – well, was ninety-nine per cent certain – that Brooks had murdered McClure: they'd got the knife from Brooks's kitchen, *without* any blood on it, agreed – but now they'd got his bike, *with* blood on it – McClure's blood on it. The only thing missing was Brooks himself. No news of him. No trace of him. Not yet. He'd last been seen by his wife, Brenda Brooks, and by Mrs Stevens – by the two of them together – on the afternoon of Wednesday, 7 September, the afternoon that the knife was stolen from the Pitt Rivers.

'Where does that leave us then?' asked Strange. 'Sounds as if you might just as well have taken a week's holiday yourself.'

'For what it's worth, sir, I think the two women are lying to us. I don't think they *did* see him that Wednesday afternoon. I think that one of them – or both of them – murdered Brooks. But not on that Wednesday – and not on the Thursday, either. I think that Brooks was murdered the day *before*, on the Tuesday; and I think that all this Pitt Rivers thingummy is a blind, arranged so that we should think there *was* a link-up between the two things. I think that they got somebody, some accomplice, to pinch the African knife – well, *any* knife from one of the cabinets there—'

'All right. You think – and you seem to be doing one helluva lot of "thinking", Morse – that the knife was stolen *the day after* Brooks was murdered.'

'Yes, sir.'

'Go on.'

Morse was very conscious that he had scarcely thought through his conclusions with any definitive clarity, but he ploughed on:

'It's all to do with their alibis. They couldn't have stolen the knife themselves – they were on a school bus going to Stratford. And so if we all make the obvious link, which we *do*, between the murder of Brooks and the theft, then they're in the clear, pretty well. You see, if Brooks's body is ever found, which I very strongly doubt—'

'What makes you say that?'

'Because if he's found, he won't have the Pitt Rivers knife stuck in him at all. It'll be *another* knife – like as not another kitchen knife. But they're certainly never going to let us find the body. That would mean the alibis they've fixed up for themselves have gone for a Burton.'

'What's the origin of that phrase?'

Morse shook his head. 'Something to do with beer, is it?'

Strange looked at his watch: just after midday. 'You know I was a bit surprised to find you here, Morse. I thought you'd probably gone for a Burton yourself.'

Morse smiled dutifully, and Lewis grinned hugely, as Strange continued: 'It's all too fanciful, mate. Stop thinking so much – and *do* something. Let's have a bit of action.'

'There's one other thing, sir. Lewis here got on to it . . .'

Morse gestured to his sergeant, the latter now taking up the narrative.

'Fellow called Davies, Ashley Davies. He's got quite a few connections with things, sir. He was on Staircase G in Drinkwater Quad when Matthew Rodway was there – had a fight with him, in fact, and got himself kicked out' – he looked at Morse – 'rusticated. The fight was about a girl, a girl called Eleanor Smith; and *she* was the girl who was Dr McClure's mistress. And now, Davies has got himself engaged to be married to her – *and* she's Brooks's step-daughter.'

'That's good, Lewis. That's just the sort of cumulative evidence I like to hear. Did *he* murder Brooks?'

'It's not that so much, sir. It's just that the Chief Inspector here . . .'

Lewis tailed off, and Morse took over.

'It's just that I'd been wondering why Miss Smith had agreed to marry him, that's all. And I thought that perhaps he might have done some favour for her. Lewis here found that he was in Oxford that Wednesday afternoon, and if it *was* Davies who went to the Pitt Rivers—'

'What! You're bringing *her* into it now? The daughter?'

'Step-daughter, sir.'

Strange shook his head. 'That's bad, Morse. You're in Disneyland again.'

Morse sighed, and sat back in the old black leather chair. He knew that his brief résumé of the case had been less than well presented; and, worse than that, realized that even if he'd polished it all up a bit, it still wouldn't have amounted to much. Might even have amounted to less.

Strange struggled to his feet.

'Hope you had a good holiday, sir,' remarked Lewis.

'No, I didn't. If you really want to know it was a bloody awful holiday. I got pissed off with it – rained all the bloody time.'

Strange waddled over to the door and stood there, offering a final piece of advice to his senior chief inspector: 'Just let's get cracking, mate. Find that body – or get Lewis here to find it for you. And when you do – you mark my words, Morse! – you'll find that thingummy knife o' yours stuck right up his rectum.'

After he was gone, Lewis looked across at a subdued and silent Morse.

'You know that "all the bloody time", sir? That's what they call – what the literati call – "hyperbole".'

Morse nodded, grinning weakly.

'And he wasn't just pissed off on his holiday, was he?'

'He wasn't?'

'No, sir. He was pissed *on* as well!'

Morse nodded again, grinning happily now, and looking at his watch.

'What about going for a Burton, Lewis?'

Chapter Fifty-Three

'Jo, my poor fellow!'

'I hear you, sir, in the dark, but I'm a-gropin –
a-gropin – let me catch hold of your hand.'

'Jo, can you say what I say?'

'I'll say anythink as you say, sir, for I knows it's
good.'

'OUR FATHER.'

'Our Father! – yes, that's wery good, sir.'

(CHARLES DICKENS, *Bleak House*)

WE MUST now briefly record several apparently disparate events which occurred between 21 and 24
September.

On Wednesday, 21, Julia Stevens was one of four people
who rang the JR2 to ask for the latest bulletin on Kevin
Costyn, who the previous day had been transferred to
the Intensive Care Unit. His doctors had become
increasingly concerned about a blood-clot in the brain,
and a decision would very shortly be taken about
possible surgery. For each of the four (including Kevin's mother) the message, couched in its conventionally
cautious terms, was the same: 'Critical but stable'.

Not very promising, Julia realized that. Considerably
better, though, than the prognosis on her own
condition.

As she lay in bed that night, she would gladly have prayed for herself, as well as for Kevin, had she managed to retain any residual faith in a personal deity. But she had not so managed. And as she lay staring up at the ceiling, knowing that she could never again look forward to any good nights, quite certainly not to any cheerful awakenings, she pondered how very much more easy such things must be for people with some comfortable belief in a future life. And for just a little while her resolution wavered sufficiently for her to find herself kneeling on the Golden Floor and quietly reciting the opening lines of the Lord's Prayer.

Photographs of the three young men involved in the Eastern Ring Road accident had appeared on page 2 of *The Star* (22 September), a free newspaper distributed throughout Oxford each Thursday. Below these photographs, a brief article had made no mention whatsoever of the concomitant circumstances of the 'accident'. But it was the dolichocephalic face of Kevin Costyn, appropriately positioned between his dead partner-in-crime, to the left, and his amputee partner-in-crime, to the right, that had caught the attention of one of the attendants at the Pitt Rivers Museum. In particular it had been the sight of the small crucifix earring that had jerked his jaded memory into sudden overdrive. Earlier the police had questioned all of them about whether they could remember anything unusual, or *anyone* unusual, on that Wednesday afternoon when Cabinet 52 had been forced. Like each of his colleagues, he'd had to admit that he couldn't.

But now he could.

Just before the museum closed, on Thursday, 22 September, he walked along the passage, up the stone steps, and diffidently knocked on the door of the Administrator (capital 'A').

Late that same afternoon Morse asked Lewis an unusual question.

'If you had to get a wedding present, what sort of thing would you have in mind – for the bride?'

'You don't do it that way, sir. You buy a present for both of them. They'll have a list, like as not – you know, dinner-service, saucepans, set of knives—'

'Very funny!'

'Well, if you don't want to lash out too much you can always get her a tin-opener or an orange-squeezer.'

'Not exactly much help in times of trouble, are you?'

'Ellie Smith, is it?'

'Yes.' Morse hesitated. 'It's just that I'd like to buy her something . . . for herself.'

'Well, there's nothing to stop you giving her a personal present – just forget the wedding bit. Perfume, say? Scarf? Gloves? Jewellery, perhaps? Brooch? Pendant?'

'Ye-es. A nice little pendant, perhaps . . .'

'So long as her husband's not going to mind somebody else's present hanging round her neck all the time.'

'Do people still get jealous these days, Lewis?'

'I don't think the world'll get rid of jealousy in a hurry, sir.'

'No. I suppose not,' said Morse slowly.

Five minutes later the phone rang.

It was the Administrator.

In the Vaults Bar at The Randolph at lunchtime on Friday, 23 September, Ellie Smith pushed her half-finished plate of lasagne away from her and lit a cigarette.

'Like I say, though, it's nice of him to agree, isn't it?'

'Oh, give it a rest, Ellie! Don't start talking about *him* again.'

'You jealous or something?'

Ashley Davies smiled sadly.

'Yeah, I suppose I am.'

She leaned towards him, put her hand on his arm, and gently kissed his left cheek.

'You silly noodle!'

'Perhaps everybody feels a bit jealous sometimes.'

'Yeah.'

'You mean *you* do?'

Ellie nodded. 'Awful thing – sort of corrosive. Yuk!'

There was a silence between them.

'What are you thinking about?' he asked.

Ellie stubbed out her cigarette, and pushed her chair back from the table. 'Do you really want to know?'

'Please tell me.'

'I was just wondering what *she*'s like that's all.'

'Who are you talking about?'

'*Mrs* Morse.'

The sun had drifted behind the clouds, and Ashley got up and paid the bill.

A few minutes later, her arm through his, they walked along Cornmarket, over Carfax, and then through St Aldate's to Folly Bridge, where they stood and looked down at the waters of the Thames.

'Would you like to go on a boat trip?' he asked.

'What, this afternoon?'

'Why not? Up to Iffley Lock and back? Won't take long.'

'No. Not for me.'

'What would you like to do?'

She felt a sudden tenderness towards him, and wished to make him happy.

'Would you like to come along to my place?'

The sun had slipped out from behind the clouds, and was shining brightly once more.

CHAPTER FIFTY-FOUR

Cambridge has espoused the river, has opened its arms to the river, has built some of its finest Houses alongside the river. Oxford has turned its back on the river, for only at some points downstream from Folly Bridge does the Isis glitter so gloriously as does the Cam

(J. J. SMITHFIELD-WATERSTONE,
Oxford and Cambridge: A Comparison)

THE TWO rivers, the Thames (or Isis) and the Cherwell, making their confluence just to the south of the City Centre, have long provided enjoyable amenities for Oxford folk, both Town and Gown: punting, rowing, sculling, canoeing, and pleasure-boating. For the less athletic, and for the more arthritic, the river-cruise down from Folly Bridge via the Iffley and Sandford locks to Abingdon, has always been a favourite.

For such a trip, Mr Anthony Hughes, a prosperous accountant now living out on Boar's Hill, had booked two tickets on a fifty-passenger steamer, the *Iffley Princess*, timetabled to sail from Folly Bridge at 9.15 a.m. on Sunday, 25 September.

The previous evening he had slowly traced the course of the river on the Ordnance Survey Map, pointing out to his son such landmarks as the Green Bank, the Gut, the concrete bridge at Donnington,

Haystacks Corner, and the rest, which they would pass before arriving at Iffley Lock.

For young James, the morrow's prospects were magical. He was in several ways an attractive little chap – earnest, bespectacled, bright – with his name down for the Dragon School in North Oxford, a preparatory school geared (indeed, fifth-geared) to high academic and athletic excellence. The lad was already exhibiting an intelligent and apparently insatiable interest both in his own locality and in the Universe in general. Such Aristotelian curiosity was quite naturally a great delight to his parents; and the four-and-a-half year old young James was picking up, and mentally hoarding, bits of knowledge with much the same sort of regularity that young Jason was picking up, and physically hurling, bits of brick and stone around the Cutteslowe Estate.

Spanning the fifty-yard-wide Isis, and thus linking the Iffley Road with Abingdon Road, Donnington Bridge was a flattish arc of concrete, surmounted by railings painted, slightly incongruously, a light Cambridge-blue. And as the *Iffley Princess* rounded the Gut, young James pointed to the large-lettered SOMERVILLE, followed by two crossed oars, painted in black on a red background, across the upper part of the bridge, just below the parapet railings.

'What's that, Dad?'

But before the proud father could respond, this question was followed by another:

'What's *that*, Dad?'

Young James pointed to an in-cut, on the left, where a concrete slipway had been constructed to allow owners of cars to back the boats they were towing directly down into the river. There, trapped at the side of the slipway, was what appeared to be an elongated bundle, a foot or so below the surface of the nacre-green water. And several of the passengers on the port side now spotted the same thing: something potentially sinister; something wrapped up; but something no longer wholly concealed.

Fred Andrews, skipper of the *Iffley Princess*, pulled over into Salters' Boat Yard, only some twenty yards below the bridge. He was an experienced waterman, and decided to dial 999 immediately. It was only after he had briefly explained his purpose to his passengers that an extraordinarily ancient man, seated in the bow of the boat, and dressed in a faded striped blazer, off-white flannels, and a straw boater, produced a mobile telephone from somewhere about his person, and volunteered to dial the three nines himself.

CHAPTER FIFTY-FIVE

It's a strong stomach that has no turning
(OLIVER HERFORD)

FROM Donnington Bridge Road, Lewis turned right
into Meadow Lane, then almost immediately left, along
a broad track, where wooden structures on the right
housed the Sea Cadet Corps and the Riverside Centre.
Ahead of him, painted in alternate bands of red and
white, was a barrier, open now and upright; and beyond
the barrier, four cars, one Land-Rover, and one black
van; and a group of some fifteen persons standing
round something – something covered with greyish
canvas.

Forty or fifty other persons were standing on the
bridge, just to the left, leaning over the railings and
surveying the scene some fifty feet below them, like
members of the public watching the Boat Race on one
of the bridges between Mortlake and Putney. And
seated silently beside Lewis, **Morse** himself would willingly have allowed any one of these ghoulish gawpers
to look in his stead beneath the canvas, at the body just
taken from the Thames.

Events had moved swiftly after the first emergency call
to St Aldate's. PC Carter had arrived within ten minutes

in a white police car and had been more than grateful for the advice of the Warden of the Riverside Centre, a dark, thick-set man, who had dealt with many a body during his twenty-five years' service there. The Underwater Search Unit had been summoned from Sulhamstead; and in due course a doctor. The body, that of a man, still sheeted in plastic, but now in danger of slithering out of its wrapping of carpet, had been taken from the water, placed at the top of the slipway – and promptly covered up, untouched. St Aldate's CID had been contacted immediately, and Inspector Morrison had arrived to join a scene-of-crimes officer, and a police photographer. With the arrival of a cheerful young undertaker, just before noon, the cast was almost complete.

Apart from Morse and Lewis.

The reasons for such a sequence of events was clear enough to those directly and closely involved; clear even to a few of the twitchers, with their powerful binoculars, who had swelled the ranks of the bridge spectators. For this was clearly not a run-of-the-mill drowning. Even through the triple layers of plastic sheeting in which the body was wrapped, one thing stood out clearly (*literally* stood out clearly): the broad handle of a knife which appeared to be wedged firmly into the dead man's back. And when, under Morrison's careful directions – after many photographic flashings, from many angles – the stitching at the top of the improvised body-bag had been painstakingly unpicked, and one pocket of the corpse had been painstakingly picked (as it were), the identity of the man was quickly established.

On the noticeboard in the foyer of St Aldate's station was pinned a photograph of a 'Missing Person' whom the police were most anxious to trace; and beneath the photograph there appeared a name, together with a few physical details. But it was not the corpse's blackened features which Morrison had recognized; it was the name he found in the sodden wallet.

The name of Edward Brooks.

Thus was a further relay of telephone-calls initiated. Thus was Morse himself now summoned to the scene.

Sometimes procedures worked well; and sometimes (as now) there was every reason for the police to be congratulated on the way situations were handled. On this occasion one thing only (perhaps two?) had marred police professionalism.

PC Carter, newly recruited to the Force, had been reasonably well prepared for the sight of a body, particularly one so comparatively well preserved as this one. What he had been totally unprepared for was the indescribable stench which had emanated from the body even before the Inspector had authorized the opening of the envelope: a stench which was the accumulation, it seemed, of the dank depths of the river, of blocked drains, of incipient decomposition – of death itself. And PC Carter had turned away, and vomited rather noisily into the Thames, trusting that few had observed the incident.

But inevitably almost everyone, including the audience in the gods, had noticed the brief, embarrassing incident.

It was Morse's turn now.

Phobias are common enough. Some persons suffer from arachnophobia, or hypsophobia, or myophobia, or pterophobia ... Well-nigh everyone suffers occasionally from thanatophobia; many from necrophobia – although Morse was not really afraid of dead bodies at all, or so he told himself. What he really suffered from was a completely new phobia, one that was all his own: *the fear of being sick* at the sight of bodies which had met their deaths in strange or terrible circumstances. Even Morse, for all his classical education, was unable to coin an appropriately descriptive, or etymologically accurate, term for such a phobia: and even had he been so able, the word would certainly have been pretentiously polysyllabic.

Yet, for all his weakness, Morse was a far more experienced performer than PC Carter; and hurriedly taking the Warden to one side, he had swiftly sought directions to the nearest loo. It was not, therefore, into the Thames, but into a lone lavatory-pan in the Riverside Centre, that Chief Inspector Morse vomited, late that Sunday morning.

'Been in the river about a fortnight, they reckon,' ventured Lewis when Morse finally emerged.

'Good! That fits nicely,' replied the pale-faced Morse.

'You OK, sir?'

COLIN DEXTER

'Course I'm bloody OK, man!' snapped Morse.

But Lewis was not in the least offended, for he and Morse were long acquainted; and Lewis knew all his ways.

CHAPTER FIFTY-SIX

He could not be a lighterman or river-carrier;
there was no clue to what he looked for, but he
looked for something with a most intent and
searching gaze
(CHARLES DICKENS, *Our Mutual Friend*)

IF A few minutes earlier it had been his stomach that
was churning over, it was now the turn of Morse's brain;
and somehow he managed, at least for a while, to look
down again at the semi-sealed body. Heavy condensa-
tion between the plastic layers was preventing any close
inspection of the knife stuck into the corpse's back. But
Morse was determined to be patient: better than most,
he knew the value of touching nothing further there;
and to be truthful he had been more than a little
surprised that Morrison had gone as far as he had.

Nothing further, therefore, was touched until the
arrival of the police pathologist, Dr Laura Hobson,
whose bright-red Metro joined the little convoy of
vehicles half an hour later. Briefly she and Morse
conversed. After which, with delicate hands, she performed a few delicate tasks; whilst Morse walked slowly
from the scene, along a track between a line of trees
and the riverbank, up to a building housing the Falcon
Rowing Club, some seventy yards upstream to his right.
Here he stood looking around him, wondering earnestly what exactly he should be looking for.

After returning to the slipway, he took the Warden to one side and put to him some of the questions that were exercising his mind. Where perhaps might the corpse have been pushed into the river? How could the corpse have been conveyed to such a spot? In which direction, and how far, could the corpse have been conveyed by the prevailing flow of the waters?

The Warden proved to be intelligent and informative. After stressing the importance, in all such considerations, of time of year, weather conditions, river-temperature, volume of water, and frequency of river-traffic; after giving Morse a clear little lesson on buoyancy and flotation, he suggested a few likely answers. As follows.

The strong probability was that the body had not been shifted all that far by the prevailing flow; indeed, if it had been slightly more weighted down, the body might have rested permanently on the bottom; as things were, the body could well have been put into the river at a point just beside the Falcon Rowing Club; certain it was that the body would not have drifted *against* the north–south movement of the tide. The only objection to such a theory was that it would have been an inordinately long way for anyone to carry such a weighty bundle. With the barrier locked down across the approach road to the slipway, no car (unless authorized) could even have reached the river at that point, let alone turned right there and deposited a body sixty, seventy yards upstream.

Unless . . .

Well, there were just over a hundred members of the Riverside Club who possessed boats, who used the slipway fairly regularly, and who were issued with a key to the barrier. Not infrequently (the Warden confessed) a boat-owner neglected to close the barrier behind him; or deliberately left it open for a colleague known to be sailing up behind. And so . . . if the barrier happened to be left open – well, not much of a problem, was there?

'You know what I'd've done, Mr Holmes, if I'd had to dispose of a body here?' Morse's eyes slowly rose to the top of Donnington Bridge, where public interest was, if anything, increasing, in spite of the makeshift screen which had now been erected around the body.

'You tell me.'

'I'd have driven here, about two o'clock in the morning, and pushed it over the bridge.'

'Helluva splash, you'd make,' said the Warden.

'Nobody around to hear it, though.'

'A few people around then, Inspector. You know who they are?'

Morse shook his head.

'Three lots o' people, really: lovers, thieves, police.'

'Oh!' said Morse.

Twenty minutes later the young pathologist got to her feet – the grim, grisly preliminary examination over.

'Mustn't do much more here,' she reported. 'Been in the river between a week and a fortnight, I'd guess. Difficult to say – he's pretty well preserved. Neat little job of packaging somebody did there. But we'll sort him out later. All right?'

Morse nodded. 'We're in your hands.'

'Not much doubt he's been murdered, though – unless he died, then somebody stuck a knife in him, then wrapped him all up and put him in the river here.'

'Seems unlikely,' conceded Morse.

Dr Hobson was packing up her equipment when Morse spoke again:

'You'll be sure not to touch the knife until—?'

'You've not got much faith in some of your colleagues, have you?'

She was an attractive young woman; and when first she had taken over from the sadly missed Max, Morse had felt he could almost have fallen a little in love with her. But now he dreamed of her no longer.

Morse had taken the sensible (almost unprecedented) precaution of refraining from a few pints of beer on a Sunday lunchtime; and at 3.15 p.m. he and Lewis stood in the path lab beside the prone body of Edward Brooks, the plastic bags in which he had been inserted lying folded neatly at his feet, like the linen wraps at the Resurrection. Apart from Dr Hobson herself, two further forensic assistants and a fingerprint expert stood quite cheerfully around the body, in which the handle of a broad knife stood up straight.

Yet it was not the handle itself, so carefully dusted now with fingerprint-powder, which had riveted Morse's attention. It was the label attached to the side of the handle; a label whose lettering, though washed and smudged by the waters of the Thames, was still partially legible on its right-hand side:

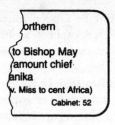

'*I just do not believe this,*' whispered Morse slowly.

'Pardon, sir?'

But Morse was not listening. He touched Laura Hobson lightly on the shoulder of her starched white coat, and for the second time that day asked for the quickest way to the nearest Gents.

CHAPTER FIFTY-SEVEN

> Karl Popper teaches that knowledge is advanced
> by the positing and testing of hypotheses. Count-
> less hypotheses, I believe, are being tested at once
> in the unconscious mind; only the winning short-
> list is handed to our consciousness
> (MATTHEW PARRIS, *The Times*, 7 March 1994)

THE FOLLOWING day, Monday, 26 September, both
Morse and Lewis arrived fairly early, just after 7 a.m., at
Thames Valley HQ.

Morse himself had slept poorly, his eyeballs ceaselessly circling in their sockets throughout the night as
the dramatic new development in the case had gradually established itself into the pattern of his thinking;
for in truth he had been astonished at the discovery
that Brooks had been murdered *after* the theft of the
Rhodesian knife; murdered in fact *by* the Rhodesian
knife.

As he had hitherto analysed the case, assessing
motive and opportunity and means, Morse had succeeded in convincing himself that two or perhaps three
persons, acting to some degree in concert, had probably been responsible for Brooks's murder. Each of the
three (as Morse saw things) would have regarded the
death of Brooks, though for slightly different reasons,
as of considerable benefit to the human race.

Three suspects.

Three women: the superficially gentle Brenda Brooks, who had suffered sorely in the role of the neglected and maltreated wife; the enigmatic Mrs Stevens, who had developed a strangely strong bond between herself and her cleaning-lady; and the stepdaughter, Eleanor Smith, who had left home in her mid-teens, abused (how could Morse know?) mentally, or verbally, or physically, or sexually even . . .

Women set apart from the rest of their kind by the sign of the murderer – by the mark of Cain.

A confusing figuration of 'if's' had permutated itself in Morse's restless brain that previous night, filtering down to exactly the same shortlist as before, since the Final Arbiter had handed to Morse the same three envelopes. In the first, as indeed in the second, the brief verdict was typed out in black letters: 'Not Guilty'; but in the third, Morse had read the even briefer verdict, typed out here in red capitals: 'GUILTY'. And the name on the front of the third envelope was – *Eleanor Smith.*

For almost an hour, Morse and Lewis had spoken together that morning: spoken of thoughts, ideas, hypotheses. And when he returned from the canteen with two cups of coffee at 8 a.m., Lewis stated, starkly and incontrovertibly, the simple truth they both had to face:

'You know, I just don't see – I just *can't* see – how Brenda Brooks, or this Mrs Stevens – how either of them could have done it. We've not exactly had a video-camera on them since the knife was stolen – but not far off. All right, they'd got enough motive. But I just don't see when they had the opportunity.'

'Nor do I,' said Morse quietly. And Lewis was encouraged to continue.

'I know what you mean about Mrs Stevens, sir. And I agree. There's somebody pretty clever behind all this, and she's the only one of the three who's got the brains to have thought it all out. But as I say . . .'

Morse appeared a little pained as Lewis continued:

'. . . she couldn't have done it. And Mrs Brooks couldn't have done it either, could she? She's got the best motive of any of them, and she'd probably have the nerve as well. But she couldn't have *planned* it all, surely, even if somehow she had the opportunity – that night, say, after she got back from Stratford. I just don't see it.'

'Nor do I,' repeated Morse, grimacing as he sipped another mouthful of weak, luke-warm coffee.

'So unless we're looking in completely the wrong direction, sir, that only leaves . . .'

But Morse was only half listening. 'Unless', Lewis had just said . . . the same word the Warden had used the previous day when he'd been talking of the red-and-white striped barrier. In Morse's mind there'd earlier been a *logical* barrier to his hypothesis that Brooks's body must have been taken to the Thames in some sort of vehicle – as well as that *literal* barrier. But the Warden had merely lifted that second barrier, hadn't he? Just physically lifted it out of the way.

So what if he, Morse, were now to lift that earlier barrier too?

'Lewis! Get the car, and nip along and have a word with the headmaster of the Proctor Memorial. Tell him we'd like to see Mrs Stevens again. We can either go round to her house or, if she prefers, she can come here.'

'Important, is it, sir?'

'Oh, yes,' said Morse. 'And while you're at it, you can drop me off at the path lab. I want another quick word with the lovely Laura.'

CHAPTER FIFTY-EIGHT

Now faith is the substance of things hoped for,
the evidence of things not seen

(*Hebrews*, ch. 11, v. 1)

COMING OUT of her lab to greet Morse, Dr Laura
Hobson appeared incongruously contented with her
work. She pointed to the door behind her.

'You'd better not go in there, Chief Inspector. Not
for the minute. We've nearly finished, though – the
main bits, anyway.'

'Anything interesting?'

'Do you call stomach contents interesting?'

'No.'

'Looks as if they've got some vague prints all right,
though – on the knife. I'll keep my fingers crossed for
you. We're all hoping, you know that.'

'Thank you.' Morse hesitated. 'It may sound a bit
far-fetched I know, but . . .'

'Yes?'

'The knife – I'm doing a little bit of hoping myself –
the knife used to murder McClure was very similar to'
– Morse nodded towards the main lab – 'to the knife
that was stolen from the Pitt Rivers.'

'Yes, I knew that.'

'What I was wondering is this. Is there any possibility
– any possibility at all – that Brooks was murdered with

another knife – one of the same type, one with the same sort of blade – *then* for the knife you've got in there – the one with the possible prints on it – to be stuck in him . . . *afterwards?*'

Laura Hobson looked at him curiously.

'Have two knives, you mean? Stick one in him, take it out, then stick the other in?'

Morse looked uneasy, yet there was still some flicker of hope in his face. 'When I said "afterwards", I meant, well, a few *hours* later – a day even?'

With a sad smile, she shook her head. 'No chance. Unless your murderer's got the luck of the devil and the skill of a brain-surgeon—'

'Or a boy with a model-aeroplane kit?'

'—you'd have some clear *external* evidence of the two incisions – and don't forget he was stabbed through his clothes.'

'And there aren't . . . ?'

'No. No signs at all. Besides that, though, you'd have all the *internal* evidence: the two separate termini of the knife-points; two distinct sets of lacerations on either side of—'

'I see, yes,' mumbled Morse.

'I don't know whether you do, though. Look! Let me explain. Whenever you have a knife-wound—'

'Please, not!' said Morse. 'I believe all you say. It's just that I've never been able to follow all these physiological labellings. They didn't teach us any of that stuff at school.'

'I know,' said Laura quietly. 'You did Greek instead. You told me once, remember, in our . . . in our earlier days, Chief Inspector?'

Feeling more than a little embarrassed, Morse avoided her eyes.

'How would it have helped, anyway?' continued Laura, in a more business-like tone.

'Well, I've been assuming all along that the theft of the knife from the Pitt Rivers was a blind: a blind to establish an alibi, or alibis; to try to establish the fact that Brooks wasn't murdered until *after* the knife was stolen.'

She nodded, appreciating the point immediately. 'You mean, if he'd been murdered on a particular day with one knife, and then, the day after, a second knife was stolen; and if the first knife was subsequently removed from the body, and the second knife inserted into the wound – people like the police, like you, could well have been misled about the time of death.'

'That's a splendidly constructed sentence,' said Morse.

'Waste of breath, though, really. *I* wouldn't have been misled.'

'You're sure?'

'Ninety-nine per cent sure.'

'Could you just rule out the other one per cent – for me? Please?'

'Waste of time. But I will, yes, if that's what you want.'

'I'm very grateful.'

'Don't you want to see the contents of his pockets? His clothes?'

'I suppose I ought to, yes.'

Again she looked at him curiously. 'It's as if you've

been putting your ... well, your *faith* in something, isn't it? And I feel I've let you down.'

'I lost all my faith a long time ago, I'm afraid.'

'Much better to have *evidence*, in our job.'

Morse nodded; and followed Laura Hobson's shapely legs into a side-room, where she gestured to a table by the window.

'I'll leave you to it, Chief Inspector.'

Morse sat down and first looked through the official 'In Possession Property' form, listing the items found on Brooks's person.

The wallet which had been removed at the river-side to establish identity (and which Morse had already looked through, anyway) was among the items, and he quickly examined its few (now dry) contents once more: one £10 note; one £5 note; a Lloyds Bank plastic card; an ID card for the Pitt Rivers Museum; a card showing official membership of the East Oxford Conservative Club. Nothing else. No photographs; no letters.

Nor were the other items listed and laid out there in small transparent bags of any obvious interest: a black comb; a white handkerchief; £2.74 in assorted coinage; what had once been a half-packet of now melted indigestion tablets; and a bunch of seven keys. It was this latter item only which appeared to Morse worthy of some brief consideration.

The biggest key, some 3 inches in length, was grimy dark-brown in colour, and looked like a door-key; as perhaps did the two Yale keys, one a khaki colour, the other shinily metallic. The other four keys were (possibly?) for things like a garden shed or a bicycle-lock or a briefcase or a box or ... But Morse's brain was suddenly engaged now: the fourth small key, a sturdy, silvery key, had the number 'X10' stamped upon it; and Morse gazed through the window, and wondered. Was it one of a set of keys? A key to what? A key to where? Would it help to spend a few hours sorting out these seven keys and matching them to their locks? Probably not. Probably a waste of time. But he ought to do it, he knew that. So he would do it. Or rather he'd get Lewis to do it.

From the dead man's clothing Morse quickly decided that nothing could be gleaned which could further the investigation one whit; and he was standing up now, preparing to leave, when Laura came back into the small room.

Phone-call for Morse. Sergeant Lewis. In her office.

Lewis was ringing from the Head's office of the Proctor Memorial School. Mrs Julia Stevens had been granted temporary leave from her duties. Well, indefinite leave really – but the terminological inexactitude had avoided any difficult embarrassment all round. She would not be returning to school, ever; she had only a few months to live; and a supply teacher had already taken over her classes. Soon everyone would have to know, of course; but not yet. She wasn't at home, though; she'd gone away on a brief holiday, abroad –

the Head had known that, too. Gone off with a friend, destination unknown.

'Do we know who the friend is?' asked Morse.

'Well, *you* do, don't you?'

'I could make a guess.'

'Makes you wonder if they're guilty after all, doesn't it?'

'Or innocent,' suggested Morse slowly.

The condition of Kevin Costyn was markedly improved. With no surgery now deemed necessary, he had been removed from the ICU the previous lunchtime; and already the police had been given permission to interview him – at least about the accident.

Very soon he would be interviewed about other matters, too. But although he was reluctantly willing to talk about ram-raiding and stolen vehicles, he would say nothing whatsoever about the murder of Edward Brooks. He may have lied and cheated his way through life, but there was one promise, now, that he was never going to break.

Seated in the sunshine outside a small but fairly expensive hotel overlooking La Place de la Concorde, Julia reached out and clinked her friend's glass with her own; and both women smiled.

'How would you like to live here, Brenda?'

'Lordy me! Lovely. Lovely, isn't it, Mrs Stevens?'

'Anywhere you'd rather be?'

COLIN DEXTER

'Oh no. This is the very best place in the whole world – apart from Oxford, of course.'

Since she'd arrived, Julia had felt so very tired; but so very happy, too.

CHAPTER FIFTY-NINE

St Anthony of Egypt (c. 251–356 AD): hermit and
founder of Christian monasticism. An ascetic who
freely admitted to being sorely beset by virtually
every temptation, and most especially by sexual
temptation. Tradition has it that he frequently
invited a nightly succession of naked women to
parade themselves in front of him as he lay, hands
manacled behind his back, in appropriately transparent yet not wholly claustrophobic sacking

(SIMON SMALL, *An Irreverent Survey of the Saints*)

AT 9.30 A.M. on Tuesday, 27 September, Morse
walked down the High from Carfax. There were several
esteemed jewellers' shops there, he knew that; and he
looked in their windows. He was somewhat uncertain,
however, of what exactly to purchase – and wholly
uncertain about whether his present errand was being
made easier, or more difficult, by his strong suspicion
now that it had been Eleanor Smith who had murdered
her step-father (the same Eleanor who had formally
identified the body the previous day). Perhaps in a
sense it was going to be easier, though, since in all
probability he wasn't looking for a wedding present any
longer, the prospect of an imminent marriage now
seeming increasingly remote. Yet for some reason he
still wanted to buy the girl a present: a personal present.

Something like Lewis had suggested.

'How much is that?' he asked a young female assistant in the shop just across from the Covered Market.

'Nice little pendant, isn't it, sir? Delicate, tasteful,
and quite inexpensive, really.'

'How much is it?' repeated Morse.

'Only £35, sir.'

Only!

Morse looked down at the representation on the tiny
oval pendant of – of somebody? 'St Christopher, is it?'

'St Anthony, sir. A well-known Christian saint.'

'I thought he was the patron saint of Lost Property.'

'Perhaps you're thinking of a later St Anthony?'

But Morse wasn't. He thought there'd only been one
St Anthony.

'If . . . if I bought this, I'd need a chain as well,
wouldn't I?'

'It would be difficult to wear without a chain, yes.'

She was laughing at him, Morse knew that; but it
hadn't been a very bright question. And very soon he
was surveying a large selection of chains: chains with
varied silver- or gold-content; chains of slightly larger
or slightly smaller links; chains of different lengths;
chains of differing prices.

So Morse made his purchase: pendant plus chain
(the cheapest).

Then, after only a few steps outside the jeweller's up
towards Carfax Tower, he performed a sudden U-turn,
returning to the shop and asking if he could please
exchange the chain (not the pendant) for something a
little more expensive. The assistant (still smiling at
him?) was happily co-operative; and five minutes later

Morse started walking once again up towards Carfax. With a different chain.

With the most expensive chain there.

He was ready for the interview.

When earlier he had rung Eleanor Smith, she had sounded in no way surprised that the police should wish to take her fingerprints – for 'elimination purposes', as Morse had emphasized. And when he'd explained that it was against the rule-book for anyone who had been at the scene of the river-side discovery (as *he* had been) to go anywhere near the homes of those who might possibly be involved with the, er, the investigation, she'd agreed to go along to Thames Valley HQ. A car would pick her up. At 11.15 a.m.

Morse just had time to call in at Sainsbury's supermarket, on the Kidlington roundabout, where he made his few purchases swiftly, and found himself the only person at the 'small-basket' check-out. Just the four items, in fact: two small tins of baked beans; one small brown loaf; and a bottle of Glenfiddich.

Chapter Sixty

When the Himalayan peasant meets the he-bear
  in his pride,
He shouts to scare the monster, who will often
  turn aside.
But the she-bear thus accosted rends the peasant
  tooth and nail.
For the female of the species is more deadly than
  the male
  (RUDYARD KIPLING, *The Female of the Species*)

'WHAT LINE are you going to take with her, sir?'

'I'm not at all sure. All I know is that if any of our three ladies actually murdered Brooks – and pretty certainly one of them did – we can forget the other two, wherever they're sunning themselves at the minute. It's odds on that one of them, or both of them, had some part to play in the plot; but I'm sure that neither of them could have murdered Brooks. It's a physical impossibility, knowing what we do about dates and times. But *she* could have done. Ellie Smith could have done – if only just. She went to Birmingham that Wednesday – you've checked on that. But we can't be sure when she came back, can we? You see, if she'd come back an hour, even half an hour earlier . . .'

'*She* could have stolen the knife, you mean?'

'Or she could have got someone to steal it for her.'

'Ashley Davies.'

'Yes. Could well have been. Then he gets his reward: he gets the hand of the increasingly desirable Miss Smith – a young woman he's had his lecherous eyes on even when she was a sleep-around-with-anybody girl.'

'What about the attendant at the Pitt Rivers, though? He says he probably saw this young fellow Costyn there.'

'It's always dodgy though – this identification business. We can't rely on that.'

Lewis nodded. 'He doesn't seem to have any real link with the case, anyway.'

'Except with Mrs Stevens. She taught him, remember. And I suppose if he's on drugs or something – got a regular habit to feed – short of cash – and if she was prepared to pay—'

'You mean she got him to steal the knife – for somebody else? For Ellie Smith, say?'

'Who else?'

'But you've always thought—'

'Give it a bloody rest, Lewis, will you?' snarled Morse. 'Do you think I get any pleasure from all this? Do you think I *want* to get Ellie Smith in here this morning and take her prints and tell her that she's a bloody liar and that she knifed her sod of a step-father?'

He got up and walked to the window.

'No, I don't think that,' said the ill-used Lewis quietly. 'It's just that I'm getting confused, that's all.'

'And you think I'm *not*?'

No, Lewis didn't think that. And he wondered whether his next little item of news was likely to clarify or further to befuddle the irascible Chief Inspector's brain.

'While you were shopping, I went down to Wolsey and had another look in Mrs Ewers' pantry.'

'And?'

'Well, something rang a bit of a bell when we found Brooks's body: those plastic bags. Do you remember when we first went to the Staircase?'

'The pile of them there in the pantry, yes.'

Lewis sought to hide his disappointment. 'You never said anything.'

'There's no end of those around.'

'I just thought that if Brooks used to take a few things home occasionally, unofficially – toilet-rolls, cartons of detergent, that sort of thing . . .'

'We could have a look in Brooks's place, yes. Where do you reckon he'd keep them?'

'Garden shed?'

'We'd need a search warrant . . . unless, Lewis—'

'Oh no! I'm not forcing any more locks, sir. Look what a mess I made of the box in his bedroom.'

'Perhaps you won't need to.' Morse opened a drawer of his desk and took out the bunch of keys. 'I'd like to bet one of these fits the garden shed; but I doubt we're going to find any bags there. They'll have been too careful for that.'

'What are you thinking of exactly?'

'Well, you'd have expected a few prints on the plastic bags, don't you think? But there aren't any, it seems. The water wouldn't have washed them off completely, I'm told. So they wore gloves all the time. And then they took good care to make sure the body wouldn't float, agreed? There's a gash in the bags, through all three layers – I don't think that was caused accidentally in the river. I think it was made deliberately, to let the air out, and get the body to sink ... at least, temporarily. That's what the Warden thought, too.'

Yes, Lewis remembered. Holmes had claimed that unless any body was weighted down it would almost certainly have come up towards the surface sooner or later because of the body's natural gases.

'Why do you think they – somebody – went to all that trouble with the bags, sir? It's almost as if ...'

'Go on, Lewis!'

'As if somebody *wanted* the body to be found.'

'Ye-es.' Morse was gazing across the yard once more. 'You know what's buggering us up the whole time, don't you? It's simply that we're going to have one helluva job making out a case against *anybody*. If somebody like Helena Kennedy, QC, was hired for the defence, she'd make mincemeat of us: we've got all the motive in the world; and all the means – but we just can't find any bloody *opportunity* ... except at about teatime on that Wednesday afternoon. They've been too clever for us. But it's not just cleverness: it's ruthlessness too. Not a blatant ruthlessness, but certainly a latent ruthlessness – latent in all three of them. Something that suddenly hardened into a cold-blooded resolve to get rid of Brooks – not just because they knew, *must* have known, that he was a murderer himself, but for an even better reason. Hatred.'

There was a knock at the door, and a WPC announced that Ms Smith was now seated in Reception.

'Bring her up, please,' said Morse, quickly opening a small, square black box, lined with white satin, and passing it across to Lewis.

'What d'you think?'

Lewis, like Dr Hobson the previous day, looked across at Morse most curiously.

'But if what you say's right, sir, she's going to have to postpone the happy day indefinitely – for quite a few years, perhaps.'

'She can still sit in a cell and twiddle it in her fingers. No law against that, is there?'

But before Lewis could remind Morse of the very strict and very sensible prison regulations regarding necklaces and the like, there was another knock at the door, and Morse swiftly took back the pendant of St Anthony – plus his golden chain.

CHAPTER SIXTY-ONE

The total amount of undesired sex endured by women is probably greater in marriage than in prostitution

(BERTRAND RUSSELL, *Marriage and Morals*)

AFTER ROLLING the little finger of her left hand across the pad, after pressing it firmly on to the fingerprint-form, Eleanor Smith had finished; and Lewis now asked her to add her signature to the form.

'That didn't take very long, did it?' said Morse patronizingly.

'Does all this mean you've found some fingerprints on the knife?' she asked.

Morse was slightly hesitant. 'We think so, yes. Unidentified prints – unidentified as yet. As I explained, though, it's just a matter of elimination.'

She looked rather weary; gone was the sparkle that had characterized the latter part of that champagne evening at the Old Parsonage.

'You think they could be mine?'

Rather weary too was Morse's smile.

'We've got to have *some* suspects, haven't we? In fact my sergeant here's got a long list of 'em.'

She turned to Lewis. 'Whereabouts am I on the list?'

'We always try to put the most attractive at the top, don't we, sir?'

Morse nodded his agreement, wishing only that he'd thought of such a splendid rejoinder himself.

'And when exactly am I supposed to have murdered that shithouse?'

She looked from one to the other, and Morse in turn looked to Lewis the Interlocutor.

'Perhaps,' said the latter slowly, 'when you got back from Birmingham that Wednesday?'

'I see . . . And did I pinch the knife as well?'

'I – we don't think you could have done that because, as you told us, you didn't get back into Oxford until after the museum had closed. We checked up on the train time: it got into Oxford Station at 16.35 – just three minutes late.'

'You still don't sound as if you believe me.'

'We don't think you took the knife,' said Morse.

The slight but perceptible stress on the 'you' was clearly not lost on Suspect Number One.

'You suggestin' somebody else pinched it – then slipped it to me on the way home from the railway station? Then I just called in to have a chat with him and decided to murder the old bugger there and then – is that what you're thinking?'

'There are more unlikely scenarios than that,' said Morse quietly.

'Oh, not you! How I hate that bloody word "scenario".'

She had touched a raw spot, for Morse hated the word too. Yet he'd not been able to come up with anything better; and he made no protest as Ellie Smith continued, changing down now into her lower-gear register of speech.

'And what am I s'posed to 'ave done with 'im then?'

'Well, we were hoping you could give us a few ideas yourself.'

'Is this turnin' into a bleedin' interview or something?'

'No,' said Morse simply. 'You're under no obligation to answer anything. But sooner or later we're going to have to ask all sorts of questions. Ask you, ask your mother . . . Where is your mother, by the way?'

'Abroad somewhere.'

'How do you know that?'

'She sent me a postcard.'

'Where from?'

'The postmark was smudged – I couldn't read it.'

'Must have had a stamp on it?'

'Yeah. I'm no good at them names of foreign countries, though.'

'Some of them aren't very difficult, you know. "France", for instance?'

She made no reply.

'Have you still got the postcard?'

'No. Threw it away, didn't I?'

'What was the picture on it?'

'A river, I think.'

'Not the Thames?'

'Not the Thames.'

'You're not being much help, you know.'

'That's where you're wrong, though.'

She produced a small pasteboard business card and handed it to Morse.

'You were asking me about that Wednesday, weren't you? Well, I met a fellow on the train, and he got a bit, you know, a bit friendly and flirty, like; said if I ever wanted any, you know, work or anything . . .'

Morse looked at the white card: 'Mike Williamson, Modelling and Photographic Agency', with a Reading address and telephone number.

'He'll remember me – for sure, Inspector. I can promise you that.'

She smiled, her eyes momentarily recapturing the sparkle that Morse could recall so well.

'Better check, Lewis.'

But as Lewis got up and moved towards the phone, Morse held up his hand: 'Office next door, please.'

'Why did you want him out of the way?'

Morse ignored the question, feeling quite irrationally jealous. 'What did this fellow offer you?'

'Oh, Christ, come off it!' Her eyes flashed angrily now. 'What the 'ell d'you think? He just thought I was an intelligent, ill-educated, expensive prostitute – which I am.'

'Which you *were.*'

'Which I *am*, Morse. By the way, you don't mind me calling you "Morse", do you? I did ask you – remember? – if I could call you something more pally and civilized but . . .'

'What about Mr Davies? When you're married—'

'To Ashley? That's all off. He came last night and we stayed up till God knows when, talking about it – going round and round in the same old circles. But I just can't go through with it. I like him – he's nice. But I just . . . I just don't fancy him, that's all; and I could never love him – never. So it's not fair, is it? Not fair on him. Not fair on me, either, really.'

'So you won't be needing me any more – for the wedding,' said Morse slowly.

''Fraid not, no. There wouldn't have been a wedding anyway, though, would there – not if you're going to arrest me?'

For a brief while the two looked at each other across the desk, their eyes locked together with a curiously disturbing intimacy.

The phone rang.

It was Strange; and Ellie got to her feet.

'Please, stay!' whispered Morse, his hand over the mouthpiece. 'Yes, sir. Yes . . . Can you just give me five minutes . . . ? I'll be straight along.'

'Why d'you want me to stay?' she asked, after Morse had put down the receiver.

He took the little black box from the drawer and handed it to her.

'It's not wrapped up, I'm afraid. I'm not much good at that sort of thing.'

'Wha—?' She held the box in her left hand and opened it with her right, taking hold of the gold chain lovingly and gently, and slowly lifting up St Anthony.

'Wha's this for?'

'I bought it for you.'

'But like I say—'

'I want you to have it, that's all. I've never bought anything like that for anybody – and, as I say, I just want you to have it.'

Ellie had been looking down at the pendant and suddenly the tears began. 'Oh God!' she whispered.

'Do you like it?'

'It's ... it's the most wonderful ...' But she could get no further. She stood up and walked round the desk, and kissed Morse fully and softly on the mouth; and Morse felt the wetness of her cheek against his own.

'I must go,' said Morse. 'My boss'll be getting impatient.'

She nodded. 'You know what I just said – about Ashley? That I couldn't marry him because I didn't love him? Well, that wasn't really the reason why I broke it off.'

In his brain Morse had become convinced that Eleanor Smith must be guilty of her step-father's murder; but in his heart he felt grieved as he awaited her words, for he knew exactly what they would be.

Yet he was wrong.

Spectacularly wrong.

'The real reason is I've ... I've fallen in love with somebody else.'

Morse wondered if he'd heard correctly. 'What?'

'You gettin' deaf or something?'

'Not – not with that charlatan from the modelling agency, surely?'

She shook her head crossly, like some unhappy, exasperated little girl who will stamp her foot until she can get her own way, her own selfish way. *Now*.

'Are you going to listen to me, or not? Can't you guess? Can't you see? Can't you *see?*' She was standing beside the door, her head held high, her sludgy-green eyes closed, trying so hard to hold back the brimming tears. 'I've fallen in love with you, you stupid sod!'

CHAPTER SIXTY-TWO

dactyloscopy (n): the examination of fingerprints
(Early Twentieth Century)
  (*The New Shorter Oxford English Dictionary*)

ALWAYS HAD Morse been a reluctant dactyloscopist, and throughout his police career all the arches and whorls and loops, all the peaks and the troughs and the ridges, had ever remained a deep mystery to him – like electricity, and the Wheatstone Bridge. He was therefore perfectly happy, on Friday, 30 September, to delegate the fingerprinting of Mesdames Brooks and Stevens to Sergeant Lewis – for the two overseas travellers had returned to Oxford early that afternoon. Immigration officials at Heathrow, Gatwick, and Stansted airports had been alerted about them; and the phone-call from Heathrow had been received at Thames Valley HQ just after midday: the two had boarded the Oxford City Link coach, scheduled to arrive at its Gloucester Green terminus in Oxford at 2.30 p.m.

Neither had appeared to show any undue surprise or discomfiture when Lewis, accompanied by a fingerprint officer, had taken them into the manager's office there, and trotted out the 'purely for elimination' line.

After his colleague had left for the fingerprint bureau at St Aldate's (where there was now a computerized search facility) Lewis had returned to Kidlington

HQ, to find Morse dispiritedly scanning some of the documents in the case.

But the Chief Inspector perked up with the return of his sergeant.

'No problems?'

'No problems, sir.'

'You're a betting man, Lewis?'

'Only very occasionally: Derby, Grand National . . .'

'Will you have a bet with *me*?'

'50p?'

'Can't we be devils, and make it a quid?'

'All right. I've got to be careful with the money, though – we've got the decorators in.'

Morse appeared surprised. 'I thought you did all that sort of stuff yourself?'

'I used to, sir, when I had the time and the energy. Before I started working for you.'

'Well, take your pick!'

'Pardon?'

'The fingerprints. Brenda Brooks or Julia Stevens – who do you go for?'

Lewis frowned. 'I can't really see his wife doing it, you know that. I just don't think she'd have the strength for one thing.'

'Really?' Morse seemed almost to be enjoying himself.

'Mrs Stevens, though . . . Well, she's a much stronger person, a much stronger character, isn't she? And she's got the brains—'

'And she's got nothing to lose,' added Morse more sombrely.

'Not much, no.'

'So your money's on her, is it?'

Lewis hesitated. 'You know, sir, in detective stories there are only two rules really, aren't there? It's never the butler; and it's never the person you think it is. So – so I'll go for Mrs Brooks.'

'Leaving me with Mrs Stevens.'

'You'd have gone for her anyway, sir.'

'You think so?'

But Lewis didn't know what he was thinking, and changed the subject.

'Did you have any lunch earlier, sir?'

'Not even a pint,' complained Morse, lighting a cigarette.

'You're not hungry?'

'A bit.'

'What about coming back and having a bite with us? The missus'd be only too glad to knock something up for you.'

Morse considered the proposition. 'What do you normally have on Fridays? Fish?'

'No. It's egg and chips on Fridays.'

'I thought that was on Wednesdays.'

Lewis nodded. 'And Mondays.'

'You're on,' decided Morse. 'Give her a ring and tell her to peel another few spuds.'

'Only one thing, sir – as I said. We're in a bit of a pickle at home, I'm afraid – with the decorators in.'

'Have you got the beer in, though? That's more to the point, surely.'

It was Lewis himself who took the call from the finger-print bureau half an hour later. No match. No match anywhere. Whoever it was who had left some finger-prints on the Rhodesian knife, it had *not* been Mrs Brenda Brooks or Mrs Julia Stevens; nor, as they'd already learned, Ms Eleanor Smith. One other piece of information. Classifying and identifying fingerprints was an immensely complicated job and they couldn't be absolutely sure yet; but it was looking almost certain now that the fingerprints on the knife-handle didn't match those of any known criminals either – well over two million of them – in the Scotland Yard library.

'So you see what it means, Sarge? Whoever murdered your fellow doesn't look as if he had any previous conviction.'

'Or *she*,' added Lewis, after putting down the phone.

There was no need to relay the message, since a glum-looking Morse had heard it all anyway.

In silence.

A silence that persisted.

The report that Lewis had written on the visit to Matthew Rodway's mother was on the top of Morse's pile.

'Hope I didn't make too many spelling mistakes, sir?' ventured Lewis finally.

'What? No, no. You're improving. Slowly.'

'I don't suppose she gives tuppence really – Mrs Rodway, I mean – about who killed Brooks. So long as somebody did.'

Morse grunted inarticulately. His thoughts drifted back to their meeting with Mrs Rodway. It seemed an age ago now; but as his eyes skimmed through the report once again he could clearly visualize that inter-view, and the room, and the slim and still embittered Mrs Rodway . . .

'I know it's probably nonsense, sir, but you don't think that *she* could have murdered Brooks, do you?'

'She had as good a motive as anybody,' admitted Morse.

'Perhaps we ought to have another little ride out there and take her fingerprints.'

'Not today, Lewis. I'm out for a meal, if you remember.'

'I'll see you there, sir, if you don't mind. About six, is that all right?'

'What are *you* going to do?'

'Lots of little things. Make a bit more progress with the keys, for a start. I'm expected at the Pitt Rivers in twenty minutes.'

After Lewis had left, Morse lit yet another cigarette and leaned back in the black leather chair, looking purposelessly around his office. He noticed the thin patina of nicotine on the emulsioned walls. Yes, the place could do with a good wash-down and redecora-tion: the corners of the ceiling especially were deeply stained . . .

Suddenly, he felt a brief frisson of excitement as if there were something of vital importance in what he'd just read, or what he'd just thought, or what he'd just seen. But try as he might, he was unable to isolate the elusive clue; and soon he knew it was of no use trying any more.

It had gone.

CHAPTER SIXTY-THREE

Fingerprints *do* get left at crime scenes. Even the craftiest of perpetrators sometimes forget to wipe up everywhere

(*Murder Ink, Incriminating Evidence*)

HER FIRST sentence, spoken with an attractive Welsh lilt, was a perfect anapaestic pentameter:

'We shall have to eat here in the kitchen, Inspector, all right?'

'Wherever, Mrs Lewis. Have no fears.'

'We've got the decorators in, see? But just go and sit down in the lounge – where I've put out some beer and a glass.' (Anapaestic hexameter.)

As he passed the dining-room, Morse stopped to look inside. The decorators had finished for the day; almost finished altogether, it seemed, for only around the main window were some paint-stained white sheets still lying across the salmon-pink carpet, with all of the furniture now pushed back into place except for a bookcase, which stood awkwardly in mid-room, a wooden step-ladder propped up against it. Clearly, though, there would be no problem about its own relocation, either, for the site of its former habitation was marked by an oblong of strawberry-red carpet to the left of the window.

Mrs Lewis was suddenly behind him.

'You like the colour?'

'Very professionally painted,' said Morse, a man with no knowledge whatsoever of professionalism in painting and decorating.

'You were looking at the carpet, though, weren't you now?' she said shrewdly. 'Only had it five years – and they told us the colours in all of their carpets would last till eternity.' (Anapaests everywhere.)

'I suppose everything fades,' said Morse. It hardly seemed a profound observation – not at the time.

'It's the sun really, see. That's why you get most of your discolouration. In the cupboards – on the lining for the cupboards – you hardly get fading at all.'

Morse moved on into the lounge where he opened a can of Cask Flow Beamish, sat contentedly back in an armchair, and was watching the *Six o'Clock News* when Lewis came in.

'You look pleased with yourself,' said Morse.

'Well, that's two more of the keys accounted for: that second Yale opens the staff entrance door at the back of the Pitt Rivers, just off South Parks Road; and that little "X 10" key – remember? – that's a Pitt Rivers key, too: it's a key to a wall-safe there that's got rows and rows of little hooks in it, with a key on each of 'em – keys to all the display-cabinets.'

Morse grunted a perfunctory 'Well done!' as he reverted his attention to the news.

Mrs Lewis produced a slightly unladylike whistle a few minutes later: 'On the table, boys!'

Morse himself had acquired one culinary skill only – that of boiling an egg; and he was not infrequently heard to boast that such a skill was not nearly so common as was generally assumed. But granted that

Morse (in his own estimation) was an exemplary *boiler* of eggs, Mrs Lewis (*omnium consensu*) was a first-class *frier*; and the milkily opaque eggs, two on each plate, set beside their mountains of thick golden chips, were a wonderful sight to behold.

As Morse jolted out some tomato sauce, Lewis picked up his knife and fork. 'You know, sir, if they ever find a body with an empty plate of eggs and chips beside it—'

'I think you mean a plate empty of eggs and chips, Lewis.'

'Well, I reckon if the fingerprints on the knife don't match any of those in our criminal library, the odds are they'll probably be mine.'

Morse nodded, picked up his own knife and fork, found (blessedly!) that the plate itself was hot – and then he froze, as if a frame on the family video had suddenly been switched to 'Pause'.

'Everything all right, sir?'

Morse made no reply.

'You – you're feeling all right, sir?' persisted a slightly anxious Lewis.

'Bloody 'ell!' whispered Morse tremulously to himself in a voice just below audial range. Then, louder: 'Bloody 'ell! You've done it again, Lewis. You've done it *again*!'

Unprecedentedly Lewis was moved to lay down both knife and fork.

'You know we had a little bet . . .' Morse's voice was vibrant now.

'When we both lost.'

'No. When to be more accurate neither of us won.

Well, I'd like to bet you something else, Lewis. I'd like to bet you that I know whose fingerprints are on that knife in Brooks's back!'

'That's more than the fingerprint-boys do.'

Morse snorted. 'I'm very tempted to report *them* for professional incompetence.' Then his voice softened. 'But I can forgive them. Yes, I can understand them.'

'I'm lost, sir, I'm afraid.'

'Shall I tell you,' asked Morse, 'whose fingerprints we found on that knife?'

His blue eyes looked so fiercely across the kitchen table that for a few moments Lewis wondered whether he was suffering from some slight stroke or seizure.

'Shall I tell you?' repeated Morse. 'You see, there's a regular procedure which you know all about; which *every* CID man knows all about. A procedure that wasn't – couldn't have been – followed in this case: that when you take fingerprints from the scene of any murder you take everybody's – including the corpse's.'

Lewis felt the blood in his veins growing cold – like the plate in front of him.

'You can't mean . . . ?'

'But I do, Lewis. That's exactly what I do mean. *The prints are those of Edward Brooks himself.*'

Chapter Sixty-Four

Gestalt (n): chiefly *Psychol.* An integrated perceptual structure or unity conceived as functionally more than the sum of its parts

(*The New Shorter Oxford Dictionary*)

As Morse well knew, it was difficult enough to describe to someone else such a comparatively simple physical action as walking, say – let alone something considerably more complicated such as serving a ball in a game of tennis. How much more difficult then, later that same evening, for him to answer Lewis's direct question about the cerebral equivalent of such a process.

'What put you on to it, sir?'

What indeed?

It was perhaps perfectly possible to describe the mental gymnastics involved in the solving of a cryptic crossword clue. But how did one explain those virtually inexplicable convolutions of the mind which occasionally led to some dramatic, some penny-dropping moment, when the answers to a whole *series* of cryptic clues – and those not of the cruciverbalist but of the criminological variety – combined to cast some completely new illumination on the scene? How did one begin to explain such a sudden, almost irrational, psychological process?

'With difficulty,' was the obvious answer; but Morse

was trying much harder than that, as he now sought to identify the main constituents which had led him to his quite extraordinary conclusion.

It was all to do with the fortuitous collocation of several memories, several recollections, which although occurring at disparate points in the case – and before – had suddenly come together in his mind, and coalesced.

There had been the report (Lewis's own) on the interview with Mrs Rodway, when he had so easily been able to re-visualize some of the smallest details of the room in which they had spoken with her, and particularly that oblong patch above the radiator where a picture had been hanging.

Then there had been (only that very evening) a second oblong, prompting memory further, when he had looked down at the pristine strawberry-red in the lounge there, and when Mrs Lewis had spoken of the unfading linings in her cupboards.

And then, working backwards (or was it forwards?) there had been the visit to the Pitt Rivers Museum, when the Administrator had pointed with pride to the fine quality of the hessian lining for her cabinet-exhibits, with its optimistic guarantee of Tithonian immortality.

Then again, a much more distant memory from his childhood of a case of cutlery, a family heirloom, where over the years each knife, each fork, each spoon, had left its own imprint, its own silhouette, on the blue plush-lining of the case. Things always left their impressions, did they not?

Or did they?

Perhaps in the Pitt Rivers cabinets, in those slightly

sombre, sunless galleries, the objects displayed there –
the artefacts, the relics from the past – were leaving
only very faint impressions, like the utensils in Mrs
Lewis's kitchen-cupboards.

No impressions at all, possibly . . .

Then, and above all, the discrepancy between the
pathologist's report on the knife used to murder
McClure, and the statement given by the Raysons about
the knife found in their own front garden: the 'blade
not really sharp', in the former; the 'blade in no
immediate need of sharpening', in the latter. Not a big
discrepancy, perhaps; but a hugely significant one – and
one which should never, never have passed unnoticed.

Yes, all the constituents were there: separate, though,
and unsynthesized – waiting for a catalyst.

Lewis!

Lewis the Catalyst.

For it was Lewis who had returned from his p.m.
investigations with the information that one of the
small keys found in Brooks's pocket fitted a wall-safe in
the museum; in which, in turn, were to be found row
upon row of other keys, including the key to Cabinet
52. It was Lewis, too, who so innocently had asserted, as
he picked up a knife with which to eat his meal, that
his own fingerprints would soon be found thereon . . .

And whither had such ratiocination finally led the
Chief Inspector, as, like Abraham, he had made his way
forth from his tent in the desert knowing not whither
he went? To that strangest of all conclusions: that on
Wednesday, 7 September, from Cabinet 52 in the Pitt
Rivers Museum in Oxford – *nothing whatsoever had been
stolen.*

CHAPTER SIXTY-FIVE

Behold, I shew you a mystery
(ST PAUL, I *Corinthians*, ch. 15, v. 51)

A COUNCIL of war was called in Caesar's tent two days later, on Sunday, 2 October, with three other officers joining Chief Superintendent Strange in the latter's Kidlington HQ office at 10 a.m.: Chief Inspector Morse, Chief Inspector Phillotson, and Sergeant Lewis. Morse, invited to put a case for a dramatic intensification of enquiries, for a series of warrants, and for a small cohort of forensic specialists, did so with complete conviction.

He knew now (or so he claimed) what had been the circumstances of each of the murders, those of McClure and Brooks; and he would, with his colleagues' permission, give an account of those circumstances, not seeking to dwell on motives (not for the present) but on methods – on *modi operandi*.

Strange now listened, occasionally nodding, occasionally lifting his eyebrows in apparent incredulity, to the burden of Morse's reconstructions.

McClure lived on a staircase where Brooks was the scout. The latter had gained access to drugs and became a supplier to several undergraduates, one of whom, Matthew Rodway, had become very friendly with

McClure – probably not a homosexual relationship, though – before committing suicide in tragic and semi-suspicious circumstances. As a result of this, McClure had insisted that Brooks resign from his job; but agreed that he, McClure, would not report the matter to the Dean, and would even provide a job-testimonial, provided that Brooks forswore his dealings in drugs.

Feelings between the two men were bitter.

Things settled down, though.

Then it came to McClure's notice that Brooks had *not* finished with his drug-dealing after all; that some of the junkies were still in touch with him. A furious McClure threatened disclosure to Brooks's new employers and to the police, and a meeting between the two was arranged (or not arranged – how could one know?). Certain it was, however, that Brooks went to visit McClure. And murdered him.

On the way home, on his bicycle, Brooks suddenly became aware that he was seriously ill. He managed to get as far as St Giles', but could get no further. He left his bicycle outside St Mary Mags, without even bothering to lock it, perhaps, and covering himself as best he could, got a taxi from the rank there up to East Oxford – and very soon got an ambulance up to the JR2, minus the bloodstained clothing which his wife disposed of.

One thing above all must have haunted Brooks's mind once he knew he would recover from his heart attack: he was still in possession of the knife he'd used to murder McClure, because whatever happened *he couldn't throw it away*. He ordered his wife to lock it up somewhere, probably in the box in his bedroom, and she did as he asked, surely having enough common sense to handle the knife – both then and later – with the greatest delicacy, pretty certainly wearing the glove she'd taken to using to protect her injured right hand. She was terrified – certainly at that point – of incurring the anger of a fearsomely cruel man who had physically maltreated her on several occasions, and who in earlier years had probably abused his step-daughter – the latter now putting in an appearance after many moons away from home, no doubt after somehow learning of Brooks's illness.

Brenda Brooks had an ally.

Two allies, in fact: because we now become increasingly aware of the unusually strong bond of friendship and affection between her and the woman for whom she cleaned, Mrs Julia Stevens, a schoolma'am who, although this fact has only recently become known to us, was suffering from an inoperable brain-tumour.

A plot was hatched, an extraordinarily clever plot, designed to throw the police on to the wrong track; a plot which succeeded in so doing.

'Let me explain.'

'At last,' mumbled Strange.

Brenda Brooks took Mrs Stevens wholly into her confidence, with both now knowing perfectly well not only who had murdered McClure but also exactly where the knife had come from – and why Brooks was unable to get rid of it.

On the Saturday before McClure's murder, the very last thing in the afternoon, Brooks had taken the knife from Cabinet 52 in the Pitt Rivers Museum, fully intending to replace it the very first thing on the following Monday morning, when he planned to turn up for work half an hour or so early and to restore it to its position amongst the fifty-odd other knives there. Nobody would have missed it; nobody *could* have missed it, since the museum was closed on Sundays.

'Why—?' Strange had begun. But Morse had anticipated the question.

Why Brooks should have acted in such a devious way, or whether he had taken the knife with the deliberate intention of committing murder, it was now only possible to guess. The only slight clue (thus far) was that one of the few books found in the Brooks's virtually illiterate household was a library copy of *The Innocence of Father Brown*, in which Chesterton suggested a battlefield as the safest place to conceal a corpse ... with the possible implication that a cabinet of weapons might be the safest place to conceal a knife.

But Brooks couldn't restore the knife. Not yet.

His great hope was that no one would notice its absence. *And no one did.* Apart from the attendant circumstance of so many other knives, one further factor was greatly in his favour: the cabinet had been recently re-lined, and there was no outwardly physical sign that any object could be missing. The normal routine, when anything was taken out, was for a printed white card – 'Temporarily Removed' – to be inserted over the space left vacant. But there *was* no space left vacant, since Brooks had only to move two or three other knives along a little to effect a balanced row of exhibits. And as day followed day, no one in fact noticed that anything at all was missing.

But, apart from Brooks, two other persons now knew of all this.

One of whom was Julia Stevens.

And the beautifully clever idea was born: if . . . if Brooks were to be murdered with the very same knife which he himself had stolen . . .

Ah, yes!

Two things only were required.

First, a knife, a different but *wholly* similar knife, *would have to be planted* – somewhere in, or near, Daventry Avenue. For when it was found – as surely sooner or later it would be – the police, with a little luck, would discover that it had been taken from one of the Brooks's kitchen drawers.

Second, the cabinet from which the actual murder weapon had been taken ('Cabinet 52' was clearly marked on the tag) *would have to be broken into* so that its contents would inevitably be checked. For then, and then only, would the pedigree of the missing knife become known.

Someone was therefore delegated to break open that cabinet, to ruffle around a few of the knives there – exactly the *opposite* of what Brooks had done earlier – and the deception was launched. The 'theft' was duly spotted, and reported; the missing knife was fairly quickly identified; and, above all, the crucial alibis were established.

How so?

Because of the wholly incontestable fact that any person found murdered by means of that stolen knife must have been murdered *after that knife was stolen.*

But the truth was that Brooks was murdered *before* the knife was stolen – probably murdered the day before, since the two women lied about seeing him alive on the afternoon when they set off with the school-party for Stratford.

The only thing now calling for some sort of explanation was the curious circumstance of Brooks's body being so elaborately wrapped up in plastic, then wrapped up again in a brown carpet, before being dumped into the Isis, just upstream from Donnington Bridge, almost certainly driven there in the boot of a car. Mrs Stevens' car? Most probably, since she was the only one of them to own such a means of transport.

Well (as Morse saw it) the reason was fairly obvious: if and when (and *when* rather than if) the body was found, such wrapping would ensure one vital thing: that the knife would still be found with the body – still be found *in* the body, it could be hoped. There would be no danger of it being lost; and thereby no danger that the alibis so cunningly, so painstakingly, devised would be discounted or destroyed.

'So you see,' finished Detective Chief Inspector Morse, 'the two women we assumed could never have murdered Brooks have overnight moved up to the top of the list.' He looked up with a fairly self-satisfied smile to Chief Superintendent Strange. 'And with your permission, sir, we shall go ahead immediately, apply for a couple of search warrants—'

'Why only two warrants?' asked Detective Chief Inspector Phillotson.

CHAPTER SIXTY-SIX

The mind is its own place, and in itself
Can make a heaven of hell, a hell of heaven
(JOHN MILTON, *Paradise Lost*, Book 1)

THE FOLLOWING day, a call was put through to Morse ('Must be Morse') from Mr Basil Shepstone, Senior Neurologist at Oxford's Churchill Hospital; and twenty minutes later the two men were seated together in Shepstone's consulting-room.

Mrs Julia Stevens (Morse learned) had been admitted at midday, having earlier been discovered unconscious at the side of her bed by her cleaning-lady. Some speedy deterioration in her mental condition had been expected; but the dramatic (the literal) collapse in her physical condition had come as some surprise. A recent biopsy (Morse learned) had confirmed *glioblastoma multiforma*, a fast-growing tumour of the neuroglia in the brain: wholly malignant, sadly inoperable, rapidly fatal.

When Julia had been admitted, it was immediately apparent that, somewhere on the brain, pressure had become intolerably severe: she had been painfully sick again in the ambulance; clearly she was experiencing some considerable difficulty with both sight and speech; showing signs too of spatial disorientation. Yet somehow she had managed to make it clear that she wished to speak to the policeman Morse.

Twice during the early afternoon (Shepstone reported), her behaviour had grown disturbingly aggressive, especially towards one of the young nurses trying to administer medication. But that sort of behaviour – often involving some fairly fundamental personality change – was almost inevitable with such a tumour.

'Had you noticed any "personality change" before?' asked Morse.

Shepstone hesitated. 'Yes, perhaps so. I think ... well, let's put it this way. The commonest symptom would be a general loss of inhibition, if you know what I mean.'

'I don't think I do.'

'Well, I mean one obvious thing is she probably wouldn't be over-worried about the reactions and opinions of other people – other professional colleagues, in her case. Let's say she'd be more willing than usual to speak her mind in a staff-meeting, perhaps. I don't think she was ever *too* shy a person; but like most of us she'd probably always felt a bit diffident – a bit insecure – about life and ... and things.'

'She's an attractive woman, isn't she?'

Shepstone looked across at Morse keenly.

'I know what you're thinking. And the answer's probably "yes". I rather think that if over these past few months someone had asked ... to go to bed with her ...'

'When you say "someone" – you mean some *man*?'

'I think I do, yes.'

'And you say she's been a bit violent today.'

'Aggressive, certainly.'

Morse nodded.

'It's really,' continued Shepstone, 'the unexpected-ness rather than the nature of behaviour that always sticks out in these cases. I remember at the Radcliffe Infirmary, for example, a very strait-laced old dear with a similar tumour getting out of her bed one night and dancing naked in the fountain out the front there.'

'But *she* isn't a strait-laced old dear,' said Morse slowly.

'Oh, no,' replied the sad-eyed Consultant. 'Oh, no.'

For a while, when Julia had regained some measure of her senses in the hospital, she knew that she was still at home in her own bed, really. It was just that someone was trying to confuse her, because the walls of her bedroom were no longer that soothing shade of green, but this harsher, crueller white.

Everything was white.

Everyone was wearing white . . .

But Julia felt more relaxed now.

The worry at the beginning had been her complete disorientation: about the time of day, the day, the month – the year, even. And then, just as the white-coated girl was trying to talk to her, she'd felt a terrible sense of panic as she realized that she was unaware of *who she was.*

Things were better now, though; one by one, things were clicking into place; and some knowledge of her-self, of her life, was slowly surfacing, with the wonderful bonus that the dull, debilitating headache she'd lived with for so many months was gone. Completely gone.

She knew the words she wanted to say – about seeing

Morse; or at least her *mind* knew. Yet she was aware that those words had homodyned little, if at all, with the words she'd actually used:

'One thousand and one, one thousand and two . . .'
But she could write.
How could that be?
If she couldn't speak?
No matter.
She could write.

As he looked down at her, Morse realized that even in her terminal illness Julia Stevens would ever be an attractive woman; and he placed a hand lightly on her right arm as she lay in her short-sleeved nightdress, and smiled at her. And she smiled back, but tightly, for she was willing herself to make him understand what so desperately she wished to tell him.

At the scene of the terrible murder that had taken place in Brenda's front room, when she, Julia, had stood there, helpless at first, a spectator of a deed already done, she had vowed, if ever need arose, to take all guilt upon herself. And the words were in her mind: words that were all untrue, but words that were ready to be spoken. She had only to repeat repeat *repeat* them to herself: 'I murdered him I murdered him *I* murdered him . . .' And now she looked up at Morse and forced her mouth to speak those self-same words:

'One thousand and three, one thousand and four, one thousand and five . . .'

Aware, it seemed, even as she spoke, of her calamitous shortcomings, she looked around her with frenzied exasperation as she sought to find the pencil with which earlier she'd managed to write down 'MORSE'. Her right arm flailed about her wildly, knocking over a glass of orange juice on the bedside table, and tears of frustration sprang in her eyes.

Suddenly three nurses, all in white, were at her side, two of them seeking to hold her still as the third administered a further sedative. And Morse, who had intended to plant a tender kiss upon the Titian hair, was hurriedly ushered away.

CHAPTER SIXTY-SEVEN

We can prove whatever we want to; the only real
difficulty is to know what we want to prove
(EMILE CHARTIER, *Système des beaux arts*)

EVENTS WERE now moving quickly towards their close.
There was much that was wanting to be found – was
found – although Lewis was not alone in wondering
exactly what Morse himself wanted to be found. Certainly one or two minor surprises were still in store; but
in essence it was only the corroborative, substantiating
detail that remained to be gleaned – was gleaned – by
the enquiry team from their painstaking forensic investigations, and from one or two further painful
encounters.

Morse was reading a story when just after 3 p.m. on
Tuesday, 4 October, Lewis returned from the JR2 where
he had interviewed a rapidly improving Costyn – to
whom, as it happened, he had taken an instant dislike,
just as earlier in the case Morse had felt an instinctive
antipathy towards Ms Smith.

Lewis had learned nothing of any substance. About
the ram-raid, Costyn had been perkily co-operative,
partly no doubt because he had little option in the
matter. But about any (surely most probable?) visit to
the Pitt Rivers Museum; about his relations (relationship?) with Mrs Stevens; about any (possible?) knowl-

edge of, implication in, co-operation with, the murder of Edward Brooks, Costyn had been cockily dismissive.

He had nothing to say.

How could he have anything to say?

He knew nothing.

If Lewis was ninety-five per cent convinced that Costyn was lying, he had been one hundred per cent convinced that Ashley Davies, whom he'd interviewed the day before, could never have been responsible for the prising open of Cabinet 52. In fact Davies *had* been in Oxford that afternoon; and for some considerable while, since between 3.45 p.m. and 4.45 p.m. he had been sitting in the chair of Mr J. Balaguer-Morris, a distinguished and unimpeachable dental-surgeon practising in Summertown.

Quod erat demonstrandum.

Lewis sensed therefore (as he knew Morse did) that the two young men had probably always been peripheral to the crime in any case. But *someone* had gone along to the Pitt Rivers; *someone's* services could well have been needed for the disposal of the body in the Isis. For although Brooks had not been a heavy man, it would have been quite extraordinarily difficult for one woman to have coped alone; rather easier for two, certainly; and perhaps not all that difficult for three of them. Yet the help of a strong young man would have been a godsend, surely?

With the Magistrates finding no objections, the three search warrants had been immediately authorized, and the spotlight was now refocusing, ever more closely, on the three women in the case:

Brenda Brooks
Julia Stevens
Eleanor Smith . . .

The previous afternoon, great activity at the Brooks's
residence had proved dramatically productive. At the
back of the house, one of the small keys from Lewis's
bunch had provided immediate, unforced access to the
garden shed. No transparent plastic bags were found
there; nor any damning snippet of dark green garden-
twine like that which had secured the bundle of the
corpse. Yet something *had* been found there: fibres of a
brown material which looked most suspiciously similar
– which later proved to be identical – to the carpeting
that had covered the body of Edward Brooks.

Brenda Brooks, therefore, had been taken in for
questioning the previous evening, on two separate
occasions being politely reminded that anything she
said might be taken down in writing and used as
evidence. But there seemed hardly any valid reason for
even one such caution, since from the very start she
had appeared too shocked to say anything at all. Later
in the evening she had been released on police bail,
having been formally charged with conspiracy to
murder. As Morse saw things the decision to grant bail
had been wholly correct. There was surely little merit
in pressing for custody, since it was difficult to envisage
that gentle little lady, once freed, indulging in any orgy
of murder in the area of the Thames Valley Police
Authority.

In any case, Morse liked Mrs Brooks.

Just as he liked Mrs Stevens – in whose garage earlier

that same day a forensic team had made an equally dramatic finding, when they had examined the ancient Volvo, *in situ*, and discovered, in the boot, fibres of a brown material which looked most suspiciously similar – which later proved to be identical – to the carpeting that had covered the body of Edward Brooks . . .

Morse had nodded to himself with satisfaction on receiving each of these reports. So careful, so clever, they'd been – the two women! Yet even the cleverest of criminals couldn't think of everything: they all made that one little mistake, sooner or later; and he should be glad of that.

He *was* glad.

He himself had taken temporary possession of the long-overdue library book found in the Brooks's bedroom, noticing with some self-congratulation that the tops of two pages in the story entitled 'The Broken Sword' had been dog-eared. By Brooks? Were the pages worth testing for fingerprints? No. Far too fanciful a notion. But Morse told himself that he would re-read the story once he got the chance; and indeed his eye had already caught some of the lines he remembered so vividly from his youth:

Where does a man kick a pebble? On the beach.
Where does a wise man hide a leaf? In the forest . . .

Yes. Things were progressing well – and quickly.

There was that third search warrant, of course: one that had been granted, though not yet served.

The one to be served on Ms Smith . . .

Of whom, as it happened, Morse had dreamed the

previous night – most disturbingly. He had watched her closely (how on earth?) as semi-dressed in a plunging Versace creation she had exhibited herself erotically to some lecherous Yuppie in the back of a BMW. And when Morse had awoken, he had felt bitterly angry with her; and sick; and heartachingly jealous.

He had known better nights; known better dreams.

Yet life is a strange affair; and only ten minutes after Lewis had returned that Tuesday afternoon Morse received a call from Reception which quickened his heart-beat considerably.

CHAPTER SIXTY-EIGHT

She turned away, but with the autumn weather
Compelled my imagination many days,
Many days and many hours
        (T. S. ELIOT, *La Figlia Che Piange*)

SHE CLOSED the passenger-seat door, asking the man to wait there, in the slip-road, for ten minutes – no longer; then to drive in and pick her up.

She walked quite briskly past the blue sign, with its white lettering, 'Thames Valley Police HQ'; then up the longish gradient to the brick-and-concrete building.

At Reception she quickly made her errand clear.

'Is he expecting you, Miss?' asked the man seated there.

'No.'

'Can I ask what it's in connection with?'

'A murder.'

The grey-haired man looked up at her with some curiosity. He thought he might have seen her before; then decided that he hadn't. And rang Morse.

'Let her in, Bill. I'll be down to collect her in a couple of minutes.'

After entering her name neatly in the Visitors' Log, Bill pressed the mechanism that opened the door to the main building. She was carrying a small package, some 5 inches by 3 inches, and he decided to keep a precautionary eye on her. Normally he would not have let her through without some sort of check. But he'd always been encouraged to use his discretion, and in truth she looked more like a potential traveller than a potential terrorist. And Chief Inspector Morse had sounded happy enough.

He pointed the way. 'If you just go and sit and wait there, Miss . . . ?'

So Ellie Smith walked over the darkly marbled floor to a small, square waiting-area, carpeted in blue, with matching chairs set against the walls. She sat down and looked around her. Many notices were displayed there, of the 'Watch Out', 'Burglars Beware' variety; and photographs of a police car splashing through floods, and a friendly bobby talking to a farmer's wife in a local village; and just opposite her a large map . . .

But her observations ceased there.

To her left was a flight of white-marbled stairs, down which the white-haired Morse was coming towards her.

'Good to see you. Come along up.'

'No, I can't stay. I've got a car waiting.'

'But we can take you home. *I* can take you home.'

'No. I'm . . . I'm sorry.'

'Why have you come?' asked Morse quietly, seating himself beside her.

'You've had Mum in. She told me all about it. She's on bail, isn't she? And I just wondered where it all leaves her – and me, for that matter?'

Morse spoke gently. 'Your mother has been charged in connection with the murder of your step-father. Please understand that for the present—'

'She told me you might be bringing *me* in – is that right?'

'Look! We can't really talk here. Please come up—'

She shook her head. 'Not unless you're arresting me. Anyway, I don't trust myself in that office of yours. Remember?'

'Look, about your mother. You'll have to face the fact – just like we have to – that . . . that it seems very likely at the minute that your mother was involved in some way in the murder of your step-father.' Morse had chosen his hesitant words carefully.

'All right. If you're not going to tell me, never mind.'

She stood up; and Morse stood up beside her. She held out the small parcel she had been carrying in her right hand and offered it to him.

'For you,' she said simply.

'What is it?'

'Promise me one thing?'

'If I can.'

'You won't open it till you get home tonight.'

'If you say so.'

Morse suddenly felt very moved; felt very lost, very helpless, very upset.

'Well – that's it then. That's all I came for . . . really.'

'I'll ring you when I've opened it, I promise.'

'Only when you get home.'

'Only when I get home.'

'You've got a note of my number, haven't you?'

'I have it by heart.'

'I have to go. Hope you'll like it.' She managed to speak the words; but only just as she picked up St Anthony and fondled him between the thumb and forefinger of her left hand. And almost, for a moment or two, as they stood there, it was as if they might embrace; but the Assistant Chief Constable suddenly came through Reception, raising his hand to Morse in friendly greeting.

She turned away; and left.

As she stepped out of the building, a red BMW was beside her immediately; and she got in, casting one lingering look behind her as she locked her safety-belt.

'I was rather hoping you'd bring her up, sir. She's getting a bit of a smasher, that one, don't you think?'

But Morse, reclosing the door quietly behind him, made no reply. Suddenly his life seemed joyless and desolate.

'Coffee, sir?' asked Lewis in a low voice, perhaps understanding many things.

Morse nodded.

After Lewis was gone, he didn't wait.

He couldn't wait.

Inside the bluebell-patterned wrapping-paper was a small, silver, delicately curving hip-flask.

Oh God!

The letter enclosed with it bore no salutation:

My mum rung me up and told me everything, but she never killed him. I know that better than anybody because I killed him.

  I'm not much cop at writing but I wish we could have gone out for shampers together again. That was the happiest night of my life, because for some cockeyed reason I loved you with all the love I've got. I hope you like the little

present. I wish I could finish this letter in the way
I'd like to but I can't quite think of the right
words, you know I'm trying though. If only you'd
known how much I wanted you to kiss me in the
taxi so some few kisses now from me

xxxx Ellie xxxx

Unmanned with anguish, Morse turned away as
Lewis came back with the coffee, folded the letter
carefully, and put it in a drawer of his desk.

Neither man spoke.

Then Morse opened the drawer, took out the letter,
and passed it over to Lewis.

The silence persisted long after Lewis had read it.

Finally Morse got to his feet. 'If I ever see her again,
Lewis, I shall have to tell her that "rang" is the more
correct form of the past tense of the verb "to ring",
when used transitively.'

'I don't think she'd mind very much what you told
her,' said Lewis very quietly.

Morse said nothing.

'Mind if I have a look at the present, sir?'

Morse passed over the hip-flask.

'Remember that crossword clue, Lewis? "Kick in the
pants?" – three-hyphen-five?'

Lewis nodded and smiled sadly.

Hip-flask.

CHAPTER SIXTY-NINE

Amongst the tribes of Central Australia, every person has, besides a personal name which is in common use, a secret name which was bestowed upon him or her soon after birth, and which is known to none but the fully initiated

(JAMES FRAZER, *The Golden Bough*)

'YOU MUST admit what a trusting, stupid brain I've got, Lewis. "Don't open it till you get home," she said, and I just thought that . . .'

'*Numquam animus*, sir, as you tell me the ancient Romans used to say.'

'We'd better get along there.'

'You think she's done a bunk?'

'Sure she has.'

'With Davies?'

'Has Davies got a red BMW?'

'Not unless he's changed his car.'

'I wonder if it's that randy sod from Reading. Where's his card?'

'The traffic boys'll be able to tell us in a couple of ticks.'

'Can't wait that long.'

He found the card, the number – and dialled, informing the woman who answered that he was ring-ing from police HQ about a stolen car, a red BMW, and he was just checking to make sure . . .

Mr Williamson was out, Morse learned. But there was no need to worry. He *did* have a red BMW all right, but it hadn't been stolen. In fact, she'd seen him get into it earlier that afternoon. Going to Oxford, he'd said.

Half an hour later, in Princess Street, it became clear that Ellie Smith had decamped in considerable haste. In her bed-sit-cum-bathroom there had been little enough accommodation for many possessions anyway; yet much had been left behind: the bigger items (perforce) – fridge, TV, record player, microwave; a selection of clothing and shoes, ranging from the sedate to the sensational; pictures and posters by the score, including a life-sized technicolour photograph of Marilyn Monroe, a framed painting by Paul Klee, and (also framed) a fading Diploma from East Oxford Senior School, Prize for Art, awarded to Kay Eleanor Brooks, signed by C. P. Taylor (Head), and dated July 1983.

'Not much here in the drawers, sir. An Appointments' Book, though, stuck at the back.'

'Which I am not particularly anxious to see,' said Morse, sitting himself down on the bed.

'You know – if you don't mind me saying so, sir – it was a bit cruel, wasn't it? Her leaving her mum for all those years and not really getting in touch with her again until—'

He broke off.

'Sir!'

Morse looked up.

'There's a telephone number here for that Tuesday the sixth, with something written after it: "GL" – and what looks like the figure "1".'

Morse got up, and went to look over Lewis's shoulder. 'It could be a lower-case letter "l".'

'Shall I give the number a go?'

Morse shrugged his shoulders disinterestedly. 'Please yourself.'

Lewis dialled the number, and a pleasing, clear Welsh voice answered, with an obviously well-practised formula:

'Gareth Llewellyn-Jones. Can I 'elp you?'

'Sergeant Lewis, Thames Valley Police, sir. We're investigating a murder, and think you might be able to help us confirm one or two things.'

'My goodness me! Well, I can't really, not for the moment, like. I'm in the middle of a tutorial, see?'

'Can you give me a time when you *will* be free, sir?'

'Could be important,' said Lewis, after putting down the phone. 'If she was . . . out all night—'

'Don't you mean "in" all night?' said Morse bitterly. 'In bed with some cock-happy client of hers – that's what you mean, isn't it? So stop being so bloody mealy-mouthed, man.'

Lewis counted up to seven. 'Well, if she *was*, she couldn't have had too much of a hand in things with Brooks.'

'Of course she did!' snapped Morse. 'I don't believe her though when she says she murdered him – she's just trying to shield her mother, that's all – because it was her mother who murdered him.'

'Isn't it usually the other way round, though?'

'What do you mean?'

'Isn't it usually mums who try to shield their kids?'

The word 'kid' did to Morse what 'scenario' did to

Ellie Smith; and he was about to remonstrate – when suddenly he clapped a cupped right hand hard over his forehead.

'What year did the Brooks marry?'

'Can't remember exactly. Twelve years ago, was it? We can soon check.'

'What time are you seeing Armstrong-Jones?'

'Llewellyn-Jones, sir. Half-past eight. After he's had dinner in Hall.'

'Good. I'm glad you're not letting our own enquiries interfere with his college routine.'

'It wasn't like that—'

'Come on, Lewis!' Morse pointed to the Diploma. 'When you said Ellie Smith must have been a bit cruel to run away from her mother, you were right, in a way. But she didn't run away from her mother at all, Lewis. She ran away from her *father*, her natural father.'

'But she could just have changed her name, surely?'

'Nonsense!'

Morse consulted the directory lying beside the phone: only one C. P. Taylor, with an Abingdon Road address. He rang the number, and learned, yes indeed, that he was speaking to the Former Head of East Oxford Senior School, who would willingly help if he could. That same evening? Why not?

After Lewis had dropped Morse ('I'll find my own way home') at a rather elegant semi-detached property in the Abingdon Road, he himself proceeded to Lonsdale

College, where his mission was quietly and quickly productive.

Llewellyn-Jones freely admitted that he'd met the young woman he'd always known as 'Kay' fairly regularly for sexual purposes: never in his college rooms; more often than not in a hotel; and twice in her own little place – as was the case on Tuesday, 6 September, when he'd spent the evening with her, and would have spent longer but for a phone-call – half-past nine? quarter-to ten? – which had galvanized her into panicky activity. *She'd* have to leave: *he'd* have to leave. Obviously some sort of emergency; but he knew no more, except perhaps that he thought the voice on the phone was that of a woman.

Lewis thanked the dark, dapper little Welshman, and assured him that the information given would of course be treated with the utmost confidentiality.

But Gareth Llewellyn-Jones appeared little troubled:

'I'm a bachelor, Sergeant, see? And I just loved being with her, that's all. In fact, I could've ... But I don't think she's the sort of woman who could ever really fall arse-orver-tit for any man – certainly not for me.'

He smiled, shook his head, and bade farewell to Lewis from the Porters' Lodge.

As Lewis drove up to his home in Headington, he realized that Morse had almost certainly been right about Ellie Smith's involvement in the murder.

With a tumbler of most welcome Scotch beside him, Morse sat back to listen.

'Kay Brooks? Oh yes, I remember *her*,' said the ex-headmaster, a thin, mildly drooping man in his early seventies. 'Who wouldn't . . . ?'

Aged eleven, she'd started at his school as a lively, slightly devil-may-care lass, with long dark hair and a sweet if somewhat cheeky sort of smile. Bright – well above average; and very good at sketching, painting, design, that type of thing. But . . . well, something must have gone a bit sour somewhere. By her mid-teens, she'd become a real handful: playing hookey, surly, inattentive, idle, a bit cruel, perhaps. Trouble at home, like as not? But no one knew. Kay's mother had come along to see him a couple of times but—

Morse interrupted:

'That's really what I've come about, sir. It may not be important, but I rather think you probably mean her *step*-mother, don't you?'

'Pardon?' Taylor looked as if he had mis-heard.

'You see, I think Brooks, Edward Brooks, the man fished out of the Isis, could well have been her real father, not her *step*-father.'

'Nonsense!' (The second time the word had been used in the past half-hour.) 'I can understand what you're thinking, Inspector; but you're wrong. She *changed* her name when her mother got remarried; changed it to her mother's new name. You see, I knew her, knew her mother, well before then.'

Morse looked puzzled. 'Is that sort of thing usual?'

Taylor smiled. 'Depends, doesn't it? Some people would give an arm and a leg to change their names. Take me, for instance. My old mum and dad – bless their hearts but . . . you know what they christened me? "Cecil Paul". Would you credit it? I was "Cess-pool" before I'd been at school a fortnight. You know the sort of thing I mean?'

Oh, yes, Morse knew exactly the sort of thing he meant.

'And I'm afraid,' continued Taylor, 'that Kay got teased pretty mercilessly about her name – about her surname, that is. So it was only natural, really, that when the opportunity arose to change it . . .'

'What *was* her surname?' asked Morse.

Taylor told him.

Oh dear!

Poor Ellie!

After gladly becoming Eleanor 'Brooks' on her mother's remarriage, so very soon, it seemed, had she come to detest her newly-adopted name. And when she had left home, she had plumped for 'Smith' – a good, common-stock, unexceptionable sort of name that could cause her pain no more.

Yes, Morse knew all about being teased because of a name – in his own case a Christian name. And he felt so close to Ellie Smith at that moment, so very caring towards her, that he would have sacrificed almost anything in the world to find her there, waiting for him, when he got back home.

'Ellie Morse'?

'*Eleanor* Morse'?

Difficult to decide.

But gladly would Morse have settled for either as he walked slowly up into Cornmarket, where he stood waiting twenty-five minutes for a bus to take him up to his bachelor flat in North Oxford.

CHAPTER SEVENTY

Then grief forever after; because forever after
nothing less would ever do
        (J. G. F. POTTER, *Anything to Declare?*)

THE SUBJECT of each of these last two enquiries, the young woman who has been known (principally) in these pages as Ellie Smith, had hurriedly wiped her eyes and for a considerable time said nothing after getting into Mike Williamson's car. Her thoughts were temporarily concentrated not so much on Morse himself as on what she could have told him; or rather on what she could never have told him . . .

It had been that terrible Tuesday night, when her mother had phoned, pleading in such deep anguish for her daughter's help; when she'd got rid of that quite likable cock-happy little Welshman; and finally reached the house – a full five minutes before that other woman had arrived in a car – to find her mother standing like a zombie in the entrance hall, continuously massaging a gloved right hand with her left, as if she had inflicted upon it some recent and agonizing injury; and when, after going into the kitchen, she'd looked down on her step-father lying prone on the lino there, a strange-looking, wooden-handled knife stuck – so accurately it had seemed to her – halfway between the shoulder-blades. Strangely enough, there hadn't been too much blood. Perhaps he'd never had all that much blood in him. Not warm blood, anyway.

Then the red-headed woman had arrived, and taken over – so coolly competent she'd been, so organized. It was as if the plot of the drama had already been written, for clearly the appropriate props had been duly prepared, waiting only to be fetched from the back-garden shed. Just the *timing*, it appeared, had gone wrong, as if a final rehearsal had suddenly turned into a first-night performance. And it was her mother surely who'd been responsible for that: jumping the starting-gate and seizing the reins in her own hands – her own hand, rather (singular).

Then, ten minutes later, following a rapidly spoken telephone conversation, the young man had appeared, to whom the red-headed woman had spoken in hushed tones in the hallway; a young man whom, oddly enough, she knew by sight, since the two of them had attended the same Martial Arts classes together. But she said nothing to him. Nor he to her. Indeed he seemed hardly aware of her presence as he began to manoeuvre the awkward corpse into its polythene winding sheet – sheets, rather (plural).

She'd even found herself remembering his name.

Kevin something . . .

As the car turned right from Park End Street into the railway station, Ellie's mind jerked back to the present, aware that Williamson's left hand had crept above the top of her suspendered right-stocking. But she would always be able to handle people like Williamson, who now reminded her of their proposed agreement as he humped the two large suitcases from the boot.

'You ring me, like you said, OK?'

Ellie nodded, adding a verbal gloss to her unspoken promise as she took his business card from her handbag and mechanically recited the telephone number.

'Right, then. And don't forget we can do real business with a body like yours, kid.'

It would have been a nice gesture if he had offered to carry her cases up the steps to the automatic doors; or even as far as the ticket window. But he didn't; and of that she was glad. Had he done so she would probably have felt obliged to buy a ticket for Paddington, for she had spoken to him vaguely of 'friends in London'. As it was, once he had driven off, she bought a single ticket to Liverpool, and with aching arms crossed over the footbridge to Platform Two – where she stood for twenty-five minutes, forgetting for a while the future plight of her mother; forgetting the minor role she herself had played in the murder of a man she had learned to hate; yet remembering again now, as she fingered the gold pendant, the man who had given it to her, the man for whom she would have sacrificed anything. If only he could have loved her.

EPILOGUE

Life is a progress from want to want, not from
enjoyment to enjoyment
(SAMUEL JOHNSON, in Boswell's *The Life of
Samuel Johnson*)

IT IS now Friday, 28 October 1994, the Feast of St
Simon and St Jude, and this chronicle has to be
concluded, with brief space only remaining to record a
few marginal notes on some of the characters who
played their roles in these pages.

On Thursday, 20 October, Mrs Brenda Brooks was
re-arrested, additionally charged with the murder of
her husband, Mr Edward Brooks, and remanded in
custody at Holloway Prison. From which institution,
four days later, she was granted temporary leave of
(escorted) absence to attend a midday funeral service
at the Oxford Crematorium, where many teachers from
the Proctor Memorial School were squeezed into the
small chapel there, together with a few relatives, and a
few friends – though the couple from California were
unable to make the journey at such short notice.

Two others completed (almost completed) the sad-
dened congregation: the facially scarred Kevin Costyn
and a pale-looking Chief Inspector Morse, neither of
whom participated in (what seemed to the latter) the
banal revision of Archbishop Cranmer's noble words
for the solemn service of the dead.

And one other mourner: a dark-suited, prosperous-looking, middle-aged man, who went last of all into the chapel; and sat down, as it happened, next to Morse, on the back row of the left-hand side of the aisle. A minute earlier, wholly unobserved, he had added his own floral tribute to the many others laid out in the Garden of Remembrance there: a wreath of white lilies. The card attached bore no salutation, no valediction – just the same words that Julia Stevens had read on a birthday card some eighteen months before:

'Don't forget we had some good times too!'

St Giles's (enforced) new home is some little way from Oxford. Yet that aristocratic cat is not displeased with his environment – particularly with the wildlife opportunities offered in the open field just behind Number 22, Kingfisher Way, Bicester; and with the soft, beige leather settee on which he now sleeps for long stretches of the day until his attractive young mistress returns from her duties at the Oxford University Press.

Janis Lawrence, only temporarily she trusts, is now unemployed once more; and her familiar, exasperated 'Stop frowin' them bricks, Jason!' is still often to be heard in the streets of the Cutteslowe Estate.

On the whole, Mrs Lewis is well pleased with the work of the decorators; and extremely pleased with her husband's present to her of a new set of five

COLIN DEXTER

black-handled knives, including one (Number 4) whose blade, unusually broad at its base, curves to a dangerous looking point.

The former dwelling of Dr Felix McClure has now been on the market for two weeks, its lounge completely re-carpeted. But Mrs (Miss?) Laura Wynne-Wilson, though maintaining a dedicated vigil behind her carefully parted lace curtains, has yet to spot any prospective client arriving to view the property. And Messrs Adkinson, renowned for their meticulous room-measurements, are a little worried that the vicious murder enacted in Number 6 has, quite understandably, postponed the prospect of any immediate purchase.

And what of Morse?

His proposed lunchtime meeting with Strange, with a view to launching a twin assault on the complexities of form-filling, has not yet been arranged; and Morse is not pursuing the matter with any sense of great urgency, since he is undecided about the 'sooner or later' of his own eventual retirement, and curiously unsettled about the immediate months ahead of him . . .

He knew, of course, that it would be utterly hopeless to ring Ellie Smith, and therefore he rang her number only three times in the week following her disappearance; only twice in the second week. After all, as Morse recalled from his believing days, Hope is one of the greatest of all the Christian virtues.

In the third week, his normal routine in life appeared to reassert itself; and at about 9.30 p.m. he was again regularly to be observed walking fairly purposefully down the Banbury Road to one of the local hostelries. He has promised himself most faithfully that he will dramatically curtail his consumption of alcohol wef 1 November; which same day will also mark his permanent renunciation of nicotine.

In the meantime there is much work still to be done in the aftermath of the case – the aftermath of both cases, rather. And above all else in Morse's life there remains the searching out of Ellie Smith, since as a police officer that is his professional duty and, as a man, his necessary purpose.

THE JEWEL THAT
WAS OURS

For my wife, Dorothy

Espied the god with gloomy soul
   The prize that in the casket lay
Who came with silent tread and stole
   The jewel that was ours away.

(*Lilian Cooper*, 1904–1981)

OXFORD UNIVERSITY COLLEGES

1 WOLFSON COLLEGE
2 ST HUGH'S COLLEGE
3 ST ANTONY'S COLLEGE
4 ST ANNE'S COLLEGE
5 GREEN COLLEGE
6 SOMERVILLE COLLEGE
7 DEPT. OF METALLURGY
8 KEBLE COLLEGE
9 INSTITUTE OF MATHEMATICS
10 RUSKIN COLLEGE
11 ST CROSS COLLEGE
12 ST JOHN'S COLLEGE
13 WORCESTER COLLEGE
14 TRINITY COLLEGE
15 BALLIOL COLLEGE
16 WADHAM COLLEGE
17 MANSFIELD COLLEGE
18 DEPTS OF ZOOLOGY AND PSYCHOLOGY
19 LAW FACULTY AND LIBRARY
20 ST CATHERINE'S COLLEGE
21 MANCHESTER COLLEGE
22 NEW COLLEGE
23 HERTFORD COLLEGE
24 ALL SOULS COLLEGE
25 RADCLIFFE CAMERA
26 LINCOLN COLLEGE
27 BRASENOSE COLLEGE
28 EXETER COLLEGE
29 JESUS COLLEGE
30 ST PETER'S COLLEGE
31 NUFFIELD COLLEGE
32 PEMBROKE COLLEGE
33 CHRIST CHURCH
34 ORIEL COLLEGE
35 CORPUS CHRISTI COLLEGE
36 UNIVERSITY COLLEGE
37 MERTON COLLEGE
38 QUEEN'S COLLEGE
39 MAGDALEN COLLEGE
40 ST HILDA'S COLLEGE

ACKNOWLEDGEMENTS

The author and publishers wish to thank the following who have kindly given permission for use of copyright materials:

Extract from *Oxford* by Jan Morris published by Oxford University Press, 1987, reprinted by permission of Oxford University Press;

Extract from the introduction by Lord Jenkins of Hillhead to *The Oxford Story*, published by Heritage Projects (Management) Ltd, reprinted by permission of the Peters Fraser & Dunlop Group Ltd;

Extract from *Lanterns and Lances* published by Harper & Row and by Hamish Hamilton in the United Kingdom and Commonwealth, copyright © 1961 James Thurber. Copyright © 1989 Rosemary A. Thurber;

Julian Symons for the extract from *Bloody Murder*;

Marilyn Yurdan for the extract from *Oxford: Town & Gown*;

Basil Swift for the extracts from *Collected Haiku*;

Martin Amis for the extract from *Other People*, published by Jonathan Cape;

Max Beerbohm for the extract from *Mainly on the Air*, published by William Heinemann Ltd;

A. P. Watt Ltd on behalf of Crystal Hale and Jocelyn Herbert for the extract from 'Derby Day', *Comic Opera*, by A. P. Herbert;

Part One

CHAPTER ONE

It is not impossible to become bored in the presence of a mistress

(Stendhal)

THE RED-SEAL Brut Imperial Moët & Chandon stood empty on the top of the bedside table to her left; empty like the champagne glass next to it, and like the champagne glass on the table at the other side of the bed. Everything seemed empty. Beside her, supine and still, hands behind his head, lay a lean, light-boned man in his early forties, a few years older than herself. His eyes were closed, and remained closed as she folded back her own side of the floral-patterned duvet, rose quickly, put her feet into fur-lined slippers, drew a pink silk dressing gown around a figure in which breasts, stomach, thighs, were all a little over-ripe perhaps – and stepped over to peer through the closed curtains.

Had she consulted her Oxford University Pocket Diary, she would have noticed that the sun was due to set at 16.50 that early Wednesday evening in late October. The hour had gone back the previous week-end, and the nights, as they said, were pulling in fast. She had always found difficulty with the goings back and forth of the clock – until she had heard that simple little jingle on Radio Oxford: Spring Forward/Fall

3

Back. That had pleased her. But already darkness had fallen outside, well before its time; and the rain still battered and rattled against the window-panes. The tarmac below was a glistening black, with a pool of orange light reflected from the street lamp opposite.

When she was in her junior school, the class had been asked one afternoon to paint a scene on the Thames, and all the boys and girls had painted the river blue. Except her. And that was when the teacher had stopped the lesson (in midstream, as it were) and asserted that young Sheila was the only one of them who had the natural eye of an artist. Why? Because the Thames might well be grey or white or brown or green or yellow – anything, in fact, except those little rectangles of Oxford blue and Cambridge blue and cobalt and ultramarine into which all the wetted brushes were dipping. So, would all of them please start again, and try to paint the colours they saw, and forget the postcards, forget the atlases? All of them, that is, except Sheila; for Sheila had painted the water black.

And below her now the street was glistening black . . .

Yes.

Everything seemed black.

Sheila hugged the thin dressing gown around her and knew that he was awake; watching her; thinking of his wife, probably – or of some other woman. Why didn't she just tell him to get out of her bed and out of her life? Was the truth that she needed him more than he needed her? It had not always been so.

It was so very hard to say, but she said it: 'We were happy together till recently, weren't we?'

'What?' The tongue tapped the teeth sharply at the final 't'.

She turned now to look at him lying there, the moustache linking with the neatly trimmed Vandyke beard in a darkling circle around his mouth – a mouth she sometimes saw as too small, and too prim, and, yes, too bloody *conceited*!

'I must go!' Abruptly he sat up, swung his legs to the floor, and reached for his shirt.

'We can see each other tomorrow?' she asked softly.

'Difficult not to, won't it?' He spoke with the clipped precision of an antique pedagogue, each of the five 't's articulated with pedantic completion. With an occasional lisp, too.

'I meant – afterwards.'

'Afterwards? Impossible! Impothible! Tomorrow evening we must give our full attention to our American clients, must we not? *Motht* important occasion, as you know. Lucky if we all get away before ten, wouldn't you say? And then—'

'And then you must go home, of course.'

'Of course! And you know perfectly well *why* I must go home. Whatever your faults, you're not a fool!'

Sheila nodded bleakly. 'You could come here before we start.'

'No!'

'Wouldn't do much harm to have a drink, would it? Fortify ourselves for—'

'No!'

'I see.'

'And it's healthy for the liver and kindred organs to

5

leave the stuff alone for a while, uh? Couple of days a week? Could you manage that, Sheila?'

He had dressed quickly, his slim fingers now fixing the maroon bow-tie into its usual decadent droop. For her part, she had nothing further to say; nothing she could say. She turned once again towards the window, soon to feel his hand on the back of her shoulders as he planted a perfunctory kiss at the nape of her neck. Then the door downstairs slammed. Miserably she watched the top of the black umbrella as it moved along the road. Then she turned off the bedside lamp, picked up the champagne bottle, and made her way down the stairs.

She needed a drink.

Dr Theodore Kemp strode along swiftly through the heavy rain towards his own house, only a few minutes' walk away. He had already decided that there would be little, if any, furtherance of his affair with the readily devourable divorcée he had just left. She was becoming a liability. He realised it might well have been his fault that she now seemed to require a double gin before starting her daily duties; that she took him so very seriously; that she was demanding more and more of his time; that she was prepared to take ever greater risks about their meetings. Well, *he* wasn't. He would miss the voluptuous lady, naturally; but she *was* getting a little too well-padded in some of the wrong places.

Double chin . . . double gin . . .

He'd been looking for some semblance of love –

with none of the problems of commitment; and with Sheila Williams he had thought for a few months that he had found it. But it was not to be: *he*, Theodore Kemp, had decided that! And there *were* other women – and one especially, her tail flicking sinuously in the goldfish bowl.

Passing through the communal door to the flats on Water Eaton Road, whither (following the accident) he and Marion had moved two years earlier, he shook the drenched umbrella out behind him, then wiped his sodden shoes meticulously on the doormat. Had he ruined them? he wondered.

Chapter Two

For the better cure of vice they think it necessary to study it,
and the only efficient study is through practice

(Samuel Butler)

MUCH LATER THAT same evening, with the iron grids
now being slotted in from bar-top to ceiling, John
Ashenden sat alone in the University Arms Hotel at
Cambridge and considered the morrow. The weather
forecast was decidedly brighter, with no repetition of
the deluge which earlier that day had set the whole of
southern and eastern England awash (including, as we
have seen, the city of Oxford).

'Anything else before we close, sir?'

Ashenden usually drank cask-conditioned beer. But
he knew that the quickest way to view the world in a
rosier light was to drink whisky; and he now ordered
another large Glenfiddich, asking that this further
Touch of the Malt be added to the account of the
Historic Cities of England Tour.

It would help all round if the weather were set fairer;
certainly help in mitigating the moans amongst his
present group of Americans:

- too little sunshine
- too much food
- too much litter

– too early reveilles
– too much walking around (especially that!)

Not that they were a particularly complaining lot (except for that one woman, of course). In fact, by Ashenden's reckoning, they rated a degree or two above average. Twenty-seven of them. Almost all from the West Coast, predominantly from California; mostly in the 65–75 age-bracket; rich, virtually without exception; and fairly typical of the *abcde* brigade – alcohol, bridge, cigarettes, detective-fiction, ecology. In the first days of the tour he had hoped that 'culture' might compete for the 'c' spot, since after joining the ranks of the non-smokers he was becoming sickened at seeing some of them lighting up between courses at mealtimes. But it was not to be.

The downpour over Cambridge that day had forced the cancellation of trips to Grantchester and the American War Cemetery at Madingley; and the change of programme had proved deeply unpopular – especially with the ladies. Yes, and with Ashenden himself, too. He had duly elected himself their temporary cicerone, pointing neck-achingly to the glories of the late-Gothic fan-vaulting in King's; and then, already weary-footed, shuffling round the Fitzwilliam Museum to seek out a few of the ever-popular Pre-Raphaelite paintings.

'They have a far better collection in the Ashmolean, Mr Ashenden. Or so I've *read*. William Holman Hunt, and – and Mill-*ais*.'

'You'll be able to judge for yourself tomorrow, won't you?' Ashenden had replied lightly, suspecting that the doom-laden lady had forgotten (never known, perhaps) the Christian names of a painter she'd pronounced to rhyme with 'delay'.

It had irked Ashenden that the Cambridge coach company would have to be paid in full for the non-outings that day. It had irked him even more that he had been obliged to forgo the whole of the afternoon in order to enlighten and entertain his ageing charges. He was (he knew it) a reasonably competent courier and guide. Yet in recent years he had found himself unable to cope properly without a few regular breaks from his round-the-clock responsibilities; and it had become his policy to keep his afternoons completely free whenever possible, though he had never fully explained the reasons for this to anyone . . .

In November 1974 he had gone to Cambridge to take the entrance examination in Modern Languages. His A-level results had engendered not unreasonable optimism in his comprehensive school, and he had stayed on for a seventh term to try his luck. His father, as young John knew, would have been the proudest man in the county had his son succeeded in persuading the examiners of his linguistic competence. But the son had not succeeded, and the letter had dropped on to the doormat on Christmas Eve:

From the Senior Tutor, Christ's College, Cambridge

Dear Mr Ashenden,   21.12.74

After giving full and sympathetic consideration to your application, we regret that we are unable to

offer you a place at this college. We can understand
the disappointment you will feel, but you are
no doubt aware how fiercely competition for places

There had been a huge plus from that brief time in
Cambridge, though. He had stayed for two nights, in
the Second Court at Christ's, in the same set of rooms
as a fellow examinee from Trowbridge: a lanky, extraordinarily widely-read lad, who apart from seeking a
scholarship in Classics was anxious to convert the University (or was it the Universe?) to the self-evident truths
of his own brand of neo-Marxism. John had understood
very little of it all, really; but he had become aware,
suddenly, of a world of scholarship, intelligence, imaginative enthusiasm, sensitivity – above all of sensitivity –
that he had never known before in his comprehensive
school at Leicester.

On their last afternoon together, Jimmy Bowden,
the Trotskyite from Trowbridge, had taken him to see
a double-bill from the golden age of the French cinema,
and that afternoon he fell in love with a sultry, husky-
voiced whore as she crossed her silk-clad legs and
sipped her absinthe in some seedy bistro. It was all
something to do with 'the synthesis of style and sexuality', as Jimmy had sought to explain, talking into the
early hours ... and then rising at six the following
morning to stand outside Marks & Spencer to try to sell
the *Socialist Worker*.

A few days after being notified of his own rejection,
Ashenden had received a postcard from Jimmy – a

black and white photograph of Marx's tomb in High-
gate Cemetery:

> The idiots have given me a major schol – in spite of that
> Greek prose of mine! Trust you've had your own good news.
> I enjoyed meeting you and look forward to our first term
> together – Jimmy.

He had never replied to Jimmy. And it was only by
chance, seven years later, that during one of his Oxford
tours he'd met a man who had known Jimmy
Bowden . . .

After gaining his pre-ordained First in both parts of the
Classical Tripos, Jimmy had been awarded a Junior
Research Fellowship at Oxford to study early Etruscan
epigraphy; and then, three years later, he had died of
Hodgkin's disease. He had been an orphan (as events
revealed) and been buried in Oxford's Holywell Cemetery, amongst many dead, but once pre-eminent, dons
– only some twenty feet or so, as Ashenden learned,
from the grave of Walter Pater. Yet though Jimmy had
died, some small part of his legacy lived on – for John
Ashenden had for many years subscribed to several
specialist film magazines, printed in the UK and on the
Continent, for cinema buffs such as he himself had
soon become. Exactly where and when the degeneration had set in (if, indeed, 'degeneration' it were) John
Ashenden could not be all that sure.

Born in 1956, John had not grown up amidst the sexually repressive mores of his own father's generation. And once he started to work (immediately after school), started to travel, he had experienced little sense of guilt in satisfying his sexual curiosities by occasional visits to sauna clubs, sex cinemas, or explicit stage shows. But gradually such experiences began to nourish rather than to satisfy his needs; and he was becoming an inveterate voyeur. Quite often, at earlier times, he had been informed by his more experienced colleagues in the travel business (themselves totally immune, it appeared, from any corrupting influences) that the trouble with pornography was its being so *boring*. But *was* it?

From his first introduction, the squalid nature of his incipient vice had been borne upon him – groping his way like a blind man down a darkened aisle of a sleazy cinema, the Cockney voice still sounding in his ears: 'It's the real fing 'ere, sir, innit? No messin' about – nuffin like that – just straight inta fings!' And it disturbed him that he could find himself so excited by such crude scenes of fornication. But he fortified his self-esteem with the fact that almost all the cinemas he attended were fairly full, probably of people just as well adjusted as himself. Very soon, too, he began to understand something of that 'synthesis' that Jimmy had tried to explain to him – the synthesis of style and sexuality. For there *were* people who understood such things, with meetings held in private dwellings, the High Priest intoning the glorious introit: 'Is everybody known?'

That Ashenden had been forced to miss such a meeting of initiates that afternoon in Cambridge had been disappointing. Very disappointing, indeed.

But the next stop was Oxford . . .

CHAPTER THREE

'O come along, Mole, do!' replied the Rat cheerfully, still plodding along.

'*Please* stop, Ratty!' pleaded the poor Mole, in anguish of heart. 'You don't understand! It's my home, my old home! I've just come across the smell of it, and it's close by here, really quite close. And I *must* go to it'

(*Kenneth Grahame*, The Wind in the Willows)

'ARKSFORD? THIS IS *Arksford*?'

Seated on the nearside front seat of the luxury coach, John Ashenden glanced across at the diminutive septuagenarian from California: 'Yes, Mrs Roscoe, this is Oxford.' He spoke rather wearily, yet wholly without resentment. Hitherto little on the Historic Cities of England Tour (London–Cambridge–Oxford–Stratford–Bath–Winchester) had appeared unequivocally satisfactory to the well-read, eager, humourless (insufferable!) Mrs Roscoe; and yet as he looked out of his own side-window Ashenden could sympathise with that lady's disappointment. The eastern stretch of the A40 could hardly afford the most pleasing approach to the old University City; and as the coach slowly moved, one car-length at a time, towards the Headington roundabout, a litter-strewn patch of ill-kempt grass beside a gaudily striped petrol station lent little enchantment to the scene.

The tour party – eighteen women, nine men (three registered husband-and-wife combinations) – sat back in their seats as the coach drove past the sign for 'City Centre' and accelerated for a few miles along the featureless northern section of the Ring Road, heading for the Banbury Road roundabout.

For some reason Mrs Laura Stratton was ill-at-ease. She re-crossed her legs and now massaged her left foot with her right hand. As agreed, it would be Eddie who would sign the forms and the Visitors' Book, and then identify the luggage and tip the porter – while she would be lying in a hot herbal bath and resting her weary body, her weary *feet* . . .

'Gee, I feel so *awful*, Ed!'

'*Relax*, honey. Everything's gonna be OK.' But his voice was so quiet that even Laura had difficulty in picking up his words. At sixty-six, four years younger than his wife, Eddie Stratton laid his hand briefly on the nylon-clad left foot, the joints of the toes disfigured by years of cruel arthritis, the toenails still painted a brightly defiant crimson.

'I'll be fine, Ed – just once I get in that bairth.' Again Laura switched legs and massaged her other foot again – a foot which like its partner had until recently commanded the careful ministrations of the most expensive chiropodist in Pasadena.

'Yeah!' And perhaps someone else on the coach apart from his wife might have noticed Eddie Stratton's faint smile as he nodded his agreement.

The coach had now turned down into the Banbury Road, and Ashenden was soon into his well-rehearsed

16

commentary: '... and note on each side of the road the cheerful orange-brick houses, built in the last two decades of the nineteenth century when the dons in the University – there, look! – see the date? – 1887 ...'

Immediately behind Ashenden sat a man in his early seventies, a retired civil engineer from Los Angeles, who now looked out of his window at the string of shops and offices in Summertown: banks, building societies, fruiterers, hairdressers, housing agents, newsagents, wine shops – it could almost have been back home, really. But then it *was* back home, decided Howard Brown.

Beside him, Shirley Brown was the second wife who had seen a smile upon a husband's lips – a smile this time of wistful satisfaction; and suddenly she felt a sharp regret.

'Howard?' she whispered. 'Howard! I *am* glad – you know I am – glad we booked the tour. *Really* I am!' She laid her right arm along his long thigh and squeezed it gently. 'And I'm sorry I was such' (*pianissimo*) 'such an ungrateful bitch last night.'

'Forget it, Shirl – forget it!'

But Howard Brown found himself wishing that for a little while at least his wife would perpetuate her sullen ill-humour. In such a mood (not infrequent) she presented him with the leeway he needed for the (not infrequent) infidelities of thought and deed which he could never have entertained had she exhibited a quarter of the affection he had known when they'd agreed to marry. But that was in 1947 – forty-three years ago – before she'd ever dreamed of checking his automobile mileage, or scrutinising the postmarks on his private mail, or sniffing suspiciously at him after his coming home from the office . . .

'. . . and here' (Ashenden was in full and rather splendid spate) 'we see the Ruskin influence on domestic architecture during that period. You see – there! – on the left, look! – the neo-Gothic, mock-Venetian features . . . And here, on the left again, this is Norham Gardens, with the famous University Parks lying immediately behind. There! You see the iron gates? The Parks are one of the greatest open spaces in Oxford – still, even now, liable to be closed to the public at the whim of the University authorities – unless, of course, you get to know how to sneak in without being noticed by the keepers at the main entrance.'

'And to sneak *out* again, surely, Mr Ashenden?'

For once, one of Mrs Roscoe's inevitable interruptions was both pertinent and good-humoured, and her fellow passengers laughed their light-hearted approval.

Howard Brown, however, had been quite unaware of the exchange. He was craning his neck to look across at the Keeper's Lodge; and as he did so, like Mole, he sensed and smelled his old home territory, and inside him something long dormant woke into sudden life. He felt his eyes welling up with nostalgic tears, before fiercely blowing his nose and looking obliquely at his wife once more, gratified to observe that her lips had once again settled into their accustomed crab-crumpet discontent. She suspected nothing, he was virtually certain of that.

As the coach drew into St Giles', the sky was an open blue, and the sunlight gleamed on the cinnamon-coloured stone along the broad tree-lined avenue. 'Here we are, in St Giles'.' (Ashenden slipped into over-drive now.) 'You can see the plane trees on either side of us, ablaze with the beautifully golden tints of autumn – and, on the left here, St John's College – and Balliol just beyond. And here in front of us, the famous Martyrs' Memorial, modelled on the Eleanor Crosses of Edward the First, and designed by Gilbert Scott to honour the great Protestant martyrs – Cranmer and Latimer and, er . . .'

'Nicholas Ridley,' supplied Mrs Roscoe, as the coach turned right at the traffic lights and almost immediately pulled in on the left of Beaumont Street beneath the tall neo-Gothic façade of the Randolph Hotel.

'At last!' cried Laura Stratton, with what might have been the relief of a prisoner learning of a late reprieve.

In retrospect, it would have seemed an odd coincidence (though not an important one) that the middle-aged man housed in a nondescript block of flats at the top of the Banbury Road had been looking out from his second-floor double-glazed windows as the long luxury coach carrying Ashenden's group had passed by that late afternoon. Inside, a recently renewed needle glided through the well-worn grooves of the Furtwängler recording of *Götterdämmerung,* but the man's mind was more closely concentrated with an almost physical hurt on the greasy wrappings discarded by the previous night's fish-and-chip brigade as they'd walked homeward from the Chicken Barbecue in Summertown.

CHAPTER FOUR

'The cockroach *Blattella germanica*,' it was observed darkly in 1926, 'was at one time recorded as present in the Randolph Hotel kitchen'

(*Jan Morris*, Oxford)

ROY, CONCIERGE OF the five-star Randolph Hotel, a cheerful, florid-faced man of sixty, had been on duty since midday, and had, as always, been fully apprised by the Reception Manager of the scheduled afternoon arrivals – especially, of course, of the biggish bus-load of American tourists at 4.30 p.m. Roy, who had started with the hotel as a page-boy in 1945 – forty-five years since – quite liked the Americans. Not that he'd ever wished to fly over there for a holiday or anything drastic like that; but they *were* a nice lot, usually, the Yanks; friendly, communicative, generous. And although an incorrigibly biased patriot himself, he had recently begun to query the automatic superiority of his own countrymen, particularly that night the previous month when he'd returned on a Euro-Ferry after an abortive 0–0 draw between England and Holland.

It was five minutes before schedule that from his cubby-hole immediately inside the main entrance he saw the patrician coach pull slowly in beside the white canopy, flanked by a pair of elegant lamp-posts, at the front of Oxford's premier hotel. And a few seconds later he was standing at the top of the steps outside, in his yellow-piped blue uniform, beaming semi-beatifically, and ready to greet the new arrivals with an appropriate degree of that 'warmth' attested to on several separate pages of the hotel's technicolour brochure. As he stood there, the flags – Union Jack, EEC, USA – fluttered lightly above him in the afternoon breeze. He enjoyed his work – always had; in fact seldom referred to it as 'work' at all. Seldom, too, did anything much go wrong in an establishment so happily and so predictably well-ordered as The Randolph. Seldom indeed.

But once in a while?

Yes, once in a while.

Phil Aldrich, a small, mournful-visaged dolichocephalic senior citizen (from California, too) moved from his habitual and lonely seat on the back row of the coach and came to sit next to Mrs Roscoe; his hearing was not quite what it had been and he wanted to know what was going on. The Deputy Manager had appeared on the coach itself to welcome them all and to announce that tea – or coffee, if preferred – was immediately available in the St John's Suite on the first floor; that all bedrooms were now ready for occupancy and that every hotel facility from telephone to trouser-press was at his guests' disposal forthwith; that even as he spoke their baggage was being unloaded, counted, checked, and portered to the appropriate rooms. It would save a good deal of time, the Deputy Manager concluded, if everyone would fill in now, on the coach, the Guest Registration Cards.

With appreciative nods observable on each side of the gangway, Ashenden duly distributed the Welcome Trusthouse Forte forms, already completed for the sections dealing with Company, Next Destination, Settlement of Account, Arrival, Departure, and Nationality. Only remaining for the tourists to fill in were the four sections headed Home Address, Telephone, Passport Number, and Signature.

Phil expressed an unqualified approval: 'Gee! That's what I'd say was pretty darned efficient, Janet.'

For once Mrs Roscoe was unable to identify any obvious flaw in the procedures, and, instead, appeared to concentrate her thoughts upon the perils of the unpredictable future.

'I do hope the people here realise the great difference between Vegetarian and Vegan—'

'*Janet!* This is one of the finest hotels in the UK—'

But Ashenden's voice now cut across their conversation:

'So! If we can all . . . St John's Suite, St *John's* – that's on the first floor, just up the main staircase – tea or coffee – right away. I know some of you will just want to settle in and have a wash and . . . So if you take your forms to Reception – that's straight ahead of you as you go through the main doors here – and just sign the documentation forms there and get your keys . . . The lift, the guest-lift, is just to your right, in the corridor . . .'

'Get a *move* on!' hissed Laura under her breath.

'. . . I shall be calling round to your rooms later, just to make sure everything's . . .'

Ashenden knew what he was doing. Experience had taught him that the first hour or so in any new hotel was always the most vital, since some small problem, dealt with promptly, could make the difference between a contented life and an anxious existence. Blessedly, Ashenden was seldom, if ever, confronted with such positive complaints as cockroaches, mice, or the disgusting habits of a room's previous occupants. But a range of minor niggles was not unfamiliar, even in the best regulated of establishments: no soap in the bathroom; only two tubs of cream beside the self-service kettle; no instructions on how to operate the knobless TV; no sign – *still* no sign – of the luggage . . .

Eddie Stratton had managed to squeeze into second spot in the queue for keys, and Laura had grabbed their own key, 310, from his hand before he'd finished the documentation.

'I'm straight up, Ed, to draw me a bairth – I can't wait.'

'Yeah, but leave the door, honey – there's only the one key, OK? I'll have a cup of tea in the Saynt Jarn Suite.'

'Sure. I'll leave the door.'

She was gone.

As Laura hobbled away towards the guest-lift, Eddie turned round and looked directly into the eyes of Mrs Shirley Brown. For a few seconds there seemed to be no communication between the two of them; but then, after glancing briefly towards her husband, Shirley Brown nodded, almost imperceptibly, and her eyes smiled.

CHAPTER FIVE

All saints can do miracles, but few can keep a hotel
(*Mark Twain*, Notebook)

'*AT LAST!*' MUTTERED Laura Stratton for the third (and final) time as she inserted her key and turned it clockwise (and correctly) in the lock.

The room itself did not open immediately off the main corridor on level three; but a small plaque fixed beside double swing-doors (a FIRE EXIT sign above them) had pointed the way to Room 310. Once through these doors Laura had found herself in a further corridor, only four or five feet wide, which ran parallel to the main corridor, along which (after she had turned left) she walked the five yards or so to the bedroom door – on her right. Just beyond this door, the corridor turned at right angles and came to an almost immediate stop in the shape of another double-doored FIRE EXIT – doubtless, as Laura guessed (again correctly), leading down some back stairs to the ground floor. It did not occur to her that a person could stand in this narrow square of space, pressed tightly back behind the wall, and remain completely unobserved from the narrow corridor leading to her room.

If anyone wished to remain thus unobserved . . .

Laura extracted the key and carefully let the door

close, or almost close, behind her, with the tongue of the lock holding it slightly ajar. The two large black-leather cases were on the floor immediately inside, and she looked around to find herself in a most pleasantly appointed room. A double bed stood immediately to her right, covered by a pale-green quilt, with a free-standing wardrobe beyond it; facing her were the three lancet windows of the outside wall, with curtains down to the carpeted floor; and in front of these windows, from right to left, a tea-maker, a TV, a low, mirrored dressing table, and a red-plush chair. Her swift glance around missed little, except for the rather fine repro-duction of Vermeer's *View of Delft* above the bed. Laura and her first husband had once seen the original of this in the Mauritshuis in The Hague, when the guide had mentioned that it was Marcel Proust's favourite paint-ing; but strangely enough she had found it disappoint-ing, and in the very few minutes of life remaining to her she was to have no opportunity of revising that rather harsh judgement.

She stepped to the window and looked across at the tetrastyle portico of Ionic columns, with the figure of Apollo, right arm raised and seated (a little precar-iously, as Laura judged) at the apex of the low-pitched pediment. Between the two central columns, a large Oxford-blue banner was suspended: *Musaeum Ashmo-leanum apud Oxonienses*. Oh yes, Laura knew quite a lot about the Ashmolean Museum, and there appeared the flicker of a smile around her excessively lipsticked mouth as she let the curtain fall back and turned to the door on her left, half-open, which led to the

27

champagne-tiled bathroom. Without for the moment entering, she pushed the door a little further open: WC to the right; bath immediately facing her, the shower-curtains half drawn across; and to the left a hand-basin with a series of heated rails beside it, fully laden with fluffy white towels.

Laura had always slept on the left-hand side of any double bed, both as a young girl with her sister and then with both her husbands; and now she sat down, rather heavily, on the side of the bed immediately beside the main door, placed her white-leather hand-bag below the various switches for lights, radio, and TV, on the small table-top next to the bed – and removed her shoes.

Finally removed her shoes.

She fetched the kettle, filled it from the wash-basin in the bathroom, and switched on the current. Then, into the bathroom once more where she put the plug in the bath and turned on the hot tap. Returning to the main room again she picked up a DO NOT DISTURB sign, hung it over the outside door-knob, and returned to the bathroom to pour some pink Foaming Bubbly into the slowly filling bath.

Beryl Reeves had noted the single arrival in Room 310. At 4.40 p.m. she had put in a final burst of corridor hovering and hoovering, and knew even from her very limited experience that before she went off duty at 5.00 there would be several queries from these Americans about the whereabouts of the (non-existent) 'ice-machine' and the (readily available) replenishments of coffee sachets. Beryl was from Manchester; and her honest, if slightly naïve attitude to life – even more so, her *accent* – had already endeared her to many of her charges on Level Three. All in all, she was proving a very good employee: punctual, conscientious, friendly, and (as Morse was later to discover) a most reliable witness.

It had been exactly 4.45 that afternoon (and who could be more accurate than that?) when she had looked in at Room 310; noticed the sign hanging over the door-knob, wondering why the door itself was slightly ajar; peered momentarily into the room itself; but immediately retreated on seeing the steam emanating from the bathroom. Yes, she *thought* she would have probably noticed a white leather handbag if it had been somewhere just inside. No, she had *not* passed beyond the door and looked around the corner beside the Fire Exit. She had seen an American guest going into Room 308 shortly after this – a man; a friendly man, who'd said 'Hi!'. Yes, of course she would recognise him. In fact she could tell them who he was straightaway: a Mr Howard Brown from California.

Just before 6 p.m. the phone rang in the office of Chief Superintendent Strange at the Thames Valley Police HQ at Kidlington. The great man listened fairly patiently, if with less than obvious enthusiasm, to his colleague, Superintendent Bell from St Aldate's in Oxford.

'Well, it doesn't sound particularly like Morse's cup of tea, Bell, but if you're really short . . . No, he's trying to get a few days off, he tells me, says he never gets his full ration of furlough. Huh! If you take off the hours he spends in the pubs . . . what? Well, as I say, if you *are* short . . . Yes, all right. You know his home number? . . . Fine! Just tell him you've had a word with me. He's usually happier if Lewis is with him, though . . . What? Lewis is already *there*? Good. Good! And as I say, just tell him that you've had a word with me. There'll be no problems.'

CHAPTER SIX

There are worse occupations in this world than feeling a
woman's pulse

(*Laurence Sterne*, A Sentimental Journey)

'YOU HERE ALREADY, Lewis?'

'Half an hour ago, sir. The Super called me. They're
short-staffed at St Aldate's—'

'Must be!'

'I've already been upstairs.'

'No problems?'

'I'm – I'm not quite sure, sir.'

'Well – "Lead on, Macduff!"'

'That should be "Lay on Macduff!", sir. So our
English teacher—'

'Thank you, Lewis.'

'The lift's just along here—'

'Lift? We're not climbing the Empire State Building!'

'Quite a few stairs, sir,' said Lewis quietly, suspecting
(rightly) that his chief was going through one of his
temporary get-a-little-fitter phases.

'Look! Don't you worry too much about me, Lewis.
If by any chance things become a bit too strenuous in
the ascent, I shall stop periodically and pant, all right?'

Lewis nodded, happy as always (almost always) to be
working with the curmudgeonly Morse once more.

31

For a few seconds Morse stood outside Room 310, breathing heavily and looking down at the door-knob. He raised his eyebrows to Lewis.

'No, sir – waste of time worrying. Four or five people been in.'

'Who's in there now?' asked Morse quietly.

'Only the quack – Doc Swain – he's been the house-doctor here for a few years.'

'Presumably the *corpse* as well, Lewis?'

'The corpse as well, sir.'

'Who else has been in?'

'The Manager, Mr Gascoigne, and Mr Stratton – that's the husband, sir. He was the one who found her – very shaken up, I'm afraid, he is. I asked Mr Gascoigne to take him to his office.' Lewis pointed vaguely to one of the lower floors.

'No one else?'

'Me, of course.'

Morse nodded, and almost smiled.

Mrs Laura Stratton lay neatly supine on the nearer side of the double bed. She wore a full-length peach-coloured dressing robe, and (so far as Morse could see) little else. And she was dead. Morse glanced briefly at the face, swallowed once, and turned away.

Dr Swain, a fresh-faced, youngish-looking man (early thirties?) was seated at the low dressing table, writing. He turned his head and almost immediately answered Morse's unspoken question.

'Heart attack. Massive coronary.'

'Thank you, Dr – *Swain*, I think?'

'And you are?'

'I am Morse. Chief Inspector Morse.'

Swain got to his feet and handed Morse a sheet of paper, headed 'Oxfordshire Health Authority', with an impressively qualified column of medical men printed top right, in which (second from bottom) Morse read 'M. C. Swain, MA, MB, BCh, MRCP, MRCGP'.

'Congratulations!' said Morse.

'Pardon?'

'Sixteen, isn't it? Sixteen letters after your name, and I haven't got a single one after mine.'

'Well, er – that's how things go, isn't it? I'll be off now, if you don't mind. You've got my report. BMA dinner we've got this evening.'

Seldom was it that Morse took such an irrationally instant dislike to one of his fellow men; but there are always exceptions, and one of these was Dr M. C. Swain, MA, MB, BCh, MRCP, MRCGP.

'I'm afraid no one leaves for the moment, Doctor. You know, I think, that we've got slightly more than a death here?'

'I'm told something valuable's been stolen. Yes, I know that. All I'm telling *you* is that the cause of death was a massive coronary. You can read it in *that*!' Swain flung his forefinger Morse's way, towards the sheet just handed over.

'Do you think that was before – or after – this valuable something went missing?'

'I – I don't know.'

'She died there – where she is now – on the bed?'

'On the floor, actually.'

Morse forced his features to the limits of credulity: 'You mean you *moved* her, Dr Swain?'

'Yes!'

'Have you ever heard of murder in the furtherance of theft?'

'Of course! But this *wasn't* murder. It was a massive—'

'Do you really think it necessary to tell me things three times, sir?'

'I knew nothing about the theft. In fact I only learned about it five minutes ago – from the Manager.'

'That's true, sir,' chipped in Lewis, greatly to Morse's annoyance.

'Yes, well, if the Doctor has a dinner to attend, Lewis – a BMA dinner! – who are we to detain him? It's a pity about the *evidence*, of course. But I suppose we shall just have to try our best to find the man – or the woman – responsible for this, er, this massive coronary, brought on doubtless by the shock of finding some thief nicking her valuables. Good evening, Doctor. Make sure you enjoy your dinner!' Morse turned to Lewis: 'Tell Max to get over here straightaway, will you? Tell him it's as urgent as they get.'

'Look, Inspector—' began Swain.

But Morse was doing a reasonably convincing impression of a deaf man who has just turned off his hearing-aid, and now silently held the door of Room 310 open as the disconcerted doctor was ushered out.

*

It was in the Manager's office, on the first floor of The Randolph, that for the first time Morse himself was acquainted with the broad outlines of the story. Laura Stratton had taken her key up to her room soon after 4.30 p.m.; she had earlier been complaining of feeling awfully weary; had taken a bath – presumably after hanging a DO NOT DISTURB notice outside her door; had been discovered at 5.20 p.m. when her husband, Mr Eddie Stratton, had returned from a stroll around Broad Street with a fellow tourist, Mrs Shirley Brown. He had found the door to 310 shut, and after being unable to get any response from within had hurried down to Reception in some incipient panic before returning upstairs to find ... That was all really; the rest was elaboration and emotional overlay. Except of course for the handbag. But who is the man, with his wife lying dead on the carpet, who thinks of looking around to see if her handbag has disappeared?

Well, Mr Eddie Stratton, it seemed.

And that for a most important reason.

CHAPTER SEVEN

Almost all modern architecture is farce
(*Diogenes Small* (1797–1812), Reflections)

THE RANDOLPH BOASTED many fine rooms for din-
ners, dances, conferences, and exhibitions: rooms with
such splendid names as Lancaster, Worcester, and the
like – and the St John's Suite, a high-ceilinged room on
the first floor where the reception had been arranged.
In the daylight hours the view from the east window
took in the Martyrs' Memorial, just across the street,
with Balliol and St John's Colleges behind. And even
now, at 6.45 p.m., with the floral, carpet-length curtains
drawn across, the room still seemed so light and airy,
the twin candelabra throwing a soft light over the
maroon and pink and brilliant-white décor. Even Janet
Roscoe could find little to criticise in such a grandly
appointed room.

Sheila Williams, a large gin and tonic in her left
hand, was trying to be pleasantly hospitable: 'Now
are we all here? Not *quite*, I think? Have we all got
drinks?'

News of Laura Stratton's death had been withheld
from the rest of the group, with only Sheila herself
being officially notified of that sad event. It was a
burden for her, certainly; but also a wonderful excuse

for fortifying the inner woman, and Sheila seldom needed any such excuse.

'Mrs Roscoe! You haven't got a drink. What can I—?'

'I don't drink, Mrs Williams!' Janet turned her head to a sheepish-looking Phil Aldrich, standing stoically beside her: 'I've already told her *once*, Phil!'

'Janet here is a deacon in our church back home, Mrs Williams—'

But Sheila had already jerked into a tetchy rejoinder: 'Well I *do* drink, Mrs Roscoe! In fact I'm addicted to the stuff. And my reasons for such addiction may be just as valid as your own reasons for abstinence. All right?'

With which well-turned sentence she walked back to the table just beside the main door whereon a dozen or so bottles of gin (Booth's and Gordon's), Martini (French and Italian), sherry (dry, medium, sweet) stood in competition with two large jugs of orange juice. She handed over her half-empty glass to the young girl dispensing the various riches.

'Gin – large one, please! – no ice – and no more tonic.'

Thus, fully re-equipped for her duties, Sheila looked down once more at the yellow sheet of A4 which John Ashenden had earlier prepared, typed up, photocopied, and distributed. It was high time to get things moving. Of the tourists, only Howard and Shirley Brown (apart from Eddie Stratton) seemed now to be missing – no, that was wrong: apart from Eddie and *Laura* Stratton. Of the two distinguished speakers (*three,* if she herself were included), Theodore Kemp had not as yet put in an appearance. But the third of the trio, Cedric Downes, seemed to Sheila to be doing a splendid job as he stood behind a thinly fluted glass of dry sherry and asked, with (as she saw it) a cleverly concealed indifference, whence the tourists hailed and what their pre-retirement professions had been.

It was 7.25 p.m. before Dr Kemp finally entered, in the company of a subdued-looking Ashenden; and it was almost immediately apparent to Sheila that both of them had now been informed of the disturbing events that had been enacted in the late afternoon. As her eyes had met Kemp's there was, albeit for a moment, a flash of mutual understanding and (almost?) of comradeship.

'Ladies and Gentlemen . . .' Sheila knocked a table noisily and repeatedly with the bottom of an ash-tray, and the chatter subsided. 'Mr Ashenden has asked me to take you through our Oxford itinerary – briefly! – so if you will all just look at your yellow sheets for a minute . . .' She waved her own sheet; and then, without any significant addition (although with a significant omission) to the printed word, read vaguely through the dates and times of the itemized programme:

THE HISTORIC CITIES OF ENGLAND TOUR
27TH OCT–10TH NOV
(Oxford Stage)

Thursday 1st November

4.30 p.m. (approx.) Arr. The Randolph
4.30–5.30 p.m.   English teas available

6.45 p.m.	Cocktail Reception (St John's Suite) introduced by Sheila Williams, MA, BLitt (Cantab), with Cedric Downes, MA (Oxon)
8.00 p.m.	Dinner (main dining room)
9.30–10.15 p.m.	Talk by Dr Theodore Kemp, MA, DPhil (Oxon) on 'Treasures of the Ashmolean'.

Friday 2nd November

7.30–9.15 a.m.	Breakfast (main dining room)
10.30–11.30 a.m.	Visit to The Oxford Story, Broad Street (100 yards only from the hotel)
12.45 p.m.	Lunch (St John's Suite) – followed by an informal get-together with our lecturers in the coffee-lounge
3.00 p.m.	We divide into groups (details to be announced later)
4.30–5.00 p.m.	English tea (Lancaster Room)
6.30 p.m.	The Tour Highlight! The presentation, by Mrs Laura Stratton, of the Wolvercote Tongue (Ashmolean Museum)
8.00 p.m.	Dinner (N.B. extra charge) in The Randolph. Otherwise group members are offered a last opportunity to dine out, wine out, and find out – wherever they wish – on our final night in this wonderful University City.

Saturday 3rd November

7.30–8.30 a.m.	Breakfast (Please be punctual!)
9.30 a.m.	Departure from The Randolph for Broughton Castle (Banbury), and thence to Stratford.

'The only thing that needs much expansion here' (Sheila was talking more confidently now) 'is the three p.m. spot tomorrow afternoon. So let me just fill in a bit there. Dr Kemp, Keeper of Anglo-Saxon and Mediaeval Antiquities at the Ashmolean – the museum just opposite us here! – will be taking his group around there tomorrow – as well as talking to us after dinner tonight, as you can see. Then, Mr Cedric Downes' (Sheila duly signified that distinguished gentleman) 'will be taking his own group around several colleges – including the most interesting of the dining halls – and addressing himself particularly to' (Sheila looked at her brief notes) ' "Architectural Design and Technique in the Sixteenth and Seventeenth Centuries". That, again, is at three p.m. ... Well, you've heard almost enough from me now ...' (Janet Roscoe was nodding) '... but I'd just like to mention that there is a *third* group tomorrow.' ('Hear, hear!' said Phil Aldrich happily.) 'You see, *I* shall be taking a group of you – perhaps only two or three of you, I don't mind – on an "Alice Tour". As most of you will know, the Reverend Charles Lutwidge Dodgson – "Lewis Carroll" – was in real life a "Student" – I shall explain that tomorrow – at Christ Church in the latter half of the nineteenth century; and we shall be looking at many mementoes of him, in the Deanery Garden, the Cathedral, and the Dining Hall; and also looking at a unique collection of old photographs, drawings and cartoons in the Bodleian Library. Well, that's what's on the menu. I'm sorry we're running just a bit late but ... Anyway, it's my great pleasure now to introduce you to Cedric here –

Mr Cedric Downes – who is going to set the scene for his talk tomorrow, in a rather light-hearted way, he tells me, by giving us a few thoughts on *modern* architecture. Ladies and Gentlemen – Cedric Downes.'

'Thank you, Sheila! I sometimes feel that some of our tourists must think that here in Oxford we're all mediaeval, Early English, Gothic, Tudor, Jacobean, Georgian, and so on. But we do have – though I'm no expert in this field – we do have a few fine examples of contemporary design. I don't want to get too serious about things – not tonight! But take St Catherine's, for example – the work of that most famous Danish architect, Arne er Johansen—'

'Jacobsen!' (*Sotto voce* from Kemp.)

'Pardon?'

'You said "Johansen",' murmured Kemp.

'Surely not! I said "Jacobsen", didn't I?'

A chorus of assorted tourists assured Downes that he had most certainly *not* said 'Jacobsen'; and for a second or two Downes turned upon his fellow lecturer a look of what might have been interpreted as naked detestation, were it not for the slightly weary resignation in his eyes. To his audience he essayed a charming smile, and resumed:

'I'm sorry! It's all these Danes, you know! You never actually meet one called "Hamlet", do you? And talking of *Hamlet*, I see you'll all be at Stratford-on-Avon—'

'I thought it was Stratford-uparn-Avon,' chirruped a shrill, thin voice.

But by now Downes was getting into his stride: 'How good it is for us all in Oxford, Mrs, er—'

'Mrs Roscoe, sir. Mrs Janet Roscoe.'

'How good it is for Dr Kemp and Mrs Williams and myself to meet a scholar like you, Mrs Roscoe! I was just going to mention – only in passing, of course – that the Swan Theatre there, in my view . . .'

But everyone had seen the door open, and now looked with some puzzlement at the newcomer, a man none of them had seen before.

'Mrs Williams? Is there a Mrs Williams here?'

The said lady, still standing beside the drinks-table, no more than a couple of yards from the door, raised the index-finger of her non-drinking hand to signify her identity.

'Could I have a quiet word with you, madam?' asked Sergeant Lewis.

CHAPTER EIGHT

Madame, appearing to imbibe gin and It in roughly equal measures, yet manages to exude rather more of the gin than of the 'it'

(*Hugh Sykes-Davies*, Obiter Dicta)

INSIDE THE MANAGER'S office, situated at the head of the first flight of stairs, Morse found his attention almost immediately drifting towards the large drinks-cabinet which stood to the left of the high-ceilinged suite of rooms wherein Mr Douglas Gascoigne, a bespectacled, intelligent-looking man in his early forties, sought, and sought successfully, to sustain the high standards of service expected from his multi-starred establishment. Early photographs, cartoons, diplomas, framed letters, and a series of pleasing watercolours, lined the walls of the main office, above the several tables on which VDU screens, print-out machines, telephones, in- and out-trays, fax machines, and file-cases abstracted from surrounding shelves, vied with each other for a few square feet of executive justifiable space. As in the St John's Suite, the curtains were drawn, this time across the window behind Gascoigne as he sat at his desk, concealing the view of the Ashmolean façade upon which, though from a higher elevation, Mrs Laura Stratton had gazed so very briefly some three hours earlier.

'It's just' (Gascoigne was talking) 'that we've never had – well, not in my time – anyone actually *dying* in the hotel.'

'Some thefts, though, I suppose?'

'Yes, a few, Inspector. Cameras left around – that sort of thing. But never anything so valuable . . .'

'Wonder why she didn't leave it in your safe, sir?'

Gascoigne shook his head: 'We always offer to lock away anything like that but—'

'Insured, was it?'

'Mr Stratton' – the Manager lowered his voice and gestured to the closed door on his right – 'thinks probably yes, but he's still in a bit of a daze, I'm afraid. Dr Swain gave him some pills and he's still in there with one of his friends, a Mr Howard Brown.' And indeed Morse thought he could just about hear an occasional murmur of subdued conversation.

Lewis put his head round the door and signified his success in securing the appearance of Mrs Sheila Williams. Gascoigne got to his feet and prepared to leave the two detectives to it.

'As I say, just make use of any of our facilities here for the time being. We may have to keep coming in occasionally, of course, but—'

'Thank you, sir.'

So Gascoigne left his own office, and left the scene to Morse.

And to Sheila Williams.

She was – little question of it – a most attractive woman, certainly as Morse saw her: mid-thirties (perhaps older?), with glistening dark-brown eyes that somehow managed to give the simultaneous impression of vulnerability, sensuality, and mild inebriation.

A heady mixture!

'Sit down! Sit down! You look as if you could do with a drink, Mrs Williams.'

'Well, I – it *is* all a bit of a shock, isn't it?'

'Anything suitable in there, Lewis?' Morse pointed to the drinks-cabinet, not without a degree of self-interest.

'Looks like he's just about got the lot, sir.'

'Mrs Williams?'

'G and T – that would be fine.'

'Gin and tonic for the lady, Lewis . . . Ice?'

'Why dilute the stuff, Inspector?'

'There's no ice anyway,' muttered Lewis.

'Look,' began Sheila Williams, 'I'm not myself in charge of this group. I do liaise *with* the group and arrange speakers and so on – but it's John Ashenden who's the tour leader.'

Morse, however, appeared wholly uninterested in the activities of Mr Ashenden: 'Mrs Williams, I'm going to have to ask everyone in the group what they were doing between about four-thirty and five-fifteen this afternoon – that's between the time Mr Stratton last saw his wife and when he got back from his walk with, er, with Mrs Brown . . .'

As Sheila tossed back the last of her G and T, Lewis thought he saw the hint of a smile about her full lips; but Morse had turned to the wall on his left where he was minutely studying a late nineteenth-century Henry Taunt photograph of some brewery drays, and his last few words may well have been spoken without the slightest hint of implication or innuendo.

'I'm sure they'll all co-operate, Inspector, but they don't know yet about . . .'

'No. Perhaps we should wait a while? After dinner? No later than that. I wouldn't want Sergeant Lewis here to be too late in bed – Ah! Another, Mrs Williams?'

'I'm sorry . . . I seem to be—'

'Nothing to be sorry about, is there?'

'Same again then, please, Sergeant. Little less tonic, perhaps?'

Lewis's eyebrows rose a centimetre. 'Anything for you, sir?'

'No thank you, Lewis. Not on duty.'

Lewis's eyebrows rose a further centimetre as he collected Mrs Williams's glass.

The tour was, as Morse and Lewis learned, a pretty expensive, pretty exclusive business really. Most of them had been to England before (not all, though) and most of them were well enough off to be coming back again before *too* long, whatever the strength of the pound sterling. One of them wouldn't be, though . . . Yes, Sheila Williams knew quite a bit about the Wolvercote Tongue, although Dr Kemp was the real authority, of course. It seemed that Laura Stratton's first husband, a real-estate man operating in California and, in later life, quite a collector, had come to find himself in possession of a jewelled artefact which, after learning of its provenance, he had bequeathed – he had died two years since – to the Curators of the Ashmolean Museum in Oxford. Oh yes, she had seen it dozens of times, though only in a series of technicolour slides, from which she had been able to sketch out a diagram of the whole jewel, buckle *and* tongue; and in fact she herself had executed the final coloured illustration which was at that moment on show at the Ashmolean. Come to think of it, she was glad she *had* done the drawings; whatever happened now, people could know exactly how the Wolvercote Jewel in its entirety *would* have appeared. Doubtless the police would find the Tongue, but . . .

'We shall certainly do our best, madam,' Lewis had interposed, the tone of his voice suggesting something less than brimming optimism.

The Tongue itself? Well, again, *Kemp* was really the one to ask. But she could certainly tell them all about the look of it: of triangular shape, some 3 inches long, and 2 inches wide at the base; of a dull dirtyish brown colour (gold!), with (originally) three ruby-stones, one on each corner of the triangle – but now reduced to just the one, and that at the narrower end of things. The great, the unique, value of the Tongue was the fact that it fitted (perfectly!) into the gold buckle which had been discovered during an archaeological dig at the village of Wolvercote in the early 1930s; and which, since 1947, had been proudly exhibited in the Ashmolean as evidence (hitherto unsuspected) of the exquisite craftsmanship of the goldsmith's art in the late eighth century AD. Laura Stratton (so Sheila had learned from John Ashenden) had carried the jewel with her, in a black velvet-lined case, and kept it in her handbag – refusing to entrust the precious artefact either to transatlantic postal services, international tour operators, or burglar-and-fire-proof safe-deposit boxes. In the same handbag, it appeared, Laura had also carried a beautiful-looking string of wholly phoney pearls, which she had worn on most evenings with her dinner-dresses. Of any other valuables which might have been stolen with the handbag, Sheila had no idea whatsoever, although she volunteered the information that from her own recent experiences – and in spite of the equally recent strength of the pound sterling – some of the Americans seemed less than fully aware of the denominational value of the English currency they carried on their persons. With almost all of the party (she suspected) several £10, £20, even £50, notes would hardly be strangers in the purses and wallets of some of California's wealthier citizens. So a casual thief might have been pleasantly surprised by the sum of the monies often carried? But Mr Stratton – Eddie Stratton – *he'd* be the man to ask about such things, wouldn't he? Really?

She turned her large, melancholy eyes upon Morse; and for a few seconds Lewis found himself wondering if his chief wasn't temporarily mesmerised. So much so that he decided not to withhold his own contribution:

'You say, Mrs Williams, that the group won't perhaps mind me asking them all where they were between four-thirty and five-fifteen? Would you mind if you told us where *you* were?'

The effect of such an innocent question was quite unexpectedly melodramatic. Sheila Williams placed her empty glass on the table in front of her, and immedi-

ately burst into tears, during which time Morse glow-
ered at his subordinate as if he had simultaneously
broken all the rules of diplomacy, etiquette, and
freemasonry.

But Morse himself, as he thought, was equal to the
task: he nodded peremptorily to the empty glass, and
immediately Lewis found himself pouring yet another
generous measure of Gordon's gin, tempered again
with but a little slim-line tonic.

Suddenly, and with a defiant glare at the two policemen, Sheila sat up in her chair, sought to regain a
precarious state of equipoise, and drank down the
proffered mixture in a single draught – much to
Morse's secret admiration. She spoke just five words:
'Ask Dr Kemp – he'll explain!'

After she was gone, guided in gentlemanly fashion
along the corridor by Sergeant Lewis, Morse quickly
opened the drinks-cabinet, poured himself half a tumbler of Glenfiddich, savoured a large and satisfying
swallow, thereafter placing the tumbler strategically on
a convenient shelf, just below the line of vision of
anyone entering. Including Sergeant Lewis.

Strangely, neither Sergeant Lewis nor Inspector
Morse himself seemed particularly conscious of the fact
that Mrs Sheila Williams had signally failed to answer
the only significant question that had been put to her.

Such is the wonderful effect of any woman's tears.

CHAPTER NINE

Often I have wished myself dead, but well under my blanket,
so that neither death nor man could hear me

(George Lichtenberg)

JOHN ASHENDEN WOULD later remember exactly
what he had done during the vital forty-five minutes
that Morse had specified . . .

It was a quarter to five when he had walked out of
The Randolph, and crossed over by the Martyrs' Memorial into Broad Street. The sun no longer slanted
across the pale-yellow stone, the early evening was
becoming much cooler, and he was wearing a lightweight raincoat. He strode fairly quickly past the front
of Balliol, the great gates of Trinity, Blackwell's Book
Shop; and was waiting by the New Bodleian building to
cross at the traffic lights into Holywell Street when he
saw them standing there outside the Sheldonian, *sub
imperatoribus*, her arm through his, neither of them (as
it seemed) taking too much notice of anything except
their mutual selves. Even more briskly now, Ashenden
walked past the King's Arms, the Holywell Music Room,
the back of New College – until he came to Longwall
Street. Here he turned left; and after two hundred yards
or so went through the wooden gate that led into Holywell Cemetery, where under the stones and crosses – so

many Celtic crosses! – were laid to rest the last remains
of eminent Oxford men, in these slightly unkempt, but
never neglected, acres of the dead. A curving path
through the grass led him to a wooden seat above which,
wired to a yew tree, was a rectangular board showing
the plot of the cemetery, with the memorials of the
particularly eminent marked by numbers:

1 Kenneth Grahame (1859–1932)
2 Maurice Bowra (1898–1971)
3 Kenneth Tynan (1927–1980)
4 H. V. D. Dyson (1896–1975)
5 James Blish (1921–1975)
6 Theodore and Sibley, Drowned (1893)
7 Sir John Stainer (1840–1901)
8 Walter Pater . . .

That was him!

It took Ashenden some twenty minutes or so, tread-
ing through overgrown grasses, and parting ivy from
many semi-decipherable inscriptions, to find the strong,
squat cross:

In te, Domine, speravi
WALTER PATER
Died July 30 1894

Then, almost immediately, he saw that other stone, the
one he was looking for – an even simpler memorial:

> JAMES ALFRED BOWDEN
> 1956–1981
> Requiescat

For several minutes Ashenden stood there silently under the darkening shadows: it seemed a wonderfully unforbidding piece of ground in which to find a final resting-place. Yet no one wanted to die – certainly not John Ashenden, as he remained standing by the grave, wondering whether Jimmy Bowden, during the pain of his terminal illness, had ever recanted the dogmatic and confident atheism he had once propounded in the early hours of one most memorable day. But Ashenden doubted it. He recalled, too, that final postcard to which he had never replied . . .

There was no one else in the cemetery; no one there to observe the strange little incident when Ashenden, after looking round about him for a last reassurance, parted the thickly twined rootage of ivy at the rear of Bowden's small cross, took something from the right-hand pocket of his raincoat, and laid it carefully at the foot of the stone before replacing the ivy and patting it, almost effeminately, back into its pristine state.

He was in no hurry, and on his leisurely way back to the cemetery gate he stopped and read several of the gravestones, including 'Kenneth Grahame, who passed the river on the 6th July 1932, leaving childhood and literature through him the more blest for all time'. Ashenden loved the wording. He looked vaguely for

'Theodore and Sibley, Drowned (1893)'; but it was too dark now, and he could find no clue as to who they were and where they had perished.

He regained the main street, and on his way back to The Randolph called in at the back bar of the King's Arms to order a pint of cask-conditioned Flowers. For which choice, Inspector Morse would have been quietly proud of him.

Shirley Brown had disengaged her arm as she and Eddie Stratton crossed into Beaumont Street at ten-past five.

'Whatever you say, Ed, I'd still like to know where he was going.'

'Like I say, *forget* it, Shirl!'

'He was trying to get out of sight – quick. You *know* he was.'

'You still reckon he saw us?'

'I still reckon he saw us,' said Shirley Brown, in her Californian drawl.

They were the only two in the guest-lift; and Eddie bade his temporary leave as they reached the third floor.

'See you in a little while, Shirl.'

'Yeah. And tell Laura I hope her feet are rested.'

Eddie Stratton had made no reply as he walked towards Room 310.

CHAPTER TEN

A foolish consistency is the hobgoblin of little minds
(*Ralph Waldo Emerson*, Essays)

TOO LONG HAD Morse been in the police business for
him to believe that a death and a theft, or (as he was
now beginning to think) a theft and a death, were likely
to be a pair of fortuitously contingent events. Not that
he was even remotely hopeful about the *theft*. He would
never mind pitting his brains against a *murderer*; but
he'd always discounted his chances against a reasonably
competent burglar – even, come to think of it, against
a reasonably incompetent burglar. And if, as seemed
the consensus of opinion now, Laura Stratton had left
her door ajar for her husband to let himself in; if she
had carelessly left her handbag on the bedside table
immediately inside her partially opened door; if someone had known of these things – even if someone had
not known of these things ... well, certainly, the odds
were pretty strong on the prompt disappearance of the
handbag. Give it fifteen minutes? At the outside,
thought Morse. We all might pray (*some* of us might
pray) 'Lead us not into temptation', yet most people
seemed perfectly happy to stick their cameras, binoculars, radios, squash rackets, handbags ... mm ... yes,
stick any of 'em on the back seats of their cars, and

then complain to the police when they found their rear windows smashed into splinters and—

Come off it!

The truth was, of course, that Morse had virtually lost all interest in the case already, his only enduring memory being the admiration he'd felt for the alcoholic capacity of a lady named Mrs Sheila Williams.

He just managed to hide the tumbler when without even a sociable knock Max put his head round the door and, seeing Morse in the Manager's chair, promptly entered and seated himself.

'They told me I'd find you here. Not that I needed much direction. Any pathologist worth his meagre remuneration tends to develop a fairly keen sense of smell.'

'Well?'

'Heart attack. Massive coronary.' (*Swain's* words.)

Morse nodded slowly.

'God knows why you ask me along here to confirm the obvious. Where's the booze, by the way?'

Reluctantly, Morse pointed to the drinks-cabinet.

'You're not paying for it, are you?'

'What do you fancy?'

'Nothing for me, Morse. I'm on duty.'

'All right.'

'Is, er, is it drinkable – the Scotch?'

Morse got to his feet, poured a miniature into a plastic cup, and handed it over. For a few minutes the two old enemies sat sipping in friendly silence.

'You *quite* sure, Max . . .?'

'Not so bad, is it, this stuff?'

'. . . about the time of death?'

'Between four-thirty and five-fifteen.'

'*Really?*' Never before had Morse heard anything remotely approaching such a definitive statement from the lips of the hump-backed police-surgeon. 'How on earth—?'

'Girl at Reception, Morse. Said the poor old dear had gone up to her room at four-thirty, on her own two tootsies, too. Then your people told me she was found by her ever-loving husband at five-fifteen.' Max took a large swallow of the Glenfiddich. 'We professionals in the Force, Morse, we have to interpret all the available clues, you know.' He drained his cup with deep appreciation.

'Another?'

'Certainly not! I'm on duty . . . And anyway I'm just off to a very nice little dinner.'

A distant temple-bell was tinkling in Morse's mind: 'Not the same nosh-up as whatshisname?'

'The very same, Morse.'

'He's the house-doctor here.'

'Try telling me something I *don't* know.'

'It's just that he looked at Mrs Stratton, that's all.'

'And you didn't have much faith in him.'

'Not much.'

'He's considered quite a competent quack, they tell me.'

'To be honest, I thought he was a bit of a . . .'

'Bit of a *membrum virile*? You're not *always* wrong, you know . . . Er, *small* top-up, perhaps, Morse?'

'You know him?'

'Oh yes. And you're *quite* wrong, in this case. He's not just a—No, let's put it the other way: he's the *biggest* one in Oxford.'

'She still died of a heart attack, though?'

'Oh yes! So don't go looking for any silly bloody nonsense here. And it's not Swain who's telling you, Morse – it's *me.*'

When, some ten minutes later, Max had departed for his BMA dinner, Morse had already performed what in political parlance would be termed a compromising U-turn. And when Lewis came in, with Dr Theodore Kemp immediately in tow, Morse knew that he had erred in his earlier thinking. The coincidence of a theft and a death (in whichever order) might often be shown to be causally connected.

But not in this case.

Lewis would have to interview them all, of course; or most of them. But that would be up to Lewis. For himself, Morse wished for nothing more fervently than to get back to his bachelor flat in North Oxford, and to listen once again to the Second Movement of the Bruckner No. 7.

But he'd better see one or two of them.

CHAPTER ELEVEN

History, n. An account mostly false, of events mostly unimportant, which are brought about by rulers mostly knaves, and soldiers mostly fools

(*Ambrose Bierce*, The Devil's Dictionary)

ALMOST IMMEDIATELY KEMP slotted into Morse's preconceptions of the we-are-an-Oxford-man, although he was aware that he could well be guilty of yet another instant inaccuracy. The bearded, clever-looking, ugly-attractive man (late thirties – Sheila's age?) who sat down only after lightly dusting the seat with a hyper-handkerchief, had clearly either been told (by Sheila?) or heard (gossip inevitable) something of what had occurred. Other persons might have been irritated only temporarily by the man's affected lisp. Not so Morse.

'Abtholutely pritheless, Inthpector!'

'Perhaps you could tell us a little more about the Wolvercote Tongue, sir.'

Kemp was well prepared. He opened his black brief-case, took out a pile of pale-blue leaflets, and handed one across the desk to Morse, one to Lewis.

The Wolvercote Jewel

During the last century or so archaeologists and historians have become increasingly conscious of the splendid workmanship of the late Saxon period, and the discovery in 1931 of a gold 'buckle' at Wolvercote had been extremely exciting. Particularly so since this buckle linked up with a corresponding 'tongue', fully documented and authenticated, known to be in the collection of one Cyrus C. Palmer Jnr, a citizen of Pasadena, California. The *cloisonné* enamel of the pear-shaped tongue, set in a solid gold frame, decorated in a distinctive type of delicate filigree, and set (originally) with three large ruby-stones, appeared to match the Ashmolean buckle with exact precision. And if further proof were sought, the tongue's lettering – [AE]LFRED[1] MEC HE[HT GEWYR] CAN – was identical in figuration and engravure to that of the gold buckle – into which (as all experts now concur) the tongue had once fitted.

That the tongue will shortly fit into its buckle once more is due to the philanthropy of Mr Palmer and to the gracious co-operation and interest of his wife, (now) Mrs Laura M. Stratton. The only major problem remaining to be resolved (according to Dr Theodore Kemp of the Ashmolean Museum) is the exact purpose of this most beauti-fully wrought artefact, henceforth to be known, in its entirety, as 'The Wolvercote Jewel'. Whether it was the clasp of some royal garment, or whether it served some symbolic or ceremonial purpose, is a matter of fascinating speculation. What is certain is that The Wolvercote Jewel – tongue and buckle at last most happily conjoined – will now be numbered amongst the finest treasures of the Ashmolean Museum.

1   Alfred the Great, AD 871–901. For a full discussion, see *Pre-Conquest Craftsmanship in Southern Britain*, Theodore S. Kemp, Babington Press, June 1991.

'You write this, sir?' asked Morse.

Kemp nodded bitterly: the whole bloody thing now cancelled (Morse learned) – the ceremony that was all fixed up – the presentation – the press – TV. God!

'We learned the dates of the kings and queens of England at school,' said Morse. 'Trouble is we started at William the First.'

'You ought to have gone back earlier, Inspector – much earlier.'

'Oh, I'm always doing that, sir.' Morse fixed his eyes on the pallid face across the table. 'What were you doing earlier this evening between four-thirty and five-fifteen, Dr Kemp?'

'What? What wath I doing?' He shook his head like a man most grievously distraught. 'You don't – you can't understand, can you! I wath probably buggering around in . . .' he pointed vaguely over Morse's head in the direction of the Ashmolean. 'I don't know. And I don't care!' He picked up the pile of leaflets and, with a viciousness of which Morse would not have thought the effeminate fingers capable, tore them across the middle, and threw them down on the desk.

Morse let him go.

Kemp was the second witness that evening who had been less than forthcoming in answering the only pertinent question that had been put to him.

'You didn't like him much, did you, sir?'

'What's that got to do with anything?'

'Well, somebody must have stolen this Wolvercote thing.'

'*Nobody* pinched it, Lewis! They pinched the *handbag*.'

'I don't see it. The handbag's worth virtually nothing – but the, you know, it's priceless, he says.'

'Abtholutely pritheless!' mimicked Morse.

Lewis grinned. 'You don't think *he* stole it?'

'I'd rather not *think* at all about that inflated bladder of wind and piss. What I *know* is that he'd be the last person in Oxford to steal it. He's got everything lined up – he's got this literature all ready – he'll get his name in the papers and his face on the telly – he'll write a monograph for some learned journal – the University will give him a D.Litt. or something ... No, he didn't pinch it. You see you can't *sell* something like that, Lewis. It's only "priceless" in the sense of its being unique, irreplaceable, crucial for historical and archaeological interpretation ... You couldn't sell the *Mona Lisa*, could you?'

'You knew all about it, did you, sir? This Wolvercote thing?'

'Didn't *you?* People come from far and wide to view the Wolvercote Tongue—'

'"Buckle", isn't it, sir? Isn't it just the *buckle* that's there?'

'I've never heard of the bloody thing,' growled Morse.

'I've never even been *inside* the Ashmolean, sir.'

'Really?'

'The only thing we learned about King Alfred was about him burning the cakes.'

'That's something though, isn't it? It's a fact – *perhaps* it's a fact. But they don't go in for facts in

History these days. They go in for empathy, Lewis. Whatever that is.'

'What's the drill then, sir?'

So Morse told him. Get the body moved quietly via the luggage-lift while the tourists were still at dinner; get a couple of DCs over from Kidlington to help with statements from the group, including the speakers, re their whereabouts from 4.30 to 5.15 p.m.; *and* from the occupants of bedrooms adjacent or reasonably proximate to Room 310. Maids? Yes, better see if any of them were turning down counterpanes or restocking tea-bags or just walking around or ... Morse suddenly felt himself utterly bored with the whole business. 'Find out the *system*, Lewis! Use a bit of initiative! And call round in the morning. I'll be at home – *trying* to get a few days' furlough.'

'We're not going to search the rooms then, sir?'

'Search the rooms? Christ, man! Do you know how many rooms there *are* in The Randolph?'

Morse performed one final task in what, by any criterion, had hitherto been a most perfunctory police inquiry. Briefly he spoke with Mr Eddie Stratton, who earlier had been sympathetically escorted up to the Browns' quarters in Room 308. Here, Morse found himself immediately liking the tall, bronzed Californian, in whose lived-in sort of face it seemed the sun might soon break through from behind the cloud of present adversity. Never particularly competent at expressing his personal feelings, Morse could do little more than mumble a few clichés of condolence, dredged up from some half-remembered funerals. But perhaps it was enough. For Stratton's face revealed little sign of grief; certainly no sign of tears.

The Manager was standing by Reception on the ground floor; and Morse thanked him for his co-operation, explaining that (as invited) he had made some, er, little use of the, er, the facilities available in the Manager's office. And if Sergeant Lewis and his men could continue to have the use of the office until . . .?

The Manager nodded his agreement: 'You know it's really most unfortunate. As I told you, Inspector, we always advise our guests that it's in their own best interests *never* to leave any unattended valuables in their rooms—'

'But she didn't leave them, did she?' suggested Morse mildly. 'She didn't even leave the room. As a matter of fact, sir, she still hasn't left it . . .'

In this last assertion Morse was somewhat behind the times, for Lewis now came down the main staircase to inform both of them that at that very moment the body of the late Laura M. Stratton was being transferred from Room 310, via the luggage-lift, en route for the Chapel of Rest in the Radcliffe Infirmary, just up the Woodstock Road.

'Fancy a drink, Lewis?'

'Not for me, sir. I'm on duty.'

The faithful sergeant allowed himself a wry grin, and even Morse was vaguely smiling. Anyway, it would save him, Lewis, a quid or two – that was for sure. Morse never seemed to think it was *his* round; and Lewis had occasionally calculated that on about three-fifths of his chief's salary he usually bought about three-quarters of the considerable quantities of alcohol consumed (though little by himself) on any given case.

Morse nodded a curt understanding, and walked towards the Chapters Bar.

CHAPTER TWELVE

Water taken in moderation cannot hurt anybody

(*Mark Twain*)

POURING A MODICUM of slim-line tonic into the large gin that her present drinking companion had just purchased for her, Sheila Williams asked the key question: 'Might you have to cancel the rest of the tour, John?'

'Oh, I don't think it need come to that. I mean, they've all *paid* for it, haven't they? Obviously we could refund if, well, if Mr Stratton or—'

'He's fine. I've spoken to him. *You* haven't.'

'I can't do everything, you know.'

'Please don't misunderstand me, John, but wasn't it perhaps a little unfortunate that you were nowhere within hailing distance when one of your charges busts her arteries and gets burgled into the bargain?'

Ashenden took a sip from his half-pint glass of bitter, appearing to acknowledge the truth of what Sheila had just said, though without volunteering any further comment. He'd once read (or heard) – Disraeli, was it? (or Jimmy Bowden?) – that a man ought never to apologise; never to explain.

He did neither now.

'We go ahead with everything, Sheila – except for the presentation bit, of course.'

'Unless they find it.'

'Which they won't.'

'Which they won't,' agreed Sheila.

'In spite of this fellow—'

'*That's him!*' whispered Sheila, laying a beautifully manicured hand across Ashenden's forearm. '*That's* Morse!'

Ashenden looked across at the greying man, of middle height and middle age, who beamed briefly at the brunette behind the bar as he ordered a pint of best bitter.

'Drinks too much – *beer*,' volunteered Ashenden, sticking in the last word rapidly as he found Sheila's eyes switch to his with a glare of displeasure. 'Bit overweight – round the middle – that's all I meant.'

'Yes! I know.' Her eyes softened, and Ashenden was aware – had *often* been aware – that he found her attractive, especially (what a cussed world it all was!) as she was now, when all that seemed required was a pair of strong arms to cart her up to the nearest bed.

But she suddenly ruined every bloody thing!

She had moved closer to him, and spoke close to his ear – softly and sensuously: 'I shouldn't really tell you this, John, but I find him awfully attractive. Sort of, you know, dishy, and . . . sexy . . .'

Ashenden removed the hand that had found his sleeve once more. 'For Christ's sake, Sheila!'

'Clever, too, John! *Very* clever – so they say.'

'And what's that supposed to mean?' Ashenden's voice sounded needlessly tense.

'I'll tell you,' replied Sheila, the clarity of her articulation beginning to disintegrate: 'He's going to wanna know wha' – wha' you were up to between – between – about – four-thirty and five-fifteen.'

'What's that got to do with *him*?'

'It's not *me* wants to know, darling. All I say is, that's . . . that's wha' he's goin' to ashk – ask you. That's wha' he's goin' to ask *everybody*.'

Ashenden looked down silently at his drink.

'Where *were* you, John?' (Was the lovely Sheila sober once again already?)

'There's no law against anyone having a look round the colleges, is there?'

'Quite a few people were wondering where you'd got to—'

'I've just told you, for heaven's sake!'

'But where *exactly* was it you went, John? Tell me! Come on! Tell mummy all about it!'

Ashenden decided to humour her: 'If you must know I went and had a look round Magdalen—'

But he got no further. A few yards away Morse was walking towards the Bar-Annexe as Sheila greeted him:

'Inspector! Inspector Morse! Come and join us!'

Morse's half-smile, grudging and potentially aloof, suggested he might have preferred his own company. But Sheila was patting the settee beside her, and Morse found himself looking down into the same dark-brown, pleading eyes that had earlier held such a curious fascination for him on the floor above.

'I, er—'

'Meet John Ashenden, Inspector – our leader!'

Morse nodded across, hesitated, then surrendered,

now positioning himself and his pint with exaggerated care.

'John was just saying he'd been round Magdalen this afternoon. That's right, isn't it, John?'

'Yep. It's, er, not a college I've ever got to know really. Wonderful though, isn't it? I'd known about the deer-park, but I'd never realised what a beautiful walk it was along the Cherwell there – those hundreds of acres of fields and gardens. As well as the tower, of course. Surely one of the finest towers in Europe, wouldn't you agree, Inspector?'

Morse nodded, seeming that evening to have a particular predisposition to nodding. But his brain was suddenly engaged, as it had never been engaged at any other point since arriving on the scene . . .

He had always claimed that when he had to think he had to drink – a dictum indulgently interpreted by his colleagues as an excellent excuse for the disproportionate amount of time the chief inspector seemed to spend at various bars. Yet Morse himself was quite convinced of its providential truth; and what is more, he knew that the obverse of this statement was similarly true: that when he was drinking he was invariably thinking! And as Ashenden had just spoken, Morse's blue eyes had narrowed slightly and he focused on the leader's face with a sudden hint of interest, and just the slightest tingle of excitement.

It was twenty minutes later, after a dinner during which they had spoken little, that Howard and Shirley Brown sat brooding over their iced tomato-juices at a table just inside the main bar.

'Well,' maintained Howard, '*you*'ve gotten yourself an alibi OK, Shirl. I mean, you and Eddie ... No prarblem! What about me, though?' He grinned wryly, good-humouredly: 'I'm lying there next door to Laura, right? If I'd wanted to, well—'

'What you thinking of, honey? Murder? Theft? Rape?'

'You don't think I'm capable of rape, Shirl!'

'No, I don't!' she replied, cruelly.

'And you saw Ashenden, you say. That gives *him* an alibi, too.'

'Half an alibi.'

'He saw *you* – you're sure?'

'Sure. But I don't reckon he thought we saw *him.*'

'Down Holywell Street, you say?'

'Uh-huh! I noticed the sign.'

'What's down there?'

'Eddie looked it up on the street map. New College, then Magdalen College – that's without the "e".'

DCs Hodges and Watson were now going systematically through their lists; and, almost simultaneously, Hodges was requesting both Mrs Williams and Mr Ashenden to accompany him to the Manager's office, with Watson asking Howard and Shirley Brown if they would please mind answering a few questions in the deserted ballroom.

*

On the departure of his two drinking companions – the lady reluctantly, the gentleman with fairly obvious relief – Morse looked again at the Osbert Lancaster paintings on the walls around him and wondered if he really liked these illustrations for *Zuleika Dobson*. Perhaps, though, he ought at last to *read* Beerbohm's book; even discover whether she was called 'Zuleeka' or 'Zuleyeka' . . .

His glass was empty and he returned to the bar, where Michelle, the decidedly bouncy brunette, declined to accept his proffered payment.

'The lady, sir. The one that was with you. She paid.'

'Uh?'

'She just said to get a pint for you when you came up for a refill.'

'She said "when", did she?'

'She probably knows your habits, sir,' said Michelle, with an understanding smile.

Morse went to sit in the virtually deserted Annexe now, and thought for more than a few minutes of Sheila Williams. He'd had a girlfriend called Sheila when he'd been an undergraduate just across St Giles' at St John's – the very college from which A. E. Housman, the greatest Latinist of the twentieth century, had also been kicked out minus a degree. A hundred years ago in Housman's case, and a thousand years in his own. Sheila . . . the source, in Milton's words, of all our woe.

After his fourth pint of beer, Morse walked out to Reception and spoke to the senior concierge.

'I've got a car in the garage.'

'I'll see it's brought round, sir. What's the number?'

'Er . . .' For the moment Morse could not recall the number. 'No! I'll pick it up in the morning if that's all right.'

'You a resident here, sir?'

'No! It's just that I don't want the police to pick me up on the way home.'

'Very sensible, sir. I'll see what I can do. Name? Can I have your name?'

'Morse. Chief Inspector Morse.'

'They wouldn't pick *you* up, would they?'

'No? Funny lot the police, you know.'

'Shall I call a taxi?'

'Taxi? I'm walking. I only live at the top of the Banbury Road, and a taxi'd cost me three quid at this time of night. That's three pints of beer.'

'Only *two* here, sir!' corrected Roy Halford as he watched the chief inspector step carefully – a little *too* carefully? – down the shallow steps and out to Beaumont Street.

CHAPTER THIRTEEN

Solvitur ambulando
(The problem is solved by walking around)
(Latin proverb)

AS HE WALKED up the Banbury Road that Thursday night, Morse was aware that by this time Lewis would know considerably more than *he* did about the probable contents of Laura Stratton's handbag, the possible disposition of the loot, and the likely circle of suspects. Yet he was aware, too, that his mind seemed – was! – considerably more lucid than he deserved it to be, and there *were* a few facts to be considered – certainly more facts than Lewis had gleaned in his schooldays about Alfred the Great.

Facts: carrying her handbag, a woman had gone up to Room 310 at about 4.35 p.m.; this woman had not been seen alive again – or at least no one so far would *admit* to seeing her alive again; inside 310 a bath had been run and almost certainly taken; a coffee-sachet and a miniature tub of cream had been used; a DO NOT DISTURB sign had been displayed on the outside door-knob at some point, with the door itself probably left open; the woman's husband had returned at about 5.15

p.m., and without reporting to Reception had gone up to the third floor, in the guest-lift, with a fellow tourist (female); thence a hurried scuttle down to Reception via the main staircase where a duplicate key was acquired. On finally gaining access to his room, the husband had discovered his wife's body on the floor, presumably already dead; the hotel's house-doctor had arrived some ten or fifteen minutes later, and the body duly transferred from floor to bed – all this by about 5.40 p.m. At some point before, during, or after these latter events, the husband himself had noticed the disappearance of his wife's handbag; and at about 6 p.m. a call had been received by St Aldate's CID with a request for help in what was now looking a matter of considerably more moment than any petty theft.

Yes, those were the facts.

So move on, Morse, to a few non-factual inferences in the problem of the Wolvercote Tongue. Move on, my son – and hypothesize! Come on, now! Who *could* have stolen it?

Well, in the first place, with the door to 310 *locked*, only those who had a key: the Manager, the house-keeper, the room-maids – namely, anyone with, or with access to, a duplicate key to the aforementioned room. *Not* the husband. In the second place, with the door to 310 *open*, a much more interesting thieves' gallery was open to view: most obviously, anyone at all who would happen to be passing and who had glimpsed, through the open door, a handbag that had proved too tempting an opportunity. Open to such temptation (if not necessarily susceptible to it) would have been the room-maids, the occupants of nearby rooms, any casual passer-by ... But just a moment! Room 310 was *off* the main corridor, and anyone in its immediate vicinity would be there *for a reason*: a friend, perhaps, with a solicitous enquiry about the lady's feet; a fellow tourist wanting to borrow something; or learn something ... Then there was Ashenden. He'd said he would be going around at some point to all the rooms to check up on the sachets, shampoos, soaps, switches. Opportunity? Yes! But hardly much of a motive, surely? What about the three guest speakers? Out of the question, wasn't it? They hadn't been called to the colours at that point – weren't even *in* The Randolph. Forget them! Well, no – not altogether, perhaps; not until Lewis had checked their statements.

So that was that, really. That set the 'parameters' (the buzz-word at HQ recently) for the crime. No other portraits in the gallery.

Not really.

No!

Or were there?

What about the husband? Morse had always entertained a healthy suspicion of anyone found first on the scene of a crime; and Eddie Stratton had been a *double-*first: the first to report both the death of his wife, *and* the theft of the jewel. But any man who finds his wife dead – dead! – surely he's not going to ... Nobody could suspect that.

Except Morse.

And what about – what about the most unlikely, improbable, unthinkable ... Unthinkable? Well, *think* about it, Morse! What about the wife herself: Mrs Laura Stratton? Could she have been responsible for the disappearance of the jewel? But why? Was it insured? Surely so! And doubtless for a hefty sum. All right, the thing was unsellable, unbuyable; the thing was useless – except, that is, as a link in a cultural continuum in a University Museum. Or else – yes! – or else as an insurance item which in terms of cash was worth far more lost than found; and if the Strattons were getting a bit hard up it might not have been so much *if* it were lost as *when*. And what – it was always going to hit Morse's brain sooner or later – what if the thing had never been there to get lost in the first place? Yes, the possibility had to be faced: what if the Wolvercote Tongue had never been inside the handbag at all? (Keep going, Morse!) Never even left America?

Morse already found himself in the Summertown shopping centre; and it was some five minutes later, as he came to his bachelor flat just south of the A40 Ring Road, that the oddest possibility finally struck him: what if the Wolvercote Tongue didn't *exist* at all? But surely there would have been all sorts of descriptive and photographic pieces of evidence, and so on? Surely such an authority as Dr Theodore Kemp could never have been so duped in such a matter? No! And he'd almost certainly flown over to see it, anyway. No! Forget it! So Morse almost forgot it, and let himself into his flat, where he played the first two movements of the Bruckner No. 7 before going to bed.

He woke up at 2.50 a.m., his mouth very dry. He got out of bed and went to the bathroom, where he drank a glass of water; and another glass of water. In truth, water – a liquid which figured little during Morse's waking life – was his constant companion during the early hours of almost every morning.

CHAPTER FOURTEEN

It is only shallow people who do not judge by appearances. The true mystery of the world is the visible, not the invisible

(*Oscar Wilde*, The Picture of Dorian Gray)

THE BACHELOR MORSE had only the wraith-like, gin-ridden spectre of a lush divorcée to share his pillow that night, unlike the male speakers scheduled for the following day's Historic Cities of England programme, both of whom, when Morse had made his first visit to the bathroom, were dutifully asleep beside their respective spouses and in their own homes – homes in North Oxford, separated by only about a quarter of a mile.

The traveller who heads north from the centre of Oxford may take, at St Giles' Church, either the fork which leads up the Woodstock Road, or the right-hand fork, the Banbury Road, which leads after a mile or so to Summertown. Here, just past the shopping area, he will come to the new, yellow-bricked premises of Radio Oxford on his left; and then, almost immediately on his right, the first of the four roads – Lonsdale, Portland, Hamilton, Victoria – which stretch between the main Banbury Road and the River Cherwell (pronounced by most of the locals 'Charwell'). At all hours, each of these roads is suitable only for one-way traffic because of the continuous lines of parked cars on either side. The majority of houses here, built in the 1920s and 30s, are without integral garages; and many an amateurishly painted sign, alongside the edges of the pavement or on boards beside front gates, urges with courtesy, warns with threats of trespass, or simply begs with a pathetic 'Please', those motorists who commute to Summertown not to park their wretched vehicles *there*. In vain! For the lifeblood along these roads ever flows, as it were, through arteries clogged with atherosclerosis.

But Dr Kemp no longer drives a car . . .

Any person meeting for the first time those two distinguished academics, Theodore Kemp and Cedric Downes, would be fairly sure to come to the following judgements. Kemp would perhaps appear to merit such epithets as artistic, flamboyant, highbrow, selfish, aloof, rakish – the list could go on and on, in much the same direction; and this impression would be formed largely from a certain arrogance in the pale features, an affected upper-class diction, the almost invariable silk shirt and bow-tie, the casual elegance of the light-beige lightweight suits which he favoured in both summer and winter to bedeck his slim and small-boned figure. And what of Downes? Certainly not by any means such a clear-cut impression: rather languid in movement, somewhat overweight, a not-quite-top-echelon-public-school-man, a slightly bored expression round the mouth, the promise of a humorous twinkle in the eyes, a semi-florid colouring, a heavyish suit with trousers sorely in need of a press, longish and lank brown hair, and a careless, unpretentious drawl in a voice which still bore the flat traces of his Midlands origins. Everything about him qualified; everything 'rather', 'quite', 'somewhat'. And finally – most importantly, maybe – the obvious impression that he was going a bit, more than a bit, deaf. For increasingly noticeable was his habit of shepherding any interlocutor to his right-hand side; his frequent cupping of the hand behind his right ear; and occasionally his use of an NHS hearing-aid, recently provided for his rapidly developing otosclerosis.

Which things being so, it might be assumed that Kemp was probably having all the fun that was going in life in general, and in Oxford in particular; whilst the seedier, world-weary Downes was slowly running out of steam, and like as not running out of luck, too. Yet such an assumption would not be wholly correct: in fact it would be some considerable way distant from the truth.

Kemp's life had not blossomed as once it had promised. After fathering (as was rumoured) almost as many illegitimate offspring as almighty Zeus himself, and after successfully disclaiming most of the responsibility for such excessive multiplication of the species, he had married a rather plain, though neatly figured woman, named Marion (with an 'o'), whose parents were rumoured to be fairly wealthy. Then, now two years since, he had managed to crash his BMW in such a way that his not-wholly fair but fully pregnant wife had lost both her child and the use of her lower limbs, whilst he himself had received only a broken collarbone, with a few slivers of glass embedded in his back. But at least Marion had survived: the driver of the other car involved, a thirty-five-year-old married woman, had been instantly killed. Definitive responsibility for the accident could not be fully determined, since the coroner found some of the evidence confusing, and far from competently reported. Yet Kemp *had* been drinking: and the charge he faced, a charge resulting in a fine and a three-year disqualification, had been one of driving whilst under the influence of alcohol, not that of reckless or of dangerous driving. Some of those who knew Kemp well, most of his University colleagues, and all of those who could never abide the man, considered him to have been extremely fortunate. Such disapprobation had probably accounted for the refusal of his college to elevate his status as a post-graduate researcher (or 'graduate researcher', as the pedantic Morse would have preferred) to that of the fellowship which had suddenly fallen vacant. Six weeks after this humiliation, he had been appointed to the post of Keeper of Anglo-Saxon and Mediaeval Antiquities at the Ashmolean. He now lived in a ground-floor flat in Cherwell Lodge, a brick-built block along Water Eaton Road – the latter stretching from the bottom of Victoria Road into the Cutteslowe Estate. The enforced move, made to accommodate his wheel-chaired wife, had taken place at exactly the wrong time in the housing market, and his property was presently worth little more than a quarter of the price likely to be fetched by that of his fellow-lecturer, the one who had temporarily forgotten the name of a Danish architect.

At the age of forty, five years previously, Cedric Downes had married Lucy, an engagingly attractive woman, eleven years his junior, fair-skinned and blonde, fully-figured and fully-sexed – though with a tendency towards a nervousness of manner on occasion – and with an IQ which was rated quite high by those meeting her for the first time, but which usually dipped a little upon more intimate acquaintance. Downes, a mediaeval historian, was a Fellow of Brasenose, and lived in a large detached house at the far end of Lonsdale Road, its beautifully tended back garden stretching down to the banks of the River Cherwell . . .

In the back bedroom of number 6 Cherwell Lodge, Marion Kemp lay supine. Marion Kemp *had* to lie supine. It would have been beneficial to the two of them, certainly would have guaranteed longer periods of sleep, if after the accident they had abandoned the double bed and settled for twin beds – perhaps even for separate rooms. Surprisingly, however, her husband would hear nothing of such a suggestion, and at first she had felt pleased and, yes!, flattered that he still wished to lie each night beside her fruitless body. And even on that Thursday night some of the hatred which for so long had been slowly coalescing in her soul had perhaps abated minimally . . .

As he had promised, he had been home at 10 p.m., had clearly not been drinking much at all, had brought her a cup of Ovaltine and a digestive biscuit, and quite definitely had *not* been with that bitchy, boozy, whore-son *Williams* woman!

Unlike Lucy Downes, Marion Kemp did not convey any immediate impression of a lively mind. Yet those who knew her well (a diminishing group) were always aware of a shrewd and observant intelligence. Earlier she had watched Theo carefully as he had spoken to her about what had occurred that evening, and she had been wholly conscious of his own colossal frustration and disappointment. But in truth she could not find herself caring two milk-tokens about the loss of the Wolvercote Tongue; nor indeed find herself unduly distressed about the death of some bejewelled old biddy from the far side of America. Yet she could find no sleep in the small hours of that Friday morning, her mind considering many things: above all the growing suspicion that the man asleep beside her was looking now beyond that bloody Williams woman . . .

And Marion thought she knew exactly where.

Cedric Downes had come home rather later than usual that Thursday evening. He had been one of the last to give the police an account of his movements from 4.30 to 5.15 p.m. ('Is this *really* necessary, officer?') God! He'd had a tutorial at that time! And now, when finally he went through into the bedroom, all was very quiet, with Lucy lying motionless along her own side of the bed. He nestled gently against the contours of her body, hoping that she might sense his need for her, but realising almost immediately that she was distanced, and would not be conjoined. He turned on to his right-hand side, as now he usually did when seeking sleep.

With his left ear becoming so deaf, he would consciously press his right ear deep into the pillow, thereafter hearing virtually nothing of the nightly groans of
the central-heating pipes, or the inexplicable creaking
of the wood, or the rushing of the wind in the towering
pine trees. Briefly his mind dwelt on the evening's
events; briefly dwelt on his loathing for Kemp; but
within a few minutes he could feel the tug of the warm
tide and soon he was floating down to the depths of
slumber.

Not so his wife, still breathing quietly and rhyth-
mically, and not so much as twitching a lumbrical
muscle.

But very much asleep that night was Sheila Williams,
the bedroom window wide open in her dingily stuccoed
semi in the lower reaches of Hamilton Road, a house
(as it happened) almost exactly equidistant from that
of Kemp and that of Downes.

At 4.45 a.m. Morse made his third visit to the
bathroom – *and suddenly he remembered.* He went into his
living room, looked along his book-shelves, extracted a
volume, consulted its index, turned to the pages given,
and read through the entry he had sought. His head
nodded a few degrees, and his dry mouth widened into
a mildly contented smile.

He was asleep when Lewis rang the doorbell at 8.30
a.m.

CHAPTER FIFTEEN

The best-laid schemes o'mice and men
    Gang aft a-gley,
And lea'e us nought but grief and pain
    For promised joy

                    (*Robert Burns*, To a Mouse)

FEW ENGLISH FAMILIES living in England have much direct contact with the English Breakfast. It is therefore fortunate that such an endangered institution is perpetuated by the efforts of the kitchen staff in guest houses, B & Bs, transport cafés, and other no-starred and variously starred hotels. This breakfast comprises (at its best): a milkily-opaque fried egg; two rashers of non-brittle, rindless bacon; a tomato grilled to a point where the core is no longer a hard white nodule to be operated upon by the knife; a sturdy sausage, deeply and evenly browned; and a slice of fried bread, golden-brown, and only just crisp, with sufficient fat not excessively to dismay any meddlesome dietitian. That is the definitive English Breakfast. And that is what the French, the Germans, the Italians, the Japanese, the Russians, the Turks . . . and the English, also, with their diurnal diet of cornflakes and a toasted slice of Mother's Pride – that is what they all enjoy as much as almost anything about a holiday.

The Americans, too, though there are always exceptions.

Janet Roscoe leaned across the table, lowered the volume switch on her abnormally loud voice, and spoke to Sam and Vera Kronquist, the third of the married couples originally registered on the tour.

'I just don't know how he' – her sharp eyes singled out Phil Aldrich, seated at the next table – 'how he can even think of eating – *that.*'

The vehement emphasis accorded to this last word might perhaps have suggested that Janet's co-worshipper in Sacramento's Temperance Hall of Christian Scientists was devouring a plateful of raw maggots or the roasted flesh of sacrificial infants, instead of his slim rasher of streaky bacon. But Sam Kronquist, though content with his croissant, was happily tolerant about the tastes of others:

'We're only on vaycation once a year, you know, Janet. So perhaps we can forgive him?'

Or perhaps not; for Janet made no reply, and in silence completed her own modest breakfast of naturally juiced grapefruit segments, and one slice of unbuttered toast smeared over with diabetic marmalade. She was just finishing her cup of black decaffeinated coffee when John Ashenden, after his peripatetic trip around the other tables, came to tell the three of them that there would be a short meeting in the St John's Suite at 9.15 a.m. in order to fit the coming day's events into a schedule that would have to be slightly revised . . .

*

'If you refer,' began Ashenden, 'to your original sheets' (he held up a copy of the yellow sheets distributed the previous day) 'you will see that quite a few amendments, sadly, will have to be made to it. But the tour will quite definitely be going ahead as normal – or as normal as it can do in the circumstances. Eddie – Eddie Stratton – wants this, wants it to go ahead, and he believes that Laura would have wished that, too. So ... First of all then: our visit to The Oxford Story, scheduled for ten-thirty. This has been put back to ten a.m. Make a note, please: ten a.m. instead of—'

'Don't you mean brought *forward*, Mr Ashenden?'

Yes, probably Ashenden *did* mean exactly what Mrs Roscoe said. And he beamed a smile towards her, in fact welcoming rather than resenting the interruption: '—has been brought forward to ten a.m. There's been a cancellation of a Spanish block-booking and it will help the people there if we take the earlier spot. Yes? No problems?'

Thereupon Ashenden duly distributed an extra sheet to each of his rather subdued audience:

The Oxford Story

It was here in Oxford that Lewis Carroll created the immortal 'Alice'; here that King Charles I held his Civil War Parliament; here where Archbishop Cranmer was burned at the stake; here where Penicillin was developed. So take a seat aboard a flying desk – Ride the Spiral! – and travel backwards through time to the earliest days of Oxford University when Friar Roger Bacon (1214–1294) sat in his rooms overlooking Folly Bridge and ... But let *Oxford* tell its own story, as you sit comfortably in your car and witness whole centuries of fascinating men and glorious events. (Wheelchair access and toilet facilities for the disabled.)

There being no murmurs of demurral, even from the customary quarter, Ashenden proceeded to extol the virtues of such a visit: to whisk oneself back to the origins of the University in the twelfth century, and thence be spiralled to the present day – seated, foothappily – with the wonderful bonus, betweenwhiles, of listening to a commentary on the passing pageants by no less a personage than Sir Alec Guinness himself. The visit had in fact figured as an 'extra' in the published brochure, but in view of the, er, the sad, *sad* events ... Well, the company had agreed that the £2 supplement should now be waived.

'That's a very kindly gesture, sir,' volunteered Phil Aldrich, and several of his fellow tourists audibly concurred.

Sam Kronquist, suffering from incipient prostate trouble, found himself wondering whether that final parenthesis signified a lack of toilet facilities for those persons as yet unwilling to label themselves 'disabled'; but he held his peace.

That meant, Ashenden continued, that there would be something of an uncomfortable gap between about 11.15 and 12.30; and he was very glad to be able to announce that Mrs Williams and Mr Downes and Dr Kemp had agreed to hold an impromptu question-and-answer session on Oxford: Town and Gown. This would be in the Ball Room, beginning at 11.30 a.m.

To the afternoon, then.

Ashenden exhorted his audience once again to consult the original sheet, confirming that, apart from the 6.30 p.m. presentation, the scheduled programme would go ahead as stated. Perhaps it would be sensible, though, to start the afternoon groups at 2.45 p.m., please, at which time Dr Kemp would meet *his* group immediately outside the main entrance to the Ashmolean; Mr Downes *his* group at the Martyrs' Memorial; Mrs Williams *her* group in the foyer of the hotel. Was that all clear? And would they all please try if possible to keep to the group they had first opted for? There was a nice little balance at the moment; not that he would want to *stop* anyone changing, of course . . .

Again the touring party appeared to find the arrangements wholly unexceptionable, and Ashenden came to his last point. Would everyone please change the time given on their sheets for dinner: this was now brought forward ('Right, Mrs Roscoe?') from 8 p.m. to 7.30 p.m. Three of the Trustees of the Ashmolean would be joining them, and he would assume unless he was informed to the contrary that everyone would be coming to this final dinner. It *had* been optional, he knew that; but in view of . . .

In the crowded hotel foyer, ten minutes later, Mrs Roscoe failed to decrease her decibel level as she called across to the Bacon Man from Sacramento: 'They tell me we sit in those cars two at a time, side by side, Phil . . .'

'Yeah! OK, Janet. Yeah, OK.'

CHAPTER SIXTEEN

As you go through, you see the great scientists, scholars, and statesmen; the thinkers, writers, actors, monarchs, and martyrs who are part of Oxford's history. By passing this doorway you have a glimpse of the people whom Oxford has moulded, and many of whom have, in their turn, gone on to help mould the world

(*Lord Jenkins of Hillhead*, The Oxford Story)

AT 9.50 A.M. Cedric Downes led the way as the tourists trooped down the front steps of The Randolph, turned right, and moved across the road. Here, just by the Martyrs' Memorial, Downes stopped.

'Here we have . . .' He pointed to the heavy iron sign on which the letters MAGDALEN STREET were painted in white, and the group gathered around him. 'Everyone – nearly everyone – knows that this is pronounced "Maudlin" Street, as if it were a sentimental, tearful sort of street. That's what the bus drivers call it. Now out in East Oxford we've got a Magdalen Road, and the same bus drivers call that one "M-a-g-dalen" Road. I only mention this, my friends, to show you that life here in Oxford is never quite so simple as it may appear. Off we go!'

'I didn't know *that*, Phil,' said Janet Roscoe quietly. '*Very* interesting.'

The group progressed to Broad Street, where Downes brought them all to a stop again, this time immediately outside the Master's Lodge at Balliol. 'Here – on your left here – the plaque on the wall – this is where Latimer and Ridley, and later Cranmer, were burned at the stake in 1555 and 1556. Not difficult to remember the date, is it? You can see the actual spot, the cross there – see it? – right in the middle of the road.'

A little silence fell on the group: those with the faculty of a visual imagination watching as the long, grey beards began to sizzle, and then the ankle-length shirts suddenly leapt up in a scorching mantle of fire, and others hearing perhaps those agonized shrieks as the faggot-fired flames consumed the living flesh ... For a few moments it seemed that everyone was strangely affected by Cedric Downes's words. Perhaps it was the way he'd spoken them, with a sad and simple dignity ...

'Here we are then! No more walking to do at all.' He pointed immediately across the way to the triple-arched entry of the three-storeyed building that housed The Oxford Story.

That same evening Miss Ginger Bonnetti (not 'Ginger', but christened Ginger) wrote a longish letter to her married sister living in Los Angeles, one Mrs Georgie (as christened!) Bonnetti, who had married a man named Angelo Bonnetti. (Morse would have had great joy in learning of this, for he gloried in coincidences; but since Miss Ginger Bonnetti was destined to play no further role in the theft of the Wolvercote Tongue, he never did.)

Hi, sis! We had a great morning in Oxford. There's a kind of tourist attraction here called The Oxford Story and we got into these sort of cars, but they're more like those old-fashioned desks from schooldays really — sitting side by side, remember? Made of some dark sort of wood with slightly sloping tops as if you'd just got to listen to the class teacher or write out the alphabet again if you didn't. Then we went up a sort of spiral gradiant at .000001 mph — no kidding! I wish I could remember all those great names we saw, and I do mean great! And you sit. You sit in these double desks and listen to a commentary from you guess who! Sir Alec Guiness. I mean, the voice So the pen was working away as we went around and I've kept a brochure for you somewhere of all

COLIN DEXTER

these people, Roger Bacon, Thomas Bodley, Charles First (what a little guy _he_ was), Hobbes and Locke, Wilkins (? — I can't read my own handwriting). Sir Christopher Wren, Boyle (you remember _our_ Physics teacher?), John Welsly (or is it Wessley?), Alice (yeah, the same!), William Ewart Gladstone and no end of those other PMs. And of course Cranmer and the Protestant Martyrs, and I'm starting to remember I've forgotten so many of the others. Does that last bit make sense, Georgie! Anyway it was marvellous— the only trouble was that the poor fellow in front of me had to put up with all this incessant chatter from a really _dreadful_ little woman who's clearly trying to trap another victim. But I've left the big news till now. You remember I told you about the jewel one of the group was going to bring to the Oxford museum here? Well yesterday this poor woman had a coronary and died and someone stole her handbag with this jewel inside it! Where _is_ safe these days? You tell me that. She'd

92

been a little poorly and her husband
said she always knew it was
going to be sooner or later but it's
a bad time just now, for the tour
I mean. Eddie, he's the husband,
doesn't want us to be too upset and
the tour goes on as sheduled, and
well he was her second! He's a
pretty nice guy really. But I reckon
she was the one with the money and
I just hope she was pretty well
insured all round. So as you can see
we're having plenty happening here!

Love to Angelo,
Ginger

P.S. I forgot to tell you it was just a
bit <u>spooky</u> for a start in that
Oxford Story.

P.P.S My room looks right out on the
Ashmolean - see that X on the
enclosed card?

In the Oxford Story Gift Shop, the group had stayed
quite some time, examining aprons, busts, chess-sets,
Cheshire cats, cufflinks, games, gargoyles, glassware, jewellery, jigsaws, jugs, maps, pictures, postcards, posters,

stationery, table-mats, thimbles, videos – everything a tourist could wish for.

'Gee! With *her* feet, how Laura would have loved that ride!' remarked Vera Kronquist. But her husband made no answer. If he were honest he was not wholly displeased that Laura's feet were no longer going to be a major factor in the determination of the tour's itineraries. She was always talking about lying down; and now she *was* lying down. Permanently.

'Very good,' said Phil Aldrich as he and Mrs Roscoe and the Browns emerged through the exit into Ship Street.

'But the figures there – they weren't nearly as good as the ones in Madame Tussaud's, now were they?'

'No, you're quite right, Janet,' said Howard Brown, as he gently guided her towards Cornmarket and back towards The Randolph.

When, five days later, Mrs Georgie Bonnetti received her sister's interesting letter, she was a little disappointed (herself a zealous Nonconformist) that with neither cartridge from the double-barrelled rifle had her sister succeeded in hitting the saintly founder of Methodism. (The unbeliever Morse would have been rather more concerned about the other four misspellings.)

CHAPTER SEVENTEEN

Clever people seem not to feel the natural pleasure of bewilderment, and are always answering questions when the chief relish of a life is to go on asking them

(*Frank Moore Colby*)

AFTER HIS *IN SITU* briefing outside Balliol, Downes left the scene of the barbarous burnings and strolled thoughtfully along to Blackwell's. An hour and a quarter (Ashenden had suggested) for The Oxford Story; then back to The Randolph where he and Sheila Williams and Kemp (the man would always remain a surname to Downes) had agreed to hold the question-and-answer session with the Americans. Downes sometimes felt a bit dubious about 'Americans'; yet like almost all his colleagues in Oxford, he often found himself enjoying actual Americans, without those quotation marks. That morning he knew that as always some of their questions would be disturbingly naïve, some penetrating, all of them *honest*. And he approved of such questions, doubtless because he himself could usually score a pretty point or two with answers that were honest: quite different from the top-of-the-head comments of some of the spurious academics he knew.

People like Kemp.

After spending fifty minutes browsing through the

second-hand books in Blackwell's, Downes returned to The Randolph, and was stepping up the canopied entrance when he heard the voice a few yards behind him.

'Cedric!'

He turned round.

'You must be deaf! I called along the road there three or four times.'

'I *am* deaf – you know that.'

'Now don't start looking for any sympathy from me, Cedric! What the hell! There are far worse things than being deaf.'

Downes smiled agreement and looked (and not without interest) at the attractively dressed divorcée he'd known on and off for the past four years. Her voice (this morning, again) was sometimes a trifle shrill, her manner almost always rather tense; but there were far worse things than . . .

'Time for a drink?' asked Sheila – with hope. It was just after eleven.

They walked together into the foyer and both looked at the noticeboard in front of them:

HISTORIC CITIES TOUR ST JOHN'S SUITE 11.30 a.m.

'Did you hear me?' continued Sheila.

'Pardon?'

'I said we've got almost half an hour before—'

'Just a minute!' Downes was fixing an NHS hearing-aid to his right ear, switching it on, adjusting the volume – and suddenly, so clearly, so wonderfully, the whole of the hotel burst into happily chattering life. 'Back in the land of the living! Well? I know it's a bit early, Sheila, but what would you say about a quick snifter? Plenty of time.'

Sheila smiled radiantly, put her arm through his, and propelled him through to the Chapters Bar: 'I would say "yes", Cedric. In fact I think I would say "yes" to almost anything this morning; and especially to a Scotch.'

For a few delightful seconds Downes felt the softness of her breast against his arm, and perhaps for the first time in their acquaintanceship he realised that he could want this woman. And as he reached for his wallet, he was almost glad to read the notice to the left of the bar: 'All spirits will be served as double measures unless otherwise requested.'

They were sitting on a beige-coloured wall-settee, opposite the bar, dipping occasionally into a glass dish quartered with green olives, black olives, cocktail onions, and gherkins – when Ashenden looked in, looked around, and saw them.

'Ah – thought I might find you here.'

'How is Mr Stratton?' asked Sheila.

'I saw him at breakfast – he seems to be taking things remarkably well, really.'

'No news of . . . of what was stolen?'

Ashenden shook his head. 'Nobody seems to hold out much hope.'

'Poor Theo!' pouted Sheila. 'I must remember to be nice to him this morning.'

'I, er,' Ashenden was looking decidedly uncomfortable:

'Dr Kemp won't be joining us this morning, I'm afraid.'

'And why the hell *not*?' This from a suddenly bristling Sheila.

'Mrs Kemp rang earlier. He's gone to London. Just for the morning, though. His publisher had been trying to see him, and with the presentation off and everything—'

'That was this *evening*!' protested Downes.

'Bloody nerve!' spluttered Sheila. 'You were here, John, when he promised. Typical! Leave Cedric and me to do all the bloody donkey-work!'

'He's getting back as soon as he can: should be here by lunchtime. So if – well, I'm sorry. It's been a bit of a disappointment for the group already and if you . . .'

'One condition, John!' Sheila, now smiling, seemed to relax. And Ashenden understood, and walked to the bar with her empty glass.

The tour leader was pleased with the way the session had gone. Lots of good questions, with both Sheila Williams and Cedric Downes acquitting themselves *magna cum laude*, especially Downes, who had found exactly the right combination of scholarship and scepticism.

It was over lunch that Sheila, having availed herself freely of the pre-luncheon sherry (including the rations of a still-absent Kemp), became quite needlessly cruel.

'Were you an undergraduate here – at Arksford, Mr Downes?'

'I was here, yes. At Jesus – one of the less fashionable colleges, Mrs Roscoe. Welsh, you know. Founded in 1571.'

'I thought Jesus was at Cambridge.'

Sheila found the opening irresistible: 'No, no, Mrs Roscoe! Jesus went to Bethlehem Tech.'

It was a harmless enough joke, and certainly Phil Aldrich laughed openly. But not Janet Roscoe.

'Is that what they mean by the English sense of humour, Mrs Williams?'

'Where else would he go to do carpentry?' continued Sheila, finding her further pleasantry even funnier than her first, and laughing stridently.

Downes himself appeared amused no longer by the exchange, and his right hand went up to his ear to adjust an aid which for the past few minutes had been emitting an intermittent whistle. Perhaps he hadn't heard . . .

But Janet was not prepared to let things rest. She had (she knew) been made to look silly; and she now proceeded to make herself look even sillier. 'I don't myself see anything funny in blasphemy, and besides they didn't have colleges in Palestine in those days.'

Phil Aldrich laid a gently restraining hand on Janet's arm as Sheila's shrill amusement scaled new heights: 'Please don't make too much fun of us, Mrs Williams. I know we're not as clever, some of us, as many of you are. That's why we came, you know, to try to learn a little more about your country here and about your ways.'

It was a dignified little speech, and Sheila now felt desperately ashamed. For a few seconds, a look of mild regret gleamed in her slightly bloodshot eyes, and she had begun to apologize when immediately next to them, on a table below the window overlooking the Taylor Institution, the phone rang.

It was 12.35 p.m. when Mrs Celia Freeman, a pleasantly spoken and most competent woman, took the call on the telephone exchange at the rear of the main Reception area. Only approximately 12.35 p.m., though. When later questioned (and questioned most earnestly) on this matter, she had found on her notepad that both the name of the caller ('Dr Kemp') and the name of the person called ('Mr Ashenden') had been jotted down soon after a timed call at 12.31 p.m. And it was at 12.48 p.m., exactly, that John Ashenden phoned back from the St John's Suite to Reception to order a taxi to meet the train from Paddington arriving 15.00, and to pick up a Dr Theodore Kemp at Oxford Station.

Chapter Eighteen

In the police-procedural, a fair degree of realism is possible,
but it cannot be pushed too far for fear that the book might
be as dull as the actual days of a policeman

(*Julian Symons*, Bloody Murder)

IT WAS NOT until 10 a.m. that same morning that
Morse had recovered the Jaguar; 10.15 a.m. when he
finally put in an appearance at Kidlington HQ.

'Hope you had a profitable evening, Lewis?'

'Not particularly.'

'Not arrested the thief yet?'

Lewis shook his head. He'd already put in three
hours' work, trying to sort out and collate various
statements, and he was in no mood to appreciate the
sarcasm of a man who had seemingly lost most of the
little enthusiasm he'd started with.

'Well?' asked Morse.

'Nothing, really. These Americans – well, they seem
a nice lot of people. Some of 'em not all that sure about
exactly where they were – but you'd expect that,
wouldn't you? Settling in, drinking tea, unpacking,
having a wash, trying to get the telly going—'

'Studying the Fire Instructions, I hope.'

'Doubt it. But as far as I could see, they all seemed
to be telling the truth.'

'Except one.'

'Pardon, sir?'

'Ashenden was lying.'

Lewis looked puzzled: 'How can you say that?'

'He said he had a look round Magdalen.'

'So?'

'He told me all about it – he was virtually reciting phrases from the guide-book.'

'He *is* a guide.'

'Pages 130-something of Jan Morris's *Oxford*. Word for word – nearly.'

'He'd probably swotted it up for when he was going round with the group.'

'Magdalen's not on the programme.'

'But you can't just say he's lying because—'

'Ashenden's a liar!'

Lewis shook his head: it was hardly worth arguing with Morse in such a mood, but he persisted a little longer. 'It doesn't *matter* though, does it? If Ashenden decided to go and look round Magdalen—'

'He didn't,' said Morse quietly.

'No?'

'I rang the Porters' Lodge there this morning. The College was closed to visitors all day: they're doing some restoration in the cloisters and the scaffolders were there from early morning. No one, Lewis – *no one* – was allowed in Magdalen yesterday except the Fellows, by order of the Bursar, an order the Head Porter assured me was complied with without a single exception – well, only a fellow without a capital "f" who

102

brought a stock of superfine toilet paper for the President.'

'Oh!' Lewis looked down and surveyed the sheets on his desk, neatly arranged, carefully considered – and probably wasted. They might just as well be toilet paper, too. Here was Morse making a mockery of all his efforts with just a single phone call. 'So he was telling us lies,' he said, without enthusiasm.

'Some of us spend most of our lives telling lies, Lewis.'

'Do you want me to bring him in?'

'You can't arrest a man for telling lies. Not *those* lies, anyway. He's probably got a fancy bit of skirt along Holywell Street somewhere. Just as well he *was* there, perhaps.'

'Sir?'

'Well, it means he wasn't in The Randolph pinching handbags, doesn't it?'

'He could have pinched it *before* he went out. Mrs Stratton was one of the first up to her room, and Ashenden was there for a good ten minutes or so—'

'What did he do with it?'

'We ought to have searched the rooms, sir.'

Morse nodded vaguely, then shrugged his shoulders.

'We wasting our time?' asked Lewis.

'What? About the handbag? Oh yes! We shall never find that – you can safely put your bank balance on that.'

'I wouldn't lose all that much if I did,' mumbled the dispirited Lewis.

'Has Max rung?'

'No. Promised to, though, didn't he?'

'Idle sod!' Morse picked up the phone and dialled the lab. 'If he still says it was just a heart attack, I think I'll just leave this little business in your capable hands, Lewis, and get back home.'

'I reckon you'd be as happy as a sandboy if he tells you she was murdered.'

But Morse was through: 'Max? Morse. Done your homework?'

'Massive coronary.'

'Positive?'

Morse heard the exasperated expiration of breath at the other end of the line; but received no answer.

'Could it have been brought on, Max – you know, by her finding a fellow fiddling with her powder-compact?'

'Couldn't say.'

'Someone she didn't expect – coming into her room?'

'Couldn't say.'

'No sign of any injury anywhere?'

'No.'

'You looked everywhere?'

'I always look everywhere.'

'Not much help, are you?'

'On the contrary, Morse. I've told you exactly what she died of. Just like the good Dr Swain.'

But Morse had already put down the phone; and five minutes later he was driving down to North Oxford.

Lewis himself remained in the office and spent the rest of the morning rounding off the dull routine of his paperwork. At 12.50 p.m., deciding he couldn't emulate the peremptory tone that Morse usually adopted with commissionaires, he took a number 21 bus down to St Giles', where he alighted at the Martyrs' Memorial and began to walk across to The Randolph. Sheila Williams was stepping out briskly, without glancing behind her, up the left-hand side of St Giles', past the columns of the Taylorian and the front of Pusey House, before being lost to the mildly interested gaze of Sergeant Lewis. And as the latter turned into Beaumont Street, with the canopy of The Randolph immediately in front of him, he stopped again. A man walked down the steps of the hotel, looking quickly back over his shoulder before turning left and scurrying along the street towards Worcester College, where he turned left once more at the traffic lights, and passed beneath the traffic sign there announcing 'British Rail'. In normal circumstances, such an innocent-seeming occurrence would hardly have deserved a place in the memory. But these were not normal circumstances, and the man who had just left The Randolph in such haste was *Eddie Stratton.*

Diffidently, Lewis followed.

It was during this hour, between 1 p.m. and 2 p.m., as Morse and Lewis were later to learn, that the scene was irreversibly set for murder.

At 3.20 p.m., to an audience slightly smaller than anticipated, Cedric Downes was pointing to the merits of the stained-glass windows in University College chapel, and especially to the scene in the Garden of Eden, where the apples on the tree of knowledge glowed like giant golden Jaffas. At 3.30 p.m., in the Archive Room of the New Bodleian, Sheila Williams was doing her best to enthuse over a series of Henry Taunt photographs taken in the 1880s – also to an audience slightly smaller than anticipated. But the slides selected by Dr Theodore Kemp, to illustrate the development of jewelled artefacts in pre-Conquest Britain, were destined to remain in their box in the Elias Ashmole Memorial Room that sunny afternoon.

At Oxford nude bathing was, and sometimes still is, indulged
in, which used to cause mutual embarrassment when ladies
passed by in boats

(*Marilyn Yurdan*, Oxford: Town & Gown)

AT 9.30 P.M. the University Parks had long been
closed – since before sundown in fact. Yet such a
circumstance has seldom deterred determined lovers,
and others slightly crazed, from finding passageways
through or over fences and hedges into this famous
precinct – the setting for countless copulations since
the Royalist artillery was quartered on its acres during
the Civil War.

Two of these latter-day lovers, Michael Woods (aged
seventeen) and Karen Jones (two years older), and
both from the village of Old Marston to the east of the
Parks, had sauntered over the high-arched Rainbow
Bridge across the Cherwell, and come to 'Mesopota-
mia', a pathway between two branches of the river,
when young Michael, encouraged by the fact that he
was now resting the palm of his right hand upon the
right buttock of the slightly forbidding Karen – and
without any perceptible opposition on her part –
steered the nymphet into the enclosure known as
Parson's Pleasure. This famous and infamous bathing

place is to be found at a point where the Cherwell adapts itself to a pleasingly circumscribed swimming area at a bend of the river, with a terrace of unsophisticated, though adequate, cubicles enabling would-be bathers to shed their clothing and to don, or not to don, their swimming costumes there. Green-painted, corrugated-iron fencing surrounds Parson's Pleasure, with the access gate fairly jealously guarded during the summer months, and firmly locked after the waters are deemed too cold for even the doughtiest of its homo-erotic habitués. But whether from an unseasonable gale, or whether from recent vandalism, one section of the perimeter fencing lay forlornly on the ground that evening; and very soon the young pair found themselves seated side by side in one of the cubicles. In spite of her seniority in years, Karen was considerably the more cautious of the two in the progress of this current courtship. And justifiably so, for Michael, as vouched for by several of the village girls, was a paid-up member of the Wandering Hands Brigade. After several exploratory fingerings along the left femur, a sudden switch of tactics to the front of her blouse had heralded a whole new manual offensive – when at that point she decided to withdraw to previously prepared positions.

'Mike! Let's get out of here, please! I'm getting a bit chilly—'

'I'll soon see to that, love!'

'And it's a bit spooky. I don't like it here, Mike.'

He'd known, really, ever since they'd slipped through the hedge at half-past eight; known when he'd kissed her briefly on the Rainbow Bridge above the swollen and fast-flowing waters, testing the temperature and finding it not warm enough for any further penetration into the underclothing of a girl who seemed dressed that balmy evening as if for some Antarctic expedition. He stood up now, and (as she thought) with a surprisingly gallant, almost endearing gesture, refastened the only button on her blouse he'd thus far managed to disengage.

'Yeah! Gettin' a bi' chilly, innit?' he lied.

The moon as they walked from the cubicle was bright upon the waters, and Karen was wondering whether she might slightly have misjudged this lively, fun-loving youth when her eyes caught sight of something lying lengthways across the top of the weir in front of them.

'Yaaaaahhhhh!'

Part Two

CHAPTER TWENTY

The moon jellyfish
like a parachute in air
sways under the waves
(*Basil Swift*, Collected Haiku)

IT WAS HALFWAY through the slow movement of Dvořák's American Quartet – with Morse mentally debating whether that wonderful work might just edge out the 'In Paradisum' from the Fauré *Requiem* for the number eight spot in his Desert Island cassettes – when the phone rang. For the second time that evening. Some while earlier, a weary-sounding Lewis had informed Morse that Mr Eddie Stratton had gone off somewhere just after lunchtime – from the railway station – and had still not returned to The Randolph. Naturally such a prolonged absence was a little worrying, especially in view of, well, the circumstances; and in fact an anxious Ashenden had rung Kidlington a few minutes previously, just in case the police knew anything. So Lewis thought he perhaps ought to mention it before going off duty ... To that earlier call Morse had listened with a grudging, half-engaged attention; but he was listening far more carefully now.

*

Both Lewis and Max were already on the scene when Morse arrived, the surgeon (incongruously suited in evening-dress) immediately putting the chief inspector into the picture – in a somewhat flushed and florid manner:

'The dead man lay there, Morse' – pointing to the moonlit water by the weir – '"something pale and long and white", as the young lady said. Rather good, eh? Somebody'd poked him along here with a punt-pole; and when I arrived his body – his naked, semi-waterlogged body – was nudging against the side of the bank – just here – just in front of the changing cubicles, face down, his head washed clean of blood – much blood, methinks, Morse! – his hair rising and falling—'

'Have you been rehearsing all this stuff, Max?'

'Just drinking, dear boy . . . hair rising and falling in the water like some half-knackered jelly-fish.'

'Very fine!'

'I read that bit about the jelly-fish somewhere. Too good to let it go, eh?'

'He needed a hair-cut, you mean?'

'You've no poetry in your soul.'

'What party was it *tonight*?'

'Oxfordshire Health Authority. Guest Speaker – no less!' Max flicked his bow-tie with the index-finger of his right hand, before pointing the same finger at the figure of a man lying covered with a plastic sheet on the splashed grass beside the water's edge.

'Who is it?' asked Morse quietly.

'Ah, I was hoping you could tell *me* that. You're the detective, Morse. Have a guess!'

'A seventy-year-old Californian whose wife died yes-terday – died, according to the best informed medical opinion, of purely natural causes.'

'And what did *he* die of?'

'Suicide – suicide by drowning – about three or four hours ago, just as it was getting dark. Crashed his head against a jagged branch as he was floating by. Anything else you want to know?'

'Back to school, Morse! I'm not sure he's an American or whether he was recently severed from his spouse. But he's certainly not in his seventies! Forties more like – you could put your pension on the forties.'

'I propose keeping my pension, thank you.'

'See for yourself!'

Max drew back the covering from the corpse, and even Lewis gave his second involuntary shudder of the night. As for Morse, he looked for a second or two only, breathed very deeply, lurched a fraction forward for a moment as if he might vomit, then turned away. It was immediately clear, as Max had said, that there had earlier been much blood; soon clear, too, that the body was that of a comparatively young man; the body of the man whom Morse had interviewed (with such distaste) the previous evening; the man who had been cheated of the Wolvercote Jewel – and the man who now had been cheated of life.

Dr Theodore Kemp.

Max was putting his bag into the boot of his BMW as Morse walked slowly up to him.

'You got here early, Max?'

'Just round the corner, dear boy. William Dunn School of Pathology. Know it?'

'How did he die?'

'Blood probably coagulated *before* he entered the water.'

'Really? I've never heard you say anything so definite before!'

'I know, Morse. I'm sorry. It's the drink.'

'But you'll know for certain tomorrow?'

'"Tomorrow and tomorrow and tomorrow."'

'It wasn't suicide, then?'

'Oh no, Morse. That was *your* verdict.'

'No chance?'

'I'm only a pathologist.'

'How long in the water?'

'Couldn't possibly say.'

'Roughly?'

'Eight, seven, six, five, four hours ... "Roughly", you said?'

'Thank you very much.'

Max walked round to the front of his car: 'By the way, I was talking to Dr Swain again this evening. He's reporting you to the Chief Constable.'

''Night, Max.'

''Night, Morse.'

When the surgeon had departed, Morse turned with unwarranted ferocity upon his ill-used sergeant: 'You told *me*, Lewis, that Mr Eddie bloody Stratton had been

missing in quite extraordinarily suspicious circumstances since early afternoon, and that a frenetically
distraught Ashenden had rung you up—'

'I didn't! I didn't say that!'

'What *did* you tell me, then?'

'Well, I did mention that Stratton had gone AWOL.
And I *also* said that Dr Kemp hadn't turned up at the
railway station when they'd arranged for a taxi to pick
him up and take him—'

'What time was that?'

'Three o'clock, sir.'

'Mm. So if there's some evidence of a whacking great
crack on his head . . . and if this had been deliberately
inflicted rather than accidentally incurred . . . about
seven hours ago, say . . . Three o'clock, you say, Lewis,
when Kemp turned up again in Oxford?'

'When he *didn't* turn up in Oxford, sir.'

So many lights; the yellow lights of the arc-lamps that
shone down on the river-bank; the white lights from
the flashes of the police photographers; the blue lights
of the police cars that lingered still around the scene.
But little light in Morse's mind. He could hang around,
of course, for the following hour or two, pretending to
know what it was that he or anybody else should seek to
discover. Or go back to HQ, and try to think up a few
lines of enquiry for the staff there to pursue – men and
women looking progressively more unwashed and
unkempt and incompetent as the small hours of the
morning gradually wore on.

But there *was* another option. He could drive down
to The Randolph, and sort out that lying sod Ashenden!

The bar would still be open, wouldn't it? At least for residents. Surely the bar *never* closed in a five-star hotel? Isn't that what you paid for? Yes! And occasionally, as now, it so happened that duty and pleasure would fall together in a sweet coincidence; and from Parson's Pleasure, after dutifully forbidding Lewis to linger more than a couple of hours or so, Morse himself departed.

It was twenty-five minutes after Morse had left the scene that Lewis discovered the first, fat clue: a sheet of yellow A4 paper on which the details of the Historic Cities of England Tour had been originally itemized; and on which the time of the final item that day had been crossed through boldly in blue Biro, with the entry now reading:

7.30 ~~8.00~~ p.m.   Dinner

118

CHAPTER TWENTY-ONE

You did not come,
And marching Time drew on, and wore me numb
(*Thomas Hardy*, A Broken Appointment)

THE PARKING PLOTS on either side of St Giles' were now virtually empty and Morse drew the Jaguar in outside St John's. It was two minutes past midnight when he walked through into the Chapters Bar, where a dozen or so late-night (early-morning) drinkers were still happily signing bills. Including Ashenden.

'Inspector! Can I get you a drink?'

After 'a touch of the malt' had been reasonably accurately translated by Michelle, the white-bloused, blue-skirted barmaid, as a large Glenlivet, Morse joined Ashenden's table: 'Howard and Shirley Brown, Inspector – and Phil here, Phil Aldrich.' Morse shook hands with the three of them; and noted with approval the firm, cool handshake of Howard Brown, whose eyes seemed to Morse equally firm and cool as he smiled a cautious greeting. The reason for such a late session, Ashenden explained, was simple: Eddie Stratton. He had not been seen again since he was observed to leave the hotel just after lunch; observed by Mrs Roscoe (who else?) – and also, as Morse knew, by Lewis himself. No one knew where he'd gone; everyone was worried sick;

and by the look of her, Shirley Brown was worried the sickest: what could a man be doing at *this* time of night, for heaven's sake? Well, perhaps supping Glenlivet, thought Morse, or lying with some lovely girl under newly laundered sheets; and indeed he would have suggested to them that it was surely just a little early to get *too* worried – when the night porter came through and asked Chief Inspector Morse if he was Chief Inspector Morse.

'How the hell did you know I was here, Lewis?'

'You said you were off home.'

'So why—?'

'No answer when I rang.'

'But how—?'

'I'm a detective, sir.'

'What do you want?'

A phone call made just before midnight to St Aldate's Police Station had been relayed to the murder scene at Parson's Pleasure: Mrs Marion Kemp, of 6 Cherwell Lodge, had reported that her husband, who had left for London early that morning, had still not arrived back home; that such an occurrence was quite unprecedented, and that she was beginning (had long begun!) to feel a little (a whole lot!) worried about him. She was herself a cripple, constantly in need of the sort of attention her husband had regularly given her in the evenings. She knew something, though not all, of his day's programme: she'd rung The Randolph at 10.45 p.m. and learned from the tour leader that her husband had not turned up at any point during the day to fulfil his commitments – and that in itself was quite out of character. After an evening of agonising and, now, almost unbearable waiting, she'd decided to ring the police.

Such was the message Lewis passed on, himself saying nothing for the moment of his own extraordinarily exciting find, but agreeing to pick up Morse in about ten minutes' time, after briefly reporting in to St Aldate's.

'News? About Eddie?' asked an anxious Phil Aldrich, when the frowning Morse walked back into the bar.

Morse shook his head. 'We get all sorts of news, sir, in the Force: good news, sometimes – but mostly bad, of course. No news of Mr Stratton, though. But I wouldn't worry too much, not about him, anyway . . .' (the last words mumbled to himself). He wondered whether to tell the four of them seated there about the death of Dr Kemp, for they'd have to know very soon anyway. But he decided they probably had enough on their minds for the moment; and swiftly tossing back the Glenlivet, he left them, making his way thoughtfully to the front entrance, and wondering something else: wondering whether any announcement of Kemp's death – Kemp's murder – would have come as too much of a surprise to *one* of the four people who still sat round their table in the Chapters Bar.

There was no time, however, for him to develop such a fascinating, and probably futile thought; for as he stood waiting on the pavement outside the hotel entrance, a taxi drew up, and with the help of the driver a very drunken man staggered stupidly into the foyer. Morse was usually reasonably tolerant about fellow-tipplers, and indeed occasionally rather enjoyed the company of slightly tipsy sirens; but the sight of this fellow pathetically fighting to extricate a wallet from an inner pocket, and then forking out and handing over three £10 notes – such a sight filled even Morse with mild disgust. Yet at least it was all a bit of a relief, wasn't it?

For the man was Eddie Stratton!

Clearly there could be little point in interviewing Stratton then and there; and already a solicitous (if censorious) Shirley Brown on one side, and a business-like (if unsmiling) Howard Brown on the other, were guiding the prodigal son to the guest-lift. No! Stratton could wait. With any luck he'd still be there the following morning.

Unlike the taxi driver.

Morse caught the man's arm, and held him back as he was walking down the steps.

'You must have brought him quite a way?'

'You wha'?'

'Thirty quid? Must have been – Banbury, was it?'

'Yeah – could a' bin. Nothin' to do with you, mate.'

'I'm not your mate,' said Morse, fishing for his warranty.

'So? Wha's the trouble?'

'Where did you pick him up?'

'North Oxford.'

'Expensive ride!'

'I didn't ask for—'

'You *took* it.'

'Not short of a quid or two though, these Yanks—'

'I quite like the Yanks.'

'Me too, officer.'

'There's a bottle there' (Morse pointed back to Reception). 'Leukaemia Fund. Doesn't look as if it's quite full yet.'

'How much?'

'Twenty?'

Shrugging, the taxi-man handed Morse two of the £10 notes.

'Where was it in North Oxford? What was the address?'

'I forget.'

'Shall we make it twenty-five?'

'Down the bottom of Hamilton Road, somewhere – ninety-seven, I think it was.'

'Name?'

'Same name as mine. Huh! Coincidence, eh?'

'I've always liked coincidences.'

'She rang up an' said, you know, take this fellah down to The Randolph.'

'Good! Thanks! Good night then, Mr, er . . .'

'Williams. Jack Williams.'

Lewis had pulled in behind the taxi, and was in time to find Morse slowly – reluctantly? – pushing two £10 notes into the slot of a Charity Bottle. He smiled happily. Morse had a *bit* of money – he knew that, but the chief's generosity, certainly in pubs, was seldom in evidence; and it was most reassuring to find that there was an unexpectedly munificent side to the chief inspector's soul. So Lewis watched, and said nothing.

CHAPTER TWENTY-TWO

Duty is what one expects from others; it is not what one does one's self

(*Oscar Wilde*, A Woman of No Importance)

IT WAS NOT difficult for Lewis to find his way to the Kemps' home in Cherwell Lodge, the ground-floor flat on the extreme right of the three-storey building, since it was the only window in the whole street, let alone the block of flats, wherein electric light still blazed at a quarter to one that morning. By this time, Lewis had shown Morse the yellow A4 sheet; and Morse had seemed so delighted with it that he'd turned on the car's internal light in transit. He folded the sheet along its original creases, and was putting it inside his breast-pocket as Lewis quietly pulled the car alongside the pavement outside number 6.

'We can ring from *there* – be easier really,' suggested Morse, pointing to the Kemps' property. 'We'll need a WPC – there should be one at HQ, don't you think?'

Lewis nodded.

'And a doc,' continued Morse. '*Her* doc, if he's not too far sunk in slumber or wine.'

Again Lewis nodded. 'You're right, sir. The more the merrier, isn't it, with this sort of thing? It's about the only time I really hate the job, you know – with

COLIN DEXTER

accidents and so on . . . having to tell the relatives, and all that.'

It was Morse's turn to nod. 'Always hard, isn't it, Lewis? I hate it too, you know that.'

'Well, at least there are the two of us tonight, sir.'

'Pardon?'

'I said, at least with the two of us—'

'No! Only *you*, Lewis. We can't waste precious resources at this unearthly hour.'

'You mean you're not—'

'Me? I'm just going to walk round to, er, talk to our other witness.'

'Who's that?'

'That, Lewis, is Mrs Sheila Williams. She could very well have something vital to tell us. It was Mrs Williams, remember, who ordered the taxi—'

'But she'll be in *bed*!'

By not the merest flicker of an eyebrow did Morse betray the slightest interest in the prospect of interviewing an attractively proportioned and (most probably) scantily clad woman at such an ungodly hour.

'Well, I shall have to wake her up then, Lewis. Our job, as you rightly say, is full of difficult and sometimes distasteful duties.'

Lewis smiled in spite of himself. Why he ever enjoyed working with this strange, often unsympathetic, superficially quite humourless man, well, he never quite knew. He didn't even know if he *did* enjoy it. But his wife did. For whenever her husband was working with Morse, Mrs Lewis could recognise a curious contentment in his eyes that was not only good for him, but

126

good for her, too. Very good. And in a strange sort of way, she was almost as big an admirer of Morse as that faithful husband of hers – a husband whose happiness had always been her own.

'Perhaps I'd better run you round there, sir.'

'No, no, Lewis! The walk may do me good.'

'As you say.'

'Er . . . just one more thing, Lewis. About the Jaguar. I left it just outside St John's, I think. If, er . . .' He held up his car-keys between the thumb and forefinger of his right hand, as if saving his nostrils the distress of some malodorous handkerchief. Then he got out of the car.

As Lewis watched him walk away up to Hamilton Road, he wondered, as he'd so often wondered, what exactly Morse was *thinking*; wondered about what was going on in Morse's mind at that very moment; the reading of the clues, those clues to which no one else could see the answers; those glimpses of motive that no one else could ever have suspected; those answers to the sort of questions that no one else had even begun to ask . . .

When Morse opened the ramshackle gate to number 97, his mind was anticipating a potentially most interesting encounter. If a diabetic patient was in need of so-called 'balance' – namely, the appropriate injection of human insulin for the control of blood-sugar levels – equally so did Morse require the occasional balance of some mildly erotic fancy in order to meet the demands of what until recently he had diagnosed as a reasonably healthy libido. Earlier that very week, in fact, as he'd filled up the Jaguar with Gulf-inflated gasoline, he'd found himself surveying the display of the semi-pornographic magazines arranged along the highest shelf above the dailies; and re-acquainted himself with such reasonably familiar titles as *Men Only, Escort, Knave, Video XXXX*, and so many others, each of them enticing the susceptible motorist with its cover of some provocatively posed woman, vast-breasted and voluptuous. And it was just after he'd flicked through one of them that Detective Constable Hodges (blast his eyes!) had come in, walked over to the newspaper stall, and picked up the top copy but one from the *Daily Mirror* pile. Morse had immediately picked up a copy of *The Times*, and proceeded to hold this newspaper like a crusader flaunting his emblazoned shield as he'd stood beside Hodges at the check-out.

'Nice day, sir?'

'Very nice.'

It had seemed to Morse, at that moment, that the dull eyes of Hodges had betrayed not the slightest suspicion of Morse's susceptibility. But even Morse – especially Morse! – was sometimes wholly wrong.

CHAPTER TWENTY-THREE

> Yet the first bringer of unwelcome news
> Hath but a losing office
> (*Shakespeare*, King Henry IV, Part 2)

LEWIS WATCHED THE silhouette gradually form behind the opaque glass in the upper half of the front door.

'Hullo? Who is it?' The voice sounded sharp, and well educated.

'Police, Mrs Kemp. You rang—'

'All right! All right! You took your time. Let me take mine!'

With much clicking of locks and a final scrabbling of a chain, the door was opened, and Lewis looked down with ill-disguised surprise.

'For Heaven's sake! Didn't they *tell* you I was a cripple?' And before Lewis could reply: 'Where's the policewoman?'

'Er, *what* policewoman, Mrs Kemp?'

'Well, I'm not going to be put to bed by *you* – let's get that straight for a start!'

Lewis might almost have been amused by the exchanges thus far, were it not for the heavy burden of the news he was bearing.

'If I could just come in a minute—'

Marion Kemp turned her chair through one hundred and eighty degrees with a couple of flicks of her sinewy wrists, then wheeled herself swiftly and expertly into the front room. 'Close the door behind you, will you? Who *are* you by the way?'

Lewis identified himself, though Marion Kemp appeared but little interested in the proffered warranty.

'Have you found him yet?' The voice which Lewis had earlier thought well under control now wavered slightly, and with her handkerchief she quickly wiped away the light film of sweat that had formed on her upper lip.

'I'm afraid—' began Lewis.

But for the moment Marion simulated a degree of hospitality. 'Do sit down, Sergeant! The settee is quite comfortable – though I have little first-hand experience of it myself, of course. Now, the only reason I rang – the chief reason – was that I need a little help, as you can see.'

'Yes, I do see. I'm, er, sorry . . .'

'No need! My husband managed to crash into another car on the Ring Road down near Botley.'

'Er, I'll just, er . . .' Lewis had seen the phone in the entrance-hall and with Mrs Kemp's permission he now quickly left the room and rang HQ for a WPC. He felt profoundly uneasy, for he'd known the same sort of thing on several previous occasions: surviving relatives rabbiting on, as if so fearful of hearing the dreaded information.

'She'll be along soon, madam,' reported Lewis,

seating himself again. 'Very dangerous that stretch by the Botley turn . . .'

'Not for the driver, Sergeant! Not on this occasion. One broken collar-bone, and a cut on the back of his shoulder – and even *that* refused to bleed for more than a couple of minutes.' The bitterness in her voice had become so intense that Lewis couldn't think of anything, even anything inadequate, to say. 'It would have been better if he'd killed me, and had done with the whole thing! I'm sure *he* thinks that. You see, he can't get rid of me – not the way he could get rid of any *normal* wife. He has to keep coming back all the time to look after my needs when . . . when he'd much rather be out having *his* needs looked after. You *do* know what I'm talking about, don't you, Sergeant?'

Lewis knew, yes; but he waited a little, nodding his sympathy to a woman who, for the moment, had said her immediate say.

'What time did your husband leave this morning?' he asked quietly, noting a pair of nervous eyes suddenly flash across at him.

'Seven-twenty. A taxi called. My husband was banned for three years after he'd killed me.'

Lewis shook his head helplessly: 'He *didn't* kill you, madam—'

'Yes he did! He killed the woman in the other car – and he killed *me*, too!'

Lewis it was who broke the long silence between them, and took out his note-book: 'You knew *where* he was going?'

131

'His publishers. He's just finished a book and now he's doing some chapters for the new *Cambridge History of Early Britain*.'

'And he actually – *went*, did he?'

'Don't be silly! Of course he went. He rang me up from London. The post hadn't come when he left, and he wanted to know if some proofs had arrived.'

'What time did you expect him back?'

'I wasn't sure. There'd been some trouble at The Randolph. You know all about that?'

Lewis nodded – ever dreading that inexorable moment when she, too, would have to know all about something else.

'They'd changed the programme – I forget exactly what he said. But he'd have been home by half-past ten. He's never later than that . . .'

The slim, dark-haired, rather plain woman in the wheelchair was beginning to betray the symptoms of panic. Talk on, Lewis! Write something in that little book of yours. Do anything!

'You've no idea where he might have gone to when he came back from London?'

'No, no, no, Sergeant! How could I? He'd hardly even have the time to see his precious Sheila bloody Williams, would he? That over-sexed, pathetic, alcoholic . . .'

Talk on, Lewis!

'He must have been pretty upset about the Wolvercote Jewel.'

'He'd been waiting long enough to see it.'

'Why didn't he go over to America to see it?'

'I wouldn't let him.'

Lewis looked down at the uncarpeted floor-boards and put his note-book away.

'Oh no! I wasn't going to be left here on my own. Not after what he did to me!'

'Mrs Kemp, I'm afraid I've got—'

But Marion was staring down into some bleak abyss. Her voice, so savagely vindictive just a moment since, was suddenly tremulous and fearful – almost as if she already knew. 'I wasn't very nice to him about it, was I?'

Blessedly the front-door bell rang, and Lewis rose to his feet. 'That'll be the policewoman, Mrs Kemp. I'll – if it's OK – I'll go and ... Look, there's something we've got to tell you. I'll just go and let her in.'

'He's dead. He's dead, Sergeant, isn't he?'

'Yes, Mrs Kemp. He's dead.'

She made no sound but the tips of her taut and bloodless fingers dug into her temples as if seeking to sever the nerves that carried the message from ears to brain.

Chapter Twenty-four

There are several good protections against temptations, but the surest is cowardice

(*Mark Twain*, Following the Equator)

'Sit down, Inspector! Can I get you a drink?'

Sheila Williams, fairly sober and fully respectable, was drinking a cup of black coffee.

'What – coffee?'

Sheila shrugged: 'Whatever you like. I've got most things – if you know what I mean.'

'I drink too much as it is.'

'So do I.'

'Look, I know it's late—'

'I'm never in bed before about one – not on my own!' She laughed cruelly at herself.

'You've had a long day.'

'A long boozy day, yeah.' She took a few sips of the hot coffee. 'There's something in one of Kipling's stories about a fellow who says he knows his soul's gone rotten because he can't get drunk any more. You know it?'

Morse nodded. '"Love o' Women".'

'Yeah! One of the greatest stories of the twentieth century.'

'Nineteenth, I think you'll find.'

'Oh, for Christ's sake! Not a literary copper!' She

looked down miserably at the table-top; then looked up again as Morse elaborated:

'It was Mulvaney, wasn't it? "When the liquor does not take hold, the soul of a man is rotten in him." Been part of my mental baggage for many a year.'

'Jesus!' whispered Sheila.

The room in which they sat was pleasantly furnished, with some good quality pieces, and several interesting and unusual reproductions of Dutch seventeenth-century paintings. A few touches of good taste all round, thought Morse; of femininity, too – with a beribboned teddy-bear seated upright on the settee beside his mistress. And it was in this room, quietly and simply, that Morse told her of the death of Theodore Kemp, considering, in his own strange fashion, that it was perhaps not an inappropriate time for her to know.

For a while Sheila Williams sat quite motionless, her large, brown eyes gradually moistening like pavements in a sudden shower.

'But how . . . why . . .?'

'We don't know. We were hoping you might be able to help us. That's why I'm here.'

Sheila gaped at him. 'Me?'

'I'm told you had a – well, a bit of a row with him.'

'Who told you that?' (The voice sharp.)

'One of the group.'

'That Roscoe bitch!'

'Have another guess.'

'Ugh, forget it! We had a row, yes. God, if anyone was going to kill themselves after that, it was me – *me*, Inspector – not him.'

135

COLIN DEXTER

'Look! I'm sorry to have to ask you at a time like this—'

'But you want to know what went on between us – between Theo and me.'

'Yes. Yes, I do, Mrs Williams.'

'Sheila! My name's Sheila. What's yours?'

'Morse. They just call me Morse.'

'All bloody "give" on my part, this, isn't it?'

'What did pass between you and Dr Kemp, Mrs – er, Sheila?'

'Only my *life* – that's what! That's all!'

'Go on.'

'Oh, you wouldn't understand. You're married, I'm sure, with a *lovely* wife and a couple of *lovely* kids—'

'I'm a bachelor.'

'Oh, well. That's all right then, isn't it? All right for *men*.' She drained her coffee and looked, first wildly, then sadly around her.

'G and T?' suggested Morse.

'Why not?'

As Morse poured her drink (and his), he heard her speaking in a dreamy, muted sort of voice, as though dumbfounded by the news she'd heard.

'You know, I was married once, Morse. That's how I got most of this' (gesturing around the room).

'It's nice – the room,' said Morse, conscious that the shabby exterior of the property belied its rather graceful interior, and for a second or two he wondered whether a similar kind of comment might not perhaps be passed on Mrs Williams herself . . .

'Oh, yes. He had impeccable taste. That's why he left

136

me for some other woman – one who didn't booze and do embarrassing things, or get moody, or stupid, or passionate.'

'And Dr Kemp – he'd found another woman, too?' asked Morse, cruelly insistent. Yet her answer surprised him.

'Oh, no! He'd already *found* her; found her long before he found me!'

'Who—'

'His wife – his bloody wife! He was always looking at his watch and saying he'd have to go and—'

She burst into tears and Morse walked diffidently over to the settee, where he temporarily displaced the teddy-bear, put his right arm along her shoulder, and held her to him as she sobbed away the storm.

'I don't know whether I'm in shock or just suffering from a hangover.'

'You don't get hangovers at this time of night.'

'Morning!'

'Morning.'

She nuzzled her wet cheek against his face: 'You're nice.'

'You've no idea why Dr Kemp—?'

'Might kill himself? No!'

'I didn't say "kill himself".'

'You mean—?' For a few seconds she recoiled from him, her eyes dilated with horror. 'You can't mean that he was murdered?'

'We can't be sure, not yet. But you must be honest with me, please. Did you know anyone who might have wanted to kill him?'

'Yes! *Me*, Inspector. Kill his wife as well while I was at it!'

Morse sedately disentangled himself from Mrs Williams. 'Look, if there's anything at all you think I ought to know . . .'

'You don't really think I had anything to do with – with whatever's happened?'

'You were seen walking up St Giles' towards North Oxford, just after lunch yesterday. And it wasn't Mrs Roscoe this time, either. It was Sergeant Lewis.'

'I was going – ' replied Sheila slowly, 'I *went* – to the Bird and Baby. Would *you* like a guess, this time? A guess about what I went for?'

'You were on your own there, in the pub?'

'Ye-es.' She had hesitated sufficiently, though.

'But you saw someone in there?'

'No. But – but I saw someone cycling past; cycling up towards Banbury Road. It was Cedric – Cedric Downes. And he saw me. I know he did.'

Morse was silent.

'You do *believe* me, don't you?'

'One of the secrets of solving murders is never to believe anybody – not completely – not at the start.'

'You don't *really* see me as a suspect, surely!'

Morse smiled at her: 'I promise to take you off the list as soon as possible.'

'You know, I've never been suspected of murder before. Thank you for being so civilized about it.'

'It'll be just as well if you don't say anything to the group about it. Not till we're a bit further forward.'

'And you're not very far forward at the minute?'

'Not far.'

'Couldn't *we* make a little more progress, Morse?' The fingers of her left hand were toying with the top button of her scarlet blouse, and Morse heard the siren voice beside his ear: 'What would you say to another little drink before you go?'

'I'd say "no", my lovely girl. Because if I'm not reasonably careful, if I do have another drink, in fact if I stay a further minute even *without* another drink – then I shall probably suggest to you that we proceed – don't forget that we don't "progress" in the police force, we always "proceed" – to, er . . .' Morse waved a hand vaguely aloft, drained his glass, rose from the settee, and walked to the door.

'You'd enjoy it!'

'That's what's worrying me.'

'Why not, then?'

Sheila had not moved from the settee, and Morse stood in the doorway looking back at her: 'Don't you know?'

A few minutes later, as he turned right into the Banbury Road, now beginning to think once more with some semblance of rationality, Morse considered whether his witness had been telling him the whole truth. Just as ten minutes earlier, as he had driven back to St Aldate's, Lewis had wondered the same about Mrs Kemp; in particular recalling the curious fact that, for a woman who had so manifestly hated her husband, she had reacted to the news of his death with such terrible distress.

CHAPTER TWENTY-FIVE

> Going by railroad I do not consider as travelling at all; it is
> merely being 'sent' to a place, and very little different from
> becoming a parcel
>
> (*John Ruskin*, Modern Painters)

AT KIDLINGTON HQ Morse and Lewis swapped notes at 7.45 a.m.: both felt very tired, but neither confessed to it; and one of them had a headache, about which he likewise made no comment. The Jaguar had been parked outside his flat that morning, with the keys found on the door-mat; but just as of his weariness and of his hangover, Morse made no mention of his gratitude.

At least the morning plan was taking shape. Clearly the biggest problem was what to do about the tour, scheduled to leave Oxford at 9.30 a.m. bound for Stratford-upon-Avon. It would certainly be necessary to make some further enquiries among the tourists, particularly about their activities during the key period between the time Kemp had arrived back in Oxford, and the pre-dinner drinks when everyone except Eddie Stratton, it appeared, was accounted for. *One* of the tourists, quite definitely, would not be able to produce his or her copy of the Oxford stage of the programme, for the yellow sheet found in Parson's Pleasure was now safely with forensics; might even produce some new evidence. And even if no fingerprints could be found on it, even if several of the tourists had already discarded or misplaced their own sheets, there would not be too many Americans, surely, who regularly wrote their sevens with a continental bar across the down stroke. Then there was Cedric Downes. He would have to be seen a.s.a.p., and would have to come up with a satisfactory explanation of exactly why and when he'd left The Randolph.

In addition it was to be hoped that Max could come up with some fairly definite *cause* of death; and it was even possible (if only just) that the surgeon might throw caution to the wind for once and volunteer a tentative approximation of the time it had actually happened.

An hour later, as he drove the pair of them down to Oxford, Lewis felt strangely content. He was never happier than when watching Morse come face to face with a mystery: it was like watching his chief tackle some fiendishly devised crossword (as Lewis had often done), with the virgin grid on the table in front of him, almost immediately coming up with some sort of answer to the majority of the clues – and then with Lewis himself, albeit only occasionally, supplying one blindingly obvious answer to the easiest clue in the puzzle, and the only one that Morse had failed to fathom. Whether or not he'd be of similar help in the present case, Lewis didn't know, of course. Yet he'd already solved a little 'quick' crossword, as it were, of his own, and he now communicated his findings to Morse. The first part of Kemp's day had probably been something like this:

Left home earlyish for his visit by rail to London to see his publishers; been picked up by taxi at about 7.20 a.m., almost certainly to catch the 07.59, arriving Paddington at 09.03; obviously with only some fairly quick business to transact, since he'd appeared confident of meeting his commitments with the tourists at lunchtime at The Randolph, and then again during the afternoon; likely as not, then, he would originally have intended to catch the 11.30 from Paddington, arriving Oxford at 12.30.

'Have you checked with BR?'

'No need.' Lewis reached inside his breast-pocket and handed Morse the Oxford–London London–Oxford Network South-East timetable; but apart from briefly checking the arrival time of the 13.30 from Paddington, Morse seemed less than enthusiastic.

'Did you know, Lewis, that before nine o'clock the third-class rail fare—'

'*Second*-class, sir!'

'—is about, what, seven times – eight times! – more expensive than getting a coach from Gloucester Green to Victoria?'

'*Five* times, actually. The coach fare's—'

'We ought to be subsidising public transport, Lewis!'

'You're the politician, sir – not me.'

'Remember Ken Livingstone? He subsidised the tube, and everybody used the tube.'

'Then they kicked him out.'

'You know what Ken Livingstone's an anagram of?'

'Tell me!'

'"Votes Lenin King."'

'They wouldn't be voting him king now, though.'

'I thought you might be interested in that little snippet of knowledge, that's all.'

'Sorry, sir.'

'Why are you driving so slowly?'

'I make it a rule never to drive at more than forty-five in a built-up area.'

Morse made no reply, and two minutes later Lewis drew up in front of The Randolph.

'You've not forgotten Ashenden, have you, sir? I mean, he was the one who took the call from Kemp – and he was the one who wasn't looking round Magdalen.'

'I'd not forgotten Mr Ashenden,' said Morse quietly, opening the passenger door. 'In fact I'll get him to organise a little something for me straightaway. I'm sure that all these tourists – *almost* all these tourists – are as innocent as your missus is—'

'But one of 'em writes these peculiar sevens, right?'

'They're not "peculiar"! If you live on the Continent it's *ours* that look peculiar.'

'How do we find out which one it is?'

Morse permitted himself a gentle grin: 'What date did the tour start?'

CHAPTER TWENTY-SIX

Wilt thou have this Woman to thy wedded Wife, to live together after God's ordinance in the holy estate of Matrimony? Wilt thou love her, comfort her, honour, and keep her in sickness and in health; and, forsaking all other, keep thee only unto her, so long as ye both shall live?

(Book of Common Prayer, Solemnization of Matrimony)

AT JUST AFTER 9.30 a.m., Morse sat with Lewis, Ashenden, Sheila Williams, and the (now fully apprised) Manager of The Randolph in a first-floor suite which the latter had readily put at police disposal. Without interruption, quietly, quickly, Morse spoke.

'I've no wish to hold up the tour a minute longer than necessary, Mr Ashenden, but I've got certain duties in this case which will involve your co-operation. Likewise, sir' (to the Manager) 'I shall be grateful if you can help in one or two practical ways – I'll tell you how in a few minutes. Mrs Williams, too – I shall . . . we, Sergeant Lewis and I, shall be grateful for your help as well.'

Morse proceeded to expound his preliminary strategy.

The tour, originally scheduled to leave at 9.30 a.m., could not now leave until well after a buffet lunch, if this latter could be arranged by the kitchen staff (the Manager nodded). A meeting of all the tourists would

144

be summoned straightaway (Ashenden felt a pair of unblinking blue eyes upon him) – summoned to meet *somewhere* in the hotel (the Manager nodded again – the St John's Suite was free), and Morse himself would then address the group and tell them as much or as little as he wanted to tell them, believing, he admitted, that Rumour had probably lost little of her sprinting speed since Virgil's time, and that most of the tourists already had a pretty good idea of what had happened. After that meeting had finished, it would help police enquiries if the tourists could be kept amused for the rest of the morning. And if Mrs Williams – and how very grateful Morse was that she'd agreed to his earlier telephone request to be present! – if Mrs Williams could possibly think of some diversion ... some talk, some walk. Yes, that would be excellent.

So! There was much to be done fairly quickly, was there not?

Ashenden left immediately, with the manifold brief of herding his flock together, of informing the coach-driver of the postponed departure, of phoning Broughton Castle to cancel the special out-of-season arrangements; of explaining to the Stratford hotel the cancellation of the thirty lunches booked for 1 p.m.; and finally of reassuring the lunchtime guest-speaker from the Royal Shakespeare Company that her fee would still be paid.

The Manager was the next to leave, promising that his secretary could very quickly produce thirty photocopies of the brief questionnaire that Morse had roughed out:

```
(a) Name ..................................................
(b) Home address ...................................
    ...........................................................
(c) Whereabouts 3–6.30 p.m., Friday 2nd Nov.
    ...........................................................
    ...........................................................
    ...........................................................
(d) Name of one fellow-tourist able to
    corroborate details given in (c)
    ...........................................................
(e) Date of arrival in UK...........................
(f) Signature ....................... Date ............
```

Sheila Williams, however, appeared less willing to co-operate than her colleagues: 'I willingly agreed to come here, Inspector – you know that. But my only specialism is mediaeval manuscripts, and quite honestly not many of this lot are going to be particularly ecstatic about *them*, are they? I could – well, I *will*, at a pinch – traipse around these inhabited ruins and try to remember whether Queens is apostrophe "s" or "s" apostrophe. But like Dr Johnson I must plead ignorance, Inspector – sheer ignorance.'

Here Lewis chipped in with his first contribution: 'What about shipping them all off on one of these circular tours – you know, on the buses?'

Morse nodded.

'Or,' pursued an encouraged Lewis, '"The Oxford Story" – *brilliant*, that!'

'They went on it yesterday – most of them,' said Sheila.

'I suppose we could just ask them to stay in their rooms and watch the telly,' mused Morse; but immediately withdrew the suggestion. 'No! People will be arriving—'

'They could just walk around Oxford, couldn't they, sir? I mean there's an awful lot to see here.'

'Christ, Lewis! That's what I suggested, at the *start*. Don't you remember?'

'What about Cedric, Inspector?' (This from Sheila.) 'I'm pretty sure he's free this morning, and he's a wonderfully interesting man once he gets going.'

'Could he do the sort of talk Dr Kemp was going to give yesterday?'

'Well, perhaps not that. But he's a bit of a Renaissance man, if you know what I mean. The only thing he's a bit dodgy on is modern architecture.'

'Good! That's fine, then. If you could ring this polymath pal of yours, Mrs Williams . . .?'

'He'd take far more notice of *you* if you rang him, Inspector. And . . . he probably won't know yet about—'

'Not unless he was the one who murdered Kemp,' interposed Morse quietly.

Cedric Downes had himself been on the phone for about five minutes, trying frustratedly to contact British Rail about times of trains to London that day; yet he could have had little notion of the irrational and

147

frenetic impatience of the man who was trying to contact *him*; a man who was betweenwhiles cursing the incompetence of British Telecom and bemoaning the cussedness of the Universe in general.

'Hullo! Is that British Rail?' (It was, by the sound of it, Mrs Downes, surely.)

'What?' answered Morse.

'Oh, I'm sorry. It's just that my husband couldn't get through to BR, and he rang the operator and I thought . . .' Clearly Mrs Downes had little idea *what* she'd thought. Her manner was rather endearingly confused, and Morse switched on what he sometimes saw in himself as a certain charm.

'I do know what you mean. I've been trying to get your number . . . er . . . Mrs Downes, isn't it?'

'Yes. I'm Mrs Downes. Can I help you?'

'If you will. Chief Inspector Morse here.'

'Oh!'

'Look, I'd much rather be talking to you than . . .'

'Ye-es?' The voice, as before, sounded a little helpless, more than a little vulnerable. And Morse liked it.

'. . . but is your husband in?'

'Ah! You want Cedric. Just a minute.'

She must, thought Morse, have put her hand over the mouthpiece, or perhaps Downes himself had been waiting silently (for some reason?) beside the phone, for there was no audible summons before a man's voice sounded in his ear.

'Inspector? Cedric Downes here. Can I be of help?'

'Certainly, if you will, sir. We have a bit of a crisis here with the American Tour. I'm speaking from The Randolph, by the way. The sad news is—'

'I know.' The voice was flat and unemotional. 'Theo's dead – I already knew.'

'Do you mind telling me *how* you know?'

'John Ashenden phoned a couple of hours ago.'

'Oh, I see!' On the whole Morse was not unhappy that Ashenden had been ringing around. 'Why I'm calling, sir, is to ask if you're free to come to The Randolph this morning.'

'This *morning*? Well ... er ... er ... Well, I've got commitments after lunch, but this morning's free, I think.'

'If you *could* get down here, sir, I'd be very grateful. We've got our hands a bit full with things.'

'Of course.'

'If you could—'

'Walk 'em round Oxford again?'

'A different route, perhaps?'

'Or I might be able to get the Oxford University Museum to open up a bit early – you know, Inspector, the dodo and Darwin and the dinosaurs.'

'Wonderful idea!'

'Glad to help, really. It's awful, *terrible* – isn't it? – about Theo.'

'You'll contact the Museum, sir?'

'Straightaway. I know someone there who's still trying to classify a few of the South American crabs that Darwin left to the Museum. Fascinating things, crabs, you know.'

'Oh yes!' said Morse. 'I'm most grateful to you, sir.'

'Anyway, I'll call in at The Randolph, so I'll see you soon.'

'Er, just before you ring off, sir?'

'Yes?'

'It's only fair to tell you that we shall be asking everyone here a few questions about what they were doing yesterday afternoon.'

'As is your duty, Inspector.'

'Including *you*, sir.'

'Me?'

'I shall be asking you why you were cycling up St Giles' towards North Oxford after lunch yesterday. So if you can have your answer ready? It's only a formality, of course.'

'Would that all questions were so easy to answer!'

'Where were you going, sir?'

'I was going home to get a new hearing-aid. I almost always carry a spare, but I didn't yesterday. At lunchtime the aid started going off and I suddenly realised that I wasn't going to get through the afternoon—'

'Your hearing's not all *that* bad, is it, sir? You don't seem to have much of a problem hearing me now.'

'Ah, but I'm very fortunate! My dear wife, Lucy, bought me a special phone-attachment – bought it for my last birthday, bless her heart.'

Something had stirred in the back of Morse's brain, and he sought to keep the conversation going.

'It sounds as if you're very fond of your wife, sir?'

'I love my wife more than anything else in the world. Can that be so surprising to you?'

'And you'd do anything to keep her?' It seemed a brusque and strange reply, but Downes seemed in no way disconcerted.

'Yes! Certainly.'

'Including murdering Kemp?'

From the other end of the line there was no manic laughter; no silly protestation; no threat of lawyers to be consulted. Just the simple, gentle confession: 'Oh yes! Including that, Inspector.'

For the moment, Morse was completely wrong-footed, and he would have discontinued the exchange without further ado. But Downes himself was not quite finished:

'It was Sheila, I know that, who saw me yesterday afternoon. And I don't blame her in the slightest for telling you. If you *have* got a murder on your hands, it's the duty of all of us to report anything, however insignificant or innocent it may appear. So I may as well tell you straightaway. As I biked up St Giles' yesterday afternoon I passed one of the group walking up to North Oxford. Would you like to know who *that* was, Inspector?'

CHAPTER TWENTY-SEVEN

It is a matter of regret that many low, mean suspicions turn
out to be well founded

(*Edgar Watson Howe*, Ventures in Common Sense)

As LEWIS SAW things, Morse's talk to the tourists was
not one of his chief's more impressive performances.
He had informed his silent audience of the death – just
'death' – of Dr Kemp; explained that in order to
establish the, er, totality of events, it would be necessary
for everyone to complete a little questionnaire (duly
distributed), sign and date it, and hand it in to Sergeant
Lewis; that the departure of the coach would have to
be postponed until late afternoon, perhaps, with lunch
by courtesy of The Randolph; that Mr Cedric Downes
had volunteered to fix something up for that morning,
from about 10.45 to 12.15; that (in Morse's opinion)
activity was a splendid antidote to adversity, and that it
was his hope that *all* the group would avail themselves
of Mr Downes's kind offer; that if they could all think
back to the previous day's events and try to recall
anything, however seemingly insignificant, that might
have appeared unusual, surprising, out-of-character –
well, that was often just the sort of thing that got
criminal cases solved. And here, sad to relate, was more
than one case – not only the theft of a jewel, but also

two deaths: of the person who was to present that jewel to the Ashmolean, and of the person who was to take official receipt of such benefaction.

When he had finished Morse had the strong feeling that what he had just implied was surely true: there *must* be some connection between the disturbing events which had developed so rapidly around the Wolvercote Tongue. Surely, too, it must be from within the group of American tourists, plus their tutors and their guide, that the guilty party was to be sought. And fifteen minutes later, with all the completed questionnaires returned, there was good reason to suppose that Morse could be right, since three of those concerned, Eddie Stratton, Howard Brown, and John Ashenden, appeared temporarily unable to provide corroboration of their individual whereabouts and activities during the key period of the previous afternoon – the afternoon when the original groups, three of them, had been re-formed slightly (following Kemp's telephone call), and when anyone wishing to absent himself for some purpose would have been presented with a wonderful opportunity so to do. And keeping check on who was doing what, and when, and where, could well have proved as complicated as calling the roll after Dunkirk.

For Morse, the information gleaned from the questionnaires was eminently pleasing; and when, at 10.50 a.m., Cedric Downes led the way out of The Randolph towards South Parks Road and the University Museum, with every single member of the group present (except Mr Eddie Stratton), he looked tolerably pleased with himself. Especially of interest was the fact that one of the two men clearly experiencing difficulty with section (c) on the examination paper, Howard Brown (Morse wondered why his wife hadn't been willing to cover for him), had filled in section (e) with the correct date of arrival, 27 October; or, to be more precise about the matter, '27 October'.

Nor would Morse be forgetting the only man who had not been present at the meeting – the man who still lay with a wicked headache and a barely touched breakfast-tray beside him in Room 201, to which room Shirley Brown had shepherdessed him when, after his unexplained absence, he had reeled into The Randolph the previous night.

But it was with Ashenden that Morse's attention was immediately engaged. Ashenden! – the man whom Cedric Downes now claimed to have passed on his bicycle; the man who had lied about his visit to Magdalen; the man who, like Howard Brown (and possibly Eddie Stratton?), was as yet unable to produce a single witness to his whereabouts the previous afternoon.

Three of them. How easy it had been almost immediately to uncover three possible suspects for the murder of Theodore Kemp!

Too easy, perhaps?

Chapter Twenty-eight

Myself when young did eagerly frequent
Doctor and Saint, and heard great Argument
    About it and about: but evermore
Came out by the same Door as in I went
             (*Edward FitzGerald*, The Rubaiyat)

'How are you, Morse?'

'Optimistic.'

'Oh!' Max appeared disappointed by the reply as he peered down again at the grisly work on which he was engaged.

The contrast between the two men would have struck any observer that morning. The stout, hump-backed surgeon – circumspect, but perky and confident; Morse – looking distinctly weary, his jowls semi-shaven by an electric razor that had seemingly passed peak efficiency, and yet somehow, somewhere underneath, a man on the side of the angels.

'There's some deep bruising here,' began Max, pointing to Kemp's left temple, 'but the main blow' – he jerked the head towards him before caressing the crushed skull with a gentle reverence – 'was *here*.'

Characteristically Morse sought to swallow back the bitter-tasting fluid that had risen in his gorge; and the surgeon, with understanding, pulled the rubber sheet over the head again.

'Bit messy, isn't it? Bled a lot, too. Whoever killed him had a bucket of blood to wipe away.'

'He *was* murdered, then?'

'What? Ah! Slipped up a bit there, didn't I?'

'But he was, wasn't he?'

'Your job, that side of things.'

'Which blow killed him?'

'Paper-thin skull like that? Either! Little knock on the right place . . .'

'Probably the blow on the back of the head, Max.'

'Oh yes – certainly could have been that.'

'Or . . .?'

'Yes – *could* have been the crack on the temple.'

'Someone could have hit him and then he fell over and hit himself on the fender or the door-jamb or the bedpost—'

'Or the kerb, if he was out in the street.'

'But you don't believe he was, do you?'

'Not my province, belief.'

'Could he have suffered either of the injuries in the water?'

'"Till that her garments, heavy with their drink, Pull'd the poor wretch from her melodious lay To muddy doom."'

'"Death", Max – not "doom". And he hadn't got any garments, had he?'

'Good point, Morse. And I've got something else to show you.' Max now exposed Kemp's torso and heaved the corpse a few inches off the table. Along the back of the right shoulder was a scratch, some five or six inches long: a light, fairly superficial scratch, it appeared, yet one made quite recently, perhaps.

'What caused that, Max?'

'Dunno, dear boy.'

'Try!'

'An instrument of some sort.'

'Not a blunt instrument, though.'

'I would suggest a sharp instrument, Morse.'

'Amazing!'

'*Fairly* sharp, I should have said.'

'Caused as he was floating along like Ophelia?'

'Oh, I couldn't possibly say.'

'Could it have been done before he was murdered – when he was wearing a shirt, say?'

'Ah! A not unintelligent question!'

Together the two men looked again at the light wound, stretching down diagonally from the back of the neck towards the armpit.

'*Could* it have been, Max?'

'I think not.'

'Then he was possibly naked when he was murdered?'

'Oh, I wouldn't go *that* far. Anyway he might have hit a willow twig in the river.'

'What other possibilities are there?'

'The evidence extends only as far as the lower scapula, does it not? He could have been wearing an off-the-shoulder toga.'

Morse now closed his eyes and turned away from the body: 'A toga pinned together with the Wolvercote Tongue, no doubt.'

'Oh no! I can assure you of one thing: that was not upon his person.'

'You don't mean – you didn't . . .?'

Max nodded. 'And he didn't swallow it, either.'

'And he didn't drown.'

'No. None of the usual muck one finds in the lungs when a man's fighting for his breath. Could he swim, by the way?'

'Don't know. I haven't seen his wife yet.'

The pathologist suddenly dropped his habitual banter, and looked Morse in the eye. 'I know you've got a lot on your plate, old boy. But I'd see her soon, if I were you.'

'You're right,' said Morse quietly. 'Just tell me, *please*, whether you think he was naked when he was murdered – that's all I ask.'

'I've told you. I don't know.'

'Not many reasons why people are naked, are there?'

'Oh, I dunno. Having a bath; standing on the weighing-scales; sun-bathing in Spain – so they tell me.'

'Having sex,' added Morse slowly. 'Not so much a willow's twig, perhaps, as a woman's talon.'

'Less likely, I'd say.'

'But you're sometimes wrong.'

'Not so often as you, Morse.'

'We'll see.'

Max grinned. 'Glad it was *you* who mentioned sex,

though. I was beginning to suspect you'd misplaced your marbles.'

'No, no! No chance of that, Max. Not yet, anyway.'

And as Morse left the pathology block, a quiet little smile of confidence could be seen around the chief inspector's lips.

CHAPTER TWENTY-NINE

There are an awful lot of drunks about these days. It wouldn't
really surprise me if you turned out to be one yourself
(*Martin Amis*, Other People)

APART FROM HIS former wife, Mr Edward Stratton
was the only one of the original group who had not
listened to Morse that morning. Although his head was
throbbing almost intolerably, he'd felt sober enough to
ring for breakfast in his room, and had done his best to
contemplate the 'Full English' he'd so foolishly ordered
for 7 a.m. His brain drew a veil over the sickening
consequences.

Edward Stratton had always been interested in
machinery, or 'working parts' as he'd always liked to
think of things. As a boy in high school he'd progressed
from World-War-I aircraft-kits to model railways, his
mind and his hands responding most happily to the
assemblage of pistons, valves, wheels, with their appropriate adjustments and lubrications. Not marrying, he
had set up a small business in specialised agricultural
machinery – which had gone bust in 1975. After a long
period of depression, and a short period of training, he
had taken on a new career – one which also demanded
dexterity with the hands: that of a mortician. Was there
ever an odder switch of professions? But Stratton had

soon grown proficient in the gruesome, sometimes disgusting, demands of his new job; and in the process of preparing an aged philanthropist for his silk-lined resting-place, he had met the man's disconsolate widow, Laura. And married her a year later. Or, perhaps, it may have been that *she* had married him. Convenience, that's what it had been for her – little more. Maybe for him, too? He'd assumed that she had money; everyone assumed that she had money. But he'd never known for certain and still didn't know now.

It was the Wolvercote Tongue which monopolised Stratton's thoughts as he sat on his unmade bed, head between his hands, that Saturday mid-morning. The thing was insured, he knew that – well insured. How otherwise? Yet insured in exactly what circumstances, under exactly what provisions, Stratton was wholly ignorant. *Why* had Shirley Brown had to mention the point on her brief visit to him earlier that morning, and sowed those slowly germinating seeds of doubt? Would it make a difference if it could be maintained that Laura had died *before* the Tongue was stolen? Would the money then go to the Ashmolean? But there could never be any proof on the matter, and if she had died *after* it was stolen, then surely the money would have to be credited to her estate, would it not? Stratton shook his aching head. He could get no real grip on the situation, and the more he pondered, the more confused his thinking became. But if he could get the police to believe it was *after* ... because that would mean it was still in her possession when she died ... wouldn't it ...?

Augh!

Stratton rose from the bed and walked to the bathroom. He was dipping his heavy, aching head into a basin of cold water when he heard the sharp knock on the door, and was soon admitting Chief Inspector Morse and Sergeant Lewis into his bedroom.

The former had immediately recognised the symptoms of a Caesar-sized hangover and offered practical aid in the form of two tablets of Alka Seltzer which he appeared to carry regularly on his person.

And almost immediately Stratton had been talking freely . . .

They must have thought him a bit insensitive – running off like that, the day after . . . But he'd seen the advert in the *Oxford Mail*, and the prospect of an Open Day at Didcot had proved irresistible. He'd walked round the engine sheds, he said, where he'd looked long and lovingly at the old locomotives, and where he'd seen schoolboys and middle-aged men carefully recording numbers and wheel-arrangements in their note-books. ('All of them apparently sane, Inspector!') And then he'd had the thrill of actually *seeing* ('a life-time's ambition') the Flying Scotsman! He'd stayed there ('in Didcart') much longer than he'd intended; and when finally he tore himself away from the Cornish Riviera and the Torbay Express he'd walked back to Didcot Parkway Station at about five o'clock, and caught the next train back to Oxford, where he'd, er, where he'd had a quick drink in the Station Buffet. Then he'd been walking back to The

Randolph when he suddenly felt he just couldn't face his excessively sympathetic countrymen, and he'd called in at a pub and drunk a couple of pints of lager.

'The pubs were open, were they, Mr Stratton?' asked Lewis.

But it was Morse who answered: 'If you wish, Lewis, I will give you the names and addresses of the three of them there that open all day. Please continue, Mr Stratton.'

Well, at about half-seven he'd gone into a restaurant in St Giles', Browns; had a nice steak, with a bottle of red wine; left at about half-nine – and was strolling down to The Randolph when he'd met Mrs Sheila Williams, just outside the Taylorian, as she was making for the taxi-rank. They had stood talking for quite some time, each of them perhaps slightly the worse for wear, and then she had invited him up to her North Oxford home for a nightcap.

And that was it.

The strong-bodied American, with his rugged features, had spoken with a quiet simplicity; and as he'd watched him and heard him, Morse thought he could well have enjoyed a pint with the fellow. Yet in Morse's view it was always a good idea to ask a few inconsequential questions. So he did.

'You say you had a drink at Oxford Station?'

'Yep.'

'Which platform would that have been on?'

'Search me! But the same side the train came in, I'd swear to it.'

'And they have booze there, do they?'

'Sure do! I had a can – coupla cans. Expensive it was, too.'

Lewis's eyebrows lifted under a frown, and he looked across at his chief: 'I'm afraid that's not right, sir. Mr Stratton couldn't have got any beer or lager at Oxford Station – not yesterday. There was a great big notice outside: "No Refreshments" or something like that, due to modernization.'

'"Owing to" modernization, Lewis.'

'I've never known the difference.'

'No need. Just say "because of" and you'll always be right.'

'As I was saying, sir, the buffet was shut.'

'Interesting point!' remarked Morse, suddenly turning again to a now distinctly uncomfortable-looking Stratton. 'So if you didn't stay on the station between about five-thirty and six-thirty, where exactly *were* you, sir?'

Stratton sighed deeply, and seemed to be pondering his position awhile. Then he sighed again, before opening the palms of his hands in a gesture of resignation. 'Your Sergeant's right, Inspector. I asked if I could get a drink – anything. But, like he says, they were refurbishing all the places there. I *did* stay, though. I stayed about half an hour – longer, perhaps. I'd gotten myself a *Herald Tribune* and I sat reading it on one of the red seats there.'

'Bit chilly, wasn't it?'

Stratton remained silent.

'Was there someone outside you didn't want to meet?' suggested Morse.

'I didn't – I didn't want to go out of the station for a while. It, er, it might have been a little awkward for me – meeting someone who might ... might be waiting for a bus, or a taxi.'

'You saw someone from the group on the train, is that what you're saying? Someone sitting in a compartment in front of you when you got on the train at Didcot?'

Stratton nodded. '*He'd* not got on at Didcot, though. He must have come from Reading, I suppose—'

'Or Paddington,' added Morse quietly.

'Yes, or Paddington.'

Morse looked across at Lewis. Paddington was beginning to loom slightly larger than a man's hand on the horizon; Paddington was where the murdered Kemp had stood and phoned The Randolph the previous day. So was it too much to believe that it was *Kemp* that Stratton had seen – about five o'clock, hadn't he said?

'You'll have to tell me, you know that,' said Morse gently.

'It was Phil Aldrich,' replied Stratton quietly, his eyes searching those of the two policemen with a look of puzzlement – and perhaps of betrayal, too.

Phew!

'Let me ask you one more question, please, sir. Do you stand to profit much from your wife's death?'

'I do hope so,' replied Stratton, almost fiercely. 'You see, I'm pretty hard-up these days, and to be honest with you I'm certainly not going to say "no" to any insurance money that might be pushed my way.'

'You're an honest man, Mr Stratton!'

'Not always, Inspector!'

Morse smiled to himself, and was walking over to the door when Stratton spoke again: 'Can I ask you a favour?'

'Go ahead!'

'Can you leave me another coupla those Alka Seltzer things?'

CHAPTER THIRTY

Precision of communication is important, more important than ever, in our era of hair-trigger balances, when a false, or misunderstood word may create as much disaster as a sudden thoughtless act

(*James Thurber*, Lanterns and Lances)

MORSE THOUGHT IT must be the splendid grand-father clock he'd seen somewhere that he heard chiming the three-quarters (10.45 a.m.) as he and Lewis sat beside each other in a deep settee in the Lancaster Room. Drinking coffee.

'We're getting plenty of suspects, sir.'

'Mm. We're getting pretty high on content but very low on analysis, wouldn't you say? I'll be all right though once the bar opens.'

'It *is* open – opened half-past ten.'

'Why are we drinking *this* stuff, then?'

'Stimulates the brain, coffee.'

But Morse was consulting the Paddington–Oxford time-table which Lewis had picked up for him from Reception, and was nodding to himself as he noted that the 13.30 arrived at Oxford 14.57, just as Kemp had claimed. Now if Kemp had been held up, for some reason, for even longer than he'd expected ... for considerably longer than he'd expected ... Yes, interesting! The train Stratton must have caught – *said* he'd caught – must have been the 16.20 from Paddington, arriving at Didcot 17.10, and Oxford 17.29. For several seconds Morse stared across Beaumont Street at the great Ionic pillars of the Ashmolean ... What time *had* Kemp left Paddington? For left Paddington he certainly had, at some point, after ringing through to The Randolph to explain his delayed departure.

But what if . . .?

'You know, sir, I was just wondering about that telephone call. What if—?'

Morse grinned at his sergeant. 'Great minds, Lewis – yours and mine!'

'You really think there's a possibility it *wasn't* Kemp who rang?'

'Yes, I do. And it would give us a whole new time perspective, wouldn't it? You know, with the best will in the world, Max will never give us too much help if he thinks he *can't*. Quite right, too. He's a scientist. But if *we* can narrow the time down – or rather, widen it out, Lewis . . .'

For a while he appeared deep in thought. Then, pushing his half-finished coffee away from him, he stood up and gave Lewis his orders: 'Go and find Ashenden for me. I shall be in the bar.'

'There we are, then!' said John Ashenden.

It was twenty minutes later, and Morse had decided (insisted) that his temporary HQ in the Lancaster

Room should be moved to more permanent quarters in the Chapters Bar Annexe. He had questioned Ashenden in detail for several minutes about the crucial phone call with Kemp, and asked him to write down in dialogue-form the exchanges as far as he could recall them. Ashenden himself now sat back in his armchair, crossed his lanky legs, and watched with slightly narrowed eyes as Morse took the sheet from him and proceeded to read the reconstructed conversation:

K. I've been held up at Paddington, John.

A. Oh no! What's you're trouble?

K. Just missed the train, but I'll catch the half-past one and be with you for quarter-past three, at the very latest. Sorry to let you down like this, and miss the drinks and the lunch and the first bit of p.m. Apologies apologies apologies, John!

A. Not the end of the world, though – not quite! (sotto voce.) I'll do my best to sort things out, of course, and let your group know. Trouble is I changed the time to quarter-to three.

K. I'm a bloody nuisance, I know.

A. It could be worse. Shall I arrange a taxi for you from the station?

K. Is it worth it?

A. Save ten minutes.

K. All right. I get in at just before three o'clock.

A. I'll ring Luxicabs just in case there's not a
taxi there.

K. Thanks.

A. Make sure you don't miss the next one!

K. No danger. Er, before I ring off can I have a
quick word with Cedric please - if he's there?

A. He's here. I'll get him. Hold on!

'You write fairly well,' said Morse, after reading
through the sheet for a second time, and still refraining
from pointing out the single grammatical monstrosity.
'You ought to try your hand at some fiction one of
these days.'

'*Fact*, Inspector – it's not fiction. Just ask that nosy
Roscoe woman if you don't believe me! She was sitting
near the phone and she misses *nothing*.'

Morse smiled, if a little wanly, and conceded the
trick to his opponent. Yet he sensed that those next few
minutes, after Ashenden had finished speaking with
Kemp, might well have been the crucial ones in that
concatenation of events which had finally led to
murder; and he questioned Ashenden further.

'So you called over to Mr Downes?'

'I *went* over to Mr Downes.'

'But he didn't want to talk to Dr Kemp?'

'I don't know about that. He was having trouble with
his hearing-aid. It kept whistling every now and then.'

'Couldn't he have heard without it?'

'I don't know. Perhaps not. The line *was* a bit faint,
I remember.'

Morse looked across at Lewis, whose eyebrows had risen a self-congratulatory millimetre.

'Perhaps you only *thought* it was Dr Kemp, sir?' continued Morse.

But Ashenden shook his head firmly. 'No! I'm ninety-nine per cent certain it was him.'

'And Sheila – Mrs Williams – she spoke to him then?'

'Yes. But you put it most accurately, Inspector. She spoke to *him.* And when she did, he put the phone down. So he didn't actually speak to *her* – that's what she told me anyway.'

Oh!

We've still only got *his* word for it,' said Lewis, after Ashenden had gone. 'Like we said, sir, if it *wasn't* Kemp, we'd have a different time-scale altogether, wouldn't we? A whole lot of alibis that wouldn't wash at all.'

Morse nodded thoughtfully. 'Yes, I agree. If Kemp was already dead at twelve-thirty . . .'

'There was somebody else who heard him, sir.'

'Was there?'

'The woman on the switchboard who put the call through.'

'She wouldn't have known the voice, Lewis! She gets thousands of calls every day—'

'She'd be a very busy girl if she got a *hundred,* sir.'

Morse conceded another trick. 'Fetch her in!'

*

171

Celia Freeman was of far greater help than either Morse or Lewis could have wished. Especially Morse. For just as he had begun to survey the picture from a wholly different angle, just as he thought he espied a gap in the clouds that hitherto had masked the shafts of sunlight – the switchboard-operator dashed any hope of such a breakthrough with the simple statement that she'd known Theodore Kemp very well indeed. For five years she had worked at the Ashmolean before moving across the street to The Randolph; and for the latter part of that time she had actually *worked* for Dr Kemp, amongst others. In fact, it had been Dr Kemp who had written a reference for her when she'd changed jobs.

'Oh yes, Inspector! It was Dr Kemp who rang – please believe that! He said, "Celia? That you?", or some such thing.'

'Mr Ashenden said that the line was a bit faint and crackly.'

'Did he? You *do* surprise me. It may be a little faint on one or two of the extensions, but I've never heard anyone say it was crackly. Not since we've had the new system.'

'He never said it *was* "crackly",' said Lewis after she had gone.

'Do you think I don't know that?' snapped Morse.

'I really think we ought to be following up one or two of those other leads, sir. I mean, for a start there's . . .'

But Morse was no longer listening. One of the most extraordinary things about the man's mind was that any check, any setback, to some sweet hypothesis, far from dismaying him, seemed immediately to prompt some second hypothesis that soon appeared even sweeter than the first.

'. . . this man Brown, isn't there?'

'Brown?'

'The continental-seven man.'

'Oh yes, we shall have to see Brown, and hear whatever cock-and-bull story he's cooked up for us.'

'Shall I go and get him, sir?'

'Not for the minute. He's on the walkabout with Mr Downes.'

'Perhaps he's not,' said Lewis quietly.

Morse shrugged his shoulders, as if Brown's present whereabouts were a matter of indifference. 'At least *Mr Downes* is on the walkabout, though? So maybe we should take the opportunity ... What's Downes's address again, Lewis?'

CHAPTER THIRTY-ONE

There is much virtue in a window. It is to a human being as a
frame is to a painting, as a proscenium to a play

(*Max Beerbohm*, Mainly on the Air)

IT WAS JUST before mid-day when Lewis braked
sedately outside the Downes's residence at the furthest
end of Lonsdale Road.

'Worth a few pennies, sir?' suggested Lewis as they
crunched their way to the front door.

'Thou shalt not covet thy neighbour's house, Lewis.
Just ring the bell!'

Lucy Downes was in, and soon stood at the door: an
attractive, slim, fair-haired woman in her early thirties,
dressed in a summerish cotton suit of pale green, with
a light-beige mackintosh over her left arm. Her eyes
held Morse's for a few seconds – eyes that seemed
rather timid, yet potentially mischievous, too – until
her mouth managed a nervous little 'Hullo'.

'Good morning, madam!' Lewis showed his ID card.
'Is Mr Downes in, please? Mr Cedric Downes?'

Lucy looked momentarily startled: 'Oh! Good Lord!
He's not here, I'm afraid, no! He's been showing some
Americans round Oxford this morning – and he's got a
lecture this afternoon, so ... Er, *sorry*! Can I help? I'm
his wife.'

174

'Perhaps you can, Mrs Downes,' interposed Morse. 'We spoke earlier on the phone, if you remember? May we, er, come in for a little while?'

Lucy glanced at her watch. 'Yes! Yes, of course! It's just' – she held the door open for them – 'I'm just off to – whoops!'

Morse had knocked his shin against a large suitcase standing just inside the door, and for a moment he squeezed his eyes tight, the whiles giving quiet voice to a blasphemous imprecation.

'Sorry! I should have – that wretched case! It's bitten *me* twice this morning already. Sorry!'

She had a pleasing voice, and Morse guessed that her gushy manner was merely a cover for her nervousness.

Yet nervousness of what?

'I'm just on my way,' continued Lucy. 'London. Got to change some curtains. A friend recommended a reasonably priced shop near King's Cross. But you really can't trust any of the stores these days, can you? I quite specifically ordered French pleats, and then – oh, sorry! Please sit down!'

Morse looked around him in the front living room, slightly puzzled to find the carpet, the decoration, the furniture, all that little bit on the shabby side, with only the curtains looking bright and new, and (in Morse's opinion) classy and tasteful. Clearly, in any projected refurbishment of the Downes's household, Lucy was starting with the curtains.

'I'd offer you both coffee but the taxi'll be here any time now. Cedric usually takes me to the station –'

175

she giggled slightly, 'I've never learned to drive, I'm afraid.'

'It's purely routine, madam,' began Morse, sitting down and sinking far too far into an antiquated, unsprung settee. 'We just have to check up everything about yesterday.'

'Of course! It's awful, isn't it, about Theo? I just couldn't believe it was true for a start—'

'When exactly *was* that?' Morse asked his question in a level tone, his eyes, unblinking, never leaving hers.

She breathed in deeply, stared intently at the intricate pattern on the carpet, then looked up again. 'Cedric rang up from The Randolph just before he came home. He said – he said he shouldn't know himself really, but one of the people there, the tour leader, told him and told him not to say anything, and Cedric' – she breathed deeply again – 'told me, and told *me* not to say anything.'

'Bloody Ashenden!' muttered Morse silently.

'His poor wife! How on earth—?'

'How many other people did you tell?'

'Me? I didn't tell anyone. I haven't been out of the house.'

Morse glanced at the phone on the table beside the settee, but let the matter rest. 'Dr Kemp tried to talk to your husband yesterday lunchtime.'

'I know. Cedric told me. He came back here.'

'What time was that?'

'One-ish? Quarter-past one – half-past?'

'He came back for his spare hearing-aid?'

Lucy was nodding. 'Not only that, though. He picked

176

up some notes as well. I forget what they were for. Well, I don't really *forget*. I never knew in the first place!' She smiled nervously, and (for Lewis) bewitchingly, and (for Morse) heart-eatingly. 'Anyway he just grabbed some papers – and he was off again.'

'With his spare hearing-aid, too?'

She looked up at Morse with her elfin grin. 'Presumably.'

'I thought the NHS only issued one aid at a time.'

'That's right. But Cedric's got a spare – two spares in fact. Private ones. But he always votes Labour. Well, he *says* he does.'

'He's not all that deaf, is he, Mrs Downes?'

'He pretends he's not. But no, you're right, he's not *that* bad. It's just that when he talks to people he gets a bit frightened. Not frightened about not knowing the answers but frightened about not hearing the questions in the first place.'

'That's very nicely put, Mrs Downes.'

'Thank you! But that's what *he* says. I'm only copying him.'

'What time did he get home last night?'

'Elevenish? Just after? But he'll be able to tell you better than me.'

The doorbell rang; and in any case the three of them had already heard the steps on the gravel.

'Shall I tell him to wait a few minutes, Inspector? He's a bit early.'

Morse rose to his feet. 'No. I think that's all. I – unless Sergeant Lewis here has any questions?'

'What are French pleats?'

177

She laughed, her teeth showing white and regular. 'Like that!' She pointed up to the curtains on the front window. 'It's the way they're gathered in at the top, Sergeant.'

'Oh! Only the missus keeps on to me about getting some new curtains—'

'I'm sure, Lewis, that Mrs Downes will be able to arrange a private consultation with Mrs Lewis at some convenient point. But some other time, perhaps? She does have a train to catch – her taxi driver is waiting impatiently on the threshold ...'

'Sorry, sir!'

Lucy smiled again, especially at Sergeant Lewis, as he carried her heavy suitcase out to the taxi.

'You know when you're coming back, Mrs Downes?' Lewis asked.

'Seven o'clock. Just before – or is it just after?'

'Would you like me to ask your husband to meet you? We shall be seeing him.'

'Thank you. But he *is* coming to meet me.'

She climbed aboard, and the two policemen stood and watched as the taxi drove off into Lonsdale Road.

'Lovely woman, that!'

For the moment Morse made no reply, staring back at the house with a slightly puzzled air. 'Thou shalt not covet thy neighbour's wife, Lewis! Exodus, chapter something.'

'I didn't mean anything like that. You've got a one-track mind, sir!'

'You are perfectly correct, Lewis: one track only. My mind wants to know what the theft of the Wolvercote

Tongue has got to do with the murder of Theodore Kemp. And I would be very surprised if that "lovely woman" of yours doesn't know a little more than she's prepared to admit – even to you!'

CHAPTER THIRTY-TWO

Man has such a predilection for systems and abstract deductions that he is ready to distort the truth intentionally, he is ready to deny the evidence of his senses in order to justify his logic

(*Dostoevsky*, Notes from Underground)

OF A SUDDEN, on the way back down the Banbury Road, Morse decided to view Parson's Pleasure by daylight. So Lewis drove down to the bottom of South Parks Road, where he was ushered through into the University Parks by a policeman on duty at the entrance to the single-track road which led down to the bathing area. Here the whole of the site was lightly cordoned off, and one of the Park Attendants was talking to (the newly promoted) Sergeant Dixon as Morse and Lewis moved alongside. The Parks had closed at 4.30 p.m. the previous day, the detectives learned, yet it was not unknown for nimble adolescents and desperate adults to gain access to the Parks from half-a-dozen possible places. And the number of expended condoms discovered in and around the bathing-area suggested that not only ingress and egress, but congress too, were not unusual there, with the cover of the night, and the cover of the cubicles, combining to promote this latter activity – even when frost was forecast. But the cubicle in which the yellow sheet had been found could reveal no further secrets, and all hope had early been abandoned of learning anything from the scores of footprints which had criss-crossed the grassy area since the murder. Two divers had gone down into the river during the morning, but had found no item of relevance; and perhaps would not have recognised its relevance had they found it. Certainly no clothes, Sergeant Dixon asserted.

Morse walked over to the water's edge, the river-level high against the banks, and there he dipped his fingers in: not quite so cold as he would have thought. Dixon's mention of clothes had pulled his mind back to the discovery of Kemp's body, and he asked Lewis much the same questions he had asked Max, receiving much the same answers.

'But I don't think he'd have been swimming here, sir.'

'Not unknown, Lewis, for people to bathe naked in this stretch.'

'Too chilly for me.'

'What about sex?'

'You don't have to take all your clothes off to do that.'

'No? Well, I'll take your word for it. I'm not an expert in that area myself.' He stood pondering the waters once more. 'Do you ever have any rows with your wife?'

'"Not unknown", as *you* would say, sir.'

'Then you patch things up?'

'Usually.'

'When you've patched things up, do you feel even closer together than before?'

Lewis was feeling puzzled now, and a little embarrassed at the course of the conversation: 'Probably a good thing now and then – clears the air, sort of.'

Morse nodded. 'We know of two people who had a row recently, don't we?'

'Dr Kemp and Mrs Williams? Yes! But she's got a whacking great alibi, sir.'

'A much better alibi than Stratton, certainly.'

'I could try to check on Stratton: Didcot – the pub he mentioned – Browns Restaurant.'

Morse looked dubious: 'If only we knew *when* Kemp was murdered! *Nobody's* got an alibi until we know that.'

'You think Mrs Williams might have killed him?'

'She might have *killed* him all right. But I don't think she could have dumped him. I'd guess it was a man who did that.'

'He wasn't very heavy, Kemp, though. Not much fat on him.'

'Too heavy for a woman.'

'Even a jealous woman, sir?'

'Yes, I know what you mean. I keep wondering if Kemp had found some other floozie – and Sheila Williams found out about it.'

'"Hell hath no fury . . . "'

'If you must quote, quote accurately, Lewis! "Heaven has no rage, like love to hatred turned, Nor Hell a fury, like a woman scorned."'

'Sorry! I never did know much about Shakespeare.'

'Congreve, Lewis.'

'He seems to have been a bit of a ladies' man—'

'And if he couldn't make love to his wife because she was paralysed from the waist down . . .'

'I got the feeling she wasn't too worried about that, perhaps. It was Mrs Williams she had it in for.'

'She might have forgiven him if it had been anyone else, you mean?'

'I think – I think you ought to go to see her, sir.'

'All *right*,' snapped Morse. 'Give me a chance! We've got these Americans to see, remember? Aldrich and Brown – find out where *they* were yesterday afternoon. Where they *say* they were.'

Morse turned to look at the waters once more before he left, then sat silently in the passenger-seat of the police car as Lewis had a final word with Sergeant Dixon. In the side panel of the door he found a street map of Oxford, together with a copy of *Railway Magazine*; and opening out the map he traced the line of the River Cherwell, moving his right index-finger slowly northwards from the site marked Bathing Pool, up along the edge of the University Parks, then past Norham Gardens and Park Town, out under the Marston Ferry Road; and then, veering north-westerly, up past the bottom of Lonsdale Road . . . Portland Road . . . Hamilton Road . . . Yes. A lot of flood water had come down from the upper reaches of the Cherwell, and a body placed in the river, say, at Lonsdale Road . . .

And suddenly Morse knew where the body had been launched into the river and into eternity; knew, too, that if Lucy Downes could so quickly arouse the rather sluggish libido of a Lewis, then it was hardly difficult to guess her effect upon the lively carnality of a Kemp.

Lewis had climbed into the driving seat, and seen Morse's finger seemingly stuck on the map, at the bottom of Lonsdale Road.

'He couldn't have done it, sir – not Downes. He was with the Americans all the time – certainly till after we found the body. If anybody's got an alibi, he has.'

'Perhaps it was your friend Lucy Downes.'

'You can't think that, surely?'

'I'm not thinking at all – not for the minute,' replied Morse loftily. 'I am deducing – deducing the possibilities. When I've done that, I shall begin to *think*.'

'Oh!'

'And get a move on. We can't keep the Americans here all day. We're going to have to let 'em get on their way. Most of 'em!'

So Lewis drove back from Parson's Pleasure, back on to the Banbury Road, down St Giles', and then right at the lights into Beaumont Street. And all the time Chief Inspector Morse sat, less tetchy now, staring at the street map of Oxford.

No doubt, as Lewis saw things, 'deducing'.

CHAPTER THIRTY-THREE

If you are afraid of loneliness, don't marry

(Chekhov)

SHEILA WILLIAMS WAS feeling miserable. When Morse, himself looking far from serene, had come into The Randolph and demanded to see Messrs Aldrich and Brown immediately, he had resolutely avoided her eyes, appearing to have no wish to rekindle the brief moments of intimacy which had occurred in the morning's early hours. And the tourists, most of them, were getting restless – understandably so. Only Phil Aldrich had seemed as placid as ever, even after being interrupted in the middle of his lunch, and thereafter being seated in the Lancaster Room, writing busily on the hotel notepaper; and being interrupted just the once, and then only briefly, by Janet Roscoe – the latter intent, it appeared, on fomenting further dissatisfaction whenever possible.

Like now, for instance.

'I really do *think*, Sheila—'

'I do *envy* you so, Mrs Roscoe. I haven't had a genuine thought in *years*! Oh, Cedric! Cedric?'

He had been trying to steal silently away from the

185

post-lunch chatter, but was stopped in his tracks at the foot of the great staircase as Sheila, glass in her hand, laid the crimson-nailed fingers of her right hand along his lapel.

'Cedric! How that bloody woman has lived this long without getting murdered . . .'

Cedric grinned his sad, lopsided grin, removed the somewhat disturbing hand, and looked at her – her upper and lower lips of almost equal thickness, moist and parted, and temptingly squashable. She was a woman he had known for several years now; one with whom he had never slept; one who half repelled, and ever half attracted him.

'Look! I've got to be off. I've got a tutorial shortly, and I ought to sober up a bit betweentimes.'

'Why do that, darling?'

'Sheila! You're a lovely girl, but you – you let yourself down when you drink too much.'

'Oh, for Christ's sake! Not you as well.'

'Yes! *Me as well*! And I've got to go. I'm meeting Lucy off the train later on anyway, and if you want to know the truth' – he looked about him with rolling eyes – 'I'm completely pissed off with the whole of this bloody set-up. I've done my best, though. First I stood in for—' Suddenly he stopped. 'Sorry, Sheila! I shouldn't have said that. Forgive me!' He kissed her lightly on the cheek, then turned and walked out of the hotel.

As Sheila watched him go, she knew that in spite of the hurtful words he had just spoken she would always have a soft spot for the man. But she knew, too, what a lousy judge of men she'd always been. Her husband!

God! A quietly cultivated, top-of-the-head English don, incurably in the grip of the Oxford Disease – that tragic malady which deludes its victims into believing they can never be wrong in any matter of knowledge or opinion. What a disaster that had all been! Then a series of feckless, selfish, vain admirers ... then Theo. Poor Theo! But at least he was – had been – an interesting and vital and daring sort of man.

Sheila walked slowly over to the window and watched Cedric as he wheeled his bicycle across Beaumont Street towards St Giles'. He never drove his car if he was having any drink with his lunch. Not like some people she'd known. Not like Theo, for instance ... He'd been over the limit, they'd said, when he'd crashed his BMW, and there could have been no sympathy whatsoever for him from the relatives of the woman killed in the other car. *Or* from his wife, of course – his bloody wife! And yet there was the suggestion that he'd been just a little unlucky, perhaps? Certainly many people had mumbled all that stuff about 'there but for the grace of God ...' And there *was* a lot of luck in life: some people would go to jail for badger-baiting; but if they'd baited just the foxes they'd like as not be having sherry the next day with the Master of the Foxhounds. Yes, Theo *may* have been a fraction unlucky about that accident.

Even unluckier now.

And Cedric? Was he right – about what he'd just said? Already that morning she had drunk more than the weekly average for women she'd noticed displayed on a chart in the Summertown Health Centre waiting-room. But when she was drinking, she was (or so she told herself) perfectly conscious of all her thoughts and actions. It was only when she was reasonably sober, when, say, she woke up in the morning, head throbbing, tongue parched, that she suspected in retrospect that she hadn't been quite so rationally conscious of those selfsame thoughts and actions . . .

God! What a mess her life was in!

She looked miserably back across the coffee-lounge, where several of the group were mumbling none too happily. Six o'clock. Morse had changed their departure-time to six o'clock, unless something dramatic occurred in the meantime.

She walked through into the Lancaster Room again, where Phil Aldrich was still scribbling away on the hotel's notepaper; and for the moment (as Sheila stood in the doorway) looking up with his wonted patience and nodding mildly as Janet propounded her latest views on the injustice of the tour's latest delay. But even as Sheila stood there, his mood had changed. None too quietly, he asked the woman if she would mind leaving him alone, just for a while, since he had something more important to do for the minute than listen to her gripes and belly-aching.

Who would have believed it?

Sheila had heard most of the exchange; and, with the volume of Janet's voice, so probably had several of the others too. It had been a devastating rebuke from the quiet little fellow from California; and as Sheila watched the hurt face of the formidable little woman from the same State (wasn't it the same Church, too?), she almost felt a tinge of sympathy for Mrs Janet Roscoe.

Almost.

Lewis, too, had been watching as Aldrich wrote out his statement; and wondering how a man could write so fluently. Huh! When Aldrich handed it to him there were only three crossings out in the whole thing.

CHAPTER THIRTY-FOUR

Thou hast committed –
Fornication; but that was in another country,
And besides, the wench is dead
(*Christopher Marlowe*, The Jew of Malta)

I was stationed in Oxford in early 1944
for training as a 22-year-old GI for the
forthcoming landings in Normandy. One night
in Chipping Norton I met a married woman
and I fell deeply in love with her. Her
husband had been serving in the British
Merchant Navy on the Russian Convoy run
but after 1943 he was receiving psychiatric
treatment in Shropshire somewhere for his
nerves. They said nobody survived that
posting without getting his nerves shattered.
Well while he was in hospital his wife
had gotten herself pregnant and she had
a baby daughter 2nd Jan. 1945. From
what I half learnt the father must have

been a forgiving sort of man because he
treated the daughter (my daughter) as if
she were his own little girl. But there was
some trouble with her in her early teens
and perhaps she'd guessed something of the
truth. The fact is she ran away from her
home in late 1962 and her mother heard
a few months later that she was living as
a common street girl near King's Cross
Station. I only knew something of all this
because the girl's mother kept in touch
with me occasionally through innocent looking
postcards and just the one phone call put
through to ~~our telephone~~ me when her
husband died in 1986. She moved soon
after that to Thetford in your E. Anglia
and I was able to phone her there a
few times. But I could tell there was no real
wish on her part to renew any old ties
of love and friendship and if I am going
to be honest no real wish on my part
either. I valued my independence too much

191

to get into any deep down involvement and particularly with a woman who goddamit I probably wouldn't have recognized anyway! But I felt so different about my daughter and tried to learn where she'd gotten to. She attended the funeral so I guess there must have been some contact there. Well then her mother died last Feb. with some awful cancer and her daughter had been beside her when she died and probably learnt then about the secret which must have burdened her poor mother's life for so many years. I guess I ought to be more honest about this because my daughter wrote me after her mother's funeral and said she'd guessed what had happened anyway. I'd never had other children of my own and somehow she seemed very prescious just then, but I never expected to see her. She'd not given any address but the stamp had a WC1 postmark. So when this tour was advertised and I saw

three days would be spent in London I
just decided to go, that's all. It would be
good to see old England again and even if
I didn't find her I could tell myself I'd
just tried that little bit. So when we were
there in London I asked around at several
centers for rehabilitating women and I struck
lucky. At one place there were about a dozen
young women having a lunch together. I don't
recall the name of the place but there was
royal blue woodwork there and grey walls
and all the pipes were bright red. It was
a biggish house in a terrace, yellowish brick
and white window frames about five or ten
minutes walk from King's Cross. The only
other thing I remember is that there was litter
everywhere in that street there. The Warden
was a wonderful guy and he mentioned my
daughter's name to those girls and one of
them knew her! There were a lot of street
walkers and petty criminals, he called
them his pros and cons, but one of them had

COLIN DEXTER

seen my daughter Pippa a week earlier in
a cafeteria somewhere near. So I left
her £10 and asked her to please tell the
warden if she saw her again so that he
could call me with any news. Yesterday
was the last possible day ~~we could have~~
on the tour that was near enough London
to get up there easily, only about an hour
away. Then I had a phone call yesterday
from my daughter herself! I'd given
the warden details of our itinerary,
and the call got put straight through to
my own room here just before we went
for lunch. So we arranged to meet in the
Bronel Bar in the Great Western Hotel
at Paddington at a quarter after two
and I just decided to go without telling
anyone in the group. I got to Paddington
just after 2 o'clock right on skedule and
I walked straight over to the hotel bar and
gotten me a big whiskey because gee was
I nervous. You see, I'd never seen my

194

own daughters before. I waited and waited and waited — until about 3 o'clock and then when the bar closed until about 4 o'clock in the lounge there. But she didn't come though I was willing and praying for any women round forty-five or so who came in to be her. So I caught the 4.20 train back to Oxford which stopped at Reading and then Didcot. I didn't see Eddie get on the train at Didcot but I now know he saw me. I only know because he told me this morning, he'd not meant to say anything but his conscience was worrying him so he told me what he'd told you. I just hope the police can come nearer solving the murder if we all tell the truth even if there are a few skeletons in the cupboard. I only ask for my secret to stay a secret. But just one more thing. I asked ~~Janet~~ Mrs Janet Roscoe to sign that she saw me yesterday

afternoon at one of the sessions. Please
don't blame her because I just told
her I'd gotten a bad headache. She
is a much nicer lady than the others may
think and I admire her such a lot.

Philip Aldrich

CHAPTER THIRTY-FIVE

> Just a song at twilight
> When the lights are low
> And the flick'ring shadows
> Softly come and go ...
> (From The English Song Book)

FOR ALL THE swiftness of his thought, Morse was quite a slow reader. And as Lewis (who had already read through the statement) watched his chief going through the same pages, he felt more than a little encouraged. It was like finding a Senior Wrangler from Cambridge unable to add seventy-seven and seventeen together without demanding pencil and paper.

'Well?' asked Morse at long last. 'What did you make of that?'

'One odd thing, sir. It's an alibi for Aldrich all right, but not really one for Stratton, is it?'

'It isn't?'

'Surely not. Aldrich didn't actually *see* Stratton – on the train, did he?'

'You mean Stratton might *not* have been on the train? Ye-es ... But if so, how did he know *Aldrich* was on the train?'

Lewis shook his head: 'I'm thinking about it, sir.'

'But you're right, Lewis,' added Morse slowly, as he sat back and stared at the ceiling for a few seconds. 'And I'll tell you something else: he writes well!'

'Clever man, sir!'

'More literate than his daughter, I should think. Only those couple or so spelling mistakes, wasn't it?'

'Only the two I spotted,' replied Lewis, his features as impassive as those of a professional poker-player, as Morse, with a half-grin of acknowledgement, started shuffling inconsequentially through the completed questionnaires.

'Bit sad,' ventured Lewis, 'about Mr Aldrich's daughter.'

'Mm?'

'Wonder why she didn't turn up at Paddington.'

'Probably met a well-oiled sheik outside the Dorchester.'

'She'd *agreed* to meet him, though.'

'So he says.'

'Don't you believe him?' Lewis's eyes looked up in puzzlement. 'He can't have made up all that stuff about the army . . . or the train—'

'Not those bits, no.'

'But you don't believe the bits in the middle?'

'As you just said, he's a clever man. I think he went up to London, yes, but I'm not at all sure what he *did* there. All a bit vague, don't you think? Just as I'm not quite sure what *Kemp* was doing, after he left his publishers. But if they *met* each other, Lewis . . .? Interesting, don't you think?'

Lewis shook his head. It was almost invariably the same: halfway through any case Morse would be off on some improbable and complicated line of thought which would be just as readily abandoned as soon as a few more facts emerged. And, blessedly, it was *facts* that Morse now seemed to be concentrating on as, forgetting Aldrich for the moment, he browsed once again through the questionnaires.

'See here, Lewis!' He passed over three of the sheets and pointed to the answers to question (e):

P. Aldrich	10–27–90
E. Stratton	27th Oct 1990
H. Brown	October 27

'Not conclusive though, is it, sir?'

But Morse appeared to have boarded a completely different train of thought: 'I was just wondering about their dates of birth . . .'

'Soon find out. I got Ashenden to collect in all their passports this morning.'

'You did?'

Lewis felt gratified to note the surprise and appreciation in Morse's eyes and voice, and very soon he was back with the passports.

'All here, are they?'

'Except Ashenden's. You're not, er, forgetting Ashenden, are you, sir?'

'Oh no! I'm not forgetting Ashenden,' replied Morse quietly, as taking out his Parker pen he wrote three d.o.b.s on a table napkin:

Aldrich:	8.4.1922
Stratton:	29.9.1922
Brown:	3.8.1918

'Two of 'em sixty-eight now, and one seventy-two ...'

'You wouldn't *think* Brown was the oldest, though, would you, sir? He trots around like a two-year-old.'

'A two-year-old *what*?'

Lewis sighed, but said nothing.

'He stayed in his room when his wife went off for a jaunt round Oxford, remember? And I still think one of the oddest things in this case is why Stratton didn't see his wife safely up to her room. It's not natural, Lewis. It's not how things *happen*.'

'What are you suggesting?' asked Lewis, vaguely.

'Brown said he stayed in his room when his wife and Stratton decided to look round Oxford. Said he was tired. Huh! As you said, he's as sprightly as a two-year-old.'

'A two-year-old *what*, sir?'

But Morse appeared to have missed the question.

In the Annexe, as if on cue, a tune could be heard quite clearly. First a few exploratory notes, presumably on the Steinway Grand that Morse had earlier admired in the Lancaster Room; then the whole melody as the pianist hired for the afternoon tea-room session fin-

gered his way through the nostalgic chords of 'Love's
Old Sweet Song'.

The two men listened in silence, before Morse
resumed:

'You know, I'm beginning to wonder exactly who
was having an affair with who.'

Lewis's eyebrows shot up yet again.

'All right! "Whom", if you prefer it. Stratton and
Shirley Brown go out together and everybody says "tut-
tut". Agreed? And we all focus our attention on the
potential scandal – completely ignoring a far more
suggestive state of affairs. Brown and Laura Stratton are
there right next to each other in Rooms 308 and 310.
It's shenanigans between the sheets, Lewis! It's a *crime
passionnel*! Stratton comes back in and catches Brown
in the missionary position – and all this Wolvercote
Tongue business is just a secondary blind.'

But Lewis would have nothing to do with such futile
speculation: 'She was tired, sir. She'd be far more
interested in a bath than . . .'

'. . . than in a bonk?'

'Well, people that age—'

'What? I've heard that sex can be very good for the
over sixty-fives.'

'Only ten years for you to go, then.'

Morse grinned, though with little conviction. 'I'm
sure of it, though. It's Love's Old Sweet Song – that
must come into things somewhere. A woman dies. An
art-work goes missing. An art-expert gets murdered.
You following me, Lewis? There's a link – there's got to
be a *link*. But for the present I can't—' He broke off,

and looked at the three dates again. 'You realize, don't you, that those three would have been – what? – twenty-two, twenty-two, and twenty-six in 1944?' His eyes gleamed with what might have been taken for some inner illumination. 'What about all of them being stationed in or near Oxford?'

'What difference would that make, sir?'

Morse seemed not to know.

Picking up Aldrich's statement, Lewis rose to his feet. 'Shall I go and get Howard Brown?'

But again Morse's mind seemed to be tuned to another wavelength. 'Why did you say he' – indicating the statement – 'he was a clever man?'

'Well, for a start, there's only the three crossings out, aren't there? And he just – well, he just sort of sat down and wrote it straight off.'

'Ye-es,' said Morse, but to himself, for Lewis had already left the Annexe to summon Brown.

He looked around at the two other tables occupied in the Bar-Annexe. At the first, a middle-aged woman with an enormous bosom was digging a fork into a plate of salad with the precision of an accountant jabbing at his calculator, before transferring the accumulated forkful up to her rapidly masticating jaws; and Morse knew that if he had married *her*, it would all have been over within the week. But there was another woman, at the second table: a woman only half the age of her executively suited escort; a woman who was having a fairly difficult time by the look of things, earnestly rehearsing a whole chapter of body language with her ringless hands. Perhaps, thought Morse, the illicit little office affair was drawing to its close. Then her sad eyes met Morse's in a sort of distant, anonymous camaraderie: she smiled across, almost fully. And Morse did the same, feeling for a few small moments an intense and splendid happiness.

CHAPTER THIRTY-SIX

Their meetings made December June

(*Tennyson*)

FACED WITH THE evidence of the tell-tale 7, Howard Brown capitulated immediately. Yes, Morse was right in one respect: Aldrich, Stratton, and himself had been stationed in or around Oxford in 1944, and he (Brown) had in fact known Stratton vaguely in those far-off days. They'd been delighted therefore to renew acquaintanceship at the beginning of the tour; and thereafter had spent many an hour together, talking about old comrades they'd known – those who'd come through, and those who hadn't . . . and reminiscing about some of the 'local talent' the GIs had been only too happy to discover, in Oxford itself and in some of the surrounding towns and villages. Brown had fallen miserably in love (so he said) with a girl named Betty Fowler, whom he'd met one Friday evening at a hop held in the Oxford Town Hall, and already on their second meeting they had vowed a mutual, eternal love.

Then, when the war ended in the summer of 1945, after being demobbed from Germany, he'd gone straight back to the US, with no possible hope of any real communication between them except for one or two impermanent and unreliable addresses. So, slowly, the memories of their idyllic times together had faded. He'd met up with a marvellous girl in Münster, anyway; then a fully consenting Hausfrau from Hamburg ... and so it had gone on. He'd gradually come to terms with the fairly obvious fact (as most of his comrades already had) that wartime associations were almost inevitably doomed to dissolution.

Back home in California, he'd met Shirley; and married her. OK, there mightn't perhaps be all that much left over now from the early joys of their marriage; yet, in an odd sort of way, the longer they'd abjured the divorce-courts, the stronger had grown the ties that bound them together: home, children, friends, memories, insurance policies; and above all, perhaps, the sheer length – the ever-increasing length – of the time they'd spent together as man and wife. Forty-three whole years of it now.

Before marrying Shirley, he'd written an honourable and honest letter to Betty Fowler, but he'd received no reply. Whatever the actual reasons for this, in his own mind he'd singled out the fact that she must have got married. She was an extraordinarily attractive girl, with a pale complexion, a freckled face, and ginger hair: a girl for whom most of the other GIs would willingly have given a monthly pay-packet. Or an annual one.

Then, only six months since, he had received a letter ('Private and Strictly Confidential'). Although sent to his 1947 address in Los Angeles, it had finally, almost flukily, caught up with him – and thereby opened a floodgate of memories upon which the years had added their sentimental compound-interest. She had (Betty confessed) received his letter all that while ago; still had it, in fact. But by that time she had married a car-worker from Cowley, was four months' pregnant, and was eventually to become the mother of four lovely children – three girls and one boy. Her husband had retired in 1988 and then, so sadly, died only seven months later. She was all right, herself. No worries – certainly no financial worries. And eight (eight!) grand-children, though she had not herself been tempted to enter the local 'Glamorous Grandmother' contest. So, the only reason for her writing was to say that if he ever *did* get the chance to come over to the UK again, well, she'd like – well, it would be nice . . .

From America, how earnestly he'd longed to reach her on the telephone! But she had given him neither an address nor a telephone number; and the com-plexities of finding either had posed rather too much of a problem on a transatlantic line. Yet here he was now – so near to her! And with his wife gone out for long enough with one of her admirers . . . So, he'd watched her go from the hotel, and then contacted Directory Enquiries from the phone-booth in the foyer. Miraculously, within a couple of minutes, he'd found himself speaking to a woman he'd kissed goodbye in the early May of 1944 – over forty-six years ago! Could she meet him? Would she *like* to meet him? The answer was yes, yes, yes. And so they *had* met (it had been *so* easy, as it happened, for him to sneak away the previous afternoon) nervously and excitedly outside the main entrance to the University Parks at 2.30 p.m.

'And *she* turned up, did she?' asked Morse.

'Yes.' Brown appeared a fraction puzzled by the question. 'Oh, yes! I'd walked up St Giles' about two o'clock, and then down Keble Road to the Parks. And, well, there she was – waiting for me.'

'Then you went to Parson's Pleasure and sat in one of the cubicles.'

'But you won't get me wrong, will you, Inspector? I want to set the record straight. We just had a quiet little kiss and cuddle together and – well, that was that, really.'

'My only wish,' said Morse, looking now with some-what irrational distaste at the remarkably well-preserved Lothario from Los Angeles, 'is to set, as you say, the record straight. So thank you for your honesty!'

Brown stood up and prepared to leave. He looked, little doubt of it, considerably relieved, but clearly there was something on his mind, for he stood hesitantly beside the table, his eyes scouting around for some object upon which to focus.

'There *is* one thing, Inspector.'

'And that is?'

'When I was walking up to Keble Road yesterday I saw someone standing at the bus-stop outside St Giles' Church, waiting to get up to Summertown. Well, I suppose it was Summertown.'

'And who was that, sir?'

'It was Mr Ashenden.'

'I just don't believe all this,' said Morse after Brown had gone.

'You mean you wonder who *Ashenden* saw, sir?'

'Exactly.'

'He sounded as if he was telling the truth.'

'They all do! But *somebody* isn't telling the truth, Lewis. Somebody stole the Wolvercote Tongue, and somebody murdered Kemp! If only I could find the connection!'

'Perhaps there isn't a connection,' said Lewis.

But he might just as well have been talking to himself.

CHAPTER THIRTY-SEVEN

Sic, ne perdiderit, non cessat perdere lusor
(To recoup his losses, the gambler keeps on
backing the losers)

(*Ovid*, Ars Amatoria)

ASHENDEN, BUTTONHOLED AS he was once again in the coffee-lounge by the diminutive dynamo from Sacramento, appeared only too glad to be given the opportunity of escaping, albeit to an interview with Chief Inspector Morse.

'Do you always get one like that?' sympathised Lewis.

'Well, she'd probably take the prize,' conceded Ashenden with a weary grin. 'But Janet's not such a bad old stick sometimes – not when you get to know her.'

'Makes you wonder how anyone ever married her, though.'

Ashenden nodded as he walked through into the Bar-Annexe: 'Poor chap!'

With this next hand (Ashenden), Morse took no finesses at all. Just played off his aces and sat back. Question: Why had Ashenden lied about his visit to Magdalen? Answer: It wasn't a lie really. He *had* gone up to Magdalen College, asked at the Porters' Lodge, discovered the grounds were closed; then just carried on walking over the bridge, around the Plain, and back

209

again down the High. Silly to lie, really. But it was only to avoid any tedious and wholly inconsequential explanation. Question: What about the previous afternoon, at about 2 p.m.? (Morse admitted his willingness to listen to a little more 'tedious and wholly inconsequential explanation'.)

'No secret, Inspector. In fact I'd told a couple of the group – Mr and Mrs Kronquist, I think it was – that I was going up to Summertown.'

'Why bother? Why explain? You're a free agent, aren't you, sir?'

Ashenden pondered the question awhile. 'I did realise, yesterday, that you perhaps weren't completely satisfied with the account of my whereabouts when, er—'

'The Wolvercote Tongue was stolen,' supplied Morse.

'Yes. That's why it seemed no bad idea for somebody to know where I was yesterday afternoon.'

'And where was that?'

Ashenden, looking decidedly uncomfortable, drew a deep breath: 'I spent the afternoon in the betting-shop in Summertown.'

Lewis looked up: 'Not a crime, that, is it?'

Morse seemed to appreciate the interjection: 'Surely Sergeant Lewis is right, sir? Certainly it's not a criminal offence to line a bookie's pockets.'

Ashenden suddenly seemed more relaxed: 'I had a tip. I met this fellow from Newmarket when we were at the University Arms in Cambridge. He said be sure to back this horse – over the sticks at Fontwell Park.'

'Go on.'

'Well, that's it, really. I picked another horse, in the race before – I'd got to the bookie's at about half-past two, I suppose. I put three pounds to win on a horse in the two-fifty, and then five pounds to win on the "dead cert" this fellow had told me about in the three-fifteen or three-twenty – something like that.'

'How much did you win?'

Ashenden shook his head sadly: 'I don't think you can be a racing man, Inspector.'

'Would they have records at the bookie's to show you'd been there, sir?'

It was Lewis who had asked the question, and Ashenden turned in his chair to face him: 'Are you suggesting I *wasn't* there?'

'No, sir. Certainly not. But it was the key sort of *time*, wasn't it? Three o'clock time? Just the time when Dr Kemp was getting back to Oxford.'

'Yes,' replied Ashenden slowly. 'I take the point.'

'Would anyone recognise you,' continued Lewis, 'if you went there again?'

'I don't know. There were quite a few there during the afternoon – eight, ten – more, perhaps, for some of the time, some of the races. But whether anyone would recognise me . . .'

'They'd have your betting-slips, surely?' suggested Morse.

'Oh yes – they'd keep those – if the horses had won.'

'Bit of bad luck you didn't pick a winner, then. You could have collected your winnings and proved your alibi both at the same time.'

'Life's full of disappointments, Inspector, as I'm sure—' Suddenly he stopped; and his eyes lit up as he withdrew a black-leather wallet from the breast-pocket of his sports jacket. 'With a bit of luck ... Yes! Thank goodness! I thought I might have torn them up.'

'They tell me betting-shops are littered with torn-up betting-slips,' said Morse, as he looked down at the two pink slips that Ashenden had handed to him.

'You might just as well tear those up as well, Inspector, I'm afraid.'

'Oh, no, sir. We mustn't destroy any evidence, must we, Lewis?'

Ashenden shrugged, and seemed for the moment somewhat less at ease. 'Anything else?'

'I think not,' said Morse. 'But it's a mug's game, betting, you know. A dirty game, too.'

'Perhaps you should go into a betting-shop yourself one day. It's quite a civilized business, these days—'

But Morse interrupted the man, and his eyes were ice. 'Look, lad! Once you've lost as much money as me on the horses – *then* you come and give me a sermon on gambling, all right?' He flicked his right hand in dismissal. 'And tell your coach-driver he can leave at *five* o'clock. That should please everybody. It's only thirty-seven or thirty-eight miles to Stratford – and Lewis here once managed it in half an hour.'

CHAPTER THIRTY-EIGHT

The west yet glimmers with some streaks of day:
Now spurs the lated traveller apace
To gain the timely inn

(*Shakespeare*, Macbeth)

ON THE COACH, as it headed north up the Woodstock Road, and thence out on to the A34, the members of the touring party were mostly silent, their thoughts monopolised perhaps by the strange and tragic events they had left behind them in Oxford. What tales they would be able to tell once they got back home again! John Ashenden, seated alone in the front nearside seat, debated with himself about reaching for the microphone and saying a few words about Somerville College, the Radcliffe Infirmary, the Tower of the Winds, the large, late nineteenth-century redbrick residences, St Edward's School . . . But he decided against it: the mood was not upon him – nor upon anyone else in the coach, as far as he could gather.

Opposite him, in the seat immediately behind the driver, sat a sour-faced Mrs Roscoe, her nicely shaped little nose stuck deep into the text of *A Midsummer Night's Dream*. Immediately behind him sat Howard and Shirley Brown, silent and sombre, each thinking thoughts that were quite impossible for any observer to ascertain – even for the two of them themselves fully to comprehend. And behind the Browns, the enigmatic Kronquists, now the only other married couple registered on the tour, reluctant, it seemed, to engage in even the most perfunctory of conversations: she now reading *Lark Rise to Candleford*; he, *The Good Beer Guide* (just published) for 1991. At the back, as if distanced to the utmost from the woman who *ab initio* had publicly sought to claim him as escort, friend, and guide, sat Phil Aldrich, slowly reading the evening's edition of the *Oxford Mail.* Nor had the sudden coolness between himself and Mrs J. Roscoe escaped most of the other tourists; indeed, this development was proving one of the few topics of conversation as the coach accelerated along the dual carriageway towards Woodstock.

Only two of the party that had arrived at The Randolph, some fifty hours earlier, were no longer in their original seats – the seats immediately behind Mrs Roscoe. One of these missing persons was still lying (lying still, rather!) in the police mortuary in St Aldate's; the other person, with Morse's full permission, had that afternoon departed by train for London, not stopping on this occasion (as he had claimed to have stopped earlier) at Didcot Parkway, but travelling straight through – past Reading, Maidenhead, Slough – to Paddington, whence he had taken a taxi to the Tour Company HQ in Belgravia in order to discuss the last wishes and the last rites of his erstwhile legal spouse, Mrs Laura Mary Stratton.

As the coach pulled powerfully up the hill away from

Woodstock, Ashenden once again looked slightly anxiously at his watch. He had rung through to the Swan Hotel in Stratford to set a revised time of arrival at 6.15 p.m.; but by the look of things it was going to be, in Wellington's words, 'a damn close-run thing'. Yet he made no attempt to harass the driver into any illegitimate speed. They'd arrive a little late? So what! Twenty-six plates of 'Mousse Arbroath Smokies' were already laid out, they'd said – with just the single carrot juice for just the single Vegan girl.

Was Inspector Morse (Ashenden pondered) quite the man most people seemed to think he was? A man with a mind that might have left even the mythical Mycroft just floundering a fraction? Ashenden doubted it, his doubt redoubling as the coach drew further and further away from Oxford along the A34.

Everything would be all right.

CHAPTER THIRTY-NINE

I feel like I done when Slippery Sun
Romped 'ome a winner at 30 to 1
(*A. P. Herbert*, 'Derby Day')

FROM THE STREET-WINDOW of the coffee-lounge, Morse and Lewis had watched them go.

'Think we shall be seeing any of them again, sir?'

'No,' said Morse flatly.

'Does that mean you've got some idea—?'

'Ideas, plural, Lewis! We've seldom had so many clues, have we? But I can't help feeling we've missed all the really vital ones—' Morse broke off and resumed the drift of his earlier thought. 'It's this wretched *love* business – and I still think that Kemp was killed because he had one too many fancy woman.'

'I know I keep on about Mrs Kemp, sir, but don't you think we ought—'

Morse ignored the interruption. '*Why* was he naked? I thought for a start it was because moving the dead body might have been a very messy business. Max said there'd have been buckets of blood, and if someone's going to get it all over a suit, or a dress ... It's a possibility, Lewis. Or he may have been stripped to delay any identification, I suppose. The longer delayed it is—'

'—the more difficult it gets for us to disprove an alibi.'

Morse nodded. 'But I don't think it was either of those reasons.'

'You think he was making love to a lady?'

'Well, a *woman*, Lewis. And since we know that woman wasn't likely to have been his wife because she'd . . . well, because of the car crash, we've got to decide who it could have been. Just think a minute! We get the husband, or whoever the jealous party was, bounding into the boudoir and catching 'em copulating. Who was *she*, though? I can't for the life of me see how it could have been Sheila Williams he was with . . . No, we've got to look down the race-card for some attractive, available, acquiescent filly – and the likeliest filly is surely—'

Suddenly Morse stopped, his mind once more six furlongs ahead of the field. He had bought a copy of *The Times* before he had come to The Randolph that morning, but hitherto had not even glanced at the headlines. Now he looked again at the two betting-slips that lay on the table in front of him; then turned to the back of the Business section for the Sport, his eye running down the results of the previous day's racing at Fontwell Park. Ashenden's stake in the 2.50 race, £3 win on Golden Surprise, had contributed further, it appeared, to the luxurious life-style of the bookmaking fraternity. But as Lewis now saw them, Morse's eyes seemed to grow significantly in circumference as they fell upon the result of the 3.15:

I THETFORD QUEEN (J. Francis) 30–I

'Bloody 'ell!' whispered Morse.

'Sir?'

'Ashenden backed a horse yesterday – a horse he said someone in Cambridge had tipped – he put a fiver on it – and it won! Thetford Queen. There! – it's on the betting-slip.'

'Whew! That means he's got a hundred and fifty pounds coming to him.'

'No. He didn't pay any tax on it, so he'd only get one hundred and forty back – including his stake.'

'I didn't realize you knew quite so much about the gee-gees, sir?'

But again Morse ignored the comment: 'He says he was there, Lewis – in the betting-shop. He's put his money on the hot tip, and the thing wins, and ... he doesn't pick up his winnings!'

Lewis considered what Morse was saying, and shook his head in puzzlement. Surely Ashenden *would* have gone up to the Pay-Out desk immediately, if he'd been there – especially since that was the only time he was going to be in the betting-shop. And if for some strange reason he'd been misinformed, been told that the horse had lost, then it was difficult to see why he'd kept the slips so carefully in his wallet. Why not tear them up like everyone else and contribute to the litter found on every bookie's floor?

Morse interrupted Lewis's thoughts: 'Shall I tell you exactly what our leader was doing in the betting-shop? Establishing his alibi! If you've backed a couple of horses, and if you'll be gone the next day, you stay there like everybody else and listen to the commentaries. But if you pick a couple of complete no-hopers, rank out-siders, well, there's no need to stay, is there? Look at the odds on Golden Surprise! 50–1! So Ashenden spent eight quid of his money *in order to buy himself an alibi.*'

'Bit of bad luck the horse won, if you see what I mean, sir.'

'Where did he *go*, though?'

'Well he can't be that "jealous husband" you're looking for.'

'No, but he went somewhere he didn't want anyone to know about. I just wonder whether it might have been somewhere like—'

The Manager walked swiftly through: 'Can you come to the phone, Inspector? Very urgent, they say.'

It was Max.

'Morse? Get over here smartish! Bloody Hell! Christ!'

'Tell me, Max,' said Morse softly.

'Mrs Kemp, that's what! Tried to cross the nighted ferry; might've made it but for a district-nurse calling unexpectedly.'

'She's not dead?'

'Not yet.'

'Likely to be?'

'Oh, I couldn't say.'

'*For God's sake, Max!*'

'Not even for His.'

Morse had never seen Mrs Marion Kemp, but from the marriage photograph that hung in the living room he realised that she must once have been quite a vivacious woman: dark, curly hair; slim, firm figure; and curiously impudent, puckish eyes. She had already been removed to the Intensive Care Unit at the JR2, but in the bedroom there seemed quite sufficient evidence that she had planned a deliberate departure. A brown-glass bottle of sleeping pills stood capless and empty on the bedside table, and beside it, lying on the top of a Georgette Heyer novel, was a short, soberly legible (though unsigned) note:

If found still alive, please let me die.
If found dead, please contact
Dr M. Davies at the Summertown
Health Centre — the only man who
ever tried to understand my
suffering.

CHAPTER FORTY

He
That kills himself to avoid misery, fears it,
And, at the best, shows but a bastard valour
(*Philip Massinger*, The Maid of Honour)

MORSE AND MAX stood for a few moments silently just outside the front door of the Kemp residence. Nothing, as both men knew, could be quite as sombre and sickening as a suicide (or, as here, an attempted suicide), for it spoke not only of unbearable suffering but also of a certain misguided fortitude. Morse had looked quickly round the flat but had found nothing much to engage his interest.

'Let's try to keep her alive, if we can, Max,' he said quietly.

'Out of my hands, now.'

'Fancy a glass of Brakspear? Only just along the road here.'

'No time, dear boy! Presumably you consider the Henley branch of the Brakspear family to be greater benefactors than that St Albans fellow?'

'Wha—?' For a few seconds even Morse was lost a little; but then he grinned acknowledgement: 'You're a cultured sod.'

'You know, Morse,' panted Max as he eased his

overweight frame into his car, 'I've always thought of myself more as a Renaissance man, actually.'

He was gone, and Morse looked around the area somewhat fecklessly. A maintenance man, with a garden fork and wheelbarrow, was tending the herbaceous border that stretched along the frontage of the flats and, in response to Morse's question, he said he was one of a small team that looked after the three blocks of flats that stood on the eastern side of Water Eaton Road. And yes, he'd been working there for several days. Had he seen anyone coming in, during the afternoon of the previous day? After three o'clock, say? But the man, looking to Morse far too young to have graduated with any glory from a landscape-gardening apprenticeship, shook his head dubiously.

'Difficult, innit? I mean, I was out the back most o' the time. There *were* some people comin' in, I remember, but they'd probably bin shoppin' and that, 'adn't they?'

'You saw this man?' Morse held up the photograph of Theodore Kemp which he had just removed from the living room. Clearly it had been taken several years earlier, but it showed, even then, the supercilious cast of a face which had looked into the camera with head held well back, and lips that seemed to smile with a curious arrogance above the Vandyke beard.

'Yea! I seen 'im before – but I dunno about yesterday. As I said, I was out the back most o' the time – doin' the bits by the river.'

The river . . .

Morse thanked the man, and walked along to the ramp at the side of the flats, and down to a concreted area where five garages directly in front of him shielded the immediate view. Then, turning to his right, he came to a stretch of well-trimmed lawn that sloped down to the river, the far bank of which was policed by a row of severely pollarded willow trees. Here the water was green-scummed and semi-stagnant. But a bridge ('Residents Only') led him across to the main channel of the Cherwell, where the water was still flowing fairly swiftly after the week's earlier rains, and where pieces of debris were intermittently knocking into the sides of the banks, and then turning and twisting, first one way then the other, like dodgem cars at the fun-fair. For several minutes Morse looked down at the turbid, turgid river; and his thoughts were as restless as the waters below him. Then, of a sudden, he nodded to himself firmly – and the look around his mouth was almost as arrogant as that of the late Theodore Kemp, who at some time, at some point, had recently been manoeuvred into these selfsame murky, swollen waters.

Lewis was waiting for him as he reached the road again.

'What now, sir?'

'What we need is a little liquid refreshment, and there's a little pub' – Morse got into the passenger seat – 'just along the road here.'

'Might as well walk, sir. It's only fifty yards.'

Morse said nothing, but sat where he was and picked up the *Railway Magazine* from the door-pocket and pretended to read it; then *did* read it – for a few seconds.

Lewis had backed the car a few feet down the ramp and was about to turn towards the Cherwell Arms when he heard his master's voice – a single hissed and incredulous blasphemy:

'Chrissst!'

'More clues, sir?'

'Look! Look at this!'

Lewis took the magazine and read through the brief article to which Morse was pointing:

GOLDEN OLDIES

Members of the GWR Preservation Society will learn with particular interest that w.e.f. 21st October the world-famous Torbay Express will be making a nostalgic return visit to a few stretches of its old track, and will first be housed for three weeks in Railway Shed 4 at Plymouth.

His eyes looked across to Morse's: 'And he said he'd seen the Torbay Express at Didcot, didn't he? It's in his statement, surely.'

Morse stared in front of him, his eyes a-glitter: 'He's a liar, Stratton is; he's a bloody liar!'

'Is – is that a 1990 magazine?' asked Lewis diffidently.

Morse turned to the colourful cover, then placed the magazine back casually into the door-pocket.

'Well, sir?'

'September 1988,' said Morse, very quietly indeed.

'What's it all mean?' asked Lewis, as he sat at the table, with a pint of Brakspear for Morse and a half of the same for himself. He had never understood why Morse almost always expected *him* to buy the beer. It was as though Morse believed that he, Lewis, was on some perpetual expense-account.

'You mean about Mrs Kemp?'

'I mean about everything. I just don't know what's happening.'

'You think *I* do?'

'I thought you might have an idea.'

'Perhaps I have.' He drained his pint with extraordinary rapidity. 'Is it your round or mine?'

Lewis walked over to the bar with the single glass – almost happily.

Whilst he was gone, Morse turned to the back of *The Times* and had filled in the whole of the bottom right-hand quarter of the crossword when Lewis returned two minutes later.

'Do you always do crosswords that way round, sir?'

'Uh? Oh, yes! I always try solving problems by starting at the end – never the beginning.'

'I shall have to try that sometimes.'

'I didn't know you did crosswords, Lewis?'

'Yes! Me and the missus, we usually try to do the *Daily Mirror* Quick Crossword of an evening.'

'Oh!' said Morse, though without much wonderment in his voice. 'Well, let me tell you something. If I'm doing a crossword, and I think I'm getting stuck—'

'Not that you *do*, sir.'

'No. Not that I do – not very often. But if by some freak mischance I *do* get a bit stuck, you know what I do?'

'Tell me!'

'I *stop* thinking about the problem. Then, when I come back to it? No problem at all!'

'Have *we* got a problem, sir?'

'Oh yes! That's why we need the break – the drinking break.' Morse took an almighty swig from his replenished pint, leaving only an inch of beer in the glass. 'Our problem is to find the connection between the theft of the jewel and the murder of Kemp. Once we find that . . . So the best thing to do is to think of something completely different. Tell me about something, Lewis – something that's got nothing to do with Mrs Kemp.'

'I was just thinking about those betting-slips, sir. They've got the time on them – the time the bet was placed.'

'I said something *different*, Lewis! Anything. Tell me anything! Tell me the name of your first girlfriend! *Anything!*'

'I can't, sir. Not for the minute. I just think I let Mrs Kemp down . . . in a way.'

'What the hell are you talking about? It's *me* who let her down! How many times did you tell me I ought to see her?'

'Why do you think she tried . . .?'

'How the hell do I know!'

'Just asked, that's all.'

'All right. What do *you* think?'

'I suppose she just felt life wasn't worth living without him – without her husband.'

'You didn't feel that, though, when you met her, did you? From what you told me, you seemed to feel the opposite: life might have been worth living if he *wasn't* there.'

Yes, Lewis knew that Morse was right. He'd felt the anger and the bitterness of the woman – far more than any sense of anguish or loss. He knew, too, that his lack of sleep was beginning to catch up with him.

'You talk about giving your mind a rest, sir, but I shall have to give my body a bit of a rest soon. I'm knackered – absolutely knackered!'

'Go home, then! What's stopping you? I can always get Dixon—'

'I don't want to go home, sir. We've got the decorators in and I keep getting nagged about getting new carpets and new curtains and—'

Morse jumped up from the table, his face radiant: 'You've done it, Lewis! You've done it again!'

Lewis too rose from his seat, a tired, bewildered expression across his honest features.

What had he just said?

CHAPTER FORTY-ONE

Light thickens and the crow makes wing to the rooky wood
(*Shakespeare*, Macbeth)

IT WAS A quarter-past six when Sheila Williams saw the police car draw up outside, and she answered the front door immediately.

'Come in, Inspector!' The colourless liquid in the glass she carried might just have been water, perhaps; but whatever it was she seemed unwontedly sober.

'No. I – we've got a lot to do. Look. I'm very sorry to have to tell you this – but Mrs Kemp tried to kill herself this afternoon.'

Sheila's right hand jumped to her mouth with a convulsive jerk: 'Oh, no!' she whispered.

'She took enough pills to kill a healthy elephant, Sheila, but fortunately a nurse found her – in time, we think. If only just.'

'Where—?'

'She's in the JR2. She's having the best care she could get anywhere.'

Sheila took a deep breath. 'Oh dear!' she managed to say in a broken voice as the tears began to trickle. Then, somewhat to Morse's embarrassment, she suddenly buried her head on his shoulder and clung tightly to him.

'Did she love him?' asked Morse gently.

'She *possessed* him!'

'But did she *love* him?'

Sheila Williams straightened herself and pulled away from him, searching her pockets for a handkerchief. Her voice was almost fierce as she answered: 'No! *I* was the only one who really loved him.'

'Do you know anyone else who loved him? Was there someone else? A *third* woman in his life?'

Sheila shook her head in deep anguish.

'You quite sure about it, Sheila? It's so very important that you're honest with me,' urged Morse.

'He said not. He swore it!'

'And you believed him?'

She nodded, and wiped her eyes. And Morse nodded, too, and looked very sad.

'All right. Thank you.' He turned to go, but she called him back, the tears springing once more.

'Inspector – please!'

Morse turned, and laid his right hand lightly on her shoulder. 'No need to tell me, really. I *know* there was another woman in his life.'

Her 'yes' was barely audible.

'And I think you knew who it was.'

She nodded again.

'It was only recently though, wasn't it, Sheila? Only recently that he'd started seeing Mrs Downes?'

Lewis, standing at the front gate, had managed to catch most of the exchanges; had watched Mrs Williams as she'd finally turned away from Morse in tearful distress. And now, as they got back into the car, both men sat in silence as they watched the light switched on in the front bedroom – and then the curtains being drawn across.

'Curtains!' said Morse, his voice sounding tired yet triumphant. 'As you said, Lewis – curtains.'

The Downes's house was in darkness, and the sound of the front-door bell seemed somehow to re-echo along empty passageways, around empty rooms. Morse looked at his watch: just after half-past six – and Downes would be meeting his wife at seven o'clock.

A wooden gate at the side of the house led to a neatly tended garden at the back, the lawn sloping down to the river, with a path of paving stones laid along the middle, ending on the edge of the waters at what looked like a small landing-stage, perhaps once used to moor a small boat or punt, but apparently (as Lewis shone his torch across it) not in recent use.

'You think . . .?' Lewis pointed down to the fast-flowing Cherwell.

'Launched from here? Yes, I do. Launched from here into eternity.'

'But *when*, sir? He wasn't back in Oxford—'

'All in good time, Lewis! For the moment, be a good Boy-Scout and shine your little torch over those back windows?'

As in the front, the windows here were fully curtained, all of them looking decidedly posh and new; and all of them with some approximation to those

French pleats whose acquaintance Lewis had so recently made – and, if truth were told, Morse too.

'You see, Lewis,' began Morse, as the two strolled back to the front of the property, 'Kemp had grown tired of Sheila Williams and was starting out on a new conquest – the delectable Lucy Downes. Unfortunately for Kemp, however, Cedric Downes discovered the guilty pair *in flagrante delicto*, which as you will remember, Lewis, is the Latin for having your pants down. He's got to have a woman, has Kemp. His motto's *amo amas amat* it again. And he's at it again when Downes hits him with whatever's to hand; kills him; wonders where he's going to dump the corpse; can't dress him – far too difficult dressing a corpse—'

''Specially for a woman, sir.'

'What?'

'Don't you think it might have been a jealous *woman*? Not a jealous man?'

'No, no, Lewis! Not Sheila Williams.'

'She left the group, though – she went to the pub—'

'She hadn't got the *time*! Whoever killed Kemp had time: time to cart him off to the river, and dump him there – *gently*, Lewis – without even a splash to startle the cygnets . . .'

'But it *couldn't* have been like that. The times are all wrong.'

'Speak on, Lewis! Like the murderer, we've got plenty of time.'

'We're waiting *here*, you mean?'

'Oh, yes! I'm very much looking forward to meeting Mr and Mrs Downes again.'

'And you think, in that suitcase of hers . . .?'

But as the two detectives stood beside the car, the radio crackled into life.

'Lewis here!'

'Bad news, Sarge. Mrs Kemp died at the JR2 – fifty minutes ago. We've only just heard.'

Morse stood where he was, listening, and staring up at the sky as if viewing the unsuspected behaviour of some distant galaxy. His shoulders were sagging, and his face looked sad, and very weary.

'You look all in, sir.'

'Me? Don't talk so daft!' Morse looked quickly at his watch.

'He's meeting her in seven minutes! Put your foot down!'

'I thought you said we were waiting here?'

'Get *on* with it, Lewis – and turn the bloody siren on!'

CHAPTER FORTY-TWO

No one came
On the bare platform

(*Edward Thomas*, Adlestrop)

THE POLICE CAR drove into the Bus and Taxi area in front of the railway station. Across on Platform 2, the train from Paddington was just pulling in; and passengers were already beginning to stream across the new pedestrian bridge as Morse and Lewis first ascended, then descended the steps, darting challenging looks around them as they dodged their way through the bustling contra-flow.

The train still stood at the platform; and a group of Post Office workers were lobbing a stack of bulging mail-bags into the guard's van. And there – yes, there right in front of them! – passing from one window to another, peering into each of the carriages, his face drawn and anxious, was Cedric Downes. Morse placed a restraining hand on Lewis's arm, and the two of them stood watching the man while two or three heavily luggaged travellers finally made their way along the platform. Soon Downes had reached the last carriage, in front of the diesel locomotive, staring quickly through the windows of the compartment as the few doors still remaining open were banged shut and a whistle blew, and with a slight chug and then with a mighty heave the long, north-bound train began slowly to move forward, gradually picking up a little speed, before moving out and away along the curving stretch of line that led to Banbury.

Downes looked down at his wristwatch, and at last turned away, walking back along the bare platform towards the footbridge – where he was confronted by the bulk of the broad-shouldered Lewis.

'Good evening, sir. We *have* met before.'

Downes seemed slightly surprised – but hardly more than that: 'It's about Theo, I suppose? Theo Kemp?'

'Er – yes.' Lewis hardly managed to climb up to any plateau of assertiveness.

'Well, I've nothing more to tell you, I'm afraid. Nothing I can add to the statement I've already—'

'Meeting your wife, Mr Downes?' interrupted Morse.

'Pardon? Just a minute, Inspector! I . . . just a minute, please.' Downes fitted a hearing-aid taken from his pocket into his right ear, the aid promptly emitting a series of shrill whistles as he fiddled rather fecklessly with the controls.

'I was asking whether you were meeting—' bawled Morse – to no avail, as it appeared.

'If you'll just bear with me a few minutes, gentlemen, I'll just nip along to the car, if I may. I always keep a spare aid in the glove compartment.' The beseeching grin around the slightly lopsided mouth gave his face an almost schoolboyish look.

Morse gestured vaguely: 'Of course. We'll walk along with you, sir.'

In front of the railway station, a second police car (summoned by a confident Morse as Lewis had driven him from North Oxford) was now waiting, and the Chief Inspector nodded a perfunctory greeting to the two detective-constables who sat side by side in the front seats as they watched, and awaited, developments; watched the three men walk over to the twenty-minute waiting-area set aside for those meeting passengers from British Rail journeys – an area where parking cost nothing at all; watched them as they passed through that area and walked into the main car-park, with the bold notice affording innocent trespassers the clearest warning:

> PARKING FOR BRITISH RAIL
> PASSENGERS ONLY.
> FOR OTHER USERS WITHOUT
> PARKING-TOKENS, £10 PER DAY

'Mind telling me, sir, why you didn't just wait in the twenty-minute car-park? Parking where you have done seems a rather unnecessary expense, doesn't it? Doesn't it . . .?'

'Pardon, Inspector? If you give me just a second . . . a second or two . . . just . . .'

Downes took a bunch of car-keys from his pocket, opened the door of a British-Racing-Green MG Metro, got into the driver's seat, and leaned over left to open the glove compartment.

Both Morse and Lewis stood, rather warily, beside the car as Downes began to fiddle (once more) with a hearing-aid – one which looked to them suspiciously like the model that had earlier given rise to such piercing oscillation.

'There we are then!' said Downes, as he got out of the car and faced them, his face beaming with an almost childlike pleasure. 'Back in the land of the living! I think you were trying to say something, Inspector?'

'No. I wasn't *trying* to say anything, Mr Downes. I *was* saying something. I was saying how odd it seemed to me that you didn't park your car in the twenty-minute car-park.'

'Ah! Well, I did in a way. I seem to have collected an awful lot of those parking-tokens over the last few months. You see, I often have to go to London and sometimes I don't get back until pretty late. And late at night the barrier here where you slip in your parking-token is often open, and you can just drive straight through.'

'But why *waste* one of your precious tokens?' persisted Morse.

'Ah! I see what you're getting at. I'm a very law-abiding citizen, Inspector. I came here a bit early this evening, and I didn't want to risk any of those clamps or fines or anything. There's an Antiques Fair this week just along Park End Street, and I'd got my eye on a little set of drawers, yew-wood veneer. Lucy's birthday's coming up, November the seventh . . .'

'And then you called in at the Royal Oxford, no doubt?'

'I did *not*! I no longer drink and drive. Never!'

'Some people do, sir,' said Morse. 'It's the most common cause of road accidents, you know.'

There was a silence between the three men who now stood slightly awkwardly alongside the MG Metro. Downes, as it appeared, had read the situation adequately, and was expecting to accompany the policemen – well, somewhere! – and he opened the driver's door of the Metro once more. But Morse, leaning slightly towards him, opened his right palm, like a North-African Berber begging for alms.

'We'd like you to come with us, sir. If you just hand over your car-keys to me, Sergeant Lewis here will see that your car is picked up later and returned to your home address.'

'Surely this isn't necessary, is it? I know where the police station is, for Christ's sake!' Suddenly, within the last few words, Downes had lost whatever composure he had hitherto sought to sustain.

'The keys, please!' insisted Morse quietly.

'Look! I just don't know what all this bloody nonsense is about, Will you please *tell* me.'

'Certainly! You can *hear* me all right now?'

Downes almost snarled his reluctant 'Yes'; and listened, mouth agape with incredulity, as Morse beckoned over to the two detective-constables from the second police car.

'Cedric Downes, I arrest you on suspicion of the

murder of Dr Theodore Kemp. It is my duty to advise you that anything you now say may be noted by my sergeant here and possibly used in evidence in any future criminal prosecution.'

But as one of the detective-constables clicked a pair of handcuffs round his wrists, Cedric Downes was apparently in no state at all to mouth as much as a monosyllable, let alone give utterance to any incriminating statement. For many seconds he just stood where he was, as still as a man who has gazed into the eyes of the Medusa.

CHAPTER FORTY-THREE

As usual he was offering explanations for what other people
had not even noticed as problems

(*Bryan Magee*, Aspects of Wagner)

AFTER DOWNES HAD been driven away, Morse and
Lewis walked back to their own car, where Morse gave
urgent instructions to the forensic lab to send a couple
of their whizz-kids over to the railway station – immediately! – and to Kidlington HQ to see that a breakdown
van would be available in about an hour's time to ferry
away a certain Metro.

'You're absolutely sure about Downes, aren't you,'
said Lewis. But it was a statement, not a question.

'Oh, yes!'

'What now, sir?'

'We'll wait for forensics. Then we'll go and see how
Downes is making out – do him good to kick his heels
in a cell for half an hour. He was lucky, you know,
Lewis. Bloody lucky, one way or another.'

'Hadn't you better start at the beginning, sir? We've
got a few minutes' wait, like as not.'

So Morse told him.

The key thing in the case was the phone call made
by Kemp. And, yes, it *was* made by Kemp, although
some doubt could quite properly have been harboured

on the matter: Ashenden knew the man, and knew his voice; and in spite of what was probably a poorish extension-line, confirmation that the call *was* from Kemp had come from the telephone-operator, someone else who knew him – knew him very well, in fact. No, the call was not made by anyone *pretending* to be Kemp. But Kemp had not made the call, as he'd claimed, from Paddington! He'd made it from *Oxford*. He was anxious about making absolutely sure that another person was present in The Randolph at the lunch session with the American tourists; and he learned quite unequivocally that this person *was* there, although he didn't actually speak to him. Furthermore, Kemp's absence that afternoon would mean that this other person – yes, Downes – would be all the more committed to *staying* with the tourists for the scheduled 'informal get-together'. This arrangement, cleverly yet quite simply managed, would give him a couple of hours to get on with what he desperately wanted to get on with: to climb into bed with Downes's beautiful and doubtlessly over-sexed wife, Lucy, and get his bottom on the top sheet before his time ran out. The pair of them had probably not been having an affair for long – only perhaps after Kemp's long infatuation with the semi-permanently sozzled Sheila had begun to wear off. But where can they meet? It has to be at Downes's place: Kemp hasn't got a room in college, and it can't be at Kemp's place because his wife is a house-bound invalid. So, that morning presented a wonderful opportunity – and just a little compensation perhaps for the huge disappointment Kemp must undoubtedly have experienced over the theft of the Wolvercote Tongue. The jewel was almost in his grasp; almost about to be displayed and photographed and written up in all the right journals: a jewel he himself had traced, and one he'd worked so hard to get donated to the Ashmolean. No wonder his interest in swapping pleasantries with ageing Americans had sunk to zero; no wonder the prospect of the lubricious Lucy Downes proved so irresistible. Now the deception practised by Kemp was a very clever one. If he was going to be late on parade – 3 p.m., he'd promised – every pressure would be on the other two group leaders, Sheila Williams and Cedric Downes, to keep the tourists adequately amused by each of them shouldering an extra responsibility. It would not, incidentally, have occurred to Kemp that a consequence of such last-minute rearrangements was that several members of the group took the opportunity this afforded to perform a strange assortment of extra-mural activities – from viewing steam locomotives to tracing lost offspring. Red herrings, all.

But then things started to go wrong. Downes is not very deaf at all yet; but sometimes, with certain kinds of background noise, and when people are asking questions, well, there can be difficulty. A deaf person, as Lucy Downes told us, is not so much worried about not knowing the answer to any question put to him; he's worried, embarrassingly so, *about not hearing the question*. And at lunchtime – there are witnesses – Downes's hearing-aid began to play up and he discovered he wasn't carrying his spare aid with him. He decided to go home and pick it up, and in fact he was *seen* going up St Giles' on his bicycle towards North Oxford. It's hardly difficult to guess the sequence of events immediately after he'd quietly inserted his key in the Yale lock. He may have had a sixth sense about the presence of some stranger in the house; more likely he saw some physical evidence – a coat, a hat – belonging to a person he knew. He picked up a walking-stick – or something – from the hall-stand, and leapt up the stairs to find his wife and Kemp *in medio coitu*, both of them completely naked. In a fury of hatred and jealousy he thrashed his stick about Kemp's head while Kemp himself tried to extricate himself from the twisted sheets, to get out of the bed, and to defend himself – but he didn't make it. He staggered back and fell, and got his head crashed – a *second* time, as we know – against the corner-post of the double bed or the sharp edge of the fireplace. He had a thin skull – a medical fact – and there was a sudden, dreadful silence; and a great deal of blood. The despairing, faithless, gaping, horrified wife looked down at her lover, and knew that he was dead. Now, sometimes it is extremely difficult to kill a man. Sometimes it is quite extraordinarily easy, as it was then ...

And Downes himself? The emotions of hatred and jealousy are immediately superseded by the more primitive instinct of survival, and he begins to realise that all may yet be well if he can keep his head. For he is suddenly, miraculously, aware that he has got a wonderful – no! – a *perfect* alibi; an alibi which has been given to him *by the very person he has just killed*. O lovely irony! Kemp had told Ashenden, and Ashenden had then told everyone else, that he (Kemp) would not be back from London until 3 p.m. And that meant that Downes could not *possibly* have killed Kemp before that time, and Downes was going to make absolutely certain – as he did – that he was never out of sight or out of touch with his group – except for the odd, brief visit to the loo – at any time that afternoon or early evening.

It is hardly difficult to guess what happened at the Downes's residence immediately after the death of Kemp. Downes himself could not stay for more than a few minutes. He instructed his panic-stricken, guilt-ridden wife to pack up Kemp's clothes in a suitcase, and to clean up the bloody mess that must have been left on the carpet, and probably on the sheets. The body was left – *had* to be left – in the bedroom. Downes himself would have to deal with that. But later. For the present he seeks to compose himself as he cycles back down to The Randolph.

That evening, at about seven o'clock, he returns to his house in Lonsdale Road, the very far end of Lonsdale Road, where the lawn slopes down directly to the bank of the River Cherwell. He manoeuvres Kemp's body down the stairs and carries it across the lawn, probably in a wheelbarrow. It was a dark night, and doubtless he covered the corpse with a ground-sheet or something. Then slowly, carefully, without even the suspicion of a splash perhaps, he slid Kemp into the swift-flowing waters of a river swollen by the recent heavy rains. Two hours later, the body has drifted far downstream, finally getting wedged at the top of the weir in Parson's Pleasure – the place where the careless Howard Brown had earlier left his yellow programme – and his continental seven . . .

It was at this point in Morse's recapitulation that the forensic brigade arrived; and soon afterwards a royal-blue BMW carrying no lesser a personage than Chief Superintendent Bell from the City Police.

'You know, Morse,' began Bell, 'you seem to breed about as many problems as a pregnant rabbit.'

'You could look at it the other way, I suppose,' replied the radiant Morse. 'Without me and Lewis half of these fellows in forensics would be out on the dole, sir.'

About an hour before these last events were taking place, the American tourists had registered into the two-star Swan Hotel in Stratford-upon-(definitely 'upon') Avon. As throughout the tour, Ashenden had observed the opportunist self-seekers at the front of the queue (as ever) for the room-keys; and in the rear (as ever) the quieter, seemingly contented souls who perhaps knew that being first or last to their rooms would make little difference to the quality of their living. And at the very back, the small, patient figure of Phil Aldrich, seeking (of this, Ashenden could have little doubt) to avoid the embarrassment of refusing to sign Janet Roscoe's latest petition.

The evening meal had been rescheduled for 8.30 p.m.; and with time to spare, after throwing his own large hold-all on to the counterpane of his single bed,

Ashenden joined a few of the other tourists in the Residents' Lounge, where he took some sheets of the hotel's own note-paper, and began to write a letter. When he had finished, he found a red, first-class stamp in his wallet, fixed it to the envelope, and walked out into Bridge Street to find a pillar-box. The letter was addressed to Chief Inspector Morse, St Aldate's Central Police Station, Oxford, and in the top left-hand corner was written the one word: URGENT.

CHAPTER FORTY-FOUR

'When my noble and learned brother gives his Judgment, they're to be let go free,' said Krook, winking at us again. 'And then,' he added, whispering and grinning, 'if that ever was to happen – which it won't – the birds that have never been caged would kill 'em'

(*Dickens*, Bleak House)

UNWONTEDLY, LEWIS WAS philosophising as he and Morse sat in the canteen at St Aldate's: 'Amazing, really: you get all these statements and alibis and secret little meetings, and then really, in the end, it's just – well, it's just the same old story, isn't it? Chap goes home and finds the missus in bed with one of the neighbours.'

'Remember, though, this is only *half* the case. And we've got to get some evidence. No, that's wrong! We've *got* some evidence – or we shall have, very soon.'

'Perhaps we shouldn't wait too much longer, sir?'

'It'll be here. Patience, Lewis! Eat your cheese sandwich!'

'I couldn't help feeling just a bit sorry for him, though.'

'Sorry? Why do you say that?'

'Well, you know, it might have been a bit sort of – *accidental*, don't you reckon?'

'I do *not*,' replied Morse, with the fullest conviction.

*

Downes sat at the table in Interview Room Two on the ground floor, spell-bound and motionless, as if a witch had drawn a circle round him thrice. Seated opposite, Sergeant Dixon was finding the silence and the stillness increasingly embarrassing.

'Like a cuppa tea?'

'No! Er, yes! Yes please.'

'Milk and sugar?'

But Downes appeared not to hear the supplementary questions, and Dixon nodded to the constable who stood at the door, the latter now making for the canteen on a less than wholly specific mission.

At the Swan Hotel in Stratford, Mrs Roscoe had just completed her evening meal, a concoction of beans so splendidly bleak as to delight the most dedicated Vegan. She immediately wrote a brief congratulatory note, insisting that the waiter convey it forthwith to the chef de cuisine himself.

At this same time (it was now 9 p.m.) Eddie Stratton was sitting on the only chair in a small third-floor room of a hotel just north of Russell Square. The facilities here were minimal – a cracked wash-basin, one minuscule bar of soap, and one off-white towel. Yet the bed looked clean-sheeted and felt comfortable; and there was a lavatory just along the corridor (the lady had said), a bathroom one floor down, and a Residents' TV Lounge beside Reception. On the bedside table was a

Gideon Bible, and beside it an entry form which, if and when completed and dispatched, would entitle the fortunate applicant to inclusion in a free draw for a ticket to one of the following summer's golfing championships. Stratton availed himself of neither opportunity.

Earlier he had visited the American Consulate, where an attractive and sympathetic fellow country-woman from North Carolina had advised him on all the sad yet necessary procedures consequent upon the death of an American national in Britain, and acquainted him with the costs of the transatlantic conveyancing of corpses. And now, as he sat staring fixedly at the floral configuration on the faded green carpet, he felt a little sad as he thought of Laura, his wife for only the last couple of years. They had been as contented together as could have been expected, he supposed, from a union which had been largely one of convenience and accommodation; and he would always remember, with a sort of perverse affection, her rather loud voice, her over-daubed war-paint – and, of course, the painful state of those poor feet of hers ... He nodded slowly to himself, then looked up and across at the lace-curtained window, like a bird perhaps suddenly spotting the open door of its cage. And an observer in that small room would have noticed the suspicion of a smile around his loose and slightly purplish lips.

It was just after 9 p.m. that a PC arrived from the railway station carrying a small brown envelope, which

Morse accepted with delight, smiling radiantly at Lewis but saying nothing as he slit open the top and looked briefly inside. Then, with smile unfading, he handed the envelope to Lewis.

'Wish me luck! I'll let you know when to come in.'

CHAPTER FORTY-FIVE

Perchance my too much questioning offends
(*Dante*, Purgatorio)

AT LEAST MORSE spared Cedric Downes the charade of a cordial re-greeting; he even forbore to express the hope that conditions were satisfactory and that the prisoner was being well treated. In point of fact, the prisoner looked lost and defeated. Earlier he had been officially advised that it was his legal right to have his solicitor present; but surprisingly Downes had taken no advantage of the offer. A cup of tea (sweetened) stood untouched at his right elbow. He raised his eyes, morosely, as Morse took Dixon's seat opposite him and pulled another chair alongside for a very blonde young WPC, who amongst other accomplishments was the only person in St Aldate's HQ with a Pitman shorthand qualification for 130 w.p.m. Not that she was destined to get any practice at such a mega-speed, since Downes, at least for the first half of the interview, was to enunciate his words with the slow deliberation of a stupefied zombie. Morse waited patiently. That was always the best way, in the long run. And when Downes finally spoke, it was to ask about his wife.

'Did someone meet the train, Inspector? The next train?'

'Please don't worry about her, sir. She'll be looked after.'

Downes shook his head in stupefaction. 'This is madness – absolute madness! There's been some dreadful misunderstanding somewhere – don't you understand that? I – I can't think straight. I don't know what to say! I just pray I'm going to wake up any second.'

'Tell me about Dr Kemp,' said Morse.

'Tell you what? Everyone knows about Kemp. He was the biggest philanderer in Oxford.'

'You say "everyone"?'

'Yes! Including his wife. *She* knows.'

'*Knew.* She died this afternoon.'

'Oh God!' Downes closed his eyes and squeezed them tightly shut. Then he opened them, and looked across at Morse. 'I think I know what you're going to ask me now, Inspector.'

Morse tilted his head to the left: 'You do?'

'You're going to ask me whether Lucy – whether my wife was . . . is aware of it, too.'

Morse tilted his head to the right, but made no reply.

'Well, the answer's "yes". Once or twice he'd – well he'd tried to make some sort of advances to her. At receptions, parties – that sort of thing.'

'Your wife *told* you about this?'

'She was a bit flattered, I suppose.'

'Was she?'

'And amused. More amused than flattered, I think.'

'And you? You, Mr Downes? Were *you* amused?'

'I could have killed the bloody swine!' So suddenly, so dramatically, the manner had changed – the voice now a harsh snarl, the eyes ablaze with hatred.

'It's not all that easy actually to kill a man,' said Morse.

'It isn't?' Downes's eyes appeared perplexed.

'What exactly *did* you hit him with? When you went home for – for whatever it was?'

'I – pardon? – you don't—'

'Just in your own words, sir, if you will. Simply what happened, that's all. The WPC here will take down what you say and then she'll read it back to you, and you'll be able to change anything you may have got wrong. No problem!'

'Wha—?' Downes shook his head in anguished desperation. 'When am I going to wake up?'

'Let's just start from when you put your key – Yale lock, isn't it? – into the front door, and then when you went in . . .'

'Yes, and I got my other hearing-aid, and some notes—'

'Whereabouts do you keep the spare hearing-aid?'

'In the bedroom.'

Morse nodded encouragement. 'Twin beds, I suppose—'

'Double bed, actually – and I keep my spare aid in a drawer of the tallboy' – he looked directly into Morse's eyes again – 'next to the handkerchiefs and the cufflinks and the arm-bands. You do want me to be *precise* about what I tell you?'

'And your wife was in the double bed there – yes, we do want you to be precise, sir.'

'Wha—? What makes you think my wife was in bed? This was at *lunchtime.*'

'Where was she?'

'In the living room? I don't know! I forget. Why don't you ask *her*?' He suddenly sprang to his feet. 'Look! I've got to talk to her! Now! You've no right to hold me here. I know you've got your job to do – I understand that. Some people get held on suspicion – *I know!* But I must speak to Lucy!'

His voice had become almost a screech of anger and frustration. And Morse was glad of it. So often the loss of self-control was the welcome prelude to a confession – a confession that was usually, in turn, a vast relief to the pent-up pressures of a tortured mind. And already Downes seemed calmer again as he resumed his seat, and Morse resumed his questioning.

'You understood, didn't you, the real point of Dr Kemp's phone call? No one else did – but *you* knew.' In contrast to the crescendo of fury from Downes, Morse's voice was very quiet indeed, and beside him WPC Wright was not absolutely sure that she'd transcribed his words with total accuracy.

As for Downes, he was leaning across the table. 'Could you please speak up a bit, Inspector? I didn't hear what you said, I'm afraid.'

It is likely, however, that he heard the loud knock on the door which heralded the entry of a rather harassed-looking Lewis.

'Sorry to interrupt, sir, but—'

'Not *now*, man! Can't you see—?'

'It's very urgent, sir,' said Lewis, in a voice of hushed authority.

WPC Wright had heard what Sergeant Lewis said all right; and she glanced across at Downes. Had *he* heard? Something in his face suggested to her that he might well have done, perhaps.

But it was difficult to tell.

CHAPTER FORTY-SIX

I do love to note and to observe

(*Jonson*, Volpone)

'I JUST DON'T believe it!' declared Morse.

It had been Lewis himself who a few minutes earlier had taken the call from the Met.

'Trying to cross over the road by King's Cross Station – about five-thirty – hit by a car. From Oxford she is. A Mrs Downes: Mrs Lucy Claire Downes according to her plastics. Lonsdale Road.'

'She – is she dead?' Lewis had asked.

'ICU at St Pancras Hospital. That's all we know.'

'Was she carrying a case?'

'No more details – not yet, Sarge. Seems she just stepped off the pavement to get in front of a row of people and . . .'

Morse sat down and rested his forehead on his right hand. 'Bloody 'ell!'

'Circle Line from King's Cross to Paddington, sir – about twenty minutes, say? She must have been going for the six o'clock train, and she was probably in a dickens of a rush when . . .' Lewis had taken the news badly.

'Yes? Dickens of a rush when she *what*?'

'When she stepped off the pavement—'

255

'An intelligent woman deliberately stepping out into the London traffic – in the rush hour? Do you really believe that? Or do you think she might have been pushed? Do you hear me, Lewis? *Pushed.*'

'How can you *say* that?'

For a few moments Morse sat where he was. Then he rose to his feet, slowly – his eyes glowing savagely. 'He did it, Lewis. *He* did it!'

'But he was in *Oxford*!'

'No he wasn't! He wasn't waiting on the Oxford platform at all. *He'd just got off the train.* And then he saw *us.* So he turned round the second he did, and made it look as though he was waiting for the woman he'd just tried to kill – when they were walking along together ... He loved her, you see – probably never loved anyone in the world except his Lucy. And when he saw her copulating with Kemp ... He just couldn't get it out of his mind, not for one second. He thought he was never going to be able to get it out of his mind.' Morse shook his head. 'And I'm an idiot, Lewis. That key! The key they found under the floor-mat in the car, or wherever. I'd guessed that Downes wanted to go back to his car to hide *something*, so I played along with all that hearing-aid rubbish. And when they brought the key, I knew exactly what it was – a left-luggage locker-key. But tell me this, Lewis! How the hell did *he* get hold of that key if he hadn't met his wife?'

'That's what it is, sir? Left-luggage key? You're sure of it?'

Morse nodded. 'And I'll tell you which station, unless you want to tell *me*.'

'King's Cross.'

'Could be Paddington, I suppose.'

'The *bastard*!' muttered Lewis, with an unwonted show of emotion.

Morse smiled: 'You like her, don't you?'

'Lovely woman!'

'That's what Kemp thought.'

'Perhaps . . .?' started Lewis.

'Oh, no! We shall waste no sympathy on Kemp. Look! I want you to get someone to drive you up to the hospital to see her. All right? You can get a bit of kip in the car. Then go to King's Cross and see if there's anything in locker sixty-seven. If there is, bring it back. And if you can get anything in the way of a statement – fine. If not, well, just try to see what she's got to say.'

'If she's . . . shall I say we've got *him* here?'

'Perhaps not . . . I dunno, though. Play it by ear!'

'OK, sir.' Lewis stood up and walked over to the door, where he halted. 'Have you ever thought it might have been *Mrs* Downes who killed Dr Kemp? What if when her husband came home he found Kemp already dead, and then he did all this stuff, you know, to cover up for *her*?'

'Oh, yes, Lewis. I've thought of every possibility in this case. Including Lucy Downes.'

'You don't think—?'

'I think you will be *completely* safe in London. I don't think you'll be in the slightest danger of being knifed as you practise your bedside-manner sitting by a semi-conscious young woman in an intensive care unit.'

Lewis grinned weakly, and felt in his pocket to make

sure that the brown envelope containing a small red key, number 67, was still there.

Janet Roscoe had finished re-reading *A Midsummer Night's Dream*, and felt just a little less certain now about her long-held view (she had earlier been an actress) that Mr Shakespeare was sometimes way below his best when it came to the writing of comedy. And she had just turned on the TV, hoping for a late news-programme, when she heard the light knock on her bedroom door. It was Shirley Brown. She had been stung by *something*, and could Janet help? But of course she *knew* Janet could help! Invited in, Shirley watched the little woman delving into her capacious handbag (a gentle little joke with the rest of the group) from whose depths had already emerged, in addition to the usual accessories, a scout-knife, an apostle spoon, and a miniature iron. And something else now: two tubes of ointment. A little bit of each (Janet maintained) could do no possible harm, unsure as Shirley was whether the offending insect had been wasp, bee, gnat, flea, or mosquito.

For five minutes after the medication, the two women sat on the bed and talked. Had Janet noticed how quiet Mr Ashenden had seemed all day? Not his usual self at all, one way or another. Janet had noticed that, yes: and he *was* the courier, wasn't he? Got *paid* for it. And Janet added something more. She thought she *knew* what might have been on his mind, because he'd been writing a letter in the Lounge. And when he'd put the envelope down to put a stamp on it – '*Face upwards*, Shurley!' – why, she couldn't *help* noticing who it was addressed to, now could she?

Suddenly, and perhaps for the first time, Shirley Brown felt a twinge of affection for the lonely little woman who seemed far more aware of what was going on than any of them.

'You seem to notice everything, Janet,' she said, in a not unkindly way.

'I notice most things,' replied Mrs Roscoe, with a quiet little smile of self-congratulation.

CHAPTER FORTY-SEVEN

Some circumstantial evidence is very strong – as when you
find a trout in the milk

(*Henry Thoreau*, unpublished manuscript)

'ARE YOU GOING to save us an awful lot of time and
trouble, sir, or are you determined to burden the
taxpayer further?'

Downes licked his dry lips. 'I don't know what this is
all about – except that I'm going mad.'

'Oh, no! You're very sane—' began Morse. But
Downes, at least for the moment, had taken the
initiative.

'And if you're worried about the taxpayer, shouldn't
you perhaps be attending to the urgent little matter
your sergeant told you about?'

'You *heard* that?' asked Morse sharply.

'He speaks more clearly than you do.'

'Even when he whispers?' For a few seconds a
bemused-looking Morse appeared slightly more concerned with the criticism of his diction than with the
prosecution of his case, and it was Downes who
continued:

'You were commenting on the degree of my sanity,
Inspector.'

WPC Wright glanced at Morse, seated to her left.

She had never worked with him before, but the man's name was something of a legend in the Oxfordshire Constabulary, and she was experiencing a sense of some disappointment. Morse was talking again now, though – getting into his swing again, it seemed, and she took down his words in her swift and deftly stroked outlines.

'Yes. *Very* sane. Sane enough to cover up a murder! Sane enough to arrange for your wife to cart off the incriminating evidence to King's Cross Station and stick it in a left-luggage locker—'

'I can't be *hearing* you right—'

'No! Not again, sir – please! It's getting threadbare, you know, that particular excuse. You used it when Kemp rang up – *rang up from your own house.* You used it again when you'd just got off the train from Padding-ton tonight, when you pretended you were waiting for Mrs Downes—'

In her shorthand book, WPC Wright had ample time to write the word that Downes now shrieked; write it in in long-hand, and in capitals. In fact she would have had plenty of time to shade in the circles in the last two letters.

She wrote 'STOP!'

And Morse stopped, as instructed – for about thirty seconds. No rush. Then he repeated his accusation.

'You got your wife to take Kemp's clothes to London—'

'Got my wife – got *Lucy*? What? What do you *mean*?'

'It's all right, sir.' Morse's tone now (thought WPC Wright) was rather more impressive. Quiet, cultured, confident – gentle almost, and understanding. 'We've got the key your wife gave you after she'd deposited the clothes and the blood-stained sheets—'

'I've been here all day – here in Oxford!' The voice had veered from exasperation to incredulity. 'I've got a marvellous alibi – did you know that? I had a tutorial this afternoon from—'

But Morse had taken over completely, and he held up his right hand with a confident, magisterial authority. 'I promise you, sir, that we shall interview everyone you saw this afternoon. You have nothing – nothing! – to fear if you're telling me the truth. But listen to me, Mr Downes! Just for a little while *listen* to me! When my sergeant came in to see me – when you yourself heard him – he'd just learned that on my instructions the locker had been opened in London. And that inside the locker was a case, the case your wife took with her to London today; a case which she told me – told me and Sergeant Lewis – contained some curtains. Curtains! We both *saw* her take it, in a taxi. And shall I tell you again what it *really* contained?'

Downes thumped the table with both fists with such ferocity that WPC Wright transferred her shorthand-book to her black-stockinged knee, and failed completely to register the next three words that Downes had thundered.

'No! No! No!'

But Morse appeared wholly unperturbed. 'Please tell me, Mr Downes, how the key came to be in your possession? Under the mat in the driver's seat, was it? Or in the glove compartment? Can you explain that?

Are you going to tell me that it was someone who came back on the train from London who gave you the key?'

'Wha—?'

'Couldn't have been your wife, could it?'

'What's Lucy got to do with—?'

'The key!' roared Morse. 'What about the *key*?'

'Key? You mean . . .?' Downes's cheeks were very white, and slowly he started to get up from his chair.

'Sit down!' thundered Morse with immense authority; and simply, silently, Downes did as he was bidden.

'Do you remember the number of the key, sir?'

'Of course.'

'Please tell me,' said Morse quietly.

'Number sixty-seven.'

'That's correct. That's correct, Mr Downes.' Morse briefly placed his right hand on WPC Wright's arm, and gave her a scarce-perceptible nod of encouragement. It would be vital, as he knew, for the next few exchanges to be transcribed with unimpeachable certitude. But as Downes spoke, with a helpless little shrug of his shoulders, the newly sharpened pencil of WPC Wright remained poised above the page.

'That's the key to my locker at the North Oxford Golf Club, Inspector.'

Suddenly, Interview Room Two was still and silent as the grave.

CHAPTER FORTY-EIGHT

Darkness is more productive of sublime ideas
than light
(*Edmund Burke,* On the Sublime and Beautiful)

THE TRAFFIC ALONG Western Avenue had been quiet,
and it was only an hour and a quarter after leaving
Oxford that Lewis was speaking to the Night Sister on
the third floor of the hospital, a neat, competent-
looking brunette who appeared rather more concerned
about the unprecedented police interest in matters
than in the medical condition of her most recent road-
casualty, now lying behind a curtained bed in Harley
Ward. A casualty not all *that* badly injured, anyway:
broken left humerus, broken left clavicle, some nasty
bruising and laceration round the left shoulder – but
no broken legs or ribs, and fairly certainly no head
injuries, either. Yes, said Sister, Mrs Downes had been
remarkably lucky, really; and, yes, Sergeant Lewis could
see her for a short while. He would find her under
sedation – a bit dopey and drowsy, and still in a state of
some disorientation and shock. Quite lucid, though.
'*And,*' added Sister, 'you'd better have something ready
to tell her if she asks you when her husband's coming.
We've put her off as best we can.'

Lewis stood by the bed and looked down at her. Her

eyes were open, and guardedly she smiled an instant recognition. She spoke softly, lisping slightly, and Lewis immediately noticed (what he had not been told) that two teeth in the upper left of her jaw had been broken off.

'We met this morning, didn't we?'

'Yes, Mrs Downes.'

'Cedric knows I'm all right, doesn't he?'

'Everything's in hand. Don't worry about anything like that.'

'He'll be here soon, though?'

'I've told you,' said Lewis gently, 'we're looking after everything. No need for you to worry at all.'

'But I want to *see* him!'

'It's just that the hospital don't want you to have any visitors – not just for the time being. The doctors, you know, they've got to patch you up a bit.'

'I want to thee Thedric,' she moaned quietly, her lips quivering and her eyes now brimming with tears as the good Lewis laid a hand on the pristine-white plaster encasing her upper arm.

'Soon. In good time. As I say—'

'Why can *you* see me if he can't?'

'It's just routine – you know – accidents. We have to make reports on—'

'But I've seen the police already.'

'And you told them—?'

'I told them it was my fault – it wasn't the driver's fault.' Her eyes looked pleadingly up at Lewis.

'Would you just repeat what you said. Please, Mrs Downes.'

265

'There was nothing *to* say. It was my fault, what else do you want me to say?'

'Just *how*, you know . . .'

'I was walking along there. I was in a hurry to catch the tube – it was the rush hour – I didn't want to miss the train – Cedric . . . you see, Cedric was waiting—'

'At Oxford, you mean? He was waiting at Oxford?'

'Of course. I was just trying to get past some people in front of me and I stepped off the pavement and the driver – he didn't have a chance. It was *my* fault, don't you believe me? He braked and . . . It was the *case* really. If it hadn't been for the case, I think perhaps . . .'

'The car hit the case, you mean? Hit the case first?'

Lucy nodded. 'It sort of, well – cushioned things, and I hit a litter bin on the kerb and . . .' She lifted her right hand and pointed vaguely across to the left-hand side of her body.

'So you still had the case with you, then? When the car hit you?'

For the first time the hitherto lucid Lucy looked a little bemused, as if she was unable to follow Lewis's last question. 'I don't quite follow . . . I'm sorry.'

'I just wanted to know if you were carrying the case, that's all.'

'Of course I was.'

'Do you – do you know where it is now, Mrs Downes?'

'Isn't it still under the bed, Sergeant?'

*

Morse took the call just after 11 p.m.

'You'll never guess what's happened, sir!'

'Don't put your bank balance on it, Lewis!'

'She's going to be all right, they think, sir. The Met got it wrong about the ICU.'

Morse said nothing.

'You are – well, pleased about *that*, aren't you?'

'I take no delight in death, Lewis, and if one thing worries me above all else it is accidents – the random concourse of atoms in the void, as Epicurus used to say.'

'You feeling tired, sir?'

'Yes.'

'You *knew* it was an accident all the time?'

'No. Not all the time.'

'You're losing me – as usual.'

'What is this news of yours, Lewis, that I shall never guess?'

'The case, sir! The case we both saw Mrs Downes take up to London.'

'We both saw her put it in the *taxi*, if we are to be accurate.'

'But she did bring it to London! And you won't guess what was in it.'

'Curtains, Lewis? Any good? Curtains with French pleats? By the way, remind me one day to explain this business of French pleats to you. Mrs Lewis would be glad if you took a bit more interest in household furnishings and interior decoration.'

'What do you want me to do about this left-luggage key, sir?'

'What are you talking about? What makes you think that's a left-luggage key?'

After Lewis had rung off, Morse sat at his desk and smoked three Dunhill International cigarettes one after the other. He'd been shaken, certainly, when Cedric Downes had invited him to go along to the North Oxford Golf Club and knock up the caretaker if necessary. And Lewis's phone call had surely hammered the last coffin-nail into the Cedric–Lucy theory. Yet Morse's mind was never more fertile than when faced with some apparently insuperable obstacle, and even now he found it difficult to abandon his earlier, sweet hypothesis about the murder of Theodore Kemp. He gazed out through the curtainless window on to the well-lit, virtually deserted parking-area: only his own red Jaguar and two white police cars. He could – should! – get off now and go to bed. He would be home in ten minutes. Less, perhaps, at this hour ... Yes, it was extremely useful to have a car, whatever people said about traffic and pollution and expense ... yes ...

Morse was conscious that his mind was drifting off into an interesting avenue of thought, but also that he was drifting off to sleep, as well. It was the cars that had started some new idea ... For the minute, though, it was gone. Yet there were other new ideas that jostled together in his brain for some more prominent recognition. First, the conviction that there was – must be! – a link, perhaps a blindingly obvious link, between the theft of the Wolvercote Jewel and the murder of

Theodore Kemp. Second, the growing belief that *two* people must have been involved in things, quite certainly in the murder. Third, the worrying suspicion that amongst the evidence already accumulated, the statements taken, the people interviewed, the personal relationships observed, the *obiter dicta*, the geography of North Oxford – that amongst all these things *somewhere* there was a fact that he had seen or heard but never fully recognised or understood. Fourth, the strange reluctance he felt about abandoning Downes as Suspect Number One. And as Morse opened his passenger door, he stood for a while looking up at the Pole Star, and asking himself the question he had been asking for the past two hours: was there *any* way in which Downes could still have been the murderer after all?

Many of Morse's ideas were either so strange or so wildly improbable that most of them were always doomed to early disappointment. Yet, as it happened, he was registering well above par that evening, for three of the four ideas he had formulated were finally to prove wholly correct.

Lewis had fallen fast asleep on the back seat of the police car and remained so for the whole of the journey back to Oxford. In his younger days, he had been a middle-weight Army boxing champion, and now he dreamed that he was in the ring again, with a right-cross from a swarthy, swift-footed opponent smashing into the left-hand side of his jaw. He had tried to feel inside his mouth to see if any teeth were broken or missing, but the great bulk of his boxing-glove precluded any such investigation.

When the car finally pulled up in St Aldate's, the young driver opened the rear door and shook Sergeant Lewis awake, failing to notice that the first action of his passenger was to run the forefinger of his left hand slowly along his upper teeth.

Part Three

Part Three

CHAPTER FORTY-NINE

Where water, warm or cool, is
Good for gout – at Aquae Sulis
(Graffito in the Pump Room, Bath, *c.*1760)

'BAIRTH? THIS IS *Bairth?*'

Seated on the nearside front seat of the luxury coach, John Ashenden glanced across at the diminutive septuagenarian from California. 'Yes, Mrs Roscoe, this is Bath.'

With less than conspicuous enthusiasm, he leaned forward for his microphone, turned it on, and began. Not quite so confidently as in Stratford; or in Oxford, of course, where he had memorised whole sentences from the Jan Morris guide.

'Bath, ladies and gentlemen, is the site of a Roman spa, *Aquae Sulis*, probably built in the first and second centuries AD. A good deal of the extensive baths has been excavated and the city presents the tourist of today with perhaps the most splendidly restored of all Roman remains in Europe.'

On either side of the central aisle, heads nodded at the buildings and streets around them as a now livelier Ashenden continued, himself (like the site, it appeared) splendidly restored from whatever malaise had affected him over the previous two days, a malaise which had been noted and commented upon by several others of the group besides Mrs Shirley Brown – the latter sitting comfortably now in her usual seat, the effects of the sting having cleared up fairly quickly under the twin application of Mrs Roscoe's unguents.

'Looks a swell place, Shirl,' ventured Howard Brown.

'Yeah. Just wish Laura was with us – and Eddie. It all seems so sad.'

'Too right! Bus seems sorta empty somehow.'

As scheduled, the tourists had lunched at Cirencester, after leaving Stratford earlier that Sunday morning. The weather was still holding, if only just: another golden day in late autumn. And perhaps in the minds of many, the memories of their tragic stay in Oxford were slowly softening at the edges.

One of the slightly younger widows, Mrs Nancy Wiseman, a librarian from Oklahoma City, was seated at the back of the coach beside Phil Aldrich. She had observed with a quiet pleasure how the strident Roscoe woman had markedly cooled towards her former partner after his refusal (and that of most of the others) to sign her petulant letter of complaint concerning Sheila Williams. Although Phil had been slightly reserved in his manner towards her (Nancy), she knew that that was his way and she was enjoying the company of that wiry, small-boned, gently spoken citizen from Sacramento who almost invariably found himself at the back of every queue that ever formed itself. Yes, the tour was definitely looking up a little, and only the previous evening she had written a card to her daughter to say that in spite of a death and a theft and a murder she was 'beginning to make one or two very nice friends on the trip'.

In truth, however, Phil himself was finding Nancy Wiseman a little too effusive for his liking and – perversely, as it seemed – would have preferred sitting next to Janet Roscoe, up there at the front of the coach, as he listened to (and indeed almost wholly managed to hear) the end of Ashenden's introduction to Bath:

'In the eighteenth century the city was transformed into a resort for English high society – being particularly associated, of course, with the name of Beau Nash, the great dandy and gamester who lived here during the 1740s and 50s. Among its many literary connections, Bath can number such great figures as Henry Fielding, Fanny Burney, Jane Austen, William Wordsworth, Walter Scott, Charles Dickens – and most famous of all, perhaps, Geoffrey Chaucer and *The Wife of Bath's Tale*.'

It was a good note on which to end.

Opposite him, he noticed that Janet Roscoe had delved once more into the deep handbag, this time producing a very slim volume, whose title it was impossible for him not to see, and which he could have guessed in any case: CHAUCER, *Tale of the Wyf of Bathe*.

He smiled across at her, and as she opened her book at the Prologue, she smiled quite sweetly back at him.

It seemed a good omen for the stay in Bath.

Only seemed.

CHAPTER FIFTY

During late visits to Stinsford in old age he would often visit
the unmarked grave of Louisa Harding
  (*Florence Emily Hardy,* The Early Life of Thomas Hardy)

ACCORDING TO THE hospital bulletin on the Monday
afternoon, the condition of Lucy Downes was now
officially listed as 'comfortable', one notch above the
'satisfactory' of the Sunday, and two above the earlier
'stable'. Three visits from her husband had helped,
perhaps (the first in the small hours of the Sunday
morning, two hours after his release from custody), but
some slight complications had arisen with continued
internal bleeding, and she had become deeply and
embarrassingly conscious of how she must appear to
everyone whenever she smiled. So she forbore to do so
altogether, even to Cedric, and as she lay in her bed
that day, her arm now beginning to give her some
considerable pain, she would willingly (she knew) have
cracked two of her ribs rather than chipped a couple
of her teeth.

Vanity, all is vanity, saith the preacher. And 'satisfactory' was arguably too favourable a judgement on her
circumstances. But that was the word Morse repeated
to the first question Lewis put to him about Lucy's
progress at 8.30 a.m. on the Tuesday. It may have been

that Morse had smiled a little at the question. But it may not.

Activity in the two days following Cedric Downes's release had hardly afforded a model of investigative collaboration, with Morse sleeping through until the late afternoon of the Sunday, then idling away most of the Monday in his office, moodily perusing the documents in the case; and with Lewis doing the converse, making what he felt had been a fairly significant contribution to the case on the Sunday afternoon, and then spending the whole of the Monday abed, where he had lain dead to the wideawake world, and where, even when Mrs Lewis had gently rocked his shoulder at 6.30 p.m. and quietly breathed the prospect of egg and chips into his ear, he had turned his head over into the pillow and blissfully resumed his slumbers. But now he felt fully refreshed.

By the look of him, however, his chief had not perhaps shared a similarly successful period of recuperation, for he sounded tetchy as he picked up the brief note Lewis had left him.

'You say Stratton *was* quite definitely out at Didcot when Kemp was being killed?'

'No doubt about it, sir. I went over there yesterday—'

'You were in bed yesterday.'

'Sunday, I mean. They remembered him.'

'Who's "they"?'

'One of 'em took a photo of him on the footplate of "The Cornishman". He'd already got it developed and was going to post it to America. Stratton gave him a fiver. He's going to get a copy and send it here.'

'And it *was* Stratton?'

'It was Stratton.'

'Oh!'

'Where does all this leave us, sir? I just don't know where we are.'

'And you think *I* do?' mumbled the ill-shaven Morse. 'Here! Read this – came this morning.'

Lewis took the envelope handed him, postmarked Stratford-upon-Avon, and withdrew the two hand-written sheets.

Swan Hotel,
Stratford,
Saturday, 3rd Nov

Dear Inspector,

My conscience has troubled me since I left Oxford. When you asked about the phone call I tried to remember everything and I don't know what else I could have told you. I want to repeat that the line was faint but it was definitely Dr Kemp on the phone and that what I wrote was as near as anyone could get to what he said. But I lied about the afternoon and I was worried when you wanted to keep the betting slips because you probably know that one of the horses won and I would have won quite a lot of money if I'd stayed in the betting shop. I wanted people to think I'd gone to Summertown and I could prove it if necessary. So I went to

Ladbrokes and picked two rank outsiders and put some money on them and left. The only reason I did this was because I didn't want anyone to know where I really went which was to a flat in Park Town where I am ashamed to say I watched some sex videos with three other people. I think one of them would be willing to back up my story and if it's necessary I will give you a name if you can promise it can all be done with no charges brought. I am worried as well about the way you asked me where I went after we'd arrived in Oxford because I didn't tell you the truth then either, I went to Holywell cemetery and went to the grave of a friend of mine. He wrote to me before he died and I didn't write back and I just wanted to make up for it in some way if I could. His name was James Braden.
I am sorry to have caused trouble.

John Ashenden

P.S. I forgot to say that I left a small memento at his grave.

P.P.S. I shall be glad if you can pick up my winnings and give the money to Oxfam.

'Well?'

'I suppose you want me to tell you how many spelling mistakes he's made.'

'That would be something.'

'Looks all right to me. There's an apostrophe missing, though.'

Morse's face brightened. 'Well done! Excellent! There is the one spelling mistake, but you're *definitely* improving ... That's a clue, by the way ... No? Never mind!'

'At least we're getting some of the loose ends tied up.'

'You mean we cross Ashenden off the suspect-list?'

'Don't know, sir. But we can cross Stratton off, I reckon. He was in Didcot most of the afternoon. That's for sure.'

'So he couldn't have killed Kemp?'

'I don't see how.'

'Nor do I,' said Morse.

'Back to square one!'

'You know where we went wrong, don't you? It was that phone call that sent me up the cul-de-sac. You see, we can't get away from the fact that if Kemp *was* in London, he could easily have caught an earlier train. That still puzzles me! He rang at twelve-thirty-five and there was a train at twelve-forty-five. Ten minutes to walk across from the phone to the platform!'

'You know, we haven't really checked that, have we? I mean the train could have been cancelled ... or something.'

Morse said, 'I've checked. It's almost the only profitable thing I did yesterday.' He lit a cigarette and sat staring gloomily out of the window.

Lewis found himself looking at the back page of *The Oxford Times* which lay on the desk. Morse had not started the crossword yet ('Ichabod' this week), but just to the right of it Lewis noticed a brief item on a fatal accident at the Marston Ferry Road traffic lights: a young student who had been taking a crash course in EFL. *Crash* course! Huh!

'Don't tell me you've done one across, Lewis?'

'No. Just reading about this accident at the Marston Ferry lights. Bad junction, you know, that is. I think there ought to be a "filter right" as you go into the Banbury Road.'

'Fair point!'

Lewis read on aloud. ' "Georgette le ... something ... daughter of M. Georges le ... something of Bordeaux ... " ' But now his eyes had spotted the date. ''Sfunny! This accident was a week last Saturday, sir, at half-past five. That's exactly one week earlier than Mrs Downes'.'

'Life's full of coincidences, I keep telling you that.'

'It's just that when you get two things happening like that, people say there's going to be three, don't they? That's what the wife always says.'

'Look, if a third accident'll please you, volunteer for the ambulance crew this morning. It's a fiver to a cracked piss-pot that some irresponsible sod—' Suddenly Morse stopped, the old tingle of high excitement thrilling strangely across his shoulders.

'Christ! What a fool you've been!' he murmured softly to himself.

'Sir?'

Morse rattled out his words: 'What's the name of Kemp's publisher? The one you rang to make sure he'd been there.'

'"Babington's". The fellow there said it was named after Macaulay' (Lewis smiled with distant memories) 'Thomas Babington Macaulay, sir – you know, the one who wrote the *Lays of Ancient Rome*. That's the one poem I—'

'Get on to the American Consulate! Quick, for Christ's sake! Find our where Stratton is – they'll know, I should think. *We've got to stop him leaving the country.*'

Morse's blue eyes gleamed triumphantly. 'I think I know, Lewis! I think I *know.*'

But Eddie Stratton had left the country the previous evening on a Pan Am jumbo bound for New York – together with his late wife Laura, the latter lying cold and stiff in a coffin in a special compartment just above the undercarriage.

CHAPTER FIFTY-ONE

At day's end you came,
and like the evening sun,
left an afterglow

(*Basil Swift*, Collected Haiku)

LEWIS WAS ENJOYING that Tuesday, the day on which Morse had suddenly spurted into a frenetic flurry of activity. Six extra personnel: Sergeant Dixon, three detective PCs, and two WPCs for the telephones. The administrative arrangement and supervision required for such teamwork was exactly the sort of skill in which Lewis excelled, and the hours passed quickly with the progressive gleaning of intelligence, the gradual build up of hard fact to bolster tentative theory – and always that almost insolent gratification that shone in Morse's eyes, for the latter appeared to have known (or so it seemed to Lewis) most of the details before the calls and corroboration had been made.

It was just after a quick, non-alcoholic lunch that Morse had sought to explain to Lewis the nature of his earlier error.

'I once did a crossword in which all of the clues were susceptible of two quite different solutions. A sort of *double-entendre* crossword, it was. Get on the wrong wavelength with one across, and everything fits except one single interlocking letter. Brilliant puzzle! – set by Ximenes in *The Observer*. That's what *I* did – got off on the wrong foot. And I did it again in this case, with Downes. You know what one across was? That bloody phone call! I'd assumed it was important, Lewis, and I was *right*. But right for the wrong reasons. When I first learned that the line was bad, I thought it possible – likely, even – that the caller *wasn't Kemp at all*. Then, because he said he'd missed the train – although there was still ten minutes to go – I thought he wasn't at Paddington at all: I thought Kemp was probably in Oxford. And it all fitted, didn't it? Except for that one single letter . . .

'But all the time, that poor line we kept hearing about *was* of crucial significance, but for a totally different reason! It was Kemp all right who made the call. But he wasn't at *Paddington*: he was still at his publisher's in London – Babington Press, Fine Arts Publications, South Kensington – and doubtless he referred to it, as anyone would, as Babington's. Oh, yes! That's where he was, and he did *exactly* what he said he'd do. He caught the next train and arrived in Oxford, dead on schedule.'

In the circumstances 'dead on schedule' hardly seemed to Lewis the happiest of phrases, but he knew that Morse was right about the call from Babington's. It had been he himself, Lewis, who had finally got on to the man there who was in the process of completing the proofs for the forthcoming seminal opus entitled *Pre-Conquest Craftsmanship in Southern Britain*, by Theodore S. Kemp, MA, DPhil; the man who had been closeted with Kemp that fateful morning, and who had confirmed that Kemp had not left the offices until about 12.30 p.m.

Sergeant Dixon (stripes newly stitched) was also enjoying himself, although initially he had serious doubts about whether he – or anyone else, for that matter – could successfully handle his assignment in the ridiculously short period of the three or four hours which Morse had asserted as 'ample'.

But he had done it.

He had not realised quite how many customers were attracted by the car-hire firms of Oxford, especially American customers; and checking the lists had taken longer than he'd imagined. In this particular respect Morse (suggesting the likelihood of the Botley Road area) had got things quite wrong, for it was at the Hertz Rent-a-Car offices at the top of the Woodstock Road where Dixon had finally spotted the name he was looking for with all the excitement of a young angler just hooking a heavyweight pike.

Tom Pritchard, the manager, went through the key points of the car-hire catechism to be faced by every client:

- Full name and home address?
- How many days' hire?
- Make of car preferred?
- Which dates?
- One driver only?

– Method of payment? (credit card preferred)
– Valid driving licence? (US licence OK)
– Telephone number of one referee?

After that, the manager went through the procedure adopted: a telephone call to the reference number cited; verification of credit card; verification of driving licence; verification of home address (the last three usually completed within ten minutes or so on the International Information Computer); preparation, presentation, and signing of the contract (including appropriate insurance clauses); then, paperwork now completed, the car brought round to the outer forecourt, with an assistant to give the client a quick run-over of the controls, and to hand over the keys. *Bon voyage*, cheerio, and Bob's your uncle.

By good fortune it had been the manager himself who had effected this particular transaction, and who remembered the occasion reasonably clearly. Well, it was only five days ago, wasn't it? The reference call to the hotel, The Randolph – that's what he'd remembered clearest of all, really: he'd looked up the telephone number and then been put through, on the extension given to him by his client, to the Deputy Manageress, who had promptly and effusively vouched for the *bona fides* of Rent-a-Car's prospective customer. Naturally, the manager had more details to offer: the car hired had been a red Cavalier, Registration H 106 XMT; it had been hired at 1.45 p.m. and returned at some time after the offices had closed at 6.30 p.m., with the keys pushed through the special letter-box, as requested. Mileage on the speedometer had been clocked as only 30.7. Probably, thought the manager, the car hadn't left Oxford at all?

Yet for all his own pleasure at tracing this evidence, Dixon could see little in his report which might have accounted for the look of extraordinary triumph he had seen on Morse's face when he reported in at 2.45 p.m.

Sergeant (with a 'g') Lewis's own, self-imposed task would, he suspected, be a fairly tricky undertaking. But even here the gods appeared to be smiling broadly on Morse's enterprise. The distinguished personage known as the Coroner's Serjeant (with a 'j') had been willing to sacrifice what he could of his time if the interests of Justice (capital 'J') were really being served. Yet it had still taken the pair of them more than two hours to assemble and photocopy the material that Morse had so confidently predicted would be found.

And was found.

But by far the most difficult and tiresome task had been that of the telephone girls, who had made scores and scores of transatlantic calls that Tuesday morning, afternoon, and early evening: calls made to one address that led to calls to another address; calls to one friend that led to another friend or colleague; from one police department to another; one State to other States; calls for one set of records that referred to another set of records that led ... *ad* apparently *infinitum.*

'Couldn't it have waited?' Chief Superintendent Strange had asked, calling in briefly in mid-afternoon. 'Waited till tomorrow?'

But Morse was a man who could never abide the incomplete; could never abide the not-knowing-immediately. One clue unfinished in a *Listener* puzzle, and he would strain the capacity of every last brain-cell to bursting point until he had solved it. And equally so, as now, in a murder case. Tomorrow was too far distanced for his mind to wait for the last piece of evidence – a mind so ceaselessly tossing, as it had been ever since Lewis – wonderful Lewis! – had mentioned that seemingly irrelevant item in the *Oxford Times.*

Those names!

And it was Morse himself who had initiated the arrest of Mr Edward Stratton as he stepped off his plane in New York; Morse himself who had spoken with the aforementioned Stratton for forty-six minutes, seven seconds – as measured by the recently installed meter in the recently constituted Telephone Room at St Aldate's. But not even the penny-pinching Strange could have complained overmuch about the price that had been paid for the extraordinary information Morse had gleaned.

It was Morse himself, too, who at 8.30 p.m. had called a halt to everything. He had not returned any copious gratitude to his staff for all the work they had put in during the day; but he always found it difficult to express his deeper feelings. However, he *had* returned all but three of the tourists' passports to the safe-keeping of the Manager at The Randolph – the latter just a fraction irked that it now appeared to be his own responsibility to return these passports to whatever location the departed tourists happened to find themselves in.

At 9 p.m. Morse, hitherto that day most remarkably under-beered, made his way up through Cornmarket to the Chapters Bar of The Randolph. There were many times in Morse's life when he needed a drink in order to think. On occasion though (such as now), he needed a drink because he needed a *drink.* What's more, having left the Jaguar down in the police car-park, he was *going* to drink.

And compulsively, happily, thirstily – he drank.

One and a half hours later, as he still sat on a high stool at the bar, he looked down and saw the fingers of a beautifully manicured hand against his left arm, and felt the ghost of a touch of the softest breast against his shoulder.

'Can I buy you a drink, Inspector?' The voice was slightly husky, slightly slurred, and more than slightly disturbing.

Morse had no need to look round. He said, 'Let me buy *you* one, Sheila.'

'No! I insist.' She took his arm, gently squeezing it

against herself, then pressed her lips – so full, so dry! – against a cheek that had been hurriedly ill-shaven some fourteen hours earlier.

For the moment, Morse said nothing. The day that would soon be drawing to its close had been one of the most wonderful he had experienced: the theft, the murder, the link *between* the theft and the murder – yes, all now known. Well, almost known. And he'd solved it all himself. He'd needed help – yes! Help in crossing the 't's and barring the '7's and dotting the 'j's. Of course he had. Yet it had been his own vision, his own analysis, his own solution.

His.

'What are you doing here?' he asked.

'Annual Dance. Lit and Phil Society. Bloody booring!'

'You with a partner?'

'You don't come to these do's without a partner.'

'So?'

'So he kept trying to get a bit too intimate during the Veleta.'

'Veleta? God! That's what I used to dance . . .'

'We're none of us getting much younger.'

'And you didn't want – you didn't want that?'

'I wanted a drink. That's why I'm here.'

'And you told him . . .'

'. . . to bugger off.'

Morse looked at her now – perhaps properly for the first time. She wore a black dress reaching to just above her knees, suspended from her shoulders by straps no thicker than shoelaces; black stockings, encasing surprisingly slim legs, and very high-heeled red shoes that elevated her an inch or so above Morse as he stood up and offered her his stool. He smiled at her, with what seemed warmth and understanding in his eyes.

'You look happy,' she said.

But Morse knew, deep down, that he wasn't really happy at all. For the last hour his progressively alcohol-ised brain had reminded him of the consequences of justice (small 'j'): of bringing a criminal before the courts, ensuring that he was convicted for his sins (or was it his crimes?), and then getting him locked up for the rest of his life, perhaps, in a prison where he would never again go to the WC without someone observing such an embarrassingly private function, someone smelling him, someone humiliating him. (And, yes, it was a *him.*) Humiliating him in that little paddock of privacy just outside the back of the house where he would try so hard to keep all that remained of his dignity and self-esteem.

'I'm not happy,' said Morse.

'Why not?'

'G and T, is it?'

'How did you guess?'

'I'm a genius.'

'I'm quite good at some things myself.'

'Yes?'

'Do you want me to make you happy for tonight?' Her voice was suddenly more sober, more sharply etched – and yet more gentle, too.

Morse looked at her: looked at the piled-up hair above her wistful face; looked down at the full and observably bra-less bosom; looked down at the taut stretch of black stocking between the knee and the thigh of her crossed right leg. He was ready for her, and she seemed to sense it.

'I've got a wonderfully comfortable bed,' she whispered into his left ear.

'So have I!' said Morse, oddly defensive.

'But we wouldn't argue *too* much about that sort of thing, would we?' Sheila smiled and reached for her drink. 'Aren't you having another one?'

Morse shook his head: '"It provokes the desire, but it takes away the performance."'

'Do you know, I've never met anyone before who's quoted that thing correctly.'

Perhaps she shouldn't have said it, for suddenly its implications stirred Morse to an irrational jealousy. But soon, as she linked her arm possessively through his, collected her coat from Cloaks, then steered him across towards the taxi-rank in St Giles', he knew that his lust for her had returned; and would remain.

'I ought to make it quite clear to you, ma'am,' he murmured in the taxi, 'that any knickers you may be wearing may well be taken down and used in evidence.'

For the first time in many days, Sheila Williams felt inordinately happy. And was to remain so – if truth is to be told – until the early dawn of the following day when Morse left her to walk slowly to his bachelor flat – only a short distance away up the Banbury Road – bareheaded in the beating rain which an hour since had obliquely streaked the windows of Sheila Williams's front bedroom.

CHAPTER FIFTY-TWO

Rigid, the skeleton of habit alone upholds the human frame
(*Virginia Woolf*, Mrs Dalloway)

MORSE AND LEWIS arrived at the Chesterton Hotel in Bath at 10.35 a.m. the following morning. Morse had insisted on travelling by what he called the 'scenic' route – via Cirencester – but, alas, the countryside was not appearing at its best: the golden days were gone, and the close-cropped fields where the sheep ever nibbled looked dank and uninviting under a sky-cover of grey cloud. Little conversation had passed between the two detectives until, an hour out of Oxford, Morse (looking, as Lewis saw him, still rather tired) had crossed those final 't's.

'All a bit unusual, though, isn't it, sir?'

'You think so?'

'I do. About as unusual as a . . .' But Lewis found himself unable to dredge up the appropriate simile.

'"Unusual as a fat postman",' supplied Morse.

'Really? Our postman looks as if he tips the scales at about twenty stone.'

Morse inhaled deeply upon yet another cigarette, half closed his eyes, shook his head, and relapsed into the silence that was customary for him on any journey.

Behind, in a marked police car, Sergeant Dixon sat beside his driver, a moderately excited PC Watson.

'Drives pretty quick, don't he?' ventured the latter.

''Bout the only thing he does do quick, I reckon,' said Dixon.

It seemed to Watson a cruel, unfair remark. And Dixon himself knew it was unfair, for a little while regretting having said it.

It had been forty-five minutes earlier when Dr Barbara Moule had parked her Fiesta at the Chesterton Hotel, finding John Ashenden waiting for her a little anxiously. The first part of her illustrated lecture was scheduled for 10–11 a.m., followed by a coffee break, and then further slides and questions from 11.30 to noon. Ashenden himself had carried the heavy projector to the Beau Nash Room at the rear of the hotel, where most of the tourists were now foregathering. The room was of a narrow, oblong shape, with the plastic chairs set out two on each side of the central gap in which, at the front, the projector was placed. Looking around, Ashenden noted yet again the readily observable fact that (doubtless like animals) tourists from very early on staked out their territories: find them sitting at one particular table for dinner and almost invariably, for breakfast next morning, you would find them sitting at the very same table; allocate them to particular seats in a coach on the first part of a journey, and as if by some proprietorial right the passengers would thereafter usually veer towards those selfsame seats. And the

Beau Nash Room might just as well have been their luxury coach: twenty-three of them only for the minute, with Eddie Stratton now being held in custody by the New York Police, distanced by only a few yards, as it happened, from the mortal remains of his former wife; and with Sam and Vera Kronquist, one of the three married couples originally listed on the tour, still in their room on the second floor of the hotel – Sam watching a mid-morning cartoon on ITV, and Vera, fully dressed, lying back lazily against the pillows of their double bed, reading the previous February's issue of *Country Life*.

'You won't forget, Birdy' (Birdy?) 'that you're supposed to be having a headache, will you?'

His wife, not deigning to look up from the page, smiled to herself slightly. 'Nobody ain't coming in here, Sam – not if we leave that notice there on the doornarb.'

In the front row of the Beau Nash Room, only one of the chairs was occupied – Number 1, if the chairs had been numbered, from left to right, 1,2,3,4 – the seat Janet Roscoe had invariably occupied on every single leg of the coach trip. Behind her the two seats were empty, a troublous reminder of where Eddie and Laura had sat side by side when the coach had first set off from Heathrow Airport ... had first arrived at the eastern outskirts of Oxford.

At the back of the room, solitary now, and perfectly prepared to be wholly bored for the next hour (or was it two?) sat Mr Aldrich. His interest in Roman remains was minimal, and in any case his ears (incipient otosclerosis, his personal physician had diagnosed) seemed to be filling up with thicker and thicker wads of cotton-wool each day. He would have liked to exchange a few words with Cedric Downes at Oxford – surely a man suffering from the same kind of trouble? But the opportunity had not arisen, and Aldrich had taken no initiative in effecting any introduction.

Odd, really: Aldrich, with his increasing hearing problems, sitting right at the back of the class; and Mrs Roscoe, whose hearing was so extraordinarily acute, ever seated at the front . . .

So be it!

Three rows in front of Aldrich, on his left-hand side as he looked at the backs of their heads, sat Howard and Shirley Brown.

'Hope these slides are better than your sister's lot on Ottawa.'

'Hardly be wurse,' agreed Shirley, as Ashenden launched into a well-rehearsed eulogy of Dr Moule's incomparable pre-eminence in the field of Romano-British archaeology in Somerset – before walking to the entrance door at the rear, and turning off the lights.

At 10.50 a.m., Aldrich looked across at the two men who had entered quietly by the same door. Surprisingly, he was hearing Dr Moule quite loud and clear, for she had a firm and resonant voice. What's more, he thought, she was good; he *wanted* to hear what she was saying. And everybody thought she was good. Indeed, only three or four minutes into her talk, Shirley Brown had leaned across and whispered into Howard's ear: 'Better than Ottawa!'

Dr Moule had been momentarily conscious, albeit with her back turned, of some silent addition to the audience, though giving this no further thought. But after she had finished the first part of her lecture; after slightly nodding her head to the generous applause; after the lights had gone up again; after Ashenden had said (as every chairman since Creation had said) how much everyone had enjoyed the talk and how grateful everyone was that not only had the distinguished speaker fascinated each and every one of them but also had agreed to answer any questions which he was absolutely sure everyone in the room was aching to put to such a distinguished expert in the field ... it was only then that Dr Moule was able to survey the two intruders. Sitting together in the back row: the one nearer the exit a burly-looking fellow, with a rather heavy, though kindly mien; and beside him a slimmer, clearly more authoritative man, with thinning hair and pale complexion. It was this second man who now asked the first, the last, question. And it was to this man that almost everyone now turned as the rather quiet, rather cultured, rather interesting, wholly English voice began to speak:

'I was a Classic in my youth, madam, and although I have always been deeply interested in the works of the Roman poets and the Roman historians I have never been able to summon up much enthusiasm for Roman architecture. In fact the contemplation of a Roman brick seems to leave me cold – quite cold. So I would dearly like to know why it is that you find yourself so enthusiastic ...'

The question was balm and benison to Barbara's ears. But then the questioner had risen to his feet.

'. . . yes, it would be extremely interesting for all of us to learn your answer. But not – not for the moment, please!'

The man now walked down the central aisle and halted beside the projector, where he turned and spoke. Was it to her? Was it to her audience?

'I'm sorry to interrupt. But the people here know who I am – who we are. And I shall have to ask you, I'm afraid, to leave the next half hour to Lewis and to me.'

Dr Barbara Moule almost smiled. She'd picked up the literary allusion immediately, and enjoyed those few seconds during which the man's intensely blue eyes had held her own.

It was Ashenden who went upstairs to knock on the door of Room 46.

'But didn't Sam here explain? I have a headache.'

'I know. But it's the police, Mrs Kronquist.'

'It is?'

'And they want everybody to be there.'

'Oh my Gard!'

CHAPTER FIFTY-THREE

And summed up so well that it came to far more
Than the Witnesses ever had said
(*Lewis Carroll*, The Barrister's Dream)

THE BEAUTIFUL IF bemused Dr Moule, invited to stay
if she so wished, took a seat in the front row. The man
spoke, she thought, more like a don than a detective.

'Let me outline the case, or rather the two cases, to
you all. First, a jewel was stolen from Mrs Laura
Stratton's room in The Randolph. At the same time –
whether just before or just after the theft – Mrs Stratton
died. What is medically certain is that she died of
coronary thrombosis: there is no question of any foul
play, except of course if the heart attack was brought
on by the shock of finding someone in her room
stealing the jewel she had come all the way from
America to hand over to the Ashmolean Museum, or
more specifically to Dr Theodore Kemp on behalf of
the Museum. I tried to find out – I may be forgiven –
who would benefit from the theft of the jewel, and I
learned from Mr Brown here' (heads swivelling) 'that
Mrs Stratton was always slightly mysterious – ambivalent, even – about her own financial affairs. So I
naturally had to bear in mind the possibility that the
jewel had not been stolen at all by any outside party,

but "caused to disappear", let us say, by the Strattons themselves. It had been the property of Mrs Stratton's first husband, and it was he who had expressed the wish, as stated in his will, that it be returned to England to find a permanent place in the Ashmolean Museum with its counterpart, the Wolvercote Buckle. As a piece of treasure of considerable historical importance, the Wolvercote Tongue was of course beyond price. In itself, however, as an artefact set with precious stones, it was, let us say, "priceable", and it was insured by Mrs Stratton for half a million dollars. I am not yet wholly sure about the specific terms of the policy taken out, but it appears that in the eventuality of the jewel being stolen, either before or after her death, the insurance money is payable to her husband – and is not to be syphoned off into some trust fund or other. At any rate, that is what Eddie Stratton believed – believes, rather – for I learned most of these facts yesterday from Stratton himself, who is now back in America.' Morse paused a moment and looked slowly around his audience. 'I don't need, perhaps, to underline to you the temptation that faced Mr Stratton, himself a virtually penniless man, and a man who knew – for such seems to be the case – that his wife had run through almost all of the considerable money she had inherited from her first husband.'

Several faces looked pained and incredulous, but Janet Roscoe was the only person who did not restrain her disquietude:

'But that could nart *be*, Inspector! Eddie was out walking—'

Morse held up his right hand, and spoke to her not ungently:

'Please hear me out, Mrs Roscoe ... It was easy to pin-point the period of time within which the theft must have occurred, and not too difficult – was it? – to find out where the great majority of you had been during the crucial forty-five minutes. Not *all* of you felt willing to be completely honest with me, but I don't wish to labour that point now. As I saw things – still see things – the thief had to be one of you here, one of the touring party, including your courier' (heads swivelling again) 'or one of the staff at The Randolph. But the latter possibility could be, and was, fairly quickly discounted. So you will be able to see where things are heading, ladies and gentlemen ...

'The immediate effects of the theft were considerably lessened both by the death of Laura Stratton and on the very next day by the murder of Dr Kemp, the man to whom the Tongue was due to be handed over that day at an official little ceremony at the Ashmolean. Now one of the jobs of the police force, and especially the CID, is to try to establish a *pattern* in crime, if this is possible, and in this instance both Sergeant Lewis and myself found it difficult not to believe there was some *link* between the two events. They may of course have been quite coincidental; but already there *was* a link, was there not? Dr Kemp himself! – the man who had one day been deprived of a jewel which he himself had traced to an American collector, a jewel for which he had been negotiating, a jewel that had been found in the waters below the bridge at Wolvercote in 1873, a jewel which once united with its mate would doubtless be the subject of some considerable historical interest, and bring some short-term celebrity, possibly some long-term preferment, to himself – to Kemp. Indeed a photograph of the re-united Buckle and Tongue was going to be used on the cover of his forthcoming book. And then, on the very next day, Kemp is murdered. Interesting, is it not? Did, I asked myself, did the *same* person commit both the theft and the murder? It seemed to me more and more likely. So perhaps I needed just the one criminal, not two; but I needed a reason as well. So my thinking went a little further in that direction – the correct direction. If the criminal was the same in each case, was not the *motive* likely to have been the same? In both crimes, the person who had suffered by far the most had been the same man, Kemp. In the first, he had been robbed of something on which he had set his heart; in the second he was robbed of his life. Why? – that is what I asked myself. Or rather that is *not*, in the first instance, what I asked myself, because I was driven to the view – incorrectly – that there could be no link between the two crimes.

'So let us come to Kemp himself. It is a commonplace in murder investigations that more may often be learned about the murderer from the *victim* than from any other source. Now what did we know of the victim, Dr Kemp? He was a Keeper of Antiquities at the Ashmolean, a man somewhat flamboyant in dress and manner, not only a ladies' man but one of the most dedicated womanisers in the University; a man who patently, almost on first sight, appeared self-centred and self-seeking. Yet life had not gone all his way: far from it. The University had recognised Kemp for what he was: his promotion was slow; a full fellowship was withheld; no family; a very modest two-bedroomed flat in North Oxford; and, above all, a great personal tragedy. Two years ago he was involved in a dreadful crash on the western Ring Road in which his wife, who was sitting beside him in the passenger seat, received such serious injuries to the lower half of the body that for the rest of her life – a life which ended tragically last week – she was confined to a wheelchair. But that was only the half of it. The driver of the other car was killed instantaneously – a Mrs Mayo from California who was in England doing some research project on the novels of Anthony Trollope. The settlements of the dead woman's Accidental Death Benefit, and of the policy covering the "passenger-liability" responsibility of the surviving driver – a driver by the way almost completely unscathed – were finally settled. But the legal tangle surrounding "culpability" was never really unravelled: no eye-witnesses, contradictory evidence on possible mechanical faults, discrepancies about the time recorded for the breathalyser test – these factors resulted in Kemp getting away comparatively lightly, being banned from driving for three years only, with what must have seemed to many the derisory fine of only four hundred pounds. What had really confused everyone was the fact that Kemp always carried a hip-flask of brandy in the car's glove compartment, and that he had given his wife – trapped by the legs beside him – several sips from this flask before the ambulance arrived; and had even drunk from it himself! Everyone who subsequently learned of this action condemned it as utterly stupid and irresponsible, but perhaps such criticism may be tempered by the fact that the man was in a deep state of shock. At least that was what he said in his own defence.

'But let me revert to the crimes committed last week. The crucial happening, whichever way we look at things, was the telephone call made by Kemp. I formed several theories about that call – all wrong, and I will say nothing about them. Kemp had reported to the group that he would be arriving in Oxford at 3 p.m. – and the simple truth is that he *did* arrive in Oxford at 3 p.m. And somebody knew about that telephone call, *and met Kemp at the railway station,* doubtless informing the taxi-driver who had been hired that he was no longer required.'

Janet Roscoe half opened her mouth as if she were contemplating breaking the ensuing silence. But it was Morse who did so, as he continued:

'A taxi, you see, would have been easily traceable, so a different plan was adopted. Someone went to a car-rental firm in North Oxford in the early afternoon and hired a Vauxhall Cavalier. There was only one real difficulty: after vehicle-licence, credit-worthiness, and so on, were formally checked, the firm required some reference to establish the *bona fides* of the client. But this difficulty was quickly and neatly overcome: the man who hired the car – a *man,* yes! – gave the telephone number of The Randolph, and as the firm's representative was dialling the number he casually mentioned

304

that the Deputy Manageress of The Randolph could be immediately contacted on a certain extension. The call was put through, confirmation obtained, and the car handed over. You will appreciate of course that an *accomplice* was essential at this juncture, but not just someone prepared to perform a casual favour. No! Rather someone who was prepared to be an accomplice to *murder*. Now, I believe it to be true that before this tour – with one exception – none of you had known each other. That exception was Mr Stratton and Mr Brown, who had met in the Armed Forces. But at the time the car was being hired, Mr Stratton was on his way to Didcot Railway Centre – of that fact there can be no doubt whatsoever. And Mr Howard Brown' (Morse hesitated) 'has given a full and fairly satisfactory account of his own whereabouts that afternoon, an account which has since been substantially corroborated.' Lewis's eyebrows shot up involuntarily, but he trusted that no one had noticed.

'There were one or two other absentees that afternoon, weren't there? Mr Ashenden for one.' The courier was staring hard at the patch of carpet between his feet. 'But he was up in Summertown for the whole of that afternoon with friends – as we've now checked.' (Lewis managed to keep his eyebrows still.) 'And then, of course, there's Mr Aldrich.' Heads were swivelling completely round this time – to the back row where sat Phil Aldrich, nodding his head in gentle agreement, a wry smile on his long, lugubrious face. 'But Mr Aldrich can't possibly have been our guilty party either, can he? He went up to London that day, and in fact was travelling on the same train as Stratton when the two of them arrived back in Oxford. Mr Aldrich himself claims, and I am fully prepared to believe him, that he did not see Mr Stratton on the train. *But Mr Stratton saw Mr Aldrich*; and so in an odd sort of way, even if we had no proof of Stratton being in Didcot, the pair of them quite unwittingly perhaps had given each other an utterly unshakeable alibi. And in addition we now *know* that Stratton was in Didcot most of that afternoon. You see, ladies and gentlemen, whatever happens in life, no person can ever be in two places at the same time, for the laws of the Universe forbid it. And the person perfecting his plans in Oxford, the person who had taken possession of the red Cavalier, that person had plenty to do, and precious little time in which to do it – to do it *in Oxford*. There is, perhaps, a brief additional point to be made. It occurred to me that if Stratton and Brown had known each other, so might their wives, perhaps. But one of these wives was already dead; and it was a *man*,' said Morse slowly, 'and not a woman, who hired the car that afternoon.

'Are we running out of suspects, then? Almost, I agree. Your tour started with only three married couples, did it not? And already we have eliminated two of these: the Strattons and the Browns.' In the tense silence which followed this remark, all eyes now turned upon the couple who had been fetched from their bedroom; the couple who had decided that any further diet of delightful architecture would have amounted to a sort of cultural force-feeding. But the pivoting glances which now fell full upon Sam and Vera Kronquist almost immediately reverted to Chief Inspector Morse as the latter rounded off his background summary.

'But Mr Kronquist, as several of you already know, was assisting Mrs Sheila Williams during most of the afternoon in question with the temperamental kaleidoscope allocated to her for her illustrated talk on "Alice". Now Mr Kronquist may be a very clever man, but *he* is not permitted, either, to suspend the physical laws of the Universe. And you do see, don't you, that Mrs Williams, too, must now be crossed off our list of suspects? And finally we shall cross the name of Cedric Downes off that same list, and for exactly the same reason. If anyone from the group here met Kemp at 3 p.m., it wasn't Downes, because nine or ten of you here will willingly testify to the incontrovertible fact that he was talking to you from that time onwards. Did I say running out of likely suspects? And yet, ladies and gentlemen, someone *did* meet Kemp at the railway station that afternoon.

'One of *you* did!'

CHAPTER FIFTY-FOUR

Either what woman having ten pieces of silver, if she lose one piece, doth not light a candle, and sweep the house, and seek diligently till she find it?

(*St Luke*, ch. 15, v. 8)

THROUGHOUT THE MORNING on which Morse was addressing his audience in Bath, and stripping away the deceptions and the half-truths which hitherto had veiled the naked truth of the case, there was much activity at the Trout Inn, a fine riverside hostelry set between the weir and the Godstow Lock in the village of Wolvercote, only a couple of miles out on the western side of North Oxford. During the summer months hordes of visitors regularly congregate there to eat and drink at their leisure on the paved terrace between the mellow sandstone walls of the inn itself and the river's edge, where many sit on the low stone parapet and look below them through the clear, greenish water at the mottled dark-brown and silvery backs of the carp that rise to the surface to snap up the crisps and the crusts thrown down to them.

But that Wednesday morning, the few customers who had called for an early drink were much more interested in other underwater creatures: four of them, with sleek black skins and disproportionately large webbed feet, circling up and down, and round and round, and sweeping the depths diligently below the weir, streams of bubbles intermittently rising to the surface from the cylinders strapped to their backs. Each of the four was an experienced police frogman, and each of them knew exactly what he was looking for – knew indeed the exact dimensions of the object and the positioning of the three great ruby eyes once set into it. Thus far they had found nothing, and above the bed of the river their searchings were stirring up a cloudy precipitate of mud as the white waters gushed across the weir. Yet hopes were reasonably high. The frogmen had been briefed – and with such a degree of certitude! – as to the exact point on the hump-backed bridge whence the Tongue had been thrown. So they were able to plot their operation with some precision as first they swam slowly abreast across the river, then turning and recrossing the current, ever feeling, ever searching, as they worked their way slowly downstream into the more placid reaches of the water.

But nothing.

After its discovery in 1873, the Tongue had found its way into the hands of a treasure-hunter, who had kept quiet about it and sold it to a London dealer, who in turn had sold it to an American collector, who had lent it to an exhibition in Philadelphia in 1922 – which latter appearance had provided the clues, sixty-five years later, for a detective-story-like investigation on the part of Theodore Kemp of the Ashmolean Museum – a man who now lay dead in the mortuary at the Radcliffe Infirmary. But the man who had agreed to tell Chief

Inspector Morse precisely where he had stood, and with what impetus thrown the Tongue back into the river at Wolvercote – this man was seated, very much alive, in the vastly confusing complex of Kennedy Airport. Beside him sat a man of such immense proportions that Eddie Stratton wondered how he could ever fit into the seat that had been booked for him on the flight to Heathrow, scheduled to leave in forty minutes' time. He wondered, too, whether the man would be willing to unlock the handcuff that chafed away at his right wrist. For he, Stratton, was contemplating no high-jinks or high-jacks in mid-Atlantic flight.

CHAPTER FIFTY-FIVE

In great affairs we ought to apply ourselves less to creating
chances than to profiting from those that offer

(*La Rochefoucauld*, Maxims)

IT WAS WAY past coffee-break time in the Chesterton
Hotel, but no one seemed to notice.

'Kemp was met at the railway station,' continued
Morse. 'He was there told something – I'm guessing –
which persuaded him to accompany the driver to his
own flat in Water Eaton Road. Perhaps he was told that
his wife was suddenly taken very ill; was dead, even.
Perhaps some less dramatic disclosure sufficed. There,
at Kemp's home – again I'm guessing – a quarrel took
place in which Kemp was struck over the head and sent
stumbling in his own living room, where his right
temple crashed against the kerb of the fireplace – and
where he died. I'm amazed how difficult it is occasionally for a murderer to despatch his victim: in the
Thames Valley we once had a case where no fewer than
twenty-three vicious stab-wounds were insufficient to
complete the sorry business. But at the same time it is
occasionally so terribly easy to rob a fellow human
being of his life: a slight nudge, let us say, from a car-
bumper, and a cyclist is knocked down and hits his
head against the road – and in a second or two a life

311

has gone. In this case, Kemp had a thin skull, and his murder was no problem. But the body? Oh yes, the body was a problem all right!

'Now, if the murder took place at about three forty-five p.m., as I believe it did, why do we find Kemp's wife, Marion, doing nothing about it? For we can be absolutely sure she was there, the whole time. Maybe the reason for this was that she was vindictively happy *not* to do anything, and it is the opinion of my sergeant here that she probably hated her husband almost as intensely as the murderer himself did. But Marion Kemp could not, in my view, have killed her husband, and quite certainly she could hardly have moved the body a single centimetre from where it lay. On the other hand, Kemp was a slimly built, light-boned man, and it *would* have been possible for most people here, let us say – anyone reasonably mobile, reasonably fit – to have moved that body at least some small distance. *Even for a woman*, if she were sturdily or athletically built.'

The innuendo in this remark proved too much for the petite figure in the front row, who during the last few words was showing signs of unmistakable distress.

'Inspector! Chief Inspector, rather! For you even to *suggest* that I, for one, could have shifted a bardy, why, that is utterly absurd! And if you think that I am going to sit here—'

Morse smiled wanly at the lady as she sat in the front row, a lady turning the scales at not much more, surely, than around five stone.

'I should never accuse *you* of that, Mrs Roscoe. Please believe me!'

Mollified, it seemed, Janet sat back primly and slimly in her seat, as John Ashenden, seated immediately opposite (beside Dr Moule), looked across at her with a troublous, darkling gaze. And Morse continued:

'In the concreted yard at the back of the flats at Water Eaton Road stood a light-weight, rubber-wheeled, aluminium wheelbarrow which one of the maintenance men had been using earlier that day. It was into this barrow, under cover of the night, at about seven p.m., that the body was put, covered with plastic sacks, themselves in turn covered with a fair sprinkling of autumn leaves, before being wheeled across the low wooden bridge there, across a well-worn path through the field, and across to the swiftly flowing current of the River Cherwell, where unceremoniously the body was tipped into the water. And as I say' (Morse looked slowly around his audience) 'it was one of your own group who performed this grisly task – a *man* – a man who would have felt little squeamishness about first stripping the dead man of his clothes – for there had been much blood, much messy, sticky blood which almost inevitably would have transferred itself to the clothes of the man disposing of the body; a man who for the last ten years of his working life had been inured to such gruesome matters, as a moderately competent "mortician" in America.'

There was a sudden communal intake of breath from the audience, and clearly no need for Morse to spell things out further. But he did:

'Yes! *Mr Eddie Stratton.*'

'*No,* sir!'

The voice from the back of the room caused every head to crane round, although the mild tones of Phil Aldrich were known so well by now to everyone.

'You have my testimony, sir, and you have Eddie's too that we—'

'Mr Aldrich! I do accept your point, and I shall explain. Let us return to Stratton briefly. He had become a small-time mortician, specializing in the beautification – please allow the word! – of corpses that had died an ugly or disfiguring death. And a bachelor. Until two and a bit years ago, that is, when he met and married the widow of a middle-bracket philanthropist. The marriage was mostly an accommodation of interests; a convenience. Eddie did the shopping, tended the garden, mended the taps and the fuses, and serviced the family car. Laura – Laura Stratton as she now was – was reasonably content with the new arrangements: she was less anxious about burglars, she was chauffeured to her twice-weekly consultations with the latest chiropodist, she forgot most of her worries about the upkeep of the household, and she still found herself able to indulge the twin passions of her life, smoking cigarettes and playing contract bridge – simultaneously, wherever possible.

'But there had been disappointed expectations, on both sides, when the estate of the late philanthropist had finally, well almost finally, been settled, with the lawyers still growing fat on the pickings. *Objets d'art* there were aplenty, but most of them were held in trust for some collection or gallery. And so the prospects of a happily-monied marriage of convenience were ever diminishing, until an idea occurred to the pair of them – certainly to Laura Stratton. The Wolvercote Tongue was insured for half a million dollars, and one of the safest ways of transferring it over to England had got to be on the person of the traveller: few people would entrust such an item to letter-post or parcel-post or courier-service; and even if they did, the insurance-risk premium would be prohibitive. So the Strattons took it themselves – *and then made sure it was stolen.* That was their plan. The reason the plan went so sadly askew was the not-wholly-unexpected but extremely untimely death of Laura Stratton herself, though whether this was occasioned by her own complicity, excitement, remorse – whatever! – we shall never really know. The plan – a simple one – was for the Tongue to be stolen immediately after Laura had installed herself in her room at The Randolph. She would be sure to make such a song and dance about her aching feet that she would get right to the head of the queue for the room-key – well, apart from Mrs Roscoe, naturally!'

For the first time during Morse's analysis, his audience was seen reluctantly to smile as it acknowledged the primacy of the perpetually belly-aching little lady from California.

'Once she had the key, and whilst her husband signed the formalities, she was to go up to her room, put the handbag containing the Tongue – and money, pearls, and so on – on a ledge as near as possible to a door which was going to be left deliberately ajar.

Meanwhile Eddie Stratton was to enthuse about a quick stroll around the centre of Oxford before it got too dark, and an invitation to accompany him was accepted by Mrs Brown, a woman with whom he'd become friendly on the tour, and who probably felt a little flattered to be asked. All he had to do then was to make it known that he had promised to leave Laura alone so that she could have a rest in peace, to make an excuse about paying a brief visit to the Gents, to go up to his room – probably via the guest-lift – to stick his hand inside the room and grab the handbag, to take out the jewel before dumping the handbag, and then . . .'

Morse stopped, but only briefly. 'Not a *terribly* convincing hypothesis, are you thinking? I tend to agree with you. Everyone would be trying to use the lift at that point – probably queuing for it. And it would be impossible to use the main staircase, because as you'll recall it is immediately next to Reception there. And where does he ditch the emptied handbag? For it was never found. However quickly he may have acted, the actual taking of the handbag must have taken more *time* than seems to have been available – since Eddie Stratton and Shirley Brown were seen walking out of The Randolph almost immediately, if the evidence of at least two of you here is to be believed, the evidence of Mr Brown and Mrs Roscoe. So! So I suggest that something a little more sophisticated may have taken place. Let me tell you what I think. The plan, whatever it was, must have been discussed well in advance of the tour's arrival in Oxford, but a few last-minute recapitulations and reassurances would have been almost inevitable. Perhaps you've noticed that it's often difficult, on a bus or a train, to assess how loudly you are talking? Yes? Too loudly? And where were the Strattons sitting?' Morse pointed dramatically (as he hoped) to the two empty seats just behind Janet Roscoe. 'If they *did* discuss things on the coach, who were the likeliest people to eavesdrop? I'm told, for example, that you, Mrs Roscoe, have quite exceptionally acute hearing for a woman of—'

This time the little lady stood up, if thereby adding only some seven or eight inches in stature to her seated posture. 'Such innuendo, Chief Inspector, is wholly without foundation, and I wish you to know that one of my friends back home is the fiercest libel lawyer—'

But, again, and with the same patient smile, Morse bade the excitable lady to hold her peace, and bide her time.

'You were not the only one in earshot, Mrs Roscoe. In the seats immediately across the gangway from the Strattons sat Mr and Mrs Brown ... and in front of them, in the courier's seat...' Eyes, including Morse's, now turned as if by some magnetic attraction towards John Ashenden, who sat, his eyes unblinking, in the front row of the seats.

'You see,' resumed Morse, 'Stratton never went up at all to his room in The Randolph – not at that point. But someone did, someone *here* did – someone who had overheard enough of the original plan; someone who had sensed a wonderfully providential opportunity for himself, or for herself, and who had capitalized upon that opportunity. How? By volunteering to steal the Wolvercote Tongue, in order that the Strattons could immediately claim – claim without any suspicion attaching to them – the tempting prize of the insurance money!

'Let me put the situation to you simply. The person who had eavesdropped on the proposed intrigue *performed Stratton's job for him*; stole the jewel; slid thereafter into the background; and disposed at leisure of the superfluous pearls and the petty cash. And *that*, ladies and gentlemen, is no wild hypothesis on my part; it is the truth. Stratton was presented with an offer he could hardly refuse. At the time, though, he was not aware – could never have been aware – of the extraordinary service he would have to render as the *quid pro quo* of the agreement. But he was to learn about it soon enough. In fact, he was to learn of it the very next day, and he duly performed his own half of the bargain with a strangely honourable integrity. As it happens' – Morse consulted his watch ostentatiously – 'he is very shortly due to take off from Kennedy Airport to fly back to Heathrow, and he has already made a substantial confession about his part in the strange circumstances surrounding the Wolvercote Tongue and Dr Theodore Kemp. But – please believe me! – it was not *he* who actually stole the one ... or murdered the other. Yet I am looking forward to meeting Mr Stratton again, because thus far he has refused point-blank to tell me who the murderer was ...'

*

At the Trout Inn, the frogmen were now seated before a blazing log-fire in the bar. The landlady, an attractive, buxom woman in her mid-forties, had brought them each a hugely piled plate of chilli con carne, with a pint of appropriately chilly lager to wash it all down. None of the four had met Morse yet, and didn't know how strongly he would have disapproved of their beverage. But they knew they were working for him, and each of them was hoping that if the jewel were found it would be *he* who would have found it. Some acknowledgement, some gratitude from the man – that was an end devoutly to be wished.

But still nothing. Nothing, that is, except a child's tricycle, an antique dart-board, and what looked like part of a fixture from a household vacuum-cleaner.

Frequently, when Eddie Stratton had flown in the past, his heart had missed a beat or two whenever he heard the 'ding-dong' tones on the aircraft intercom. Indeed, he had sometimes felt that the use of such a system, except in times of dire emergency, should be prohibited by international law. No one Eddie had ever met wished to be acquainted with the pilot and his potential problems. So why not keep an eye on the steering, and forgo any announcement to interested passengers that there was now, say, a splendid view of the Atlantic Ocean down below? *No* announcements, *no* news – that's what passengers wanted. But now, ten minutes before take-off, Stratton felt most curiously relaxed about the possibility of an aerial disaster. Would such an eventuality be a welcome release? No, not really. He would speak to Morse again, yes. But Morse would never learn – at least not from *him* – the name of the person who had murdered Theodore Kemp.

CHAPTER FIFTY-SIX

And as the smart ship grew
In stature, grace, and hue,
In shadowy silent distance grew the Iceberg too
    (*Thomas Hardy*, 'The Convergence of the Twain')

SERGEANT LEWIS HAD been gratified by the brief
mention of himself in despatches, and he was in any
case revising (upwards) his earlier judgement on
Morse's rhetorical skills. All right, he (Lewis) now
knew the whole picture, but it was good to have the
details rehearsed again in front of a different audience.
He had never been near the top of the class in any
of the subjects he had been taught at school, yet
he'd often thought he wouldn't have been all that
far below the high-fliers if only some of the teachers
had been willing to go over a point a second time; or
even a third time. For once Lewis *did* get hold of a
thing firmly – suggestion, idea, hypothesis, theory – he
could frequently see its significance, its implications,
almost as well as anyone; even Morse. It was just that
the initial stages were always a bit of a problem; whereas
for Morse – well, *he* seemed to jump to a few answers
here and there before he'd even read the question-
paper. That was one of the big things he admired most
about the man, that ability to leap ahead of the field

almost from the starting-stalls – albeit occasionally finding himself on completely the wrong race-course. But it wasn't the *biggest* thing. The biggest thing was that Morse appeared to believe that Lewis was not only usually up with him in the race, galloping happily abreast, but that Lewis could sometimes spot something in the stretches ahead that Morse himself had missed, as the pair of them raced on towards the winning-post. It was ridiculous, of course. But Lewis ever found himself trusting that such a false impression might long be perpetuated.

The man's diction is slightly pedantic, thought Dr Moule, but he actually speaks in *sentences* – unusual even for a preacher, let alone a policeman. And – heaven be praised! – he doesn't stand there with his hands jingling the coins in his pockets. He reminded her of her Latin master, on whom she'd had an extra-special crush, and she wondered whether she wouldn't have had the same for this man. He looked overweight around the midriff, though nowhere else, and she thought perhaps that he drank too much. He looked weary, as if he had been up most of the night conducting his investigations. He looked the sort of man she would like to be going with, and she wondered whether he'd ever been unfaithful to his wife . . . But surely no wife would allow her husband abroad in such an off-white apology for a laundered shirt? Dr Moule smiled quietly, and trusted she was looking her attractive best;

and tried to stop herself hoping he had holes in his socks.

As the TWA Tristar turned slowly at the head of the runway, Lieutenant Al Morrow tried to pull out a final inch or two from the safety-belt that clamped his enormous girth to the seat. At the same time he unfastened the handcuffs which united him to his fellow-passenger. Morrow had a good deal of experience of the criminal classes, but this particular villain was hardly one of the potentially-dangerous-on-no-account-to-be-accosted variety. OK. He'd accompany him to the loo. But for the rest, the fellow would be fine, imprisoned in his window-seat between the fuselage on the one side and the mighty mountain of flesh that was Morrow on the other. The lieutenant opened his reading matter, *The Finer Arts of Fly-Fishing*, and, as the great jet raced and roared its engines, glanced quickly once again at the man who sat beside him: the features immobile, yet in no way relaxed; the eyes staring, yet perhaps not seeing at all; the forehead unfurrowed, yet tense, it seemed, as though his mind was dwelling on unhappy memories.

'You want sump'n to read, pal?'

Stratton shook his head.

It was as the lieutenant had suspected . . .

*

. . . It had been extraordinary how the two things had synchronised so perfectly at Oxford: a bit like the iceberg growing as the SS *Titanic* drew ever closer.

It was Laura's fault, of course! The woman could never keep her voice down – a voice that was usually double the decibels needed in normal conversation; and in whispered, conspiratorial communication, just about as loud as normal speech. And particularly on any form of public transport the dotty but endearing old biddy could never seem to gauge the further limits of her penetrating tones. Constantly, had she been fitted with a volume-control attachment somewhere about her person, Stratton would have turned it down. Frequently, as it was, he had enquired of his fairly recently acquired bride whether she was anxious for *the whole world* to know her business! Well, perhaps that was a bit of an exaggeration. Yet someone *had* overheard their plan; or heard enough of their plan to make a firm four out of two and two. And the glory of the thing had been that this someone had been just as anxious – more anxious! – to spirit away the Wolvercote Tongue as Laura was. As *he* was.

It had been the night at the University Arms in Cambridge that Plan B had been agreed. Such a *simple* plan, that 'plan' seemed far too grand an appellation: audibly (not a difficult task!) Laura would complain about her feet on the journey to Oxford; quite naturally (for her regular seat was on the row second to the front) she would be first in the queue at Reception in The Randolph – even Mrs Roscoe probably conceding her customary prerogative; she would leave her handbag immediately inside the allocated, unlocked bedroom; she would take a bath; she would leave the thief the childishly simple assignment of putting a hand inside the door. His own rôle? Principally to keep as far away from his room as possible. The police (no way in which they could not be involved) would be primarily interested in who was going to profit from any insurance, and he, Stratton himself, would have to vie with Caesar's wife in immunity from any suspicion. As it happened, he'd already prepared the ground for that by making something of a fuss of Shirley Brown; not at all difficult, because he *wanted* to make a fuss of Shirley Brown; and that lady had been flattered to follow his suggestion for a twilit stroll round Radcliffe Square – a stroll on which they'd seen their courier, Ashenden, and in turn been seen by the all-seeing Roscoe, a woman whom no one could abide, yet one whom everyone believed. Clever little touch, that! The problem that had worried Stratton about the earlier (now discarded) Plan A was where on earth he was going to dispose of the handbag. But need he have worried? Would it really have mattered if the bag had been found fairly soon in the nearest litter-bin? No, it wouldn't! The only thing that had to be disposed of was the jewel itself – not only because the insurance money must not be put in jeopardy, but also because someone else desired *Kemp* to be deprived of it. Desired it desperately.

Then Laura had to put her foot in it! Put her goddamned, aching, corny, foot right in it.

She'd gone and died.

Not that he (Stratton) had been involved in any way in that first death. No! But as far as the second death was concerned? Ah! That was a different matter. And whatever happened he would never tell the whole truth about that to anyone – not voluntarily – not even to that smart-alec copper, Chief Inspector Morse himself.

Yet he respected the man; couldn't help it, remembering the initial broadside on the transatlantic telephone, when Morse had immediately breached the outer fortifications.

'No, Inspector. There's nothing I can tell you about Kemp's death. Nothing.'

'I was more interested in the jewel, sir.'

'Ah! "The jewel that was ours", as Laura used to think of it.'

'Come off it!'

'Pardon, Inspector?'

'I said "Bullshit!"'

326

CHAPTER FIFTY-SEVEN

What's in a name? that which we call a rose
By any other name would smell as sweet
(*Shakespeare*, Romeo and Juliet)

ALTHOUGH IT HAD been a rather chilly morning, several of the people seated in the Beau Nash Room wished that the central heating could be turned down a few degrees. Howard Brown wiped his high forehead with a large handkerchief, and John Ashenden brushed the sleeve of his sports jacket across his upper lip where he felt the sweat-prickles forming. Morse himself drew a forefinger half a circuit round the neck of his slightly over-tight collar, and continued:

'I know who stole the Wolvercote Tongue. I know where it is, and I am quite sure that it will soon be recovered. I also know which one of you – which one of you here – killed Dr Kemp.' The hush was now so intense that Lewis found himself wondering whether his involuntary swallow had been audible, as for thirty seconds or so Morse stood silent and still, only his eyes moving left and right, and left and right again across the central aisle. No one in the audience moved either. No one dared even to cough.

'I'd hoped that the guilty person would have come forward by now. I say that because you may have read of several cases in England recently where the police have been criticized – in some cases rightly so – for depending for a prosecution on the uncorroborated confessions of accused persons, confessions which, certainly in one or two cases, might have been extorted in less than safe and satisfactory circumstances. How much better it would have been, then, if Kemp's murderer came forward – *comes* forward – in the presence of his friends and fellow tourists ...' Morse again looked around the room; but if there were any one person upon whom those blue eyes focused, it was not apparent to the others seated there.

'No?'

'No?' queried Morse again.

'So be it! There is little more to tell you. The biggest single clue in this case I passed over almost without reading it, until my sergeant jogged my memory. It was contained in a police report of the road accident in which Kemp crippled his wife – and also killed the driver of the other car, a Mrs P. J. Mayo, a thirty-five-year-old woman from California: Mrs Philippa J. Mayo, whose husband had earlier been killed in a gunnery accident on the USS *South Dakota*. That would have been bad enough for Philippa Mayo's parents-in-law, would it not? But at least the man had been serving his country; at least he'd died for some *cause* – whether that cause was justified or not. What of Philippa's own parents, though, when *she* is killed? Their daughter. Their only daughter. Their only child. A child killed needlessly, pointlessly, tragically, and wholly *reprehensibly* – by a man who must have appeared to those parents, from the reports they received, as a drunken, selfish, wicked swine who deserved to be as dead as their daughter ... Above all, I suspect, the parents were appalled by what seemed to them the quite extraordinary leniency of the magistrates at the criminal hearing, and they came over to England, father and mother, to lay the ghost that had haunted them night and day for the past two years. But why only then, you may ask? I learn that the wife had been suffering from cervical cancer for the previous three years; had just endured her second massive session of chemotherapy; had decided that she could never face a third; had only at the outside six more months to live. So the pair came over to view the killer of their daughter, and if they deemed him worthy of death, they vowed that he would die. They met him the once only, on the night before he died: a cocky philanderer, as they saw him; a cruel, conceited specimen; and now a man who, like Philippa Mayo's mother, had so very little time to live. The link between the two crimes, and the motivation for them, was clear to me at last, and the link and the motivation merged into a single whole: the implacable hatred of a man and his wife for the person who had killed their daughter.

'For Theodore Kemp.

'I keep mentioning "man *and* wife" because I finally persuaded myself that no one single person on his own could have carried through the murder of Kemp. It could have been *any* two people, though, and we had to try to find out as much about all of you as we could. When you signed in at The Randolph, you all filled in a form which asked overseas visitors to complete full details of nationality, passport number, place passport issued, permanent home address, and so on. But, as you know, I also had to ask Mr Ashenden to collect your passports, and from these, my sergeant here' (the blood rose slowly in Lewis's cheeks) 'checked all the details you had given and found that two of you lived in the same block of retirement flats. But these two were not registered as man and wife; rather they had decided to play the waiting game, to take advantage of anything that might crop up, to "optimize the opportunity", as I believe you say in America. And that opportunity materialized – in the person of Eddie Stratton.

'Stratton had been out at Didcot on the afternoon Kemp died, and what is more he could prove his presence there conclusively – with photographic evidence. And I – we – were led to believe that his quite innocent statements about his train journey back to Oxford were equally true. *But they weren't.* Cleverly, unwittingly, as it seemed, he gave a wholly unimpeachable alibi to a man he saw in the carriage ahead of him – a man to whom he owed a very great deal. But he did *not* see that man, ladies and gentlemen! Because that man was *not* on the Didcot–Oxford train that afternoon. He was in Oxford . . . murdering Dr Kemp.'

The last few words sank into the noiselessness of the stifling room. And then Morse suddenly smiled a little, and spoke quietly:

'Can you hear me all right at the back, Mr Aldrich?'

'Pardon, sir?'

'Don't you think it would be far better if you ...'
Morse held out the palm of his right hand and seemed
to usher some invisible spirit towards the front row of
the seats.

Aldrich, looking much perplexed, rose from his seat
and walked forward hesitantly down the central aisle;
and, turning towards him, Janet Roscoe smiled expect-
antly and pointed her hand to the empty seat beside
her. But Aldrich ignored the gesture, and slipped
instead into one of the empty seats immediately behind
her.

'As I say,' resumed Morse, 'the person Stratton
claimed to have seen was never on the train at all. That
person told me he'd been to London to see his daughter; but he'd only ever had the one daughter ... and
she was *dead.*'

Morse's audience was hanging on his every word, yet
few seemed able to grasp the extraordinary implications
of what he was saying.

'Names, you know' (Morse's tone was suddenly
lighter) 'are very important things. Some people don't
like their own names ... but others are extremely
anxious to perpetuate them – both Christian names
and surnames. Let's say, for example, that Mr and Mrs
Brown here – Howard and Shirley, isn't it? – wanted to
christen their house, they might think of sticking half
of their two names together. What about "W-a-r-d" from
his name and "l-e-y" from hers? Make a reasonable
house-name, wouldn't it? "Wardley"?'

'Gee, that's exactly—' began Shirley; but Howard laid a hand on her arm, and the embarrassed lady held her peace.

'Not much good trying to perpetuate a surname, though – not if your daughter gets married. She *can* keep her maiden name, of course. Can't she? *Can't* she . . .? But it's easier with Christian names, especially sometimes. A father whose name is "George", say, can call his daughter "Georgie", "Georgina", "Georgette".' (Lewis glanced up at Morse.) 'And the woman who was killed in the road accident was called Mrs Philippa J. Mayo, remember? Her father couldn't give her his own name exactly, but he could give her the female equivalent of "Philip". And Philippa Mayo was the daughter of the only man here who has that name.

'*Wasn't she, Mr Aldrich?*' asked Morse in a terrifying whisper.

CHAPTER FIFTY-EIGHT

> ... that fair field
> Of Enna, where Proserpin gathring flowrs
> Her self a fairer Flowre by gloomie Dis
> Was gathered, which cost Ceres all that pain
> To seek her through the world...
>
> (*John Milton*, Paradise Lost, Book IV)

'YOU'RE *SERIOUS* ABOUT all this, sir?' Phil Aldrich cocked his head to one side and his sad features seemed incredulous, and pained.

'Oh, yes,' said Morse, with a quiet simplicity – perhaps also with some pain. 'You've no daughter in London – or anywhere else now, I'm afraid. You've lost your alibi, too – the very clever alibi provided by Eddie Stratton as the first of his services for you ... before he performed his *second* service, later that same day, by disposing of Kemp's body in the River Cherwell.'

Momentarily, it seemed, Aldrich was on the point of protesting, but Morse shook his head wearily:

'No point – no point at all in your saying anything to the contrary, Mr Aldrich. We've been in touch with the police department in Sacramento, with your neighbours, with the local institutions there, including the High School your daughter attended. We've got your passport, and we've checked your home address, and it's perfectly correct. You carried through all your details accurately on to the t.h.f. Guest Registration Card at The Randolph, and doubtless here too, in Bath. But *your wife*? She was a little "economical with the truth", wasn't she? Your wife – *your accomplice*, Mr Aldrich – she made just a few little changes here and there to her details, didn't she? It was all right for it to be seen that you both lived in the same district, the same street, even – *but not in the same apartment.* Yet you do, don't you, live in the same apartment as your wife? You've been married together, happily married together, for almost forty-two years, if my information is correct. And apart from your daughter, there has only ever been one woman in life you have loved with passion and tenderness – the woman you married. She was a gifted actress, I learned. She was well known on the West Coast of America in many productions in the fifties and sixties – mostly in musicals in the earlier years, and then in a series of Arthur Miller plays. And being an actress, a successful actress, it was sensible for her to keep her stage name – which was in fact her maiden name. But she gave her Christian name to her daughter, just as you did. Philippa J. Aldrich – Philippa *Janet* Aldrich – that was her name.' Morse nodded sadly to himself, and to the two people who sat so near to one another now.

Then a most poignant and exceedingly moving thing occurred. Only a few minutes since, Phil Aldrich had rejected (as it seemed) the blandishments of a diminutive, loud-mouthed, insufferable termagant. But now he accepted her invitation. He rose, and moved forward, just the one row, to sit beside the woman in the front, and to take her small hand gently into his – the tears now spilling down his cheeks. And as he did so, the woman turned towards him with eyes that were pale and desolate, yet eyes which still lit up with the glow of deep and happy love as she looked unashamedly, unrepentantly, into her husband's face; the eyes of a mother who had grieved so long and so desperately for her only daughter, a mother whose grief could never be comforted, and who had journeyed to England to avenge what she saw as an insufferable wrong – the loss of the jewel that was hers.

CHAPTER FIFTY-NINE

Je ne regrette rien
(French song)

AFTER THE ARRESTS, after the statements from the two Aldriches and from a repentant Stratton, after a second search of the Kemps' residence, the case – at least from Morse's point of view – was finished.

The major statement (the statement to which Morse awarded the literary prize) was made by Mrs Janet Roscoe, who properly insisted on vetting the transcription of her lengthy evidence typed out by WPC Wright. Except at one point, this agreed with the parallel statement made by Mr Phil Aldrich, with each, in turn, substantially corroborated by Mr Edward Stratton's testimony about his own collusion with the Aldriches. The one colossal discrepancy arose from the two wholly contradictory accounts of Kemp's death. Neither Mr nor Mrs Aldrich was willing to give any detail whatsoever about what, as Morse imagined, must have been a savagely bitter altercation between Kemp and themselves before the fateful (though maybe not immediately fatal?) blow struck with the stick that originally had rested across Marion Kemp's knees as she sat in her wheelchair, her eyes (in Janet's splendid phrase) 'glowing with a sort of glorious revenge'. So much was agreed. Kemp had stumbled blindly against a chair and then fallen heavily, the back of his head striking the corner of the fireplace with 'a noise reminiscent of a large egg trodden underfoot – deliberately'. So much was agreed. Then there was all that blood. Such a surprising amount of it! And the carpet where most of it had dripped; and his clothes 'sticky and messy with the stuff'. So much was agreed. But which of the two it was who had lashed out ferociously at Kemp with that stick ('Please return to the Radcliffe Infirmary' branded upon it) – ah! that was proving so difficult to decide. It had been *Phil*, of course – Janet confessed: 'He must have gone quite berserk, Inspector!' But no! It had been *Janet* all the time, as Phil had so sadly admitted to Morse: a frenetic Janet who had been the happy instrument of eternal Justice. But when Morse had told Janet of the wild discrepancy, she'd merely smiled. And when Morse had told Phil of the same ridiculous discrepancy, he too had merely smiled – and lovingly.

There had been one or two minor surprises in the statements, but for the most part things had happened almost exactly as Morse had supposed. What finally, it appeared, had transmuted an intolerable grief into an implacable hatred, and a lust for some sort of retribution, was the fact that in all the reports the parents had received of the coroner's proceedings and the magistrates' hearing, *Philippa's name had never once occurred*. A curious catalyst, perhaps, and yet what a devastating one! But the name of Dr Theodore Kemp had been mentioned many, many times; and when they had read of the Historic Cities of England Tour, *they had seen that name again.* Their plans were made (for what they were) and they duly took their places on the tour – almost enjoying the distanced yet sometimes friendly roles they had assumed. And it was on the coach that Janet had learned of the deceit that the Strattons were plotting ... And after Janet had taken Laura Stratton's handbag, and put it immediately into her own, far more capacious one, she had gone to her own room, on the same floor, and happily discovered that the Wolvercote Tongue fitted almost perfectly into the small case she'd brought with her containing her portable iron ...

Then it was the telephone call ...

Janet had heard everything, *clearly!* And a plan was immediately formulated. Eddie Stratton was despatched somewhere – anywhere! – so long as he could establish a firm alibi *for himself*; and Phil sent off to a nearby car-hire firm, whilst she, Janet, remained seated by the extension-phone in her bedroom to deal with the necessary reference for the car firm. The confusion caused by Kemp's delay that day was a godsend; and Phil, after picking up Janet from Gloucester Green, had met Kemp at the railway station (his train two minutes early) informing him that his wife had been taken ill, that his duties were fully taken care of, and that he (Aldrich) was there to drive him directly up to his North Oxford home ...

After the deed was done, Janet had found herself waiting anxiously for the return of Eddie Stratton; and as soon as she – and no one else! – had spotted him, she steered him away from The Randolph, handed him the Wolvercote Tongue and acquainted him with the *second* of his duties in the criminal conspiracy in which he was now a wholly committed accessory: the disposal of the body.

Marion Kemp (this from Stratton's evidence now) had admitted him at Water Eaton Road, where he had divested the corpse of its clothes – how else shift the body without staining his own? And ... well, the rest was now known. It had not been an unduly gruesome task to a man for whom such post-mortem grotesqueries had been little more than a perfunctory performance. He had wrapped the carpet round the clothes of the murdered man, depositing the bundle behind the boiler in the airing-cupboard. And what of Marion Kemp? Throughout she had sat, Stratton claimed, in the hallway. In silence.

'And greatly disturbed,' opined Morse.

'Oh no, Inspector!' Stratton had replied.

After leaving Water Eaton Road, Stratton had walked via First Turn and Goose Green to the Trout Inn at Wolvercote where he had thrown the Tongue into the river – and then caught a Nipper Bus back to St Giles', where he'd met Mrs Williams.

Sheila's evidence tallied with Stratton's account. She had invited Stratton back to her house in North Oxford, and he had accepted. Anxious as he was to drink himself silly, and with a co-operative partner to boot, Stratton had consumed considerable quantities of Glenfiddich – and had finally staggered into a sum-moned taxi at around midnight ...

Such was the picture of the case that had finally emerged; such the picture that Morse painted on the Friday morning of that same week when Chief Superintendent Strange had come into his office, seating himself gruntingly in the nearest chair.

'None of your bullshit, Morse! Just the broad brush, my boy! I'm off to lunch with the C.C. in half an hour.'

'Give him my very best wishes, sir.'

'Get *on* with it!'

Strange sat back (and looked at his watch) when Morse had finished. 'She must have been an amazing woman.'

'She was, sir. I think Janet Roscoe is possibly the—'

'I'm not talking about *her*! I'm talking about the Kemp woman – Marion, wasn't it? Didn't the Aldrich pair take a huge gamble though? You know, assuming she would play along with 'em, and so on?'

'Oh, yes. But they were gambling all along – with the very highest stakes, sir.'

'And you just think, Morse! Staying in that house – with that bloody corpse – in her bedroom – in the hall – wherever – I don't know. *I* couldn't do it. Could *you*? It'd send me crackers.'

'She could never forgive him—'

'It'd still send me crackers.'

'She *did* commit suicide, sir,' said Morse slowly, beginning only now, perhaps, to see into the abyss of Marion's despair.

'So she did, Morse! So she did!'

Strange looked at his watch again and tilted his heavily jowled head: 'What put you on to 'em? The Aldriches?'

'I should have got there earlier, I suppose. Especially after that first statement Aldrich made, about his fictional trip to London. He wrote it straight out – only three crossings-out in three pages. And if only I'd looked at what he'd crossed out instead of what he'd left in! He was writing under pressure and, if my memory serves me, he crossed out things like "*we* could have done something" and "*our* telephone number". He was worried about giving himself away, because he was writing like a married man ... He *was* a married man ... And there was another clue, too. He even mentioned his daughter's name in that statement: "Pippa" – which as you know, sir, is a diminutive of "Philippa".'

Strange rose to his feet and pulled on his heavy winter coat. 'Some nice bits of thinking, Morse!'

'Thank you, sir!'

'I'm not talking about *you*! It's this Roscoe woman. Very able little lady! Did you know that a lot of 'em have been *little* – these big people: Alexander, Augustus, Attila, Nelson, Napoleon ...'

'They tell me Bruckner was a very small man, sir.'

'Who?'

The two men smiled briefly at each other as Strange reached the door.

'Just a couple of points, Morse. How did Janet Roscoe get rid of that handbag?'

'She says she walked round the corner into Cornmarket, and went into Salisbury's, and stuck it in the middle of the leather handbags on sale there.'

'What about the murder weapon? You say you've not recovered that?'

'Not yet. You see, she walked along to the Radcliffe Infirmary, so she says, and saw a notice there about an Amnesty – for anything you'd had from the place which you should have returned: "Amnesty – No Questions Asked", it said. She just handed it in.'

'Why haven't you got it, then?'

'Sergeant Lewis went along, sir. But there were seventy-one walking sticks in the Physio department there.'

'Oh!'

'Do you want any forensic tests on them?'

'Waste of money.'

'That's what Sergeant Lewis said.'

'Good man, Lewis!'

'Excellent man!'

'Not so clever as this Roscoe woman, though.'

'Few cleverer.'

'She'd be useful in the Force.'

'No chance, sir. She had a thorough medical yesterday. They don't even give her a fortnight.'

'Any doctor who tells you when you're going to die is a bloody fool!'

'Not this one,' said Morse quietly – and sadly.

'Think you'll get that jewel back?'

'Hope so, sir. But *they* won't, will they?'

'Say that again?'

'The jewel that was theirs, sir. They won't ever get *her* back, will they?'

Was Morse imagining things? For a second or two he thought that Strange's eyes might well have glistened with a film of tears. But there was no way of telling this for certain, for Strange had suddenly looked down fixedly at the threadbare carpet beside the door, before departing for his lunch with the Chief Constable.

CHAPTER SIXTY

Accipe fraterno multum manantia fletu,
Atque in perpetuum, frater, ave atque vale

(*Catullus*, Poem CI)

A WEEK AFTER his meeting with Strange, Morse took
the bus down from North Oxford to Cornmarket. He
had managed two complete days' furlough, had re-read
Bleak House, listened again (twice) to *Parsifal*, and
(though he would never have admitted it) begun to
feel slightly bored.

Not today, though!

When he had said farewell to Sheila Williams the
previous week, he had suggested a second rendezvous.
He was (he assured her) a reasonably civilized sort of
fellow, and it would be pleasant for both of them to
meet again fairly soon, and perhaps have lunch
together: the Greek Taverna, perhaps, up in Summertown? So a time and a place were carefully agreed: 12
a.m. (twelve *noon*) in the foyer (the *foyer*) of The
Randolph.

Where else?

As usual (for appointments), he was ten minutes
early, and stood for a while in the foyer talking to Roy,
the bespectacled Head Concierge, and congratulating
this splendid man on his recent award of the BEM. A

quarter of an hour later, he walked down the hotel steps and for several minutes stood immobile on the pavement there, some of his thoughts centred on the Ashmolean Museum opposite and on its former Keeper of Anglo-Saxon and Mediaeval Antiquities; but most of his thoughts, if truth be told, on Mrs Sheila Williams. At 12.20 p.m., when he found himself looking at his wristwatch about three times per minute, he returned to the foyer, and stood there rather fecklessly for a further few minutes. At 12.25 p.m., he asked the concierge if there'd been any messages. No! At 12.30 p.m., he abandoned all hope and decided to drown his disappointment in the Chapters Bar.

As he came to the door, he looked inside – and stopped. There, seated at the bar, a large empty glass held high in her left hand, her right arm resting on the shoulder of a youngish (bearded!) man, sat Sheila Williams, her black-stockinged legs crossed provocatively, her body disturbingly close to her companion's.

'If you insist!' Morse heard her say, as she pushed her glass across the bar. 'Gin – large one, please! – no ice – just *half* a glass of tonic – slim-line.'

Morse held back, feeling a great surge of irrational and impotent jealousy. About which he could do nothing. Absolutely nothing. Like a stricken deer he walked back to the foyer, where he wrote a brief note ('Unavoidable, urgent police business'), and asked the concierge to take it through to the bar in about five minutes or so, and hand it to a Mrs Williams – a Mrs *Sheila* Williams.

Roy had nodded. He'd been there in the hotel for

forty-five years, now. That's why he'd been honoured by the Queen. He understood most things. He thought he understood this.

Morse walked quickly along the Broad, past the King's Arms, the Holywell Music Room, the back of New College, turned left at Longwall Street, and after two hundred yards or so went through the wooden gate that led into Holywell Cemetery. He found the grave far more quickly than Ashenden had done; and behind the squat cross the envelope that Ashenden had left there, with the four lines written out neatly on a white card therein. After replacing the envelope, Morse left the cemetery and walked slowly back along Holywell Street to the King's Arms, ordering there (as Ashenden had done before him) a pint of Flowers Bitter. He found himself ever thinking of Sheila, and at one point had been on the verge of rushing up to The Randolph to see if she were still there in the Chapters Bar.

But he hadn't.

And gradually thoughts of Mrs Williams were receding; and instead, he found his mind lingering on the sad quatrain he'd found beside the small stone cross in the Holywell cemetery:

> Life divided us from each other,
> Depriving friend of friend,
> Accept this leave-taking – with my tears –
> For it is all I have to bring.

At the Trout Inn, the frogmen had given it four days, then called off the search for the Wolvercote Tongue.

Sensibly so, as Eddie Stratton (now facing charges of perjury and perverting the course of justice) could have told them from the beginning. It had been a sort of back-up insurance, really – prising out that single remaining ruby, and hiding it privily beneath the white-silk lining of Laura's coffin. In New York his plans had been thwarted, but the jewel would still be there, would it not? Whenever, wherever they finally buried her. Was *anyone* ever likely to suspect such duplicity, such ghoulish duplicity? Surely not. Surely not, reflected Stratton. Yet he found himself remembering the man who had been in charge of things.

Yes, just the one man, perhaps . . .